MY IMMOVABLE OBJECT

My Immovable Object

OBJECT

Michelle Kay

To: Zoe's
always
Michelle Kay

ISBN: 0-9986716-0-4
ISBN-13: 978-0-9986716-0-4

FOR MY BUTT CLUB

01: ALISTAIR

The tiny nook Alistair had found at the back of the club was poorly hidden—he only had to shift a foot to the right to see the corner of the bar. It didn't matter, though. He wouldn't be there long.

The bass of the music thumped in his chest, keeping time with the clumsy thrusting of the Mediterranean hottie he'd lured into that corner. He'd given up on the goth club he'd taken Cole to a month ago, and now he frequented this pop-centered dance club. There were fewer gay men at this one, which had never slowed Alistair down before, though it did explain his partner's mediocre performance. In the end, even mediocre sex was better than wasting away in the prison they were calling "Haven."

Alistair wrapped a fist around his own straining erection, pressed his brow into his forearm where he braced himself against the wall, and tried to focus on the good points. His partner—he'd not made out his name over the volume of the music—was big, and he was rough. Alistair could work with that. He gasped as the dark-haired boy pressed a hand into the back of his neck. Even though Alistair knew he could snap every bone in this man's arm with one hand, it still made his slowly leaking cock jump with excitement against his palm. Moaning loudly for show, he told the man behind him to fuck him harder, knowing exactly what to say to get a straight guy's gears turning. It was never difficult to get what he wanted.

"God, I've never felt a woman squeeze me like this." His voice was hot against Alistair's ear—was his name Joseph?

Alistair didn't answer. He was getting close and had to continually remind himself not to squeeze too hard around the thick rod that pushed inside him. He'd gotten good at controlling his hands, but other body parts were less obedient, especially in the throes of excitement. He moaned an obligatory half-answer and closed his eyes, focusing on his own hand as he fought to wring the orgasm out of himself.

Then, as Joseph—Jason? Maybe it was Jason—gripped his hips with bruising fingers, as he yanked him back to press as deep inside as he could, Alistair felt himself suddenly forced to the precipice of his end.

"Ah! Wait, pull out. Pull out!" His voice was shaking, but loud enough he knew the other man would hear him, and he tried to hold back until his partner was safely detached. But Jason ignored the command, hammering into him even harder than before, planning to ride him through the wave of his orgasm. It was kind of sweet of him, really, but he should have learned to follow orders.

Oh well.

Alistair stopped fighting. Instead, he let the wave of breathlessness freeze time for just a few seconds, and for that moment he forgot about his imprisonment and his loneliness. He drowned in the fuzziness that clouded his brain and made his skin prickle with life as every muscle in his body quivered and tightened.

Then he heard Jason screaming. He'd been too caught up in his own pleasure to hear the unnatural popping sound that meant he'd broken the blood vessels in the other man's suddenly wilted pride—he might have even torn some tissue this time.

As soon as Alistair's body relaxed, freeing his partner-turned-victim, Jason collapsed to the ground behind him, a gurgling sob escaping the man that had been playing tough only moments earlier. Alistair didn't think any less of the other boy for crying—he knew it didn't make him any less of a man—but he also didn't really feel sorry for him. He'd warned him to pull out. He'd given him the opportunity.

Alistair released the corner of the wall he'd been holding, taking only a second to admire the finger-shaped dents he'd left behind. Jason was still shouting, but the music drowned him out as Alistair refastened his pants around his narrow hips.

"Sorry about your dick," he called to his writhing partner. "Next time you should probably listen when someone tells you to stop."

As he was leaving the club, Alistair thought he heard some commotion coming from the corner near the bar where he'd left Jason—maybe it was Jackson. He didn't wait for them to start looking around for him.

It wasn't quite fall yet, but the weather was getting cooler outside, which meant the air of freedom was cool as Alistair breathed deep. He hated how stale the air was in the dorms, hated how stagnant *everything* was. He checked his watch, knowing better than to take his cellphone with him. Marla and Venja let them keep phones, but they all knew they were bugged to next week and back. It was just past one—he'd scored his tryst with Jackson faster than he'd expected—which meant he had almost two hours to kill. Shift change back at Haven happened at three. Sneaking in was always easiest when the guards were doing change-over.

Wanting something a bit quieter, Alistair made his way to a small bar he'd begun frequenting. It was just classy enough that he felt at home, and since it was a gay-friendly bar, it was also a good place to score a few free drinks while he killed time. Turning down a smaller side road, Alistair approached the unmarked storefront. The best gay bars were always the ones that had no signage. It meant that only people who were interested in what the bar offered would know where to find it. Alistair had never been one to feel uncomfortable with his sexuality, but it still felt good to be in a "safe place."

As he let himself in, he nodded to the bartender—a man in his forties who he usually saw working there. He was quiet, stayed out of Alistair's business, and didn't card him when other patrons bought him drinks, which meant that Alistair had grown fond of him.

Normally, he would scan the room to find the right person to bum drinks off of, but this time he didn't need to look. While small groups and couples peppered the room, his attention was pulled immediately to a man sitting at the bar. He could only see his back and a sliver of his profile, but already his interest was piqued. The man's shoulders were broad, accentuated by the perfect cut of his suit. Dark hair was styled neatly away from the pale skin of his face. He was older—in his early thirties maybe—which surprised Alistair since this bar catered mostly to younger men. It meant that he was probably some pervert who liked picking up younger boys. Alistair grinned; he could work with that.

Putting on his game face, Alistair approached his new target.

"Hey, Mister." Softly, Alistair brushed one hand over the man's shoulder as his slid up to the bar beside him. He could tell just by the fabric that the suit was expensive—the sort of thing that had been tailored to his body. It certainly *looked* like it had been made just for him.

While Alistair was still admiring the shape of this man's clothes, pale, blue-grey eyes turned toward him, and for just a second, even Alistair was awed. He'd made the right choice. This man had amazing features. His cheekbones were high but balanced perfectly by the masculine cut of his jaw. His brows, like his neatly

4

swathed hair, were a dark, warm brown, making the arch they drew look so defined that he might have cut someone with them—especially as one brow quirked just slightly up his forehead.

"I think you're overdressed for this place," Alistair said to hide the hint of wonder he'd felt. "You won't pick anyone up looking like you'll take them to court."

The man chuckled, the sound rumbling in his throat, and when the corner of his mouth turned up in a smirk, Alistair realized it wasn't the suit that was warding the others off. Even he felt just a little intimidated.

"Well, rest assured, there are much better places I could take you than a courthouse."

Alistair had expected the man to sound more exotic—his marble-white skin and angled features made him look Scandinavian—but his accent was American, though admittedly very well-spoken American. He could also tell that this man was a professional when it came to flirting.

"Aren't you a little old to be here? You aren't here to prey on innocent little boys like me, are you?"

He put a hand over the lapel at his chest, his fingers long, but powerful looking. "You wound me! Old..." He clucked his tongue around a smile that looked like it belonged in a magazine. "I'm only thirty, you know. Calling me old..."

Alistair was shocked to realize he was actually smiling without forcing himself. This man seemed to have some wit about him. "So you're telling me that if you bought me a drink, you wouldn't slip me some sort of nasty drug?" He used the kitten-like smile that he knew drove men nuts when he was insulting them—they were all masochists if you had a pretty enough face, and he thought this one might be exceptionally interested in the banter.

The man shook his head, returning his hand to his drink. He was still smiling though. "I'm insulted you think I would need to resort to something as shady as that. I think you already know that you and I could get whomever we liked without nasty games like that."

So he thought they were on equal footing. Alistair scoffed playfully to hide the fact that, for the first time, he thought he might be right. Alistair would be the first person to label himself a perfect ten, and in a different situation he may have thought the same thing about his man, but he was also being cocky. That meant he would have to be stuck as a nine.

"If you think so, then why don't you just give in and let me have what I want?"

The man turned toward him more fully. "And what is it you want, exactly?"

Alistair bit his lip and looked to the wall of liquor on the other side of the bar. After a perfunctory glance, he pointed to the decorated bottle of amber liquid on the top shelf.

"That cognac, there, on the top shelf. I want that. On the rocks."

He watched the bartender look uncertainly at the man in the suit. Alistair knew the bottle was worth a few thousand dollars, easily, and even though he'd only be getting a small portion, it would probably run at least a hundred dollars. He looked back at his partner and smiled expectantly, waiting to see what he would do now that the ball was in his court. He looked only vaguely surprised, then chuckled again as he motioned for the bartender to do as Alistair had asked. Neither of them spoke as the bottle was opened and the deep liquid was poured.

Alistair smiled at the man over the rim of his glass as he took his first, slow sip.

"How is it?"

Alistair licked his lips and set the crystal glass on the bar, though his fingers didn't leave the delicate rim. "Not bad."

The man laughed for real this time, finished off what remained in his own glass, then motioned to the bartender again. "I'll have one as well."

So he *was* rich. Alistair wouldn't mind taking advantage of *that*, but he would never get the chance to keep a partner long enough to make it worthwhile. He would just have to settle for his expensive drink.

"You have a lovely accent. Where are you from?" The coy phase of their flirting seemed to be over—surely he thought he'd just bought his way out of it.

"Germany."

He nodded, as though he'd already known that. He looked like the type to be well traveled, which meant he was only asking out of politeness.

"And your name?"

"Alistair." He sipped his drink again, watching him as he accepted his own glass from the bartender, watching his pale fingers wrap around the glass. "And yours?"

"Luca. But I feel like you may forget it by tomorrow."

"Well whether that's true or not, niceties are important, don't you think?"

"It's true. Manners *can* get you pretty far." Luca paused to take a slow sip from his own glass, his expression unchanging, giving Alistair the impression that he'd tried that particular cognac plenty of times before. Then he nodded to the bartender who left them to enjoy their drinks.

Alistair had already reeled in his catch for the night, but the coolness of this man's attitude was quickly waking his body back up. Luca was definitely a step up from the inept encounter he'd had in the dance club. Maybe this would be a lucky night for him. "And if I used extra manners, how far would that get me?" He crossed his legs, smiling just a little when he saw grey eyes flick down to catch the movement.

"I have a feeling you already know the answer to that."

Alistair smirked more suggestively now, shifting a little closer as Luca moved a hand to Alistair's knee, as though he needed to still those long limbs before they drove him crazy.

"Well then, why are we still stumbling around all of these formalities?"

Luca smiled this time, the expression a little more sultry than the good natured grin he'd worn earlier. There was something more promising in the way his eyes squinted now. Alistair wet his lips as he watched the older man take one more long sip from his glass before setting it aside, and despite Alistair's show, his heart skipped just a little when Luca's hand moved from the glass to the hair at the base of his neck. Alistair hadn't realized how badly he wanted this man. Now he watched the pale, sculpted face bow toward his. He let his lips part as hot breath passed over them, and he dropped his eyes to watch the pale pink of the other man's mouth descend.

Then Luca stopped. He smiled, and his voice was so low that Alistair thought he could feel the vibration against his mouth, though they'd never touched.

"If you're going to seduce someone, maybe do it when you don't already smell like cheap sex."

Luca was still grinning as he pulled away, the hand in his hair moving to the pen he used to sign for his tab.

"We'll play again next time, Alistair. When you're not feeling quite so greedy."

Then he walked out of the bar, leaving his half empty glass of cognac on the counter.

02: ALISTAIR

It was five minutes past two in the afternoon when Alistair woke up for the fourth time. He'd been in such a bad mood when he'd fallen into bed the night before that all he wanted was to sleep through the day, though he was starting to think he wouldn't be able to wring much more sleep out of himself. It was unfortunate, because already, in the few moments he'd been awake, he could feel the humiliation creeping back up on him.

Rejection was *not* something he usually stood for.

Only men on the extreme hetero end of the sexuality scale ever turned him down, or men who were taken, and even then it was only because Alistair chose not to press them. His face was hot with anger and embarrassment and he turned over to press it into his pillow.

The next time I see that asshole, I'll break his dick with my bare hands.

Hurting a partner on purpose was never something Alistair set out to do. He always took precautions—he faced away from them so he couldn't break any bones with gripping hands, he told them to pull out before he came, he spent more time thinking about relaxing than he did about anything that felt good—but damn he wanted to tear Luca, apart. He'd never seen him before, though, so maybe he was only passing through. As much as he would enjoy revenge, it would be easier for Alistair if he never saw him again.

Of course the devastatingly handsome one is a complete ass.

Deciding that lying alone in bed would only make things worse, Alistair finally talked himself into getting up. He would dress properly after his shower, so for the time being he skipped the underwear, pulled on a thin pair of house pants, and a wide-necked sweater—his own personal Haven uniform.

After collecting his late-afternoon breakfast, Alistair made his way to the largest of the three TV rooms, wanting to rest in some silence. Two feet inside the room, though, he noticed Sabin lounging on the couch. He was just turning around to sneak away when the other boy spoke up.

"I've got something for you."

Alistair didn't dislike Sabin—if anything the other boy's tendency to keep to himself had quickly moved him toward the top of Alistair's list of people he liked. Bastian was nice to hang out with because he was quiet for the most part and because he humored his interest in ballroom dancing, but it was intimidating to spend time with someone you couldn't lie to. And now he was insufferable with his goo-goo love story.

"A present? For me? I didn't know you liked me so much." Despite his initial intentions to sneak away, he walked toward the couch as Sabin flapped a stack of papers over his head without bothering to turn around to look at him.

"I like you enough to give you homework."

Things between the two groups of boys had settled down, and for the most part they all go along. *For the most part.* Taking the stack of printed pages, Alistair planted himself in the couch where Sabin's feet used to be—he'd pulled them out of the way to make room for him.

"What is this?"

"I dunno," he was already half way through his stack. "Something to do with our next mission."

"What? You mean she's not going to just throw us out into the woods this time?"

"Her ways are not our ways," Sabin joked.

Despite his bad mood from that morning, Alistair smiled. Really, Sabin had made his good list way back when he'd hexed Berlin.

"We'll be having our first briefing about it tonight after dinner," Sabin continued.

"Mm. Do the others know already?"

"Mostly."

"Let me guess, everyone knows but Berlin."

"I threw his in the garbage."

Alistair smiled behind his papers. "What's he done to upset you this time?"

"Nothing. I just hate him."

"That's beautiful."

Honestly, Sabin and Berlin's constant fighting was the only source of entertainment Alistair had now that things were settled between Cole and Bastian.

No one else came into the TV room once Sabin left—he'd said he'd had enough studying for a while—and Alistair was glad for the quiet. He'd seen Sabin spend hours reading old, ratty looking books, but his attention span for the report they'd been given wasn't as good. Alistair, at least, found it interesting, if not a little over his head. As best he could figure, it focused on viruses, fungi, and parasites that caused personality changes in their hosts. As interesting as it was, he wondered what it had to do with Haven. They dealt with the paranormal, after all, not with outbreaks.

Alistair flipped back to the front page of the paper and saw that it was written by a professor L. Shipton. It certainly sounded like a stuffy professor name. He wondered what someone so smart might look like. He'd always supposed that a nerd of this level would be all pock marks and buck teeth, but Milo was a bona fide genius and he certainly wasn't hideous. In the end it didn't matter, he supposed. If the paper would help them on their mission, then this man could look however he liked.

Alistair was half way through the article for the second time when he heard a knocking on the open door to the TV room. He jumped, unused to anyone taking the time to knock—after all, aside from their bedrooms, none of the extracurricular rooms belonged to anyone. When he looked over the back of the couch, though, he saw one of the workers—a guard—standing in the doorway. The guards wore black pants—kept in place around their ankles by combat boots—and black button ups with patches and badges on their chest and sleeves. They didn't carry assault rifles or anything like that, but they always had a pistol on their hip, and despite the casual feel of the uniform, Alistair could make out the bullet proof vests they wore underneath. It made him wonder what they were afraid of. He'd never heard of anyone trying to break into Haven before—in the U.S. or in Germany.

"Ms. Clairemonte's asking for you."

Alistair dropped back onto the couch for a second, the papers on his chest. This wasn't going to be a good conversation, he could feel it already. Still, he was never the type to be intimidated. She was probably going to slap him on the wrist again for sneaking out, just like all the other times she had over the past month. He would say he was sorry, jump through a few of her hoops, and then go about his business.

"Alright, I'm coming." After dropping the papers onto the cushion he vacated, Alistair followed the guard out of the room. The light-haired guard didn't seem that much older than Alistair or the others on his team, and for a moment he wondered how someone got a job like this. Then he followed the man through one of the hidden doors and into the back passages of the facility.

He'd heard Bastian talk about the office full of monitors he'd seen after his fistfight with Milo in the research wing, but this was Alistair's first time seeing it. Normally, when Marla wanted to give him her perfunctory lecture, she did it at the dining room table or just standing in the doorway of whichever room he'd planted himself in for the day. Now, as the door shut behind him, he was surprised to see that Venja wasn't with the woman who sat behind the massive black desk. Usually the two seemed inseparable, Venja acting as Marla's sensible half. Now Marla Clairemonte sat alone behind her desk, her red painted lips turned down in a serious expression that they rarely saw on her face. She looked surprisingly powerful.

"Yes?" Alistair rarely meant to sound as curt as he usually did, but he didn't feel bad for it this time. There was no way that he would give up any ground to someone who was keeping him grounded like a child.

"Come sit down, Alistair." Despite her serious expression, her voice was gentle.
He wasn't sure if that was a good sign or a bad one, but he did as he was asked.

"Did you get the report I asked Sabin to hand out?"
Small talk.

"I did. It's interesting," he said as he leaned his weight onto one armrest, not wanting to show any signs of the nervousness he absolutely wasn't feeling.

"I'm glad. This next mission will be a change of pace for us, so it makes me happy to hear that you're invested already."

"Was there something about the mission you wanted to discuss with me?"

"No. I'm sure you know that already, though. I want to talk to you again about you steaking out."

"Is it really 'sneaking' if you already know about it?"

"Alistair, don't joke. This is a serious issue."

"It's not seemed that serious the last eight times you've talked to me."

Marla sat up a little straighter, laced her fingers in front of her on the desk. "Listen to me, Alistair. To be frank, the only reason I've turned a blind eye to what you're doing is because Venja asked me to, and because she insisted that you were responsible. That you would never cause trouble or go out of your way to hurt anyone."

"Excuse me?" Alistair sat up straight too now. "I *haven't* ever gone out of my way to hurt anybody, unless *you* tell me they're someone worth hurting."

"So you *didn't* send a boy to the E.R. last night?"

The pause in Alistair's voice probably gave him away, but he raised his chin, refusing to admit any guilt. "I didn't do anything to intentionally hurt that boy."

"Alistair, do you understand how serious his injuries are? There's a good chance they won't be able to repair him. He could be impotent the rest of his life; how can you not take this seriously?"

"I *told* him to pull out. I told him to stop and he didn't. This isn't my fault."

"You *know* how dangerous what you did is. You know what you can do to people. You don't get to play innocent here."

"So, what? I have to be abstinent the rest of my life because my partner might go against my wishes after I ask him to stop?"

"It means you need to take responsibility for what you know you're capable of. It means doing what's right and foregoing the things you want if it means keeping people safe. After this incident was brought to my attention I went back over the E.R. records for the past two months. Since you got here there have been three boys admitted to the hospital with similar injuries. You've hurt *three* innocent people in the past two months. How can you think this behavior is okay?"

"I always warn them! I *always* tell them to stop before they get hurt! This isn't my fault!"

"So you would be okay telling Felix that it wasn't your fault? That you're not doing something wrong?"

Ice dumped into Alistair's veins and he knew that his face went white.

"You don't get to talk about Felix." When he finally forced the words out of his lungs they wheezed through his frozen throat.

"Alistair, listen to me--"

"No! Venja promised me that Felix would *not* be brought up again."

"You are *hurting* people, Alistair. Just like you hurt him, and you don't get to pretend you're not doing it." Her voice finally rose above Alistair's. "I was letting you out because I thought I could trust you, but I refuse to put the safety of the local population in jeopardy just so you can go prowl around for boys!"

Alistair's chest hurt, his ribs quivered and his felt something that might have been tears aching behind his eyes.

"I'm leaving."

Without waiting for a response, Alistair stood up and made his way to the door, his hands shaking as they closed around the knob. The guard who had escorted him to Marla's office was waiting outside and jumped as he erupted from the room. From behind him, and through the muffling sound of his heart as it pounded in his ears, he heard Marla's order to follow him, but he didn't stop. He didn't even bother turning around. He wouldn't stay there anymore. He wouldn't sit around and let someone who knew nothing more about him that what was written down in some dossier tell him that he was a monster.

His dossier had obviously gotten around, too, because no one tried to stop him—though every time he passed a startled looking guard they would fall into line behind him. By the time he arrived at the locked door that would take him back to the dorms, Marla was being trailed by three agents.

"Alistair, you need to calm down. Come back to my office and we can talk about this."

Instead of answering, Alistair ripped the handle off the locked door, then punched it once, and it swung open, a wide dent in the center of it.

"Alistair!" Marla sounded like an owner shouting at a cat who had just tipped a glass of water off the edge of the table. "Stop this right now! You need to settle down."

"You and this whole place can fuck yourselves! Dieser Ort ist ein Gott verdammt Gefängnis!

As he tore through the dorms, he saw Sabin poke his head out of his room, but he didn't pause for even a second. Even the thought of losing his teammates and friends wasn't enough to keep him there. He made a beeline for the main exit that would lead him to the higher levels. It was more secure than the last door, and when he heard Marla demanding that he stop and not damage any more property, he took a step back, braced himself, and kicked the door clear off its hinges. His pursuers quieted for a few seconds as the slab of metal slid to a halt, but as he marched over the discarded door, they surged forward to follow him, none of them stupid enough to lay hands on him.

He knew they wouldn't be able to do anything to stop him, but he was getting tired of being followed, so as he turned the corner he broke out into a sprint, determined to get through the next set of doors before them. Marla was shouting, and boots hammered through the hall behind him, but after he forced the next door open, he turned around and slammed it shut again. Pressing his fingers as hard as he could into the metal that surrounded the door, he managed to crimp the seam shut. It rattled a little as the guards tried to force it open, but snagged on the bent steel and stayed in place.

Shaking the pain from his fingers, Alistair took off for the main exit at a jog. His heart was pounding, but from a cocktail of nerves and exhilaration this time. He was leaving. He was *really* leaving. This is what he wanted, but now the idea was terrifying. What was he supposed to do with himself on his own? Without Berlin or Bastian, without Venja, who had basically adopted him? He shook his head as he turned the last corner, ignoring the sirens that had started ringing in the hallway. He would figure it out. Nothing was worth staying in a place that, at its barest bones, was a fancy prison.

The light of the alleyway blinded him for a second as pushed the final barrier between himself and his freedom open. That freedom, unfortunately, only lasted a second before he bumped against an unexpected blockade. The chest he hit was broad, and the man it belonged to didn't even sway as Alistair plowed into him. Instead, hands moved up to catch Alistair by his arms.

"Slow down, there, kitten. It's the middle of the day. I thought they only let cats out at night."

"You?" Alistair felt the heat in his face rise, humiliation flooding in to join the rage and fear he was already struggling with.

"I'm afraid so." Luca smiled at him, his narrowed eyes the same color as the cool grey of his new suit.

He didn't try to hold onto him as Alistair yanked away, feeling like this man's hands were made of hot coals.

"What the hell are you doing here? If you're stalking me, I really don't have time for this shit right now!" From behind him, Alistair heard the guards break through the temporary lock he'd made on the door.

"I think you should probably calm down." Luca held his hands up as though he could do something to stop Alistair from fleeing.

"I *told* you—" Before Alistair could say anything else, he heard Marla shout as she and the guards turned the last corner, connecting their lines of vision.

"Shipton, stop him!"

Alistair's eyes snapped back to the man he'd met in the bar the night before and his vision went red.

"You know her?"

Luca made a soft hissing noise as he breathed in through his teeth. "Yeah."

Alistair's hands were fisting the other man's suit lapels before he'd even finished speaking.

"You! You were the one that ratted me out, weren't you?"

"I think it would be for the best if you calmed down now, kitten. Things are going to get messy if you don't."

Alistair rarely struck anything, let alone any*one*, with full force. For him, losing his temper and punching another human being could mean murder charges. But now his hand balled into a fist. He wanted to decimate this man. Partially because his smug attitude pissed him off, but also because he had no reason *not* to be a monster if that was how Marla was going to treat him.

His mind was blank, save for a maddening buzz of rage, but as he reeled back, ready to seal his fate with this man's crushed skull, he saw Luca's grey eyes move over his shoulder. He looked curious, then startled. And just as the word "stop" left his perfectly shaped lips, Alistair felt a sharp pain in his shoulder blade. Instantly, his body seized, an electrical current freezing him and driving the breath from his lungs. Then, as the current ebbed, fog filled his head and his legs crumpled beneath him. The last things he recalled as his vision began to fail him, were the supple material of Luca's suit on his cheek and the feel of strong arms lifting him up. He was cradled against the hard plain of Luca's chest when he finally blacked out.

03: BASTIAN

It took everything Bastian had to not bury his hand in Cole's feathery hair and thrust hard into the mouth that worked around him so diligently—it always took everything he had.

Cole whimpered so softly as he came up for air, only to wrap wet lips around the sensitive head of Bastian's cock again seconds later. He squirmed where he lay between the blond's legs, and when Bastian saw him rock his hips against the mattress, he shuddered. His head dropped back, and a growl escaped from deep in his chest. Even his wings quivered as his hands gripped onto the sheets again, using them to tether himself to his own sanity.

Immediately, he regretted the sound, because Cole slowed, then paused. When he looked down his own body at the smaller boy who he'd only come to love more over the past month, he saw his black, star-speckled eyes watching him, his narrow brows turned up in uncertainty. He looked so innocent, even as he licked the shine of pre-cum from his reddened lips.

Patience was hard when he could feel the heat of this boy's breath across the suddenly neglected head of his dick, but instead of hurrying him along, Bastian moved his hand to Cole's cheek, brushing the corner of his mouth with his thumb.

"Alright?

Cole sucked his bottom lip into his mouth and nodded in a way that made him seem bashful. "Yeah…"

Finally, the horned boy looked down, shame coloring his face. Even after all the tests which proved Bastian immune to Cole's toxins, he still worried that he might be slowly driving the man he loved insane. Maybe he was, in a way, because even though it hurt Bastian to see him struggling with this, in that moment, it was hard for him calm his lust.

Reaching down, Bastian's hands closed around the smaller boy's deceptively thin arms. Cole didn't struggle as he was hauled up Bastian's body until they were lying chest to chest, though his back arched just slightly when the blond rocked his hips forward, grinding himself against the matching hardness he felt on top of him.

"Cole, Mein Liebling, light of my life…" His hands moved to either side of Cole's face, cupping his cheeks and forcing him to meet his stare. "You know I'd die for you, but you're driving me crazy." Cole's eyes dropped and his fingers traced patterns on Bastian's chest. Worried that he may have actually hurt the other boy's feelings, Bastian brushed his lips over his temple, whispering against his skin "And you know, if we don't concentrate now, I'm going to have to flip you over and fuck you until you can't walk. And then we'll miss our mission briefing."

Cole's face flashed hot under Bastian's hands, though he could feel the smaller boy's prick jump at the threat. No matter how innocent he looked, he always responded well to a certain level of dirty talk, and somehow that only made Bastian love him more.

Sliding his hands down the curve of Cole's body, Bastian gripped his backside, holding him steady as he rocked his hips up against him, and, despite the uncertainty he seemed to feel, Cole gasped against the other man's collarbone.

"The only thing that makes me hungry for you is love, Cole. Please believe me."

As Cole's mouth moved up the length of his neck, he pressed his own hips down, matching his lover's every move. Cole really would drive him mad someday, but Bastian knew it wasn't because of toxins; it was because he loved him so damn much.

It was impossible to keep from smiling as he watched Cole burrow his face into his pillow. No matter how many nights they spent together, his tiny black-haired lover always burned with embarrassment afterward. Not that they'd spent very many nights together. Even now, Cole rarely became receptive to Bastian's advances unless he was hungry. Today had been an exception, and he'd only agreed after Bastian promised not to go all the way. It wasn't that sex was the most important thing for Bastian, but he hated watching Cole continue to beat himself up over it.

Softly, Bastian ran two fingertips from the nape of Cole's neck down the curve of his spine, smiling when he saw the other boy jump as his fingers eased over the swell of his backside. He winked when Cole turned to peek at him. He was rewarded with shy, but thrilled smile, then Cole mumbled against his pillowcase.

"How do you feel?"

Bastian sighed around his smile and leaned down to kiss his temple.

"I feel perfect, love. Just like I always do."

Cole let out a matching breath and moved so his cheek was resting on the pillow, watching his winged lover. He looked like he wanted to believe him, and Bastian was thankful for that much.

"I just worry." His voice was quiet, but he reached for Bastian's hand as his other arm moved to prop himself up so he could look at the blond man more directly. "Milo changed so slowly that I didn't even notice until it was too late."

Bastian never held Cole's past against him, or the things he'd done to stay alive and fed, but it still hurt him a little to hear his lover talk about another man while he laid, debauched and red-lipped, in bed beside him. He knew the connection he had to Milo was important, though, so he brushed his thumb over the backs of Cole's knuckles.

"I don't know what else to tell you, Cole. We can go run blood tests again, but they're going to say the same thing. I just need you to trust in me."

"I'm sorry, Bastian. I do believe you. I'm just scared."

"I know." Rolling onto his back, he collected Cole into his arms, drawing him close so the other boy lay with his head resting on his chest. It was always a warm, calming feeling to have the smaller boy pressed against his side—it dissipated any frustration he may feel. "Milo seems to be coming around, though. I mean, you guys were talking at dinner the other night, weren't you?"

"Yeah. It still wasn't the same though. It's hard to explain, but he seemed so reserved."

"It'll just take time for everything to work out of his system. You'll see. He'll be right as rain in just another month or two."

"I just want him to be happy."

"I know you do."

Cole had a hopeful smile on his face when he folded his arms on Bastian's chest, propping his chin up so he could look the blond in the face. "Maybe he just needs someone else, you know? Don't people say the best way to mend a broken heart is to fall in love again?"

"Do people say that?" Bastian couldn't help but laugh. "Are you suggesting we hook him up with someone down here?"

"It would be perfect, though. Right?"

"Who on earth would you want to hook him up with? We don't exactly have a wide range of choices."

"I dunno. He seems to get along well with Alistair."

"Alistair wouldn't touch him with a ten foot pole."

"Why not?" Cole actually sounded offended. "Milo is really handsome." When Bastian raised a brow at him he rolled his eyes. "You know what I mean. There isn't anything wrong with him."

"I'm not saying there's anything wrong with Milo, but you've seen the sort of place Alistair goes to pick up guys. Do you honestly think that Milo falls into his interest group?"

Cole made a face, probably trying to imagine Milo in the middle of the noisy night club he'd followed Alistair to the month before. It was a pretty funny visual if Bastian was going to be honest.

"Well what about Berlin? You know him better than I do..."

"Milo's too good for Berlin."

Cole pressed his lips to Bastian's chest to muffle his laugh. "Are you guys even friends?"

"Yeah. But he's still a piece of shit."

"I think he's probably a better person than he lets on."

"Maybe." Bastian couldn't deny the times Berlin had put himself in danger to protect him or their other teammates. "But he's just barely a good person. I mean, he's good, but he's a jerk. And I can't imagine Milo putting up with that. Wouldn't Sabin be a better choice? They know each other better."

"I don't think Sabin would be interested. He's never said a word about wanting to be with anyone, and I think he has a crush on this long term pen pal he has."

"You're allowed to have pen pals?"

"If you knew someone before you came to Haven you are. At least Marla lets us. Sabin said their letters get pretty heavily censored though."

Bastian supposed it made sense that Haven would want to block out information that might give away their location, but it still felt weird to know that a third party read every letter. It felt creepy.

I'm sure it's important, though. We can't have the public finding out about the things we deal with. There would be hysteria.

Planting one last kiss on Cole's forehead, he moved to sit up.

"We're going to be late if we don't hurry."

04: ALISTAIR

The light was dimmed when Alistair came to, and for a second he thought he'd just woken up after a bad night of partying. His head hurt, and his body ached, but he was in his room. Then he tried to rub his eyes and he realized his arms and legs were completely immobile. Panic shook him for a second—he'd never been tied down before, not by anything he couldn't break. His heart hammered hard enough to hurt, and when he realized he couldn't even lift his head he started shouting.

Instantly, the door opened and Venja hurried in to his bedside.

"Shh. Calm down, Alistair. You're fine."

He could feel her warm hands on his arm as he tried to slow his suddenly ravenous lungs.

"Why am I tied down?" The tremor in his voice sounded alien.

"Honey, you're not tied down. You're sedated. Just relax."

"Sedated? Why am I sedated?"

"It's just until we sort out what happened earlier today."

"What?"

"Sweetheart, you tried to run away. You broke thousands of dollars of equipment…"

"So you're drugging me? You're holding me hostage?"

"You aren't a hostage. Just relax." Her hand moved to pet the hair off his forehead, and, despite the situation, the sensation calmed him.

He wanted to hold onto Venja, or at least have her hold onto him. He wanted something, anything to make him feel secure. He didn't like the way sedatives made him feel. After a few breaths, he realized he could move his head from side to side— though he couldn't lift it off the pillow—and if he really tried, he could move his arms and legs the tiniest bit.

"Am I going to be punished?"

Venja's brown eyes softened and her lips thinned a little. "I don't know. If they insist, then I'll make sure it's fair. I won't let anything bad happen to you."

Alistair took a deep breath, doing his best to keep his anger and fear hidden. Venja said he wasn't a prisoner, but he would be punished for trying to leave. Alistair wasn't a brainiac like Milo, but he was pretty sure that was the definition of "prisoner."

"She blamed me for Felix." Alistair hadn't wanted his voice to sound so small.

"Oh sweetheart." Her hand cupped his cheek. "I know. She feels horrible about it. She just doesn't want you to wind up in the same situation. She wants to keep you safe. Just like I do."

It was hard to disagree with Venja when she spoke so gently to him. She was his mother after all—not by blood, maybe, but she'd shown him more love than his real mother ever had.

"I'm going to tell her that you're awake so we can decide on a course of action. The sooner we do that, the sooner we can get you off these sedatives."

Alistair managed a small nod, though his heart raced as he watched her go. His bedroom felt different now that he lay defenseless inside it. It felt like a vault, like a coffin he would be trapped in forever. Taking a few breaths, he occupied his mind by assessing himself for real. Now that he wasn't panicking, he had a better idea of where he stood—so to speak. His limbs felt weighted, like two sandbags that had been roughly sewn onto his body. His chest and lungs were unhindered, though. He knew what muscle relaxers and over the counter sedatives felt like. This was different. It was like his limbs had been targeted. It made him wonder what was going on in the research labs under the facility.

He was just beginning to regain some motion in his knees and elbows when the door opened again. Heat flooded Alistair's body when he saw Luca enter the room instead of Venja.

"Get out," he barked before the man had finished closing the door behind himself. Alistair felt the anger coloring his face, but Luca only clucked his tongue at him and walked to his bed, sitting casually on the edge of the mattress.

"You sure do change your tune quickly, don't you? I mean, just last night you were ready to crawl inside my skin and now I can't even get a pleasant 'hello' out of you."

"That's because I'm only here thanks to you. Now leave. This is *my* room." His body jerked as he tried to lash out at the man. Instead, all he could do was turn his head away from the hand that moved to brush some hair from Alistair's face.

"I'm pretty sure this room belongs to the big bad government. They own it and this whole rodeo, kitten. They're just lending it to you. And, unfortunately, they were the ones who finally blew the whistle on you. I'm afraid I had nothing to do with that one."

"I don't believe you." His limbs were dead weight, but Alistair's heart was pounding hot in his chest, rattling his ribcage and making him shiver all over. The fingers that brushed down his jawline were cool and very lightly calloused. And while Luca had looked handsome in the bar, hearing the low reverberation of his voice in the silence of a private room—*his* private room—made every cell in his body hum.

"Are you still upset that I turned you down?" The cattish grin he wore only made his cheekbones sharper.

"Like I give a shit about that. I could get anyone I want."

"I bet you could." Luca stared at him a few moments and Alistair refused to drop his own eyes. He would *not* let this man take an inch from him, even as he felt more heat seep traitorously into his face and neck.

The backs of cold fingers pressed against his heated cheek, and though Alistair was able to shift his head away from them, he could do little else.

"You look warm," Luca said. "Let me help."

Carefully, Luca used both hands to pull the blanket down, folding it across Alistair's knees.

"What do you think you're doing?" Alistair's body jerked when he tried to swat Luca's hands away.

"Just helping you out." With his body uncovered, Luca took a moment to admire the narrow lines that were only hidden by Alistair's thin shirt and house pants. "You're very prickly, Alistair, but you're easy to read."

"So you're reading me? Have you gotten to the part where I put my fist through your skull?"

Luca laughed, and the sound was like a drug that went straight to the redhead's most private parts.

"You're upset with Marla, right? You feel like a prisoner?"

That wasn't the response Alistair was expecting. Even Luca's tone seemed a little more understanding than it had seconds before, and, for a moment, Alistair thought he'd like to have some commiseration—he'd like to have someone who could validate the unease that had been growing inside him.

"Wouldn't you feel the same way?"

The other man seemed to soften a little in response. His steady gaze easing just enough to make Alistair feel like maybe he understood—like maybe Luca was a safe place for him to turn. Then he remembered who he was talking to.

"But you're in the same pocket Marla's in, aren't you? You'd have no idea what this feels like." He made sure his words were sharp enough to make up for his moment of weakness.

The new teacher didn't argue. He didn't try to defend himself or his position within Haven. He only smiled as his eyes dropped down the helpless body that lay beneath him.

"So prickly," he said again, his fingers brushing the tiny strip of skin that peeked out between Alistair's shirt and pants. "You hardly know me but have already decided I'm a villain."

It was only his hip bone, but lightning shot through Alistair's body as fingers pressed over the small protrusion of bone. This was *not* good. The thin fabric of his pants would do nothing to hide any reaction he might have.

"Don't touch me." He clenched his teeth to hide his shiver of arousal. The last thing he wanted was for this man to know exactly how badly he craved his hands on him. If only this had happened in the bar, before Luca had humiliated him—before he'd learned that he worked for Haven.

"I think you'll feel much better if you relax a little." With steel eyes watching his every reaction, Luca's fingers trailed over the band of his pants, and after a helpless jerk of Alistair's legs, he outlined his treacherously growing shape through the fabric.

Alistair grit his teeth, determined to not make a sound.

Shit. Why do I want this so bad? I hate this guy so much, but...

Alistair's limbs trembled and his feet pushed against the sheets with the strength of an infant. He'd imagined what it would be like to be helpless under the hands of a lover before, but had never been able to separate the imagined sensation from the time he'd spent drugged as a child. Now, however, instead of feeling terrified, he felt exhilarated. Maybe it was simply because Luca was so handsome, but Alistair was completely, painfully hard, and he'd barely even been touched.

"Your mouth has a sharp tongue, Alistair. But this part of you seems much more honest." Luca squeezed him through his pants, and Alistair's head rolled back on its own, though he managed to bite his lip against the moan at the back of his throat.

"Fuck you."

Luca laughed as he watched every twitch of Alistair's face. "Well I don't usually let my partners do the fucking, but for someone as gorgeous and defiant as you...maybe someday I'd make that exception."

"I hate you..." The words somehow lost their bite as his voice quivered.

"I know, kitten." As though he were unwrapping something fragile and expensive, Luca's fingers pulled the waistband of the boy's house pants down until his unambiguous arousal was left exposed, hard and jumping against his stomach. "What? No underwear? Don't tell me this is how you dress when you go out to that bar." Luca's voice dropped a little deeper, if that was even possible, and Alistair had to close his eyes against the sound, his face burning.

"So what if it is?" He tried to move again, his arms sliding over the mattress, but still refusing to lift.

"Well I'd have to say I was disappointed." Luca's fingers traced the underside of Alistair's cock. "Look how perfect you are. There's not a man in this whole city who deserves to see even an inch of you. Let alone touch you."

"Then why are you putting your grubby hands all over me?"

Luca smiled at him, wide and genuine, and for a second Alistair felt himself swoon.

"Well obviously, I'm the exception."

"Don't be so full of yourself, you fucking geezer."

"So mean." With a smile on his lips, Luca's long fingers finally wrapped around Alistair's length, and instantly the redhead's mouth dropped open, all the air in his lungs rushing out of his body. "Let me show you what a bit of age can teach you."

Alistair's fingers scraped helplessly against the sheets of his bed, his hands still too weak to actually grab hold of anything. If someone were to ask him what it was that Luca did differently from any other person who had ever touched him, Alistair would probably have been at a loss for an answer, but Luca was doing *something,* that was sure. He squeezed him just hard enough to make him tremble, he outlined his shape like it was made to fit in his hand.

Weakly, Alistair tried to tell him to stop, but the sound only came out in a pathetic warble and was met by a soft chuckle.

"Just beautiful." With his free hand, Luca pushed Alistiar's shirt up his torso, his fingers spreading out across his narrow chest until he'd tucked the fabric under the boy's chin. "You can hate me for it later, but for now just let go a little and enjoy yourself."

Before Alistair could tell him to go fuck himself, fingers found the already hardened buds of his nipples and rolled them gently under calloused pads. There was something about not being able to move, not being able to grab hold of his partner and guide him to where he really wanted to be touched that made the simple sensation so extraordinary.

Like his body were some tightly strung instrument, Luca pulled the most disgraceful sounds from him. He bit his lip in an attempt to keep quiet, not wanting to let this man know, for even one second, that, with a single hand, he'd aroused him more than most of his previous lovers had ever managed. Luca was working in earnest now, though, palm smearing the tiny beads of pre-cum down over his length as his fist began pumping around him. Alistair wanted to come so badly, but he didn't want to give this man the satisfaction.

As though he could read Alistair's mind, Luca's free hand moved to his face, catching him by his jaw. When the redhead forced his eyes open, he found his senses flooded as Luca leaned down close to him, his mouth coming so near to his that he could feel his breath and the vibration of his voice against his lips.

"You're such a proud little thing." Luca didn't move away as Alistair shivered helplessly. His thin lips brushed over the younger man's cheek, then teeth caught his earlobe and when he spoke again, his lips tickled his ear. "Let that go. Show me what you look like helpless and desperate. If you're good, I won't make you beg this time."

The arrogance in his voice was infuriating, but somehow it made Alistair gasp, it made his resolve melt, and with a soft, wordless quivering of his voice he did exactly what Luca wanted. His back arched as he shot a thin ribbon of white into this man's waiting hand, and through his own breathing he heard Luca chuckle against his ear.

"Truly gorgeous." His lips brushed a soft kiss against his damp temple, and as Alistair lay trembling on the mattress, riding out the last tendrils of his climax, Luca found a discarded shirt Alistair had left on the floor the day before. Using it as a rag, he wiped the few drops from where they'd landed on the pale expanse of Alistair's flat stomach, then he wiped his own hand clean. He had already rearranged the redhead's clothes back to a state of normalcy when the younger man finally came around enough to glare at him. "Don't look at me like that. You'll make me ravish you."

"Why did you do that?" His voice sounded weak, even in his own ears.

Luca smiled at him as he folded the soiled shirt into a small bundle. He looked knowing somehow, and amused.

"Because you wanted me to."

A more indignant sound had never passed Alistair's lips, but as he stumbled to tell him he was full of shit, the older man stood, pulled his blankets back up around him, brushed a few strands of hair from his eyes, then left, all the while smiling at him as though he knew every secret on the planet. It wasn't until the room had been quiet for a few minutes that he realized the man had taken his shirt with him.

05: COLE

"What are you doing?" Cole shook Bastian where he was sitting beside him on the couch, both hands fisted in the sleeve of his shirt.

"Stop shaking me! I'm trying to put some distance between us!" The controller jostled in his hand as Cole continued to yank at him.

"You can't do that! You have to get close! You have to get in from the back, and—"

Before he could finish his sentence, Bastian's hunter was blasted with a stream of blood as Ebrietas, Daughter of the Cosmos, caught him in her sites. A bright red "YOU DIED" materialized on the screen and they both sank back into the couch. They had gotten Bloodborne just over a week ago and had been playing every free moment they had, when they weren't occupying themselves with something a little more naked.

"You can't shake me like that while I'm playing, Cole. You got me killed."

"I did *not!* You wouldn't be dead if you'd listened to me. If you hang back too far she'll hit you with the blood spit thing. You have to roll in close to her side and hit her tail."

"I've tried that. It doesn't work."

"You just have to keep trying. Look." Cole took a second to bring up a how-to video on his phone. They sat shoulder-to-shoulder watching a hunter similar to theirs flawlessly roll between the creature's body and her canopy of tentacles to get at the slug-like body behind her. "See? That doesn't look so hard."

"Says the one who just sits and shouts in my ear the whole time."

"Excuse you! I do a lot more than just sit around. I am your navigator, strategist, and—" He stopped when he saw the grin on Bastian's face. He tried to look annoyed as he shoved his teasing boyfriend.

"No, don't push me away," Bastian cooed, winding his arms around Cole as the smaller boy squirmed and swatted at him. "I need my strategist. Navigate me, Cole."

Bastian leaned all his weight on his boyfriend, making him topple back into the arm of the couch. He still struggled to get out from under him, but Cole couldn't stop the bubbling laughter that Bastian's arms wrung out of him. It was moments like this that made Cole happiest. Playing games, laughing, teasing each other— Cole felt like a normal teen. Well, as normal as it could feel with the other boy's pristine white wings unfurling above them.

Wandering hands drew him out of his thoughts as Bastian snaked his fingers up under Cole's shirt, sending shivers up his spine.

"What are you doing?" Cole laughed, even as his stomach churned a little.

"Getting in from the back, like you told me too." Bastian mouthed playfully at his neck as his hands continued to trace lines across his back, the sensation breaking goosebumps out across Cole's skin.

"Stop it, or I'm gonna spit blood at you." He was still laughing at his own joke when Bastian's head turned and he leaned down, his breath washing over Cole's lips. In a panicked reflex,

Cole turned his head, leaving Bastian's kiss landing on his cheek near the corner of his mouth.

The laughter stopped. Cole braced himself, ready for Bastian to get angry at him for denying him a kiss *again*. Instead, Cole felt Bastian sigh against his cheek. Then he kissed it again, kissed his temple, kissed his forehead—he sat up, one arm propped up on the back of the couch, a soft smile on his face as he looked down at his lover.

Cole could see the disappointment in his eyes, even as his lips formed that perfect arc on his face. Even when Cole gave into Bastian's advances, kissing still terrified him. His blond lover had done everything they could think of to ease his fear—blood tests, hours of conversation, regular checkups to monitor his hormone levels, therapists, doctors—but nothing seemed to shake the queasy anxiety he felt.

"I'm sorry." Cole's voice came out soft and pathetic.

Bastian just sighed again and guided Cole's hand up to kiss his knuckles.

"I know, Cole. Take your time."

It was stupid to dig his heels in there when just that morning Basitan had brought him to a shattering orgasm with just his fingers, when Cole had desperately sucked the ecstasy from the other boy's body. Yet, somehow, kissing was a problem.

Cole was about to apologize again, when he was cut off by the piercing wail of a siren. The lights and television flicked off, and for a second everything in the room was still and silent. Bastian grew still, and they both held onto each other for a second. Then the siren rang again and an automated voice came on.

"Facility breach on dorm level. Standby for further information."

Cole was on his feet immediately, his hand on Bastian's wrist to guide him through the dark. Emergency lights had come on, but the TV room was nearly pitch black, and the hallways were dim save for the flashing lights at the junction of each corridor. His eyes were made for this, and he would use whatever advantage he had to keep Bastian safe and find his teammates.

They had never had a real security breach before, but they had trained for them. And there was still a possibility that this was only a drill. Then a low growling reverberated through the hallways, and they both knew this wasn't practice.

Every member of the American Haven team knew the first thing to do in the face of any fight was arm themselves. That meant taking one of the secure lifts down to the hanger. Cole knew the other boys would make their way to the same place, so he didn't waste time looking for them.

06: ALISTAIR

Venja didn't come back to check on him as the sedatives slowly worked their way out of Alistair's body. That meant he'd been stuck playing his encounter with Luca over and over in his head. No matter how attracted he was to the man, he hated him for his arrogance. Though, admittedly, if that cool attitude was dealing out insults to someone else, Alistair may have admired it. Still, for a few moments during their interaction, he had seemed to understand Alistair in a way that his teammates and house mother never had. He wondered if that had all been part of his cocky act as well.

When he was finally able to move his limbs for real, Alistair sat up. He was horribly thirsty and needed the bathroom. Luckily, the toilet was only a short distance from his bed, and no one was around to see his legs wobbling like a baby deer. By the time he'd finished, his strength had returned enough that he thought he could walk without falling. Which was good. All he had left was his dignity, and he didn't want to do anything in front of his teammates that might jeopardize that.

He didn't know what Marla might have planned for him, but he figured she would find him when she figured it out. For now, he would go to the kitchen, eat, drink, and try to regain a bit of normalcy.

Alistair had only just slipped out of his door when the whole level went black. A quaking heartbeat later, the emergency lights came on. They were dim and red, and further down the hall he saw a white light flashing. A loud siren shook the floor, followed by a recording.

"Facility breach on dorm level. Standby for further information."

The announcement played on repeat, presumably while the security team tried to locate the intruder and assess the problem. Whatever the problem may be, though, Alistair was surprised that security hadn't flooded the level yet. He stayed still, waiting for them to come, but the minutes stretched on, and his heart beat faster with every passing moment.

The halls were quiet, and Alistair was surprised that none of his teammates had come out to check the situation. Then he looked at his watch and realized it was dinner time. The others must have been in the dining room, or one of the TV rooms, probably keeping still just like he was, waiting for more information. Maybe it was all just a test. After all, since when had an *intruder* ever made it into Haven? Alistair couldn't even make it *out* of the place. The chances of someone getting *in* were exceedingly lower.

When the main lights failed to come back on the way they would after a test, Alistair knew he couldn't just hang around. If this wasn't a drill, then he would have to find the others. His knees shook and tried to buckle as he began down the hall, the weakness that still hung in his body making his hands shake with an unease he wouldn't have admitted even if there had been someone there to admit it to. Helplessness was not something he had much experience with, but questioning whether he'd be able to defend himself made his body feel even weaker than it already was.

He'd only made it a few yards when a figure shuffled into sight at the end of the hall. One of the emergency lights flashed in Alistair's eyes, making it hard to see who it was, but he was tall and broad shouldered.

"Bastian?" Alistair called only loud enough to be heard, not wanting anyone else who might be lurking in the area to hear him. The figure paused and turned toward him, ambling in a drunken, swaying path toward him. "Luca?" He tried again, wondering if the man who had already proven troublesome was playing a trick on him. Then the light above him flashed again and, for just a second, it lit up the man's face.

It wasn't Luca *or* Bastian. It was hard to even call it a "man" at all. Obviously human, but with blackened eyes and a jaw that seemed detached from the rest of its skull, gaping and swaying with its slow, wide pace. Its clothes were normal enough—jeans and a dark blue t-shirt—but they were stained black down the front as a thick, tar-like liquid dripped down the dislocated chin. A low gurgle sounded from the thing, and it paused in the flashing light.

Alistair heard his own breath over the rushing of blood in his ears, and realized his own mouth hung open in a vague mockery of the creatures dangling mandible. They were both still for a few seconds, waves of stink rolling down the hallway—putrescence and rotten eggs. Obviously this would-be man was the intruder, but it looked like something out of a zombie flick. He had seen a fair share of strange creatures, but they all been just that—creatures. They never looked like people.

"Hello?" Alistair's voice was barely a whisper. "Do you understand me?"

The creature's back muscles seemed so spasm, jerking its torso back, its arms curling up toward its chest for a few seconds. The motion looked painful, but Alistair only heard a mild, gurgling grunt from the creature parading as a human.

"Are you okay?"

Alistair knew it was a stupid question to ask, but before he could think of anything better, the man-creature lurched toward in him at a speed that betrayed the jerky, feeble movements from earlier. Alistair could feel the weakness in his body still, but he ran. He knew that if he could avoid the intruder for just a few more minutes, his body might finish its recovery. But finding the others was also a good option.

The gurgling he'd heard from the creature—which, despite his skepticism, he'd already labeled as "zombie" in his head—had turned into a wet screeching. He had no idea how strong this thing was, or if the gross-out show was all it had. Either way, Alistair's limbs still felt too weak for him to take on this movie-monster hand-to-hand. No matter how strong you are, close proximity meant biting. And biting meant infection. And the last thing Alistair wanted was his good looks to go down the drain. "Undead" wasn't really his aesthetic. Managing to push his still shaky legs into a sprint, Alistair slid around a corner, heading to the lift that would carry him down to the equipment room.

No matter how gross this thing was, an accurate shot from his rifle would blast its brains right back to Hollywood. The elevator had just come into view when the intercom crackled to life again, and this time it was Marla.

"Hey kiddies. So, not a huge deal, but it looks like our latest creature of interest from the research level has accidentally escaped its holding cell."

If Alistair wasn't running for his life, he would have been angrier about their leader's blasé attitude over the flesh-hungry *zombie* she'd accidentally let loose. He knew they studied creatures they'd collected from various missions on one of the levels of their underground beehive, but most of them where things they'd brought home with them—like the Daaparu from Lechugilla. He'd always assumed the containment facilities were built to keep things like this from happening.

Then again, they'd been intentionally air-dropped into murder-dog-robot territory, so he shouldn't be that surprised.

He didn't bother slowing down until he caught himself against the wall beside the lift and mashed the down button with the heel of his hand.

"We've deactivated all of the lifts to keep it from wandering away again."

"Are you serious?" Alistair wouldn't be surprised if Marla had heard him. He'd certainly shouted loud enough.

"Our friend's name is Charles, so if you guys could take care of him for me, that would be great."

Alistair pressed his back to the closed elevator doors, watching *Charles* barrel toward him, arms slashing at the air in front of him, jaw extending to show the long black tongue that whipped back and forth like an independent, Lovecraftian mini-monster, slinging black tar on the walls where it smoked and bubbled.

"Fuck, Charles. You've really let yourself go."

When the man lunged toward him, Alistair ducked under his arm and took off in the other direction, not pausing to appreciate the thump as the infected man stumbled into the closed, steel doors. So his rifle was out of the question. What else did he have to use as a weapon? He spent so much time relying on his strength that he'd never put much time into weapon training. He could feel the effects of the tranquilizer wearing off, but was still far from his full potential. Of course, he probably had enough of his strength back to accomplish *something*.

Following a gut instinct, Alistair led his new friend toward the kitchen, hoping to find the others. Emergency lights flashed in the empty room, and for the hundredth time in the past five minutes, Alistair wondered where the others had gone. The more time that passed without running into them, the more Alistair began to feel like this was some additional, elaborate punishment Marla had concocted just for him. Ducking around the side of the seven-foot fridge, Alistair waited until the garbling, rank man was just about to hook him with his crooked fingers. Then, in one motion he thrust the freezer door open, catching the thing in the face, toppling it onto its back. Before it had a chance to recover, Alistair braced himself against the wall and pushed, forcing the refrigerator up onto its edge, ready to topple it onto the already decaying body.

Then Marla's voice stopped him again.

"By the way, Charles is an important part of our next mission. So please refrain from killing him."

Alistair was rocked back against the wall as he let the fridge fall back onto its flat bottom.

"Son of a bitch! Are you serious?"

He was convinced now that Marla could hear him. His only hope was that she knew just how pissed off he was. Not only did he have to find a way to keep from being bitten, but now he had subdue this Romero reject without killing it—she had to be fucking with him. Trying to take advantage of Charles' temporary concussion nap, Alistair made for the door. As he stepped away from the still body, a hand caught his ankle, and in true B-rated horror fashion, Alistair fell to the ground. His weakened legs tried to kick the man's slobbering mouth away from him as a thick, black tongue wrapped around his sock, the tar that oozed from it hot against his skin even through the fabric. He was shouting, flailing, his gut churning from the unfamiliar feeling of helplessness.

Then light flashed between himself and the creature, heat hitting his face like a wave of coal, threatening to burn his skin. His arm flew up to shield his eyes. At the same time, the raspy, wheezing sounds rose to a screech, and his ankle was freed. Squinting against the light and heat, Alistair moved his arm, only to be met with a wall of fire between himself and his zombie admirer. He scrambled away, the flames close enough to catch his socks and—consequently—his feet ablaze.

"Watch your toes, sweetheart."

Alistair, still on the ground, turned to see a boy standing over him—a stranger with a wide line of blue hair striping the top of his head in a thick, short Mohawk. Dots of metal in his eyebrow and nose reflected the light, and, for a second, Alistair wondered if Sabin had dyed his hair. But this boy was taller and broader than their resident witch, even if they seemed to shop at the same place.

"Who the fuck are you?" Alistair didn't bother getting up, his muscles quivering now that he'd stopped running, ready to rest while Charles shuffled about in the ring of fire that acted as his cage now.

A low growl came from behind the new boy, and at his side a massive black dog—*no, definitely a wolf*—stalked toward him, teeth bared and eyes shining.

07: BASTIAN

Cole had not seemed as surprised as Bastian had upon hearing that Marla's research team had accidentally let something loose. Then again, he'd not been surprised about the robot dog either, and Bastian had to just assume that these sorts of surprises were normal for his American teammates. Personally, he could do without them.

"Come on," Cole said, leading Bastian by the hand away from the lifts. "We have a set meeting place in case of emergencies."

"What? Why haven't I heard anything about this?"

"Oh." Cole didn't stop, but Bastian could hear the smile in his voice. "I guess it slipped our minds. It's more of an understanding between us. We don't want Marla to know because then she'll take our plans into account when she tests us."

"Is that what this is?" The more time he spent in the American facility, the more he began to question their leader's methods. "A test?"

"Well better to stay on our toes than get caught off guard, right?"

As they turned another corner, orange light flooded the hallway, radiating from the open archway that lead into the dining room. The space was empty, its chairs sat quietly around the table, but through the connecting opening they heard the thrum of a fire, voices rising up over it.

Cole stopped in his tracks as they entered the space, Bastian bumping into him as they both brought up an arm to shield their faces from the heat and light of the fire. Inside the blazing ring was a shuffling, moaning creature, its features shrouded by the impossibly bright flames. Silhouetted between them and the burning cage was the new comrade they'd met during their briefing that morning and Alistair, collapsed on the ground, near enough to the flames that his pant-leg looked singed.

Bastian had just reached for Cole, wanting to protect him from the wolf whose attention they'd drawn, when the smaller boy pushed past the hackled dog. It must have been as surprised as Bastian was, because the canine softened immediately, a small whine escaping it as it fell back on its haunches. Hooking his hands under Alistair's arms, Cole dragged their friend further away from the heat of the fire.

"Oh good, you guys finally got here. I'd hoped someone else would get to enjoy the nice fire I made." The blue-haired boy seemed unbothered by the flames that licked at the ceiling, yet somehow didn't spread.

"Who the fuck is this kid?" Alistair tried to shake Cole's hands off, but he was still shaky and was glad for the help he had getting to his feet.

"He came with Professor Shipton. Are you hurt? Did you get burned anywhere?" Cole steadied the taller boy, looking him over as he spoke.

"Shipton? You mean Luca? You're here with that asshole?" Alistair's lip curled, even as his cheeks pinkened.

"Well, for starters, the name's Jett." The other boy grinned despite the contempt in his voice. "And last I checked, I just saved your life."

"By lighting a fire in a sealed building?"

Jett cocked his head, gestured to the fire, then to the unharmed room around them, then to the smokeless air around them. "I'm failing to see the problem here. But if magical, smokeless fire isn't enough and you're still going to be salty about it, I'll go ahead and give you the authentic experience." He snapped his fingers, and black smoke curled off the peaks of the flame, choking the room.

Bastian's lungs seized and he ducked low, grabbing Cole and leading him and Alistair both out of the smothering haze of ash. Their coughing ricocheted down the corridor and was answered by a familiar voice.

"What happened?" Running up on them, Berlin grabbed Bastian's arm and pulled them further from the bellowing room. Milo and Sabin weren't far behind.

He shook his head, unable to talk through his coughing. As he caught his breath, he wiped Cole's eyes for him, trying to ease the sting that had them watering.

"This asshole kid lit a fire, what does it look like?" Alistair snapped at his teammate, rubbing at his own eyes.

"You guys were the ones who wanted smoke." Jett materialized out of the grey fog that began retreating as he walked toward them.

"Like hell we did," Bastian barked at him. He wouldn't have cared so much if this new boy's immature prank hadn't put Cole in danger.

"Well your pretty friend should keep his mouth in check when talking about my boss, then."

"Well, I'm sorry that your boss is a piece of shit," the redhead interjected.

Beside Jett, the black wolf took a step toward Alistair, the rumble in the creature's chest louder than it was last time.

"Oh shut up!" Alistair, shouted at the dog, his hands finally feeling strong enough that he felt like he could snap the thing's neck if it lunged for him.

To the others' surprise, the dog's head drooped and turned to give Jett a forlorn look.

"Fuck your boss," Alistair continued. "And fuck *your* boss." He jammed a finger against Cole's collarbone—only because he was the closest member of the original American team to him. "I'm over these stupid games she's playing with us!"

To everyone's surprise, it was Milo who spoke up, his voice stronger than they'd heard it in weeks. "I hardly think you can call a security breach a 'game.'"

"Oh please, you think this is an actual security breach? Sie dumme Amerikaner." He paused a second, his eyes narrowing at their bespectacled teammate. "And now that I think about it, you're always down there on the research level. Maybe you're in on this stupid prank. How do we know *you* didn't set this thing loose?"

Bastian looked at the brunette.

"That's a good question," Jett, of all people, chimed in. "We haven't seen you since the mission briefing."

Alistair turned on him, too. "Shut up! Don't act like you know what's going on around here."

Jett only raised both hands in surrender, chuckling under his breath at the explosive temper tantrum Alistair was having. Even Bastian was surprised. He'd known Alistair almost as long as he'd known Berlin, and very rarely did the redhead lose his cool this badly. Then his friend turned back to Milo, jabbing his finger at him this time.

"Go on then. Did you know she was going to send this thing up here to get us?"

Milo swatted the other boy's sharp finger away, his brows drawing into a hard line over the rim of his glasses. "Did I know this thing was down there? Yes. We've been running tests on it for about a week. Did I know that it had escaped? Of course not. But really, what goes on down in the research lab is none of your business."

"None of my business? Are you kidding? You guys are hoarding *zombies* down there and it's none of our business?"

"We aren't *hoarding* anything. And he isn't a zombie."

"Oh yeah, then explain to me what that thing is?" Alistair swept a hand back at the doorway where they saw Charles shuffling back and forth behind the line of fire, his contorted hands reaching for them only to recoil from the heat.

Milo seemed to take pause now. "We're not sure what it is yet."

"But you still think this thing got out all on its own?"

Bastian didn't like seeing his teammates turning on one another, but he couldn't help wondering the same thing. Haven was an extremely secure stronghold. It was hard to imagine that some shuffling movie-monster could break its way out.

"I'll tell you what." Alistair's tone had gone from angry to insultingly sarcastic. "You prove to me that this thing wasn't set loose on purpose, and I'll retire and move to *Kansas.*"

Bastian couldn't help but exchange looks with Cole and Berlin, each of them obviously too afraid to tell Alistair what he'd missed in their mission briefing.

08: ALISTAIR

As it turned out, Alistair had been completely correct. Charles hadn't been a security breech at all—he had been their training wheels. With the kitchen fire still burning, but smokeless again, the security guards had swarmed the dorm level and taken the man-creature back into custody. Unfortunately for Alistair, though, his win was immediately transformed into a loss, and his wager came back to bite him in the ass. The following morning they had all been packed onto a commercial-looking plane and shipped off on their next mission. Sure, they'd not been sent to Kansas, but when Alistair was caught up on the things he'd missed in their briefing, he felt the civilized part of his soul whither. They were on a one way flight to Hastings, Nebraska.

To make matters worse, before the flight, Alistair had been pulled aside by Marla and Venja, where he was told that the damage caused by his tantrum the day before had capped in the six-digits. He was pretty sure they were exaggerating, but when he asked Marla how much money her friend Charles had racked up in damages, the atmosphere had grown notably chillier, and she had doled out his punishment with a look that might have been satisfaction.

Two months under strict supervision.

Supervision wasn't the worst punishment—they were all subject to the security cameras that were hidden throughout the facility anyway. But seeing as they'd be spending who-knows-how-long in the middle of corn country, they wouldn't really have access to security cameras, unless she wanted to spend a few million for satellite surveillance. So, instead, he would have a chaperon. And since Marla seemed to like making him suffer, his chaperon would be Luca Shipton.

Alistair had almost walked out again.

It was hard not to, especially when Luca had given him a roguish grin while he boarded the plane. He wouldn't give his new teacher the satisfaction of victory though, so he went without a fuss, though he sat himself at the back of the cabin, as far away from Shipton and Marla as he could manage.

Given the events of the night before and their short foray into the monster movie business, they had all been wanting a few more answers than they had gotten from the regular briefing, and once the plane had leveled out, Marla took the front of the cabin and gave them just that.

"So I guess the biggest question you all probably have rolling around in those cute little heads of yours is, 'Was Charlie a zombie?'" She sounded more excited about the prospect than Alistair cared for, but in front of him he saw Sabin sit up a little straighter. "Unfortunately, as far as we can tell, he's not."

"I'm disappointed," Sabin said, slouching in his seat again.

"I'm a little disappointed too," Marla agreed with a smile. "But the good news is that we've run tests on our friend, and whatever he has doesn't seem to be contagious, either through saliva, blood, or sweat—it doesn't even seem to be an airborne contagion. Yet, somehow more and more people are turning up in the hospital like this. And they've all been coming from the same area. Trumbull, Nebraska, as far as we can tell, sits at the epicenter of the outbreak. We've been ordered to place it under quarantine, but first we want to get you on the inside. With you inside and everyone else kept from coming or going, we'll have a better opportunity to find out what's going on.

"I'm sending you in as a group of agricultural engineering and cultural anthropology students who are interested in the crop growing techniques of small town America. So if they ask, we're from the University of Nebraska. Since we're trying to blend in, there will be no power use of any kind—save for in emergency situations—and Sabin has put together a glamour spell for those of us who stick out a bit too much." She glanced at Bastian and Cole. "Hopefully, people will be more likely to talk to *you* than they would be with a bunch of HazMat guys."

They had all seen Sabin work magic, but usually it had been in the middle of a fight or simply an annoying hex he'd used on Berlin to make his lips swell or his face break out in hives. Alistair wondered what sort of magic he could do that would make Bastian and Cole look normal again. The wings had been an interesting addition to his friend, and he'd be lying if he said he'd not enjoyed watching him knock things off counters with them or accidentally close the tips in doors. But slowly the blond had learned to keep them tucked close to his body. They looked funny now, crammed behind him in the seat. For a while, they'd waited for them to go away on their own, but they seemed to be there to stay.

"So this guy is our weird-shit expert?" Berlin broke Alistair's train of thought as he motioned to Luca.

"I suppose that could be a less elegant way of describing him, yes." Marla seemed fine with pandering to Berlin's stupid jokes. "He's an expert in the transmission methods of abnormal conditions. Usually he works out of the west coast Haven, but we've recruited him for this mission."

"What sort of abnormal are we talking about? Like rare rainforest shit? Or do you mean like paranormal?" Berlin seemed more interested than Alistair had expected, but with his fear of

Sabin using witchcraft to turn him into a voodoo zombie, it did sort of make sense that he would want an expert on his side.

"A little bit of both," Luca said with a smile that seemed far too professorly. "Working with Haven, I've had opportunities that most people in my field never get. So I have worked a few very unusual cases. Though, in the end, most cases end up being—as you put it—weird rainforest shit."

Alistair watched Berlin turn to Bastian with a grin, as though saying "I like this guy."

It pissed him off, but what sort of argument could he make? "Don't like that guy! He turned me down when I tried to fuck him and then gave me the best hand-job of my life!" *He* wasn't even sure if that was a bad thing yet. The others seemed taken by him too. Milo looked like he was vibrating with attention—no doubt eager to exchange notes with another researcher. And Sabin had been buzzing about the possibility of a real movie-quality zombie since he'd gotten a look at the thing the night before. He'd been asking all morning if they were bringing Charles with them. Not that Alistair was particularly attached to Sabin, but it was good to see him joking again. He'd been quieter than usual over the past week, and with Bastian wrapped up in his mushy love affair, Milo still nursing a broken heart, and Berlin being Berlin, he was missing the little bit of company the witch had offered him.

And in any case, he wasn't interested in turning to Jett either. There was only enough room for *one* person with an attitude that big in any group, and Alistair wasn't willing to give up his seat.

"Now, the good news is that this contagion has proven to have a low transmission rate," Luca went on. "The bad news is, we have no idea how it spreads. From what I've been able to tell, I would guess we're dealing with some sort of parasite."

"Will it lay eggs inside you?" Sabin sounded excited.

"What the hell is with you and things laying eggs inside people?" Berlin turned around in his seat, looking disgusted, which was normal when he was talking to Sabin.

"Because if it lays eggs inside someone, you can get infected if you come in contact with them, you muttonhead."

"Oh, please. You probably just want some fucking zombie eggs to keep in jars under your bed."

"I'll keep your dick in a jar under my bed if you really want to be that far up my ass. Get it? Cause you're a fucking dildo."

Then Berlin jumped over the back of the seat, fists swinging. Alistair stayed put as his remaining teammates struggled to separate them. Once Berlin started swelling all over—presumably from a hex they'd missed in the blast of shouting—Marla and Venja finally stepped in. This wasn't that unusual anymore, but it was fun to see Luca and Jett look so surprised. When Luca glanced his way, Alistair just smiled faintly and raised one brow, as though wishing him luck.

Though their final destination was Trumbull, they landed in Hastings, because that was the closest place they could manage that had an airport. And really, "airport" was a generous term for the tiny airstrip and drugstore-sized office they landed at. With their luggage in tow, they were herded into two vans that would be taking them to their final destination.

Things seemed bleak. Hastings, after all, was a small town. The driver in Alistair's van said the population was only about twenty-four thousand. Certainly not even close to the population of New York. But the real joke was—

Trumbull was even smaller.

A twenty minute ride through fields and fields of farmland took them to their final destination, and when they stopped, Alistair thought he was going to faint.

"What is this?" It was impossible to keep the pure disgust from his voice as the driver pulled into the broken concrete parking lot of a miniscule, run down motel.

"This is where you'll be staying for the next week or two," Marla said from the front of the van, and Alistair swore he heard a smile in her voice.

"You've got to be shitting me," he mumbled to himself as he took in the L shaped building. Dark red doors faced the empty parking lot, paint chipping from them and bits of gutter hanging broken from the eaves of the flat roof.

Trumbull, Nebraska, Alistair quickly realized, was his own personal hell on Earth. It had been labeled a "village" but was barely that. There were two hundred people living in the tiny knot of buildings. Alistair had been in a nightclub with ten times that many people less than forty-eight hours ago. And to top it all off, the elderly man who gave them keys to their rooms spent nearly twenty minutes telling them about the history of the motel. Not the town—just the motel.

Alistair shaded his eyes with his free hand, the other holding his duffel bag as the drivers unloaded the rest of their luggage into one of the rooms. They all stood by the van as the motel worker refused to release Marla from their conversation of niceties. He leaned back against the side of the vehicle as the geezer went on.

"Weren't even s'posed to keep it open, y'know?" He was fiddling with his massive keyring, apparently looking for the ones that would belong to them. "As a town, we funded the construction o' this place back in the fifties when the healing revivals were goin' on. Our Reverend Blackholly was a right expert. People came from miles to sit in with him. Had to build a bunch a tents to make room fer 'em all."

"Is that right?" Despite the bluntness she relied on sometimes, Marla was incredibly patient. "Well, we really appreciate you opening up for us. We promise to stay out of everyone's hair."

"Don't be coy now," he said with a few barks of laughter. "You lot'r welcome to stay s'long as ya like. We'll set up some extra chairs down at the church for ya come Sunday."

"Thank you, we appreciate the hospitality."

A light flashed beside Alistair and he saw Sabin inspecting a picture that had just ejected from his Polaroid camera. He must have gotten it recently because Alistair hadn't seen him with it before. When he noticed the redhead looking at him he leaned over and said, "So I heard that the local currency here is a home-made lemon square."

Alistair couldn't stop the snort that had a few of the other boys looking at him, but the adults seemed to ignore the tiny bit of commotion.

"Careful, this guy probably has his dead mother stuffed and waiting for him back at home."

"Or a meat locker full of hands. I swear I've seen this motel in a slasher flick before." Sabin handed him the photo he'd taken: a macabre looking shot of the motel. Alistair thought the other boy could make a living in the film industry if he ever got out of Haven.

They'd not heard the final conclusion of Old McDonald's story, but he seemed to be finished and was sauntering back toward the office when Venja got their attention again.

"Alright, class," Venja waved her arms just a little. "Let's all head to room 103 now for a quick meeting."

As they moved away from the van, Alistair finally had a chance to look around properly. The motel was situated at the very edge of town, and across the poorly kept road was a giant dirt patch with massive silos of some kind standing behind a partially built chain link fence. There was no telling what was inside those silos, but Alistair figured it was grain and small town charm.

Beyond those, and beyond the motel and the other small buildings that specked the road leading north, were expansive fields of green. He had no idea what they were growing—probably corn and freakish Devil-worshipping children. Still, it was a wide open space, with wind that blew into his face from across the field. Big city or not, it felt good to be outside.

Alistair hung back, ready to be the last one to file into the dimly lit motel room, but Luca slid in behind him, smiling faintly when the redhead jerked away from him and shot him a glare over his shoulder.

"Can't have you slinking off when we're not looking." He was whispering, but the sound still straightened Alistair's spine, and once the door was shut behind them, he snaked his way through his teammates until he was standing on the opposite side of the room, one of the double beds standing between them like a guard.

The space was small already, but felt even smaller with all the people crammed into it. It smelled stale and the air was clammy, like there was some unseen moisture growing mold inside the walls. The two beds were covered in scratchy quilts, and the TV at the other end of the room was set inside a wooden stand, suggesting it had been bought at the time of the revivals as well. There was a tiny bathroom attached, and Alistair thought he heard a faucet leaking from the other side of the door.

"Alright, you guys. For better or worse, this is home for a while. We'll get you sorted into rooms here in a few minutes." Slowly the room settled, and Marla was able to talk in a lower voice. "Our guys are going to come in with the quarantine announcement in twenty-four hours. That means we get to play school for a little while to get ourselves integrated with the locals. Marla and I will leave right before the quarantine hits. I need to be on the outside to deal with the external attention this will draw.

"We want them to see you as bystanders caught in the wrong place at the wrong time. They need to like you in order for us to gain access to whatever information they have. That means being nice to everyone. I'm looking at you two." She shot a pointed finger toward Sabin and Alistair. Apparently she'd heard them talking outside. "Tomorrow morning we'll start some general recon. Remember the symptoms we talked about. We're looking for people who are detached, violent or forgetful. Just remember that we have a lot of old people here. Let's try to not file a report every time we meet a grandma with Alzheimer's."

Alistair wondered how they could tell the difference, but before he could decide if he wanted to grace Marla with the lovely sound of his voice, Cole asked for him.

"How do we tell them apart?"

"Unfortunately, until we get a better idea of what this outbreak is exactly, it's going to be a judgement call. Professor Shipton, who will be staying inside the quarantine with you, will have the final say before we act on anything. That also means that even though we need to be friendly with our hosts here, we should also avoid getting too intimate with any of them." Her eyes passed over Alistair for a split second, as though she couldn't help herself. "Transmission rates are low, but we should play it safe."

Something in between outrage and shame passed through Alistair. Did she really think so little of him that she thought he would prowl a bunch of farmers during a mission? And Alistair wasn't the only one who seemed to catch her little glance, either, because some of the other boys turned to look at him too. At the very least, they looked a bit surprised, as though they were waiting to see if he was going to retaliate. Before he could decide what his reaction would be, though, Luca broke the tension, his voice edged in a way that may not be obvious to everyone, but sounded defiant to Alistair.

"Yes. Things like sharing drinks or eating utensils should be avoided until we know what we're dealing with more fully."

Alistair looked at the strap of his duffle bag where he was still holding onto it. Had Luca really just defended him? It was probably his imagination, but the room was quiet for a second until Venja chimed in, her voice a little higher than normal, trying to soften the atmosphere with a little motherly charm.

"Why don't we just get settled for tonight and we'll worry about everything else tomorrow?" Alistair looked up at the sound of her voice and was pleased to see that the others seemed to be soothed by her as well. She looked shorter than usual with Luca and Marla standing beside her, the lines of her body soft—a perfect match for her personality. "I have all the keys here so we'll just relax and order some pizza or something."

Alistair was pretty sure there were no pizza places in Trumbull, but he never liked being a downer if it meant bringing Venja down with him, so he scooted in with the other boys as she began assigning rooms.

09: COLE

Alistair had been right—there were no pizza places in Trumbull. But it turned out dinner wasn't an issue. Just as Venja had finished handing out the keys, they had been interrupted by an impromptu dinner buffet in the parking lot. It was hard to tell how it had been arranged so quickly, but five women showed up with fold-out tables and stacks of food containers. It was a surprise, for sure, and several of the other boys seemed put on guard by it, but Cole couldn't see why.

It was wonderful.

It was comforting even—having these women, who were perfect strangers, doting on them this way. As the three younger women—all of them in their thirties or forties by the looks of them—filled plates with meatloaf, mashed potatoes, and macaroni—the two older women went around to greet each of the boys in turn. From the looks of them, Cole thought they may be put off by Berlin's tattoos or Sabin's piercings, but instead of avoiding them, they fawned over them. They touched the metal in Sabin's nose, and squeezed Berlin's bicep as they made surprisingly risqué jokes. Even Jett was getting positive attention as the ladies insisted on touching his Mohawk.

And when they got to Cole they pinched his cheek and talked about how little he was—about how he needed to eat more meat to build some muscle. Cole rarely left the compound, so any interaction with outsiders was novel, but to be fawned over—to not have to worry about his horns—was a gift he'd not ever expected to receive. Maybe it was Sabin's glamour spell, but since he'd stepped off the van into this miniscule town, he'd felt strangely at home.

If Marla was like a mother to him, he was sure that these women were what grandmothers felt like.

The women's arrival had been sudden, but their departure was slow, and the quick dinner turned into a two hour ordeal. Hoping they could gain some insider information, Marla, Venja, and Luca humored the local women by listening to their gossip. But they got nothing about sickness or violence, just a lot of small town gossip—who was expecting, when the next church meeting was scheduled, whose dog had been caught rifling through a neighbor's garbage. Save for a possible divorce that was brewing between the man who ran the small hardware store in town and his wife who was head of the PTA, Trumbull seemed like a drama—and subsequently epidemic—free sort of place.

It was dark by the time the women finally packed up, and everyone seemed eager to get back to their rooms—save for Alistair, who was stuck with his chaperon, and Berlin, who insisted Sabin would hex him in his sleep. Eventually, they all accepted their fate and dispersed.

The accommodations Cole and Bastian had were no different than any of the others. It was a small, musty space with two full-sized beds. The silence once they'd closed the door behind them was a bit of a relief after their bustling dinner guests.

"Which bed do you want?" Cole set his duffle bag on the foot of the nearest bed. I know you run kind of warm at night, so maybe you should take the one closer to the air con—"

Before he could finish his sentence, Bastian was pressed flush against his back, his arms snaking around his waist. A shiver ran from Cole's tailbone to the shell of his ear where Bastian's lips brushed against him.

"Well, I had kind of hoped we could share one." One hand traced lines up Cole's chest, settling over his heart, which hammered his sudden panic against his ribs.

"Oh," was all Cole could manage.

His mouth was dry. It had been a month since Bastian had dragged Cole out of that night club, a month since their first declarations of love, and only a day since Bastian had driven him to mind-blowing sexual heights, even if it had only been with his fingers. Hell, as thanks, Cole had even drawn the blond's own orgasm out for him—he still reveled in the feel of Bastian's dick jumping excitedly against his tongue. But he'd been hungry a day ago.

He reminded himself again about the bloodwork—playing the words Bastian repeated every time he sought intimate contact over and over in his head.

He's immune.

"Do you not want to share a bed with me?" Bastian's voice wasn't accusing——it was soft. And it was that softness that made him ache all over.

Cole took a deep breath. It was such a hard line to walk. If he clung too hard, he was convinced, even after the blood tests, that he would poison his lover. But, if he pulled away too far, he would hurt him. He wanted Bastian to be happy more than anything, but he still couldn't believe that he was the one who could give him that happiness. He tried to decide how to answer—to decide what the right answer even *was*—but his brain fizzled as Bastian's mouth moved from his ear to his neck. A shiver threatened to crumple Cole's body as hot breath passed over his collarbone. Sometimes, he thought *Bastian* was the toxic one.

"Maybe we shouldn't..." Cole had to pause to swallow the lump in his throat. "I mean, the walls are thin, so..."

"So we'll have to be very, very quiet." Bastian used the excuse of privacy to whisper into Cole's ear again, making the black-haired boy tremble. "Unless you really don't want me touching you."

"You know that's not..." Cole sighed to hide the moan he felt trying to escape him.

"It's fine. We won't do it all if you don't want."

This was what made it so hard for Cole to know whether Bastian was really falling the way Milo had. He pushed so hard, but in the end, he always compromised. Cole didn't know what was right anymore, but he knew what he wanted. He wanted to throw his concerns aside and absolutely drown under the blond's touch. He wanted to embrace the hunger he felt inside himself and devour his lover until he was perfectly sated.

Bastian seemed to read the desire in him and pulled away long enough to yank his own shirt off over his head, his warm, bare arms wrapping around him again before the garment even hit the floor. He shuffled them toward the bed, toeing off both of their shoes before toppling them onto the mattress. The air froze in Cole's lungs as one thigh pressed into the junction between his legs, Bastian's hips rolling down against him. Cole was a goner; there was no way he could pull himself out of this spiral.

Just as he was accepting his fate, there was a pounding at the flimsy door of their motel room.

It was loud enough to make Cole's stomach clench, but Bastian didn't stop. If anything, his arms wrapped more tightly around Cole. His mouth opened and teeth scraped across the soft skin at the dip behind Cole's collarbone. How did he make Cole's entire body feel weak with just the heat of his tongue?

"Bastian, the door." He didn't sound very convincing, breathless like he was.

"Ignore it." Bastian's voice was low in his ear, and the air drained momentarily from Cole's lungs.

His whole body seemed to vibrate under the soft groan Bastian hummed against his skin as he rolled his hips down against the other boy, the heat almost unbearable, even through two layers of pants.

Then the door shook again, the hammering sound finally knocking the ecstasy loose from Cole's head. He squirmed a little in his lover's arms, twisting his neck away from the other boy's hot mouth.

"It sounds important." He needed Bastian to stop. If he didn't, Cole wouldn't be able to stop either.

Finally, Bastian's mouth stilled, and he sighed into the crook of Cole's neck—even that sent a tingle all the way to his toes. He was still for a moment, like he was annoyed, but then he kissed Cole's cheek, making a loud smacking sound as he did.

"I love you, but if this is Berlin, I'm going to bury him."

"Why would it be Berlin?"

"Because he's a fucking idiot."

Cole straightened his top as Bastian marched to the door, not bothering with his discarded shirt. From the bed, Cole watched him look briefly through the peephole before giving Cole the tiredest look. He opened the door like he was presenting some grand circus act, and standing under the yellow light of the walkway was Berlin. Cole could *feel* the "I told you so" radiating off his lover.

"They are out of their fucking minds if they think I'm sharing a room with some kind of voodoo-creep Devil worshiper." Berlin barged his way into the small motel room without waiting for an invitation.

Cole couldn't decide if he was annoyed or relieved to have him there. Either way, he was getting tired of the mean things he usually had to say about Sabin. "You know he doesn't worship the devil, right? And if I remember correctly, he was really concerned about you while we were in Lechuguilla."

"Well of course a *demon* would be on his side."

"That's enough, Berlin." Bastian's voice had taken on the deeper tones it did when he was getting angry. He never spoke like that to Cole.

"Come on, Bastian. Let me sleep in here. Cole can go stay with Sabin; they're part of the same team, anyway. It makes more sense."

"No. We're all on the same team now, so you need to get over whatever issues you have with Sabin and learn to get along. The sooner you do that, the sooner Marla will stop pushing you guys on each other. I mean, you know that's what she's doing, right?"

"Well she obviously succeeded with you two." As though he just had an idea for a new tactic he smiled and moved straight to Cole, putting both hands on his shoulders. "Come on. Aren't you tired of being stuck with this stick in the mud?" He tilted his head toward Bastian. "You should spend more time with your other teammates. You and Sabin could have loads of fun. "

He knew it was just a trick, but maybe Berlin was actually right in a way. He had been spending most of his time with Bastian. Maybe he should stay with Sabin for a while. If nothing else, it would keep him from succumbing to Bastian's appetizing advances.

"I mean... if it'll make things easier for everyone, I don't really—"

"Absolutely not." Bastian's voice was louder now and Cole was a little taken aback by his sudden anger. It reminded him of the way Milo had started shouting at him when he'd hit the bottom of his spiral. "Du bist einfach nur ein Arsch darüber. Müssen Sie erwachsen werden." He jabbed a finger toward Berlin.

"Und du lässt ihn kontrollieren! "

Bastian was still shouting in German as he shoved Berlin toward the door.

"Oh, come on, Bastian! He unpacked a jar full of spiders! He's gross! What if they get out? They'll lay eggs in my—"

The blond boy slammed the door in his friend's face before they could find out exactly where the spiders might lay eggs. Cole hoped he was going to say "luggage" but he had the impression it was going to be somewhere a little more mucosal than that.

"I swear to God, I'm going to smother him in his sleep someday."

"It's really not a huge deal if we need to change rooms."

"It *is* a big deal. Berlin is the way he is because he's used to getting his way. Venja was way too soft on him. He's gotten spoiled."

At the very least, the intimate mood from earlier seemed to be gone. Bastian moved to the far bed and threw himself across it.

"I was half the problem though. I always gave in to what he wanted. That's why I feel like I really need to make a stand now."

Cole could definitely see what Bastian was saying, but Berlin's issues with Sabin seemed more persistent.

"Can he sense auras like you? He seems bothered by me and Sabin in particular. I know you said we both had kind of questionable auras." He sat down beside the other boy, placing a hand on his stomach in an attempt to ease his frustration.

"No. He was brought up by a bunch of psycho Catholic monks. They were always talking about demons and dark magic and possession. Stuff like that. Now he's paranoid and always thinks there's something evil out to get him."

"Considering the things that've happened, do you ever think that maybe he's right?

"What do you mean?"

"Well, your wings, my horns, our shared dreams... sometimes it feels like we were somewhere else."

"I still don't really buy the angel thing, if that's what you're asking. And there's no way you could be a demon."

"You sound so sure."

Bastian's hand moved to Cole's face, his fingertips warm on his cheek. "Of course I'm sure. You're too sweet to be something evil."

It was corny, but Cole couldn't stop the smile that split his face. He leaned into his hand as Bastian continued.

"You look so different without them…"

Cole had almost forgotten Sabin's glamour spell. Slowly, Bastian's fingers raked through his hair until they met the invisible base of one horn and couldn't go any further.

"Do you like me better without them?" He tried to sound casual about it, but knew he'd failed to keep the uncertainty from his voice when Bastian showed him that sad, understanding smile.

"I like you most exactly how you're meant to be."

Cole chuckled for real. "You are the king of corny."

With a small bark of laughter, Bastian yanked the smaller boy down on top of him. "Don't act like you hate it. You can't fool me when your face gets all red like that."

"Well, you have that effect on me." With a sigh, Cole surrendered his weight to his lover, settling against his broad chest. "Can we stay like this tonight?"

This time it wasn't an excuse to keep the other boy from ravishing him. He wanted to stay just how they were for as long as he could.

"Of course."

10: BASTIAN

Bastian could sense the uncertainty in his lover. He'd almost given into his soft touches, but he'd been fighting it, just like he did every time. Bastian was in a state of constant uncertainty these days. He knew the other boy loved him, and he didn't want to rush him into anything he wasn't ready for, yet at the same time, he was sure Cole would lose himself in his anxiety if he let him. So he pushed for intimacy, sometimes harder than he wanted to. He was sure, though, that he could free Cole from the self-loathing he felt if he could just get him to accept the normal sort of lust that lovers were meant to feel for each other.

Still, sex aside, having his dark-haired lover tucked into his chest the way he was felt perfect—made him think he could go the rest of his life without the carnal embrace of another person so long as he had Cole's cheek pressed against his skin.

Cole had just begun to drift off, his breath slowing and his lips parting, when Berlin came pounding on their bedroom door again. He sounded more panicked this time as he shouted for Bastian through the thin barrier, and Cole sighed as he moved to let his lover up off the bed. When he opened the door, his friend looked panicked, but exhilarated at the same time.

"I told you not to come back here." Bastian was too tired to raise his voice this time. "I don't care about Sabin's jar spiders."

"Oh no. This is so much worse than jar spiders, okay? He's doing some shady shit."

"Jar scorpions?"

"I'm being serious, Miststück. He just snuck out of our room!"

"So? He's probably just trying to get away from your judgmental staring for a few minutes."

"I'm being serious, Bastian. We need to follow him."

"We? Why do I need to go with you?"

"Because he'll hex me again if you're not there."

"If you're so worried about it, why not go to Venja or Marla about it?

"Well—" Berlin paused, as though the thought hadn't crossed his mind, which was a bit of a relief. "Obviously I need to have some sort of evidence before I go to them, or they'll think I'm just being paranoid again."

Bastian sighed for what must have been the tenth time in the last two minutes. "Look, Berlin. Whatever Sabin is doing, he obviously wants to keep to himself. You're not his mother. You don't have to worry about every little thing he does."

"What if he's doing something to hurt our mission? What if he gives us away while he's out sneaking around? What if he's out casting spells on the townspeople?"

"Why would he do *any* of that, Berlin?" His voice grew loud again, tired of dealing with Berlin's refusal to work as a team.

"I don't know, Bastian! Why did he pack six suitcases full of weird shit to bring with him?"

Before Bastian could finish throwing his hands into the air in pure disinterest, Cole interrupted them.

"I think we should go." Bastian was sure his face looked utterly betrayed as he looked back to his still-drowsy lover. "If he's sneaking out, he must have a reason. If we don't check on him I'll worry."

Bastian took a breath. Giving in to Berlin's stupid requests was going to make living with him unbearable, but Cole had a point. "Okay. I guess we should find out what he's doing before *someone* reports it to Venja or Marla."

"And don't think I won't if we find him doing something freaky."

"Whatever. Cole, you stay here." The last thing he wanted was to listen to Berlin bitch about having to bring Cole along. His lover didn't argue as Bastian retrieved his shirt and kissed the other boy on the top of his head.

"Make sure he's okay?" Cole *did* look worried, Bastian realized once he'd gotten close.

"Of course. Get some sleep." He brushed a hand down Cole's cheek, then turned and left with Berlin.

If making sure Sabin was alright would put the other boy at ease, then he would humor Berlin's stupid requests one more time.

The town at night had an eerie quality to it. Dark, like the woods they'd sometimes slept in during missions, but spotted with lonely streetlamps too far apart to be anything more than isolated specks highlighting empty rings of street.

"This way," Berlin left the small spot behind a row of trashcans they'd ducked behind.

"I could be romancing my adorable boyfriend right now. I hope you appreciate this."

"Well, maybe instead of letting that demon sex you up and brain wash you, you should pay more attention to all this creepy bullshit that's getting out of hand here."

"The only thing getting out of hand here is your paranoia."

As the words were leaving his mouth, Berlin yanked him around the side of a building, hissing for him to be quiet. They were still for a few seconds before Berlin leaned out to look around the corner.

"There, see? He was looking over his shoulder. He's worried about being watched, which means he's *sneaking*."

"Berlin, *we're* sneaking." Bastian leaned over his friend to look down the street as well, catching a final glimpse of Sabin before he turned a corner going further into town.

"It's not the same. Come on." He didn't wait for Bastian as he hurried after the other boy.

Sabin led them further into town, the fields that surrounded the relative speck of buildings dropping out of sight behind the squat structures that made up the heart of the community. Whether Berlin was right about Sabin being up to some sort of Salem witch plotting or not, it was obvious that he wasn't interested in anyone else knowing his whereabouts. He checked around corners, looked over his shoulder, hung in the shadows along the sides of buildings. Bastian wondered what he might be hiding from, since the town and most likely everyone in it was asleep. He would never tell Berlin this, but the longer they followed the young witch, the more curious Bastian became.

Finally, Sabin stopped by one of the lonely lamp posts. This one lit up a plain, blue mailbox. When he fished an envelope out of his jacket, Bastian elbowed his friend in the ribs where they hunkered behind another parked car.

"A letter? You drug me out here for a letter?"

Berlin swatted at him, hissing to keep quiet. "You can't tell me for sure that letter isn't something nefarious."

"Using a big word won't make you more correct, Berlin."

"Just shut up."

Sabin stood in the light of the street lamp, looking at his envelope for a second. He seemed reluctant to put it in the slot, though once he did, he stuffed his hands into his pockets and started his trip back to the motel. Berlin didn't move to follow him this time. Instead, he waited until the other boy was gone before leading Bastian to the mailbox. Pulling his jacket off, Berlin made a point with his fingers, flattening his hand out like the blade of a sword. When his fingers passed just beyond the shadow of the slot, black rivulets of ink slithered from their normal home wrapped about his arm. Trailing down his fingers, the little vines of black ink snaked into the depths of the mailbox.

"Seriously? You're going to use your power to fish out a private letter?"

"Shh. I'm concentrating."

"I can't believe I'm out here doing this with you. I could be in bed with Cole right now."

"Whatever. It's not like he's going anywhere." After another second, the writhing tattoos began receding again, moving back to the scarred tissue they'd left behind. "Here we go."

Both of the boys moved away from the box so they were standing more comfortably in the light of the street post. Despite his complaining, Bastian peered over his friend's shoulder, eager to see what was so secret it had to be mailed out in the dead of night.

The front of the envelope had no return information, but the address scribbled in Sabin's slanted handwriting was for Vancouver. The name on the front was "Noah Clark."

"Cole said he had a pen pal," Bastian suggested. It felt wrong when Berlin turned it over to open it, but he held his breath as the other boy unfolded the paper inside. The plain notebook paper just said "I'm worried about you. Please contact me." There was no name at the bottom, leaving Sabin completely detached from the letter. That also meant that whoever it was being sent to would recognize his handwriting and would know HOW to contact him, which was exceedingly difficult for anyone staying in Haven.

"Is that it?" Berlin said it first, but Bastian had already been thinking it. He flipped it over, like he was expecting more on the back.

"I guess so."

Berlin seemed disappointed. "But what does it mean?"

"I think it means he's worried about Noah Clark, and he wants him to contact him."

"Shut up. You know what I mean. Why send it in secret?"

"Who knows? I guess you'll have to ask him."

"I'm not going to tell him that I fished his letter out of the mailbox and opened it. He'll curse me! He'll make me infertile or something."

"Well I guess it'll just be a mystery then." He slapped his friend on the shoulder, then started back toward the hotel and the warm body of his lover. It only took Berlin a few moments to follow, though he'd actually been kind enough to reseal the envelope and stuff it back into the box.

11: ALISTAIR

Alistair's head and neck ached as he pulled the musty-smelling blanket up over his face—the light from the window drilling into his eyes and reminding him how poorly he'd slept. The room had swung back and forth between sweltering and frigid all night, and with Luca in the bed next to his, he did little more than doze most of the night. Every time the man shifted in bed, Alistair's heart sprinted across his ribs, preparing his body to fend off any advance the teacher might have in mind. Luca had not slinked into his bed, though. He had slept, seemingly well, the whole night through.

Thinking of Luca, Alistair peeked out from under his scratchy fortress, needing to check on the man to ease his worry. The bed by the window was empty, its blankets still ruffled, and Alistair sat up in a flash, needing to check the man before he got the upper hand. But Luca was nowhere to be seen—that is, until the door to the bathroom opened, releasing steam into the cramped room. Alistair must have slept through the sound of the shower.

Despite the instinctual distrust he felt toward Luca—his urge toward flight peaking when the other man's aura filled any space—he was struck motionless as he reentered the room. The suits Luca wore—particularly the one he'd worn in the bar the night Alistair had first laid eyes on him—suggested an amazingly constructed body. The seaming and structure attested to broad shoulders and a narrow waist.

The suits did him no real justice.

Alistair clenched his jaw to keep his mouth from falling open as Luca scrubbed a towel into his wet hair, seeming oblivious to the eyes that raked down his bare chest, tracing the lines of his body down to the V that disappeared into a precariously tucked towel at his waist. The damp fabric seemed to be held up by the sheer angles of his body and a prayer. Despite the dislike he had for the man, Alistair urged the cover to drop.

"If you're going to stare that hard, you could just ask to see what's underneath the towel, you know."

He'd not even looked at Alistair, and it was exactly that cocky attitude that infuriated him. In the end, Alistair *had* been staring—and who wouldn't have? He was gorgeous, and when he tossed the towel he'd been using to dry his hair onto the foot of his bed, it was all Alistair could do to keep from blushing. Luca was a piece of art at any given moment, but just then, with his wavy hair untamed and swooping over one eyebrow, the strands seeming to catch on his eyelashes, he looked beautifully feral.

"I promise you, I am one hundred percent uninterested in what you're keeping under that towel."

Luca only smiled at him, then walked to the side of his student's bed. He stood directly beside Alistair, staring down the straight line of his nose, his eyes seeming illuminated in the shadow cast by his mussed hair. Alistair didn't move, refusing to abandon the disinterested slouch in his posture. He held his gaze, his eyes trained on the two mercurial pools that watched him like he could cleave flesh from him. He would not even *glance* at the body that was so close to him he could feel the radiating heat of the shower coming off him in waves. No matter how gorgeous, Luca would *not* intimidate him.

Though the redhead *did* feel like his heart was moments away from either stopping, or blowing out.

"Touch me and I'll break your arm." It was a tiny loss, to be the first one to break silence. But his voice was rock steady, and caused Luca to drop his gaze as he laughed through his nose.

"So I don't get a broken arm for our *last* encounter?"

Heat finally crept into Alistair's face. To hide it, he shrugged and pulled his hair into a knot, tying it with a band he kept on his wrist. "Well, it's not like you got anything so great out of that stupid stunt you pulled. And I've never been one to turn my nose up at some free service." He hoped the humiliation he'd felt didn't show through his words.

"Hm. I bet you *are* used to servicing, aren't you. Sitting by and letting people flock to you." Luca looked like he wanted to reach out and touch Alistair as he spoke, his voice subdued, but his lips turned up into the smallest of grins. "It'll be interesting to see you do the begging for a change."

The small embers of embarrassment in Alistair's cheeks burst into real flames, and he threw the blankets from himself. "You're more delusional than I thought if you think I'd beg *you* for *anything*."

Luca only laughed as Alistair snatched a fresh set of clothes from his suitcase. "We'll see how long your stubbornness lasts, kitten."

"Kill yourself." Alistair slammed the bathroom door shut behind him, then took the time to ensure it was locked.

Trumbull was small enough that using the van they'd come in on to go anywhere seemed like a waste of time. Even for someone like Alistair, who avoided more physical labor than necessary, thought walking made more sense. But walking meant giving them some kind freedom, and based on the way Marla was watching Alistair in particular, she obviously didn't trust them.

Instead, Alistair bumped between Sabin and Milo at the back of the van, hot and annoyed.

Back in the motel room, Luca had been dressed and waiting when Alistair had finally emerged from his shower. It had been nearly an hour since then, and he was still kicking himself for the way he'd handled the situation. Not wanting Luca to think he held any sort of power over him, he'd dressed right there in front of him—like it was an act of defiance and not just a free peep show. While the teacher had not moved an inch from where he'd perched himself on the foot of his own bed—let alone lay a hand on him— it still felt as if he'd had complete control over the situation. In retrospect, the slow, almost teasing way he'd dressed himself probably hurt his cause.

At the front of the van, Luca turned to glance over his shoulder. He gave the whole group a sweep with his eyes, as though pretending that he was just being a responsible chaperone, but when his eyes fell on Alistair, he paused and the tiny bend at the corner of his mouth told Alistair that he was probably looking straight through his clothes. The redhead was getting very acquainted with that look. Like he knew how attracted Alistair was to him without the boy ever admitting it.

The tour that Mayor Barrett gave them was a short—yet still pointless—one. And even though they were there under the guise of agricultural interests, they were led through the "historical" buildings that made up the local political system— something most likely there for show and ego. In fact, the system was so small that even the local post office made it into the lineup for the tour. Barrett seemed so excited about the history of his little town-speck that everyone, without exception, listened patiently to him. Even Alistair found it cute, in a way.

Next came the tour of their fields and grain bins—the huge cylindrical structures they had seen lining the road they'd driven in on. If they really had been from a university interested in the subsistence of small town America in the grain belt, as they'd suggested, then it might have been the interesting part of the tour. As it stood, though, it was worse than the post office. The things he was talking about may have also made more sense if they'd actually been from a university.

By the time they'd completed the tours in mid-afternoon, the mayor had stopped seeming so nervous. He even seemed used to Kiyiya, who had been fitted with a service dog vest. It was a lie, of course, and Alistair wasn't even sure why they were bringing this dog around with them, but Luca and Jett seemed unyielding when the subject of leaving him behind was brought up. It didn't really matter to Alistair—the dog behaved well enough, trotting quietly behind Jett and sitting with his body leaned against Luca's leg when they stood to listen to more and more information about corn.

The last stop on the tour was a massive white tent at the edge of town. The rectangular field it had been erected in was bordered on two sides by farmland, the other sides marked by residential homes and a warehouse that sat cattycornered at its northern edge. At the front of the pavilion was a podium and stands for what were probably mobile amps. It was obvious that these tents were usually used for church service, which was strange, considering they'd passed by an attractive little church on their way there.

Whether they were usually used for church or not, there were no pews to be seen. Instead the space was full of picnic and buffet tables. The space was already teeming with people, some of them serving others, some sitting out in the grass enjoying the sun, others huddled in the shade, all of them taking and laughing, looking like some sort of small town republican campaign commercial. As they unloaded from the van, it looked like the entire town had turned out for it, and then some. Alistair remembered being told that there were only about two hundred people who lived in Trumbull, and if he was guessing right, he would say there were almost twice that many people swarming the field.

Before Alistair could decide if anyone else had noticed, or if it was even important, they were approached by a man Alistair assumed was the Pastor. He didn't wear black robes or anything like Catholics did, but he had one of those faces. He was young...ish—probably in his thirties, but he looked spry, with the overly neat hair, white button up and store-bought slacks Alistair imagined when he thought of Mormons or something.

"Pastor Blackholly." The mayor greeted the other man with a firm handshake and then a squeeze to his shoulder. "This is our very own local pastor. His daddy was the man who gave us our little boom back in the fifties with the revivals. We know he's gonna do the same for us now."

"You think too highly of me, Mr. Mayor."

"You're too humble, John." He clapped the other an on the back.

Already, Alistair disliked Blackholly. He was too wholesome. Like the pastors from megachurches who played the pinnacles of righteousness, but wound up snorting crack off a hooker's ass. To his credit, he did smile at each of them, and for once Alistair didn't see the look of disgust he was used to seeing when meeting men of the cloth. It wasn't like his sexuality was that hard to discern. Still, there was something that left him feeling uneasy.

Pulling his attention away from the charismatic pastor, Alistair watched Luca's face instead. Marla and Venja had masterfully excused themselves half way through the tour, saying they had to return to Hastings to retrieve equipment that had been shipped to them. If Luca felt the same uneasiness he did, the man hid it as he shook hands with the Pastor and made small talk. The draw of food seemed to have caught his teammates' attention too, because no one else seemed particularly bothered.

Inside the tent, the tables were covered in barbecued *everything*. Pulled pork, ribs, brisket—the women piled mountains of beans or coleslaw onto their plates as well—it was hard to guess where all the food had even come from now that he'd seen how remote the place was. In the end, he regretted even thinking the question. As they piled food onto his plate, every person he brushed by seemed determined to tell him exactly how much of the food had been grown "right here in good ol' Trumbull."

"Yokel" was the word he finally settled on to describe the majority of people he met.

As he was herded through the buffet line, the paper plate in his hand growing heavier by the second, Alistair noticed a distinct lack of anyone their age in the sea of babbling people. Maybe that was why everyone was fawning over them—their own teen children had left for college, ready to flee the map-speck they'd grown up in. There were a few younger kids wandering through the crowd, though, sneaking food from the buffet before being shooed away to play outside the tent. A few of them sat at a table on the edge of the others, and as Alistair and the rest of his "class" found their own table, he noticed a persistent stare coming from their young neighbors.

Sitting beside a girl who was swinging her legs and grinding a crayon into the white tabletop was a boy who couldn't have been older than thirteen—maybe fourteen. Whatever his age, he was obviously on the brink of puberty, and Alistair could tell by the way the boy stared at him, that the worst of the hormones had already started to trickle in. He was a cute kid—sandy blond hair that stuck out in funny places since he'd not figured out how to tame curls yet, freckles, blue eyes—in about five years he would be a real catch.

Alistair ignored him for a while, not bothered by the feeling of eyes on him, but after the kid had been watching him for nearly ten minutes he decided he could have a little fun. Pulling some of his hair behind his ear, he made eye contact with the kid—trying not to laugh as his eyes went big—and he swept his tongue suggestively over his top lip. It was low in Alistair's arsenal, but the kid's face lit up like a stop light. Even from a distance, Alistair could see the boy's spine go straight, and for a second he thought he saw a small squirming under the table. *How innocent.* Alistair didn't miss those years—when a gust of wind could have him rock hard if it hit him the right way. He, at least, had been lucky enough to have Felix with him during those years—someone who understood. Someone to explore with.

"I didn't know you were into minors." Jett had sat down next to Alistair when they'd first arrived, and with Sabin on his other side, Alistair wasn't going to complain, since that left nowhere for Luca to sit. But now the teasing grin on the new boy's face made Alistair wish he'd sat somewhere else.

"Like I would ever be interested in a kid. I'm just doing him a favor is all." He looked back to where the boy was sitting, but saw him staring at his plate now, face still radiating heat.

A weight settled in Alistair's gut. Alistair never thought about Felix. He didn't *allow* himself to, and it was something he'd become rather good at. Music, magazines, fashion blogs, sex; he drowned himself in whatever it took to keep those thoughts away. And now, Marla and some horny country boy had messed up all the hard work he'd put into his distractions.

"I mean, you *do* strike me as the type of guy who lost his virginity at thirteen anyway, so maybe it doesn't seem like a big deal to you." Jett's tone suggested he was trying to be funny, but that maybe he was being honest too. "But a kid that age around here? He's probably never even seen *porn*. And what would his *parents* think about him getting a boner because of another *man*. This whole revival business makes me think they wouldn't be too chuffed to find out their kid was a fa—ow!" He jerked, and his knees hit the underside of the table.

For a second, Alistair wondered if he had reached out and hit the other boy without thinking, but when he looked under the table he saw Kiyiya, the massive black wolf-dog holding Jett's hand in his teeth. For a second he looked like he was threatening him, because when Jett tried to pull away the dog tightened its grip. He wasn't growling, just holding onto him. Just reminding him that he could hurt him if he wanted.

"Fine! Fine, I'll shut up. Jesus."

With that, the dog released his hand, and for a second Alistair wondered what sort of training the dog had received.

"Smart dog."

"*Wimp* dog." Jett corrected, rubbing his hand.

"I don't know. He seems to have you under his paw."

"I'll stop calling him a wimp when he can actually sleep on his own at night."

Alistair wasn't exactly thrilled with his new teammates, but he figured he might as well take advantage of the opportunity while he had it.

"So what's with you and this dog, anyway? Luca was brought here because he's an expert. What about you guys?"

Jett smiled at him, the look surprisingly charming. Getting a closer look at him, the other boy had a gentle face for someone with multiple facial piercings and flashy blue hair. His jaw was wide and his lips were full, a bit of scruff spackling his chin.

"We both owe Luca a sort of debt. He's helped us out in the past. So we go where he goes. Besides, we couldn't trust his safety with some unknown group of freaks." He winked at Alistair even as he insulted him. "Kiya in particular." Jet flicked the dog's pointed eat just hard enough for it to give him a short warning growl.

"I thought his name was something else."

"Technically it's Kiyiya. Native American names are a pain in the ass to pronounce, though. So he's been saddled with the nickname Kiya, because he's just so cute." Jett pursed his lips for the last few words, pinching the loose skin of the dog's cheek and jiggling it.

Kiya snapped halfheartedly at his hand, then huffed and laid down in the grass.

Alistair couldn't help but snort. Maybe the new kid wasn't as bad as his first impression had suggested. Of course, being friends with Luca made it much harder to be friendly with him, but at the very least Alistair decided he wouldn't waste his energy hating the other boy.

Before he could decide on the level of civility Jett deserved, however, the tents shuttered as the sound of helicopters filled the field around them.

The quarantine was starting.

12: COLE

Cole knew that this was the reason they were there. They'd had this quarantine planned from the beginning. But now, as the townspeople left their plates of food and wandered to the edges of the tent where they watched twenty cargo choppers encircle the town, then land, he wished they could have handled things differently. He reminded himself that they were there to help these people, even if he could see the panic ripple through the crowd as soldiers swarmed out of the grounded helicopters. In the span of a few minutes, the men had erected small towers with lights and speakers mounted to the top—they weren't huge, maybe twenty feet tall, but the speed with which they were built was stunning.

By the time the towers were constructed, several townspeople had flocked around the mayor, demanding answers. Before the man could give them more than "I'm sure there's no reason to panic," a voice boomed across the fields from the halo of speakers.

"Attention, citizens of Trumbull. We are with the United States Center for Disease Control and are here to enforce a quarantine of the area."

Cole heard the word echoed behind them as all of the attendees began talking quietly amongst themselves. Everyone knew what a quarantine was, and what it meant. It meant someone was sick, and that it was bad enough for the government to think it could cost the country too many lives if it spread. They knew from the exaggerated Hollywood movies that the government might even let them all die before risking further exposure. And the part that scared Cole the most was that he knew the Hollywood version might just be right.

The voice was skewed by static as the unseen officer continued.

"We ask that you please remain calm. Provisions and information will be sent to you immediately, and we will have workers in to clear the area within the next seventy-two hours. For the time being, all phone and satellite connections to the area have been disabled, though we will provide you with a short wave radio which you may use to contact us with any needs or concerns you have."

The nervous whispers erupted into a noisy roar as some of the townspeople rushed from the field, hurrying back toward their homes, presumably to check their phone connection, or to protect themselves from whatever illness they imagined might be going around now.

"What a surprise; everyone's panicking."

Cole had stood up when the helicopters had arrived, feeling unexpectedly scared. But when he heard Jett's dry words, he turned back to look at the new boy. He sat slouched in his chair, one hand on Kiyiya's head which rested on his hip, and Professor Shipton standing behind his chair. They were the only ones left at the table—the rest of his teammates had moved to watch the landing just like he had. None of them had been surprised, but they were solemn, and somehow seemed colder to the panic around them than any of the others. Even Alistair—who was known for his uncaring stare—looked worried, his brows knit uncomfortably on his forehead.

Cole turned around, not wanting to draw too much attention to the uncertainty he was suddenly feeling toward his new teammates. With his back to them, he heard Shipton respond quietly.

"Well just remember that panic can be fabricated. And more panic than is necessary can be a marker. I'm sure we'll suss the liars out eventually."

Fabricated panic? What does he mean?

They were there to look for people who were sick. What did liars have to do with illness? Cole tried to tamp down the uncertainty, reaching for Bastian's hand out of habit. Marla and Venja might be gone now, but they wouldn't have left them with someone they didn't trust. And whether Cole knew much about their new teacher or not, if Marla trusted him, then he would too.

13: BASTIAN

That evening—after the mayor had retreated to his office with the short wave radios that had been delivered as the soldiers promised—there was a town meeting. Because of space issues, they had moved the meeting from town hall to the gymnasium located inside the community center. The bleachers that lined the walls were full of people, and the basketball court was blanketed in rows of fold-up chairs. Every person in town was probably squeezed into that room, which was lucky for Bastian and the others, since it gave them all a chance to observe the town as a whole. But it was tiring.

From the moment they'd arrived, something had seemed off about the town. Some of the others, like Cole, hadn't seemed to notice it at all, but no matter how hard he tried, Bastian couldn't shake the discomfort. Unfortunately, since he'd met Cole, he'd begun to doubt his senses when they showed him darkness surrounding certain people. Cole's aura still hung around him in gentle ripples of black and purple, but Bastian now saw the beauty in those cosmic swells. And when they rolled off his lover they left a sensation of calmness inside him rather than fear. But Cole was the exception, wasn't he? Could he trust his senses now, knowing that they had been wrong about the boy he loved?

Then again, if one person with a dark aura could be an anomaly, then what about a whole town?

The meeting was pure chaos. People were shouting and crying, and all Bastian and the others could do was stand toward the back and graciously accept the apology they were offered by the mayor after his townspeople had finally filed away back to their homes.

"When I took this position, I never imagined I would have to go through anything like this," he said, entire body looking exhausted.

"Not many people ever do," Shipton said, bracing the other man by his shoulder. "For what it's worth, I think you're handling it well."

Bastian heard the lie in his voice, but figured anybody with a heart would have told the obviously shaken man the same thing. But then the Mayor said:

"We're just a bunch of farmers."

And something prickled inside Bastian. It wasn't a deception or a half truth. It *was* true. But it was *also* false. It was both.

"The officer I talked to on the radio said whatever it was might be a biological weapon. Who here would know how to make something like that? We grow *corn* for Pete's sake."

There it was again. Both true and false.

"Well," Shipton continued. "Please let us know if there's anything we can do. We'll do whatever we can for you."

A lie. Bastian felt his brows come together, unable to keep the confusion from showing on his face. The whole reason they were there was to help these people, how could that have been a lie? He was still mulling over the strange sensations turning over inside him him when Cole's fingers slipped into the crook of his elbow.

"Bastian? Are you okay?"

"I think I ate too much," he said, patting his stomach. That was the truth, his gut ached. But it also kept him from having to explain the suddenly strange developments he'd stumbled upon.

That night, after the panic in the town had settled down to an uneasy quiet, the team met again in the motel room Luca and Alistair were sharing. Bastian thought he should ask about the strange truth-lie that he'd heard from the mayor, but every time he thought to, the lie he heard from Shipton replayed in his mind. He wasn't ready to trust this man, even if he *was* supposed to be their leader while Marla was away.

In an attempt to get a closer look at the townspeople as individuals—presumably so they could identify those who were carrying the sickness without causing mass hysteria—Shipton split them into pairs and assigned them to different people and groups whom they would shadow the next day. The mayor, the pastor, the homeschool group, the field workers—they would divide and conquer. Or, rather, divide and observe. It felt strange encroaching on their daily lives, which the mayor had insisted would go on as normal. At least as normally as possible.

14: ALISTAIR

Now that the mission had started for real, Luca was more tolerable. Though Alistair refused to admit that the dependable, leaderly side of the man's personality just made him that much more attractive. Showing any interest would only inflate the teacher's head to an infuriating size, though, so Alistair did everything he could *not* to notice.

Though he was starting to wonder if he needed to fake it anymore.

The previous night had been quiet. Luca had gone to sleep early, saying they should be well rested for the next day. Alistair had laid awake, once again expecting the man to slink into his bed, but once again being wrong. Alistair woke up with the light shining in his eyes again and an empty bed. Once he'd checked the bathroom and found that empty as well, he started to wonder if Luca wasn't interested in him at all. Which was absolutely unacceptable.

After pulling a long sleeve shirt on over the tank top he'd slept in, he left the room, tying his hair up into a knot as the door swung shut behind him. Despite the towers he saw on the horizon as he exited into the parking lot, the day was beautiful. The sky was clear, and the wind blew just enough to send rolling waves across the fields of corn. It was deceptive, knowing that past all that green was a swarm of armed soldiers who would probably shoot anyone who tried to leave.

No one answered when he knocked at Bastian's door, or Berlin's. So Alistair walked barefoot to the office. Inside was a small unmanned counter and two metal waiting chairs with magazines from the sixties strewn across them. Past the counter was a doorway swathed in beads, and Alistair heard his friends' voices coming from the other side. There was no welcome meal this time, but in the back room he found his teammates gathered around small plastic tables eating cereal and muffins.

"What? No barbeque for breakfast?" After grabbing one of the single wrapped blueberry muffins and a banana from the counter along the wall, Alistair pulled a chair away from the table Luca sat at, and forced his way in with Bastian, Berlin, and Cole.

"You don't want to sit with your babysitter?" Berlin was grinning with his food packed into one cheek.

"I guess you're the lesser of two evils now," Alistair said, batting his eyelashes at Berlin and smiling as innocently as he could. The insult-based banter he shared with the tattooed boy was annoying but comfortable. He liked that he didn't have to hide his flaws around his two original teammates, but he also never had to question their allegiance. They would risk their lives to save his, and he would do the same for them. There was a trust there that he didn't have with Luca and Jett. Hell, that feeling still wasn't even secure with the other three, even though he'd already spent months with them. Venja had told him once that he was slow to trust people. He glanced at Luca who winked at him. He didn't figure it was a bad trait to be cautious.

"Have you had a chance to talk with him much?" Ever since their trip to the club together, Cole tried to be friendly toward Alistair.

The outfit sharing and occasional dance lessons probably left a feeling of closeness in him. It wasn't that Alistair disliked him, but he didn't hold much stock in those sorts of things. And since he'd gotten together with Bastian, he'd found the boy's depressive ups and downs tiring. If anything, he got along with Sabin the best out of his three new teammates. The witch kept to himself most of the time, and had a sharp tongue that impressed Alistair whenever he got to see it unleashed—usually on Berlin.

"I've made it a point to talk to him as little as possible, actually. Why? Do you have a crush on him?"

"I, for one," Berlin Began. "Think you would make a much better couple with Shipton than you would with Bas—urk."

Bastian's hand closed around the other boy's throat before he could finish. "Let me stop you there." He wasn't holding him tight enough to hurt him, but Berlin dropped the subject.

"Sure, sure. Whatever you say."

While Berlin was still sarcastically groveling, Cole stole a look in Luca's direction. That was when he noticed how serious both he and Bastian looked.

"So if it's not a crush. Why are you so curious?" Alistair asked, dropping his banana peel on the table in front of him.

"Well," Cole glanced at Bastian. "Something about this mission just seems a bit strange. Like we aren't being told something. Maybe it's just our imagination, but--" He paused, giving him a look that suggested his next words had a bit more meaning to them than what showed on the surface. "Bastian feels like there's more to this too."

Obviously, Cole was referring to the blond's sometimes-inconvenient ability to detect even the best crafted lies.

"Is that right? With Shipton?" The chances of him getting a private moment to talk to them was slim, especially if his babysitter was the subject.

"Mostly," Bastian said.

"I'm not surprised." Alistair did what he could to not look over at the teacher whose eyes he felt on the back of his head. "I'll keep my eyes open."

There wasn't much more he could do. But it was a relief to know that he wasn't the only one having issues with the man. Suddenly, he wondered if Luca was harassing any of the other boys as well. The idea of the man leaned over another boy's body, his hand touching his skin, or even stroking him into bliss had his blood boiling. Jealousy was not the right emotion to be feeling at the time, so he settled on calling it disgust and ensured himself that that was all he felt.

Alistair trusted Bastian's gut more than he trusted his own most of the time, so if he said that Luca was up to something, then Alistair had no doubt that it was true. Now he just had to look past the annoying flirtation to see what the man was really planning.

After breakfast, Alistair and Luca made their way to the community center where the town meeting had been held the night before. There was a small homeschool group that used one of the back rooms for their classes, but with the rest of the town shut down, and children unable to be bussed to public schools in neighboring towns, they had moved classes into the auditorium instead. As soon as they entered the auditorium, the two women who were in charge flocked to Luca's side.

Alistair hated it.

He hated how Luca smiled at them, tricking them into thinking he was some sweet teacher. He hated the way he cupped one woman's hand in both of his as he thanked them again for being so hospitable. He hated how charming his was, and that these women were getting to bask in it.

"Don't be jealous," Luca whispered in Alistair's ear as the women left to get the children quieted down. One warm hand came to the nape of the redhead's neck, long fingers brushing his collarbone as his breath passed over the shell of his ear. "Shall I kiss you to make you feel better?"

Doing what he could to keep his strength in check, Alistair swatted the man's hand away from him. "Keep talking and I'll tell these ladies that you're molesting one of your students. We'll see how much they fawn over you then."

"Well go on, then." He lifted his chin in the direction of the two women who were on their way back over. "If you want to keep me to yourself that badly, go ahead and tell them everything. Don't forget the part where you came, shivering in my hand from just a little bit of teasing. That's my favorite part, after all."

Alistair's face flashed hot, and the best excuse he could find was "Marla would just punish me for ruining our mission if I did that. You're not worth it."

"I'm sorry about all the noise," one of the women said over the murmur of two dozen kids. "We don't usually have so many. We're not used to this."

"It's no problem at all, Caroline." The woman actually clutched for her pearls as Luca used her first name. "We're here to help in any way we can."

Caroline was probably in her fifties, with salt and pepper hair pulled into a puffy bun, but she blushed like a schoolgirl. "Well, it's rare for us to have a man's help around here. Maybe you could help me carry some things from our usual room into here. We're not really properly equipped."

"Fantastic. Just show me what you need and I'll cart it wherever you want me to." Luca turned back to Alistair. "Why don't you stay here and give Margaret a hand? You know, he might not look it," Luca said to the other woman. "But this one is a wiz with children."

Then he winked at Alistair and left with Caroline.

"What a…" she trailed off as Luca walked away, seeming to be at a loss for words for a few moments. "Kind man."

Alistair could tell she'd used "kind" to keep from saying anything about how dashing he was.

"Your name is Alistair, is that right?" She continued when she got a polite "yes" in response. "So stylish," she continued, a hand on her flushed cheek. "We don't ever see people like you and your friends around here. It's been so wonderful. Well, you know, save for all the quarantine business."

"Yeah, I guess that does put a damper on things." He wondered where the panic from the night before was.

"Oh! Where are my manners? My son is in here somewhere. Let me introduce you." She scampered off before Alistair could come up with a polite way to tell her he didn't care.

The auditorium did a horrible job at absorbing any of the noise made by the shouting, laughing children. The bleachers along one wall had been folded back out of the way, though the other side was left open for seating. Still groups of kids sat on the floor in circles, and several chased each other in laps around the room. The sound echoed in the open space and made Alistair's head throb. At the base of the bleachers, set apart from the boisterous children, there were a few young teens. Alistair might have stooped to sharing their company—the way he figured, even young teens would be better company than brats—but the girls were dressed in skirts down to their ankles and the boys all wore polo shirts and khaki shorts, sure signs that Alistair wouldn't have anything in common with them either.

It wasn't until Margaret dragged a shy-looking blond kid in Alistair's direction, that he realized he was in the same room as the boy who had been ogling him at the barbecue. Now his face was red as his mother led him by his arm toward the stranger who had caught him staring.

"Alistair, this is my son, Lakelyn." The woman all but planted the boy's hand in Alistair's.

"That's a trendy name for a place like this," Alistair said, trying not to laugh at the amount of sweat on this boy's palm.

"Oh, well I was a much different person when I had my son. Dreams of moving away to a big city, you know. But Trumbull is where we belong." She wrapped an arm around her son's shoulders, already about an inch shorter than the kid Alistair decided—now that he was close up—was probably thirteen. "Staying here was the best choice I ever made."

Lakelyn shifted in his mom's grasp, looking anywhere but at Alistair. She probably had no idea that her son was capable of looking at another boy with the sort of arousal Alistair had seen in his eyes the day before. Trumbull didn't seem like the sort of place to let that information slip, either.

"Mom, why do you keep telling people that?"

"Shush, sweetheart. Don't embarrass me in front of our guests. We need to make a good impression for our hometown. Don't want these college kids in here thinking we're a bunch of hillbillies!" Her laugh was louder than it needed to be, and Lakelyn shifted again.

"Well every town has its flaws. I'm sure Trumbull has a few skeletons in its closet, just like any other," Alistair said.

"Well that's where you're wrong. Trumbull is unlike any other. You mark my word. By the time this whole mess is sorted out, even you won't want to leave."

It was hard not to pull a face as the Children-of-the-Corn vibes washed over the room. Something seemed strange, but he couldn't exactly go to Luca and say that some lady gave him the willies because she liked her town *too much*. Even Lakelyn looked a little creeped out, but before Alistair could decide if he was imagining it, Margaret brought a hand up to her mouth to cover a few wet sounding coughs.

"Oh, excuse me," she said, patting her own chest and smiling before doubling over, coughing even harder.

"Mom?" For the first time, Lakelyn looked at his mother the way you would expect a child to. He took her by the shoulders, trying to steady her as she rode out the convulsive coughing fit.

Adrenaline dumped into Alistiar's system—was this how it had started for Charles? He couldn't imagine this sweet looking woman turning into the movie monster that had chased him around just a few nights ago. The children in the room had grown silent, and as Alistair stalled, weighing his options, the woman's hand latched onto her son's neck. She screamed--a distinct gurgling low in her throat that Alistair remembered from his encounter with the escapee back at haven--and Lakelyn struggled to pull his mother's hands from his restricted airways.

"Let go of him!" Alistair tore the two apart, pulling the boy toward him and shoving his mother with his free hand. Keeping the thirteen-year-old tucked behind him, Alistair watched Margaret stumble and then fall to her knees. She shook and stared at her hands as if they weren't hers. Her breathing came in phlegm filled rasps.

"Mom?" Lakelyn asked again, the room dead silent—even the youngest children frozen where they sat with their friends.

Then she started screaming, her hands moving to her the neck of her shirt, ripping it open before clawing at her exposed chest.

"Get it out. Get it out!"

The children erupted into a panic, screaming and crying as some of the older ones tried to get the smallest to leave, but Margaret kept screaming, kept ripping at her own skin as blood began to pool around her.

"Mom, stop!" Lakelyn tried to run to her side, but Alistair stopped him, shoving him as gently as he could away from the woman who had started ripping hair from her head in handfuls.

"Go get help, I'll stop her."

Her son watched her for a second before turning and sprinting out of the room. When he was safe, Alistair ran to the woman's side, capturing her wrists in his hands, careful not to break bones as he did so. She lunged for him, her teeth clacking together as they tried to catch his face between their blood-slicked edges. He'd not noticed the blood that had come up with her coughing, and now up close he could see the deep wounds she'd scratched into her own body. Deep gashes from her neck down over her collarbones, white from the tendons and ribs peeking through the shredded skin.

Flecks of blood spattered across Alistair's face as she tried to catch him in her teeth, and his hands slipped in the blood covering her wrists. He couldn't squeeze any harder or he would cause damage, but he had to subdue her. A low growling sounded from her throat that was interrupted by a gurgling, then she heaved once and blackened, clotted blood surged from her mouth and ran hot down Alistair's chest and across his lap.

As he fought the wave of disgust that burned the back of his throat, Margaret slipped her hand away from him, the blood lubricating her body. Alistair grappled with her, fighting to control his strength as he tried to pin her flailing arms and snapping jaws. Children were screaming behind him still, and when he made the mistake to look back at them to ensure they were safe, she caught his forearm in her mouth, his skin tearing as if her teeth had been replaced with knives. Not wanting to risk her slipping away, instead of trying to free his arm, he hooked her with it, pressing her head against his chest so she couldn't get away as he wrapped his free arm around her neck. He would squeeze just hard enough to knock her out.

He would just squeeze a little.

Just...

He felt a cracking under his arm and Margaret's body went limp in his arms. He dropped her like she'd caught fire and shuffled away from her, his hands and shoes sliding in the pool of blood that had formed around them.

He was cradling the bite wound on his arm when Luca ran into the auditorium, Caroline's scream punctuating his arrival. Instead of checking the woman's body where she lay in her own blood, Luca descended on Alistair.

"Are you alright?"

It was the first time Alistair had heard anything but confidence in the man's voice, but he was too shaken to enjoy it.

"I killed her. Oh god, I think I killed her. I didn't mean to. I just—I didn't mean to squeeze that hard and I broke her neck. I didn't mean to."

"Hey!" Luca's hands closed on either side of Alistair's face, forcing him to look him in the eyes, and for a second, the panic eased in Alistair's head. He blinked and took a second to appreciate the flecks of dark blue in the pools of steel that made up the other man's eyes. "Are you hurt?" Luca asked.

"I'm okay." Alistair's voice was steady now, and his lungs finally relaxed enough for him to take a full breath of air. "She bit me, but that's it." He moved his hand to uncover his wound, allowing Luca to examine it.

"I've seen worse." He smiled encouragingly and wiped a bit of blood from the boy's cheek, then stood up. "Wait here while I go check on her."

Somehow, Luca's presence had calmed Alistair, but as he watched him crouch over the woman's body, he began shaking again. He tried so hard to not hurt anyone, especially after Felix, but things didn't always work out that way. Still, he'd never *killed* anyone before. Not a regular person, anyway.

He held his breath as Luca's fingers passed over Margaret's face and neck, and that's when he saw Lakelyn, standing beside Caroline, frozen where they'd reentered the auditorium. There were tears on the boy's face, and something icy settled in Alistair's stomach. What would he do if he was the one responsible for the loss of this kid's mother?

"Someone bring me one of the fold-out tables." Luca's authoritative voice seemed to break the stillness that had fallen on all of them. "She's alive. We'll use the table as a stretcher to get her to Dr. Adler's office."

There was one doctor who lived in town—a decrepit old man who was more or less retired, but still diagnosed colds and prescribed arthritis medicine to the other seniors in town. They'd met him briefly at the barbecue the day before, but the only impression Alistair had gotten from him was one of infirmity. The man seriously looked like he would keel over at any second. Still, he was a doctor, and if Luca thought he was the one who could help, he was willing to do anything to save himself from the label of "murderer."

With Luca's instruction, Alistair, Lakelyn, and a trembling, weeping Caroline helped move Margaret's body onto the table-turned-stretcher. Strips of torn fabric were used to stabilize her head to keep her neck still, and with the bite wound on his arm throbbing, Alistair helped carry the woman to the doctor's house.

Townspeople swarmed them, and soon, Alistair had been shooed away—told that he looked like he needed a doctor himself. When they reached Dr. Adler's, the man did little more than Luca had done before deciding that she would need to go to a real hospital. That's when the mayor showed up.

Then the preacher.

Then, about twenty minutes later, in a military jeep and clad in a full HazMat suit, Marla.

Alistair sat on the stairs in front of Dr. Adler's house, most of his teammates loitering in the general area as well. He could feel their questions hanging in the air around them, but they at least had enough tact not to ask. Even Jett kept his mouth shut, though it seemed more like he was disinterested than thoughtful. He leaned against a short fence that surrounded the house, thumbing through the music on his phone, Kiyiya laying in the grass by his feet.

Milo was inside with the adults—unsurprising—and Sabin was staring at the bite wound on his arm like it physically pained him *not* to ask if he was going to turn into a zombie. Tired of the awkward silence, Alistair kicked a small rock toward his pierced friend.

"Hey, Sweetheart. Let me tell you something." Alistair could see the confusion on Sabin's face, but went on. "You, uh, you have my permission. I ever turn into one of those things? Do me a favor, blow my fucking head off."

A second passed, and then recognition passed over Sabin's face. He laughed and then finished the quote. "Oh yeah, you can count on that."

"Oh good. Dawn of the Dead quotes." If Berlin were any more on edge he would tip off the side. "We're in the real life prequel to the zombie apocalypse and they're quoting Romero movies."

"That was a Zack Snyder flick, dip shit. It's from the remake."

"Oh! I got the director wrong? On a movie from like ten fucking years ago? I'm so sorry. I guess I was kind of distracted by the *real* fucking zombies we have running the fuck around."

Before Sabin could go into the history-of-zombie-movie-directors rant they could all see brewing inside him, the door behind Alistair opened. Marla led a group of townspeople out who were carrying Margaret on a real stretcher this time.

"Clear a path, boys."

Luca came out behind her. "We got in touch with the guys in charge. They've offered to take her for medical attention." They all knew that was a lie. The "guys in charge" was code for "Marla."

Alistair stood up, but only managed to plant one foot off the porch before Marla stopped him.

"*You* stay." The look she gave him matched the harsh edge of her words, but she softened a second later when she realized her other wards were watching her. "Get your arm looked at. We'll take care of this."

15: ALISTAIR

They all stood quietly as the townspeople loaded their friend into the back of Marla's jeep and then watched her drive away, out toward the towers of the quarantine line. It wasn't until the dust had settled that people started dispersing, and Luca said in a solemn voice, "Let's call it a night, you guys. Everyone back to the motel."

It wasn't until Alistair had walked the whole way back to his room—until Luca instructed him to have a seat on the side of his bed—that he remembered the blood and what he could only assume was vomit that covered the front of his shirt and pants.

"Don't worry about it," Luca said as he came out of the bathroom with a bowl of water. "I'll pull the blankets off and have them cleaned. Just sit down."

As he followed the man's instructions, Alistair was just thinking he was being too complacent when Luca grinned at him, settling on the edge of the mattress across from him.

"You're being awfully obedient."

He didn't even feel like arguing, so he just stared at him a second before presenting his still-throbbing arm.

"I didn't expect you to be so torn up about this." Luca's smile was faint as he opened the packets of gauze, some of its teasing luster gone. "It's pretty cute, to be honest."

"Accidentally breaking someone's neck isn't cute, *professor*. I could have killed her. I'm not really in the mood for your harassment."

"No, it isn't cute. But it's good to know that underneath that gorgeous, prickly exterior, there's a nice soft center."

"The only soft center you're interested in is my asshole."

"Well *that's definitely* not cute."

"I'm doing what I can."

The quiet that settled between them was a relief. All that Alistair wanted to do was wallow for a while longer. This was exactly why Marla had made him so angry: he didn't *want* to hurt people. If he had the choice to be normal, to have boyfriends, to make love without fear of hurting anybody, he would take it in a heartbeat. He wondered how Lakelyn was doing—if he hated him now.

I don't even know that kid. Why would it even matter?

"You know, the breaking sound you heard was probably just cartilage." Luca's voice was low, missing its usual teasing edge. Alistair didn't answer as he watched the man slowly wipe the blood away from the two arched lines of teeth marks that were blooming into spectacular red and purple bruises. "At worst, her hyoid might be fractured. A painful recovery, but she won't be paralyzed or anything."

"Are you trying to comfort me?"

"Do you need comforting?" His hands were warm where he was cradling Alistair's wrist, which felt very thin all of a sudden.

"I don't."

"Well that wasn't the impression you gave me in the auditorium. Do you have any idea how badly you were shaking?" His hand tightened slightly on the thin white wrist in his hand. What could he even say to that? "I get the impression that you think Marla sees you as a threat, as a bad person, maybe, but—"

"Look, you can stop there, okay? I don't need you to pep talk me. I'm tired of you and Venja telling me what Marla *meant*. She's a grown-ass woman and she can take responsibility for the things she *actually* says to me."

Luca just smiled, the slightly crooked smirk that had weakened Alistair's knees the first time he'd seen it in the bar.

"Actually I was going to tell you to not listen to a damn thing she says." After applying some unidentified ointment to the wound, he wrapped a waterproof bandage around his forearm like a bracer, then slid his fingers up a soft trail of skin until they passed under the sleeve of his shirt. "It's good to know that you still have some fire in you."

"It's a shame it's not literal like it is with Jett. Then I could actually burn you to death."

Luca only laughed and stood up. "Come on then. You need to clean up. I have a special soap for you to use just in case this thing is more contagious than we think."

Alistair had almost forgotten about that, and felt his stomach turn over as he looked down at the stains covering his clothes. He didn't argue as Luca followed him into the bathroom where he ran the water for him.

"We have to make sure it's as hot as you can manage so it can kill any bacteria." He placed a clear bottle of soap on the side of the tub. "There you go. Try to stay under the spray as long as you can."

A few moments passed as Alistair waited for the man to leave, but Luca only lifted himself onto the sink counter where he sat facing the shower.

"What are you doing?"

"Me?" He smiled. "Well I have to ensure that you clean properly."

"Like hell you do. Get out."

"Now, Alistair, don't be difficult. It's quarantine protocol. Anyone who has been exposed must be disinfected to the satisfaction of a licensed agent. Honestly, you're lucky I'm not cleaning you myself."

"Do you really think I'm going to believe that?" Despite his words, Alistair was happy to pull the filthy, sticky shirt off over his head. He wasn't ashamed or embarrassed to be seen naked, he just hated the way the man's eyes cut such sharp lines down his body. "Are you going to start wiping my ass for me too?"

"Watching you try to turn me off with rough language only arouses me more, you know."

Alistair hoped the man didn't notice him swallow so hard.

"So now I arouse you?" Alistair tried to regain his teetering composure. "You had a funny way of showing it in the bar."

"Is your pride still bruised over that? How adorable. Seems like you're just not used to people telling you 'no.'" He crossed his legs and leaned back against the mirror. "Don't close the curtain."

He almost threatened to report Luca to Marla and Venja, but he didn't want to hear the man tell him what he already knew—that Marla would never believe him. He knew exactly what sort of person Marla thought he was. Promiscuous, slutty, dangerous. Somehow he didn't want to hear that come from the perfectly shaped lips that were turned up in a leering grin. So Alistair said nothing and kicked his pants and underwear into the corner of the bathroom as they hit the floor.

He heard Luca mutter a quiet "gorgeous," but ignored it as he stepped into the tub. He was already sweating slightly, just from the heat of the steam coming off the spray. A hiss escaped him as he eased his legs into the spray, his skin turning pink where the water hit him. Luca had been right—the water was nearly unbearable—but it was just cool enough that it wouldn't cause real burns.

"Now make sure to wash everywhere. Even places blood didn't touch."

Alistair did as he was told, wanting to be done with the whole ordeal, but he could feel the other man's eyes on him, hotter than the water he was slowly growing accustomed to. As he lathered the stringent soap into his hair, the suds that fell over his chest trailed down his body like fingertips, and he could feel Luca's eyes following them down over the slight angle of his hip. And when his own hands slicked the soap over his skin, his breath began to shorten.

He'd showered in front of his teammates countless times, but he'd never felt exposed like he did with Luca sitting rapt, only feet away. He stared straight ahead, refusing to look where he sat at the periphery of his eye, like a shadow of lust causing his skin to prickle. Luca could stand up and in two steps be in the shower, pushing Alistair against the cool tiled wall. In seconds he could be ravishing him, his wide hands mapping his body with the same skill he'd felt in his room where he'd been helpless under his touch.

"Alistair."

He wasn't sure when his eyes had drifted shut, but as he heard his name roll off the other man's lips in a voice lower than he remembered, he realized that he'd already started reacting. Looking down his own body he could see the proof of his arousal stirring, and when he finally turned toward Luca he saw the man leaning forward, hands gripping the edges of the counter, legs uncrossed, leaving the obvious answer to his desire exposed where his trousers strained against him.

"I told you to clean everywhere, didn't I?"

There was something in the timber of his voice that bypassed the defiant part of Alistair's brain, and in a fog of arousal, the redhead turned to press his back against the tiled wall, pretending that it was Luca who had pushed him there. Facing the man, he tipped his head back as both hands slid over his soap-slicked body to where he really wanted the other man to touch him. A sigh escaped him as he wrapped his fingers around his hardening cock, squeezing just enough to force a gasp past his lips.

"Perfect. Show me how you do it when you're alone."

Buried somewhere in his mind was a voice reminding Alistair that he'd just broken a woman's neck—that he'd just watched a person tear parts of their own skin away. This was inappropriate on more levels than he could count, but when he eased his eyes open again and saw Luca watching him, he didn't care.

"Are you regretting turning me down now?" The sense of power Alistair always felt when men fawned over him made his dick jump in his hand. "Because now, watching me do this is the closest you'll ever get."

"Well." His voice sounded rough, and just a little breathless. "If this is really all I'm going to get, you're going to take mercy on me and show me everything, right?"

"Why would you even deserve that much?" Talking was becoming difficult as Alistair's long fingers twisted around his shaft, pulling slow and hard. He watched the tenting in his teacher's pants grow as his free hand traced lines up his body before passing each of his fingertips over the sensitive peak of his nipple. He would make Luca watch him. He would refuse to succumb to the urge he felt for the man's touch.

"Because if you show me, I'll be good and keep my hands to myself." He was obviously humoring him, the grin on his face giving him away. "Show me all the places I'm not allowed to touch."

Who was in control of whom stopped mattering when Luca's hand moved to rub himself through his pants. Alistair let his head fall back with a long, soft moan—one that was less for show than he wanted to admit—and leaned against the shower wall, starting working himself for real. Stealing glances at Luca, whose attention was so focused on him he could *feel* his eyes passing over his skin, Alistair tried to remember the things he liked. He squeezed himself just hard enough to make his spine jump, pressed a fingertip into the sensitive slit at the tip, cupped the tightening pouch between his legs. He did everything his body craved, but still struggled to push himself over the edge.

"Having problems, kitten? You're starting to look desperate." Luca sat leaned back against the mirror on the counter now, his fingers lazily tracing himself through his pants, seeming content to enjoy the show.

The last thing Alistair would admit is that Luca was right. After the magic the man had worked on him in his bedroom, Alistair found himself struggling on his own. Still kneading soft, tightening skin between his legs, his fingers moved further, seeking the part of him that was really begging to be touched. The muscles in his stomach tensed as fingertips passed over the tight ring of muscle. He looked away from Luca as he pressed a finger inside, his body quaking as his skin gave way to the hot, slick walls inside him.

"Now, now. Don't hide anything from me. Let me see where you're touching that feels so good."

If Alistair had any sense left, he would have told Luca to fuck himself. But his head was buzzing, his face was hot, and the twisting appetite for more was muddling his brain. Instead, he leaned back against the wall and spread his feet so Luca could see just how far back he was reaching.

"Oh, now. What sort of view is that? Why don't you turn around and let me see?" His voice was a low rumble in the room, and even though he sat several yards away, it sent goosebumps across Alistair's skin. "Turn around and spread your legs for me." His words were a command this time, and Alistair couldn't deny him.

The tile felt like ice on the heated skin of Alistair's chest and face, but he pressed into them, his back bowing and his legs spreading so Luca could see where he had his middle finger buried inside himself. He wanted Luca to look, to watch him as he worked his finger in as far as his body would let him, guiding it inside himself in slow thrusts. He was glad that Luca couldn't see the desperate look on his face.

"Don't tell me that's all you can fit. One little finger? You know I'm much thicker than that."

"Fuck off." His voice cracked, ruining the attempt to sound tough.

Luca only chuckled as Alistair followed his commands, pressing his forehead against the tile as he pushed another finger inside himself. The slow, warm stretching sensation started a tremor in his knees, and soon he groaned in frustration, the angle of his wrist where it was hooked between his legs preventing him from reaching the spots inside himself he knew would send him to the moon. Sliding the digits out of himself he shifted, bracing himself with one forearm as he reached around himself, his still slick fingers rubbing over the loosened muscle before pressing in again. This time he brushed the places that really wanted to be touched and his head fell to his forearm with a weak moan.

"Beautiful."

Alistair's dick jumped where it stood neglected, Luca's voice wrapping around him like an extra hand. It wasn't impossible for Alistair to work himself to completion without ever touching his front, but he'd never been pushed to the edge so quickly. Already his legs shook and he felt pre-cum slide down the underside of his cock, his body jerking every time the tip brushed against the cold tile of the shower. He could barely hear Luca any more, his eyes shut as he thrust into himself, desperately trying to get to the nirvana building inside him. Then the other man's voice broke through the haze, seizing Alistair's breath in his throat.

"More, Alistair." He didn't sound amused any more, he sounded predatory. "Two isn't enough. Get yourself ready for me."

The keening that escaped Alistair's lips was pathetic, but he couldn't deny him anything. Pressing his chest against the tile wall to free his other hand, he wrapped his fingers around his own seeping arousal. He *did* want more. He wanted Luca to force him open, to grip his hips and fuck him to tears against the wall. But that wouldn't happen. Even if he did grab him, push him into submission, his strength would still overpower the other man. He would still end up hurting him.

All he could do was hold his breath as he urged a third finger inside himself and pretend. He could imagine it. Closing his eyes again, he worked his fist around his cock and spread his fingers, as though preparing himself to be taken the way he imagined. He didn't want to let

Luca win, he didn't want to succumb, but right that second, he was waiting for it to happen. Any second. He just had to get himself that much closer, then the game would be over and Luca would fuck him.

Just a little bit more.

Then his fingers pressed against the small node inside himself and he shouted, his knees buckling as he came hard against the tile wall, thin strip of white painting the ceramic like tears of frustration. Alistair sank to his knees in the shower, his fingers sliding out of himself as his body pulsed around them, as though trying to keep them from leaving.

For a while, all he could hear was the sound of his own breathing as the tingling sensation drained from his face. Luca hadn't touched him. He had let him drive himself over the edge.

With a squeak, the shower was turned off and a towel was presented to him. Alistair looked up at the pale, brunette man, his grey eyes shining around the satisfied grin that lit his face. Suddenly angry, Alistair snatched the towel from him, pushing himself up onto still shaking legs.

"Why didn't you touch me?" It was hard to say why he was so offended. Normally, when Alistair touched himself in front of another person it was to control them. He would make them shake with desire before inviting them over. But this time he hadn't felt any control. He'd simply been following directions.

"Because you told me not to, of course." Using one finger, Luca guided a few strands of wet hair out of the boy's face. "Did you *want* me to touch you?"

The dissipating heat in Alistair's face flared back up and he swatted the man's hand away before wrapping the towel around himself. "Don't make me laugh. I just did you a favor."

"Oh yes, it was quite the favor." With one step, he extended an arm between Alistair and the doorway, blocking his escape. "Maybe next time I can do more than just watch. Back at base, you came awfully fast too. Does the idea of being helpless turn you on? Would you have come even faster if I'd pinned you to the wall? Hm? What would have happened, I wonder, if you were held down? If you were completely powerless."

A shiver wound up Alistair's back, and he had to use every bit of strength he had left to steady his voice, and at the same time a weight settled in his stomach, dissipating the last winding highs of his orgasm. Kinks and longings aside, any lover Alistair touched would be in danger. And that included Luca.

"That'll never happen." He didn't have to fight for the dead-level voice this time. It wouldn't happen, because he wouldn't let it. He lifted his chin a little, trying to regain some of power over the situation. "You can enjoy the show, but the real thing would leave you crippled. Get it?" He held up the fingers that had been inside him only minutes ago. "I'm a death trap." Then he bent his fingers to illustrate the sort of damage he'd done to prior partners.

"And you're baited with pure honey, aren't you?" If the promise of a crushed dick bothered him, Luca didn't show it. Instead, he ran a few fingers down the soft curve of Alistair's cheek. "Does it make you lonely?"

Alistair grinned. "Not lonely enough to fall for *you*. I'll make you a deal though. You let me walk out of this motel room, alone, and I won't tell Marla about all the sexual harassment I've been putting up with."

Luca laughed and leaned down, his nose and lips brushing along the wet hair above Alistair's ear. When he spoke, his voice vibrated Alistair's skull, turning his bones soft. "How could I say 'no' to you?" When he stood back up, his face seemed softer, warmer than what Alistair was used to. "Just don't get caught, okay?"

Alistair had to take a moment to catch his breath under the shine of his smile.

16: ALISTAIR

The sun felt warmer on his face than it had earlier that day. Of course, it was the same, but, as he crossed the parking lot, he felt like the wide expanse had finally hit him. The town was terrible—minuscule and too country for him to handle—but the sky went on forever, and for the first time in years, he felt like he could breathe. Probably because he knew he could go anywhere he wanted just then—at least anywhere inside the quarantine line.

Not that there was anywhere in particular that he wanted to go. He just wanted to enjoy the open space for a while.

Crossing the street, the gravel crunched under his feet as he skirted the chain-link fence that surrounded the massive silos he'd seen when they'd first arrived. If nothing else, they would act as a good hiding place.

As he turned the corner, though, he saw that he wasn't the only person looking for some relief. Sitting in the shadow cast by the silo, at the border where the gravel stopped and grass started, sat Lakelyn. For a second, Alistair thought about turning around. He wanted to be alone, not stuck with the boy whose mom he'd just assaulted. But then he was struck by the way his sandy-blond curls waved in the breeze coming in off the fields, the way his freckles looked so warm even in the shade, and he was reminded of Felix.

Lakelyn jumped as Alistair dropped himself into the grass beside him. It was definitely a good spot. The wind moved the tall stalks of corn, rolling them in waves that looked like some vast, green ocean. The horizon would have looked endless if not for the black stains caused by the quarantine officers.

When he gave the kid beside him a sideways glance he saw him staring at his shoes, his hands holding his knees like they were going to run off without him.

"Sorry about what I did to your mom." There was no sense in beating around the bush.

A few more beats of silence passed between them.

"I'd apologize for the way my mom acted, but... I don't even know what happened anymore."

It was at that point that Alistair realized why Lakelyn had come all the way out to the edge of town to sulk. There was a clear view down the road that led out of town, probably the road they'd driven the ambulance out of.

"Well, nothing she did was her fault. She was obviously sick. I'm just sorry I ended up hurting her more than she already was."

"If she's sick, this whole fucking place is doomed."

Alistair couldn't help but smile at the language this thirteen-year-old kid was using.

"I've heard it's not that contagious."

"I'm not even worried about that. It's this stupid town. It's ruined everything."

"I imagine growing up here is hard."

"Are you kidding? I grew up in Chicago."

That would explain the trendy name and the lack of the mid-western drawl he heard from some of the older people in town. But it still didn't make much sense.

"That's not what you mom said."

"My mom was going nuts. It started like two months ago. She started acting weird, then packed me and two suitcases into the car and just drove us out here. Like, there's nothing out here. At all. She doesn't even have a job out here. She just fucks around with the PTA and the church ladies." Now that the dam had broken, Lakelyn seemed ready to purge as much as he could manage. "It's like she woke up in the middle of her midlife crisis and decided she wanted to be a yokel Stepford Wife!"

Alistair just propped his elbow on his knee and watched the younger boy unload. That was definitely an interesting tidbit, probably something Marla would want to know.

"Why tell everyone she grew up here then?"

"I don't know. All the new people have been saying that."

"All the new people?"

Lakelyn snorted through his nose. "This place is like a roach house, and all the crazies are scurrying in. And now I feel like the only way out is the way my mom went."

"Can you tell me who else is lying about growing up here?"

Lakelyn turned to look him, but his eyes drifted over his shoulder. "I think your teacher is looking for you."

Turning back the way he'd come, Alistair saw Luca standing at the edge of the chain-link fence, hands in his pockets and a smile on his face.

"Are you shitting me?"

"Look, don't worry about what you did to my mom. You probably did her a favor. She's out of here now because of you." He stood up. "See ya."

Lakelyn walked in the opposite direction of Luca and disappeared around the fence and silos.

"What the hell?" He waited until Lakelyn was out of earshot before he snapped at his new stalker. "You said you'd let me go out on my own."

"No, no. If you remember, I agreed to let you walk out the door on your own. You did that all by yourself. You said nothing about whether or not I could follow you."

Alistair just glared at the black towers at the far edge of the field. He refused to look at Luca as he sat down beside him.

"Well, joke's on you. I was getting really great information from that kid. And you just ran him off."

"I've had my eyes on him and his mom since we got here. They matched the description of two missing persons reports from the Chicago area. The boy's father filed them about a month ago."

"He said a lot of people in town are new. You think they're the same? Do you think maybe they're infected?"

"Well if *she* was, then there's always a chance that they are. Trumbull's population is usually two hundred. We've been doing a low-key estimation since we got here, and as best we can tell it's in the four hundreds now. And we're still matching a bunch of them to missing reports."

"Hm. I estimated something similar at the barbecue. Popular vacation spot, I guess."

"Well it's no Disneyland. But that kid could be a good way in. I'll make sure you have more chances to talk to him."

"Mm. I feel bad for him."

Luca only smiled a little, as though impressed that Alistair could actually feel sympathy. Neither of them bothered saying anything else, and though Alistair had gone out there to be alone, sitting in silence with the man beside him wasn't so bad.

17: BASTIAN

"Do you have any idea how cute Cole was being when you interrupted us?" The night was quiet, just like it had been the night before when Berlin had come banging on Bastian's motel room door. And just like the night before, he had just reduced Cole to a shivering, panting mess beneath him when his friend had disturbed them. "For the second night in the row, I might add."

"Oh shut up, Bastian." They weren't ducking behind trashcans like they had been the last time, since they weren't actually *following* Sabin this time. Now they were hunting for him. Berlin had woken up to find the other boy's bed empty, and had all but beat Bastian's door down in the panic that followed. "You and your stupid boyfriend can suck face some other time. This is important."

"As important as the super scary letter he was sending to his friend last night?"

"Well sorry for being worried about you. If he's up to something, it's not just me who might be in danger. I mean, I know we had a lot of shit we went through, but you're still important to me, you know?"

Bastian narrowed his eyes at the back of Berlin's head as they turned off the lit main street onto one of the darker roads. "You aren't trying to talk me into a hand job or anything, are you?"

The tattooed boy shot him an indignant look over his shoulder. "Obviously, I'm not *that* desperate."

"I don't know, I've seen you pretty desperate before."

Before the other boy could decide on a comeback, a low grunt and a muffled ripping sound neither of them could place caught their attention. They fell into silence, pausing a moment to get their bearings as the sound of a strained breath led them to an empty lot that stood between two brick buildings. The space had probably once been a building attached to the two on either side, but now was overgrown with vines and shrubs.

They inched up to the corner of the building beside it. Berlin was the first to peer around the corner, though Bastian pushed him down to a kneel so he could lean over him to look. Sitting in the center of the lot was Sabin, sleeves rolled up, on his knees in the dirt, and the grunting sound they'd heard made sense. With his bare hands, Sabin had dug a wide trough in the dirt. He was slightly winded, hauling dirt up out of the ground and onto a pile beside him

"What is he doing?" Berlin's voice was a little hoarse.

"Digging?"

"Well, obviously!" Berlin hissed at him. "But why? What if he's digging a grave?"

It was Bastian's turn to be annoyed, and he dug his elbow into the top of his friend's skull. "Don't be stupid. He'd never be able to dig something that big with just his hands."

Then Sabin pulled hard on something he found inside the hole, and the strange ripping noise they'd heard earlier made sense as he pulled a tangled root from the ground, the threads snapping and flinging dirt into his lap. With a sigh, Sabin sat back on his feet, brushing dirt off the tangle of roots. When it was relatively clean, he stuffed it into a sack that lay beside him.

"Are you happy now? He's gardening. So spooky."

"In the middle of the night?"

Just then, a dragon fly buzzed by Sabin's head, and with well-trained reflexes, he dropped his bag and snatched the bug out of the air with both hands.

"And he likes catching bugs." Bastian continued, his voice weaker now.

A telling twist of Sabin's wrist told Bastian he wasn't planning to release the unsuspecting insect, and when he produced a jar they'd not seen and dropped the lifeless thing inside, Bastian felt a chill run up his spine. Holding the jar up to his face, Sabin squinted at the heap of bodies inside it.

"Okay, yeah. That was creepy." Bastian worried that his friend's paranoia was rubbing off on him. But a jar full of dead bugs was where he drew the line.

"See? This is what I have to sleep with! He has more jars too. Ones with live things in it. This isn't normal!"

Stuffing the jar into the bag with the roots, Sabin pushed all the dirt back into the hole he'd dug and hoisted the sack onto his shoulder.

18: COLE

It wasn't surprising when Berlin came running back into the room Cole and Bastian shared with wide eyes and a sheen of sweat, but it *was* surprising when Bastian came tumbling into the room behind him, looking equally shaken.

"What's going on?" Cole's heart rate soared in preparation. Surely, if they both looked *that* upset, something terribly must have happened. In answer they both began talking over each other.

"We found him, he wasn't sending letters this time," Bastian began.

"He was digging things up out of the ground."

"And he has a jar full of dead bugs!"

"He killed a dragonfly and threw it in."

"And he's hauling it all back into his room."

Cole blinked at them a second, trying to let it all settle in his head. "Well, what'd he say?"

"Say?" It was Bastian's turn to pause.

"I mean, did you ask him what he was doing?" Cole looked between the two blank stares he got from his lover and his teammate.

"Well…" Bastian looked a bit sheepish, but Berlin cut him off before he could admit that they *may* have gotten carried away.

"Of course we didn't ask him what he was doing! He'd hex us if he knew we were following him. And considering what we just saw, he might do something even worse!"

"Because he killed a bug and dug a hole?" Cole felt like he was talking to a child. "You know what, move out of the way." Tired of Berlin slowly dragging his lover into his paranoid fantasies, Cole decided it was time to set things straight, and he marched to the door.

"What are you doing?" Bastian, at least, scampered after him.

"I'm going to talk to Sabin. You know, the way normal people handle situations?"

Bastian and Berlin ran after him, nearly toppling into him when he stopped outside of Sabin's door, knocking politely. There was a pause and a hissed warning from where Berlin stood behind him before the door opened. Sabin looked disheveled, dirt smudging his face and coating his hands, but he looked over Cole's shoulder at the two taller boys and just sighed.

"I figured you were up to something when I found your bed empty." Despite his obvious annoyance, he moved aside and let everyone in.

"Sorry," Cole apologized before continuing. "But these two seem to be under the impression that you're up to something. They followed you tonight." He paused to look at Berlin who was making a cutting motion across his own throat with his hand. "*And* last night." He was tired of Berlin bossing him around. "I want to set it all straight though. So, who were you sending a letter to? And why are you sneaking around and digging things up?"

Sabin laughed a little and leaned against the dresser where his dirty bag was sitting. "Man, what ever happened to privacy, huh?"

"I know," Cole said. "I'm sorry. But I'm tired of Berlin spreading rumors and getting all worked up on his own. We're a team, so we should all be able to talk to each other when we have uncertainties."

Sabin scraped some dirt out from under his thumbnail, though he was smiling a little. "You're starting to sound like Bastian now, all leaderly and stuff."

Cole knew the witch never liked people prying into his business, but he didn't want to see the sorts of disconnects between Sabin and the others that he felt. Sabin might be a witch, but even popular media had "good" witches. He at least had a chance.

"I just thought I'd give you the chance to explain, so these two don't get the wrong idea."

The whole room was quiet for a few moments, then Sabin sighed and pushed himself off the dresser, taking his bag and walking toward a stack of weathered trunks near his bed.

"I was out collecting spell ingredients. Usually I have to go through Marla to get what I need, and that always comes with lots of explanations. I miss going out and collecting them on my own." He paused to flash them a derisive smile. "And sometimes that means I need icky bugs."

"And the letter?" Cole pressed.

"What? You guys have never sent a letter?" He dropped his bag to the floor and opened the top trunk.

"Look, just tell us who this Noah person is, okay?" Berlin was talking big, but he was still hiding behind Cole and Bastian.

The trunk lid slammed down hard, and when Sabin turned to look at them again the exasperated look he'd been wearing was gone. His eyes were wide now, his brows drawn down into straight, angry lines.

"Did you shitheads seriously fish my letter out of that box?" When they didn't answer, he surged toward them, Bastian and Berlin both retreating behind Cole like he would protect them. "That letter was important!"

"Hold on!" Cole raised his hands and placed himself between the witch and the other two who probably deserved whatever punishment was coming. But he didn't want to see his friends fight. "They put it back," he insisted. "It was still mailed out yesterday." Sabin was quiet as he glared over Cole's shoulder. "They shouldn't have read it, but they didn't keep it at least."

"You guys are assholes." His voice shook a little, and Cole thought the witch's eyes might have looked a little watery.

The stillness in the room made Cole think the others might feel bad for what they did—he knew that at least Bastian would—but his own curiosity was still piqued. In the softest voice he could muster he asked, "Who's Noah?"

As though he'd forgotten that his hands were filthy, Sabin pushed them through his hair, leaving smudges of dirt on his forehead. After a sigh, he relented. "A friend I have in Vancouver. He took care of me for a while before I was brought to Haven. I learned most of my magic from him." Sabin swallowed, and his face darkened a little, the ring in his lip flicking like a nervous twitch. "I haven't heard from him in a while, so I'm worried."

"Why do it in the middle of the night then?" Berlin didn't sound as moved as he should.

"Have you ever tried sending a letter at Haven?" Sabin practically spit the words at the tattooed boy. "At least half of everything either of us writes gets redacted. And sometimes, letters just never make it through. I sent it here, in secret, so I knew for sure it would get to him. I thought that maybe Marla had just stopped sending them."

Cole's heart ached. He'd known Sabin just as long as he'd known Milo, but admittedly knew very little about him. They'd all been vaguely aware of his pen pal, but this was the first time he'd ever heard Sabin actually talk about him. Still, hearing the spite in his voice when talking about Marla censoring his letters still made Cole bristle a little.

"I'm sure she wouldn't do that. And if she's censoring something, it must be for good reason. I mean, we *are* a top secret facility. There are probably rules she has to follow."

"I don't care." Sabin's tone was quieter—like he'd checked out. "Marla's in charge because she's the queen of secret keeping."

"Not from us though." Cole's stomach twisted, even as the words left his mouth. Marla was his mother. She'd saved him. She was odd sometimes, but she always did what was best for them, even if it was a tough sort of love.

"That's cute that you think that, Cole." Sabin walked back to the beat up leather trunk at the foot of his bed and popped it open. "But I've been with Marla longer than you have. If she wants you to believe something, she'll make you believe it. Whether it's real or not. And she'll tell you whatever she needs to." Crouching by the open trunk, he dug through it, the clinking sound of glass filling the room.

"Well even if she's keeping secrets, it doesn't change the fact that she cares about us."

"Maybe." He opened a small rusted tin box, smelled it, then put it back before continuing his search.

The room was quiet again, and Cole wondered if Bastian or Berlin would back him up. Of course, they hardly knew Marla, so he didn't figure they could weigh in even if they wanted to. When Sabin opened another, similar looking tin he made a face as his nose neared the powdered substance inside. It was apparently what he was looking for, because he set it on the floor beside him, followed by a small drawstring bag, and a glass jar full of a yellow, congealed substance. Cole swallowed and heard Berlin whispering to Bastian, though he couldn't make out what he was saying.

"What are you doing?"

"Putting the ingredients I found tonight to use." He shot a nasty look at Berlin and Bastian. "I'm not just a hoarder, you know. I collect things for reasons."

"Yeah, in the middle of the night…" Berlin muttered to himself more than to anyone else, but Cole was surprised he didn't get hexed when Sabin narrowed his eyes at him.

"You're going to do a spell?" Cole had never seen him actually work magic before. He'd seen him cast spells during fights and things like that, but there was apparently much more to his magic than that. He'd talked before about having to "load" spells—whatever that meant—and to do that he needed ingredients. Usually, he did that in the privacy of his own bedroom.

"Not tonight. I'm still missing a few things I need."

"Like what? What are you trying to do?" He eased closer as Sabin pulled his large, worn mortar and pestle out from under his bed.

Sabin looked at him as Cole crouched on the other side of the large stone bowl, eyes hooked on the few ingredients. Bastian and Berlin hung back.

"Well, since Marla is a secret keeper, naturally none of this is holding up to the story she told us." Grabbing two more jars from the far side of the bed Sabin took a seat by his pestle, setting the jar with a single, angry black spider in front of Cole.

"What is *that*?" Berlin's voice cracked, despite his effort to sound angry.

"Don't be such a baby. It's just little ol' spider."

Cole picked up the jar and looked inside. It really wasn't very big, but it was jet black with long spindly legs.

"Is this a black widow?" Cole tilted the jar until he caught site of the red hourglass shape on the arachnid's back. "Oh wow, it *is!* I've never seen one in person before." He watched as it tried over and over to climb the smooth sides of the jar.

"A black widow? A *black widow?*" A vein bulged in Berlin's forehead when Cole glanced over his shoulder at him. "Are you kidding me right now? If that thing escapes it could *kill* one of us!"

Even Bastian's eyes were wide as he stared at the jar in his lover's hands.

"Oh give it a rest." Sabin took the jar from Cole and, without hesitating, he unscrewed it and dumped the spider into his pestle. Berlin had just started screaming when he crushed the spider with the dull end of his mortar. "See? Now it can't get you."

"Are you crazy? Why did you get it if you were just going to kill it?"

"Because it's an ingredient, obviously."

Cole watched with morbid fascination as Sabin added a handful of small, dark berries to the pestle, then a bit of the powder and congealed, yellow liquid.

"What is all this?"

"Cole," Bastian's voice sounded a little weak. "Maybe you shouldn't sit so close."

"Well, there's the black widow, nightshade, this stuff is snake venom, and I forget what this is." He shook the tin of powder. "But it's poisonous too."

"Jesus, Mary, and fucking Joseph, he has a poison collection." Berlin crossed himself as though it would keep him safe. "Bastian, he has a poison collection."

Cole didn't have to look at Berlin to know that he was pale.

"What are they for?"

"Well," Sabin started pounding the ingredients together, a wet slapping sound filling the room. "It's complicated to explain. Whatever is going on in this town isn't a sickness. It's magic."

"What sort of magic?" Cole's eyes were wide with fascination as he edged closer to his teammate, watching him work and ignoring Bastian's uneasy requests that he be careful.

"That's the problem. I'm not sure. It's not good though. Whatever it is, it's *definitely* evil. I just don't know what sort of evil yet."

"And this will tell you?"

"Well, it'll tell me what it's not."

Berlin scoffed, though he was still hanging back by the door. "And how is a poisonous paste supposed to help?"

"Well, dip-shit. It turns out if I mix this poisonous paste with the ashes of a certain Chinese talisman, it will become a sort of banishing balm. If whatever evil is hanging around here happens to be of the Buddhist persuasion, it'll react. Knowing what we're fighting is the first step in defeating it."

"Wow." Cole had a thousand questions, but before he could get to any of them, Bastian intervened with a much more level headed approach.

"Why not tell us about this sooner?"

"And why would some Chinese ghost monk being hanging around Nebraska?" Berlin jumped as Bastian stomped on his foot. "What?"

"Well, chances are it won't be a Buddhist spirit. That's why I'm going to put together a bunch of other tests for it. But that also means I need something to test. So now that you guys know my plan, you can help me."

"Fuck that, I'm not helping." Berlin made a sound like he'd been jabbed in the side. "What? Why should I help him?"

In the few beats of silence that followed, Cole wondered if there was anything Sabin could do to make Berlin change his mind about him. Maybe if he showed him some sort of spell that did really good things for people, the Catholic boy's opinion would ease a bit. It would be nice to see them getting along. He held out hope for the two of them, though any hope he'd had for himself and Berlin becoming friends had long since disappeared. He knew what Berlin thought of him, and in the end, Berlin was right about most of it.

"Well if you have a better way to sort this out, feel free. But I'd like to take care of this before the rest of us get a zombie barf shower, okay?"

"I'll help," Cole offered, and he gave Bastian a grateful smile when his lover offered his assistance as well.

"Okay. Tomorrow we'll probably get assigned to different groups again like last time. Right after assignment, meet me at the church. We can finalize our plans, get the last ingredients I need, and get back to our assignments before we're missed."

Cole wondered why Sabin thought they need to sneak around to do this. Surely, if he had a way to figure out what they were up against, Marla and Shipton would want to know. It seemed counterproductive to leave them out of the loop. But he also liked the idea of calling Marla on the radio and surprising her with the information they'd gathered. He smiled to himself, even as he watched Sabin scrape the poisonous goop out of his pestle and into a small tin.

He liked the idea of surprising Marla.

19: ALISTAIR

Sunlight woke Alistair again the next morning. Squinting at the crack in the curtains, he wondered why Luca insisted on keeping them open. Maybe he should have invested in a sleeping mask or something, but then his lecherous chaperon might mistake it for some sort of kinky blindfold. He immediately stamped down the jump of excitement he felt in his gut at the idea of being blindfolded and helpless under the other man. Instead he took a few seconds to try and smother himself with his own pillow.

What am I thinking?

Memories from the day before, from the way he had laid himself open in the shower for the other man, swirled in his sleep drunk brain. He was still surprised that Luca hadn't touched him, and the more he thought about it, the more he wished he had. Whenever that thought popped up, though, his pride was never far behind, chastising him for falling under the man's spell. Still, physical attraction aside, Luca's company had been pleasant the night before, as they'd sat on the edge of the crop field, simply enjoying being as close to free as he'd been for years.

Alistair tucked his hands under his pillow, resting his cheek on the scratchy fabric, and watched Luca sleeping. He'd initially struck Alistair as the type to get up with the sun, but he was starting to think the dear professor wasn't as perfect as he seemed. He grunted in his sleep a lot, especially when he was turning over. And Alistair could tell by just looking at him that he was going to have an intense case of bedhead once he woke up. Still, all that just seemed to make him more charming.

Ugh. What is wrong with me?

Not wanting to let his drowsy brain wander off any more than it had, he levered himself out of bed and shuffled into the shower. At the very least he should keep Luca from seeing the shamefully frizzy braid he'd tied his hair into.

Luca was out of bed and composed by the time Alistair was done, and the others showed up not long after, gathering in their cramped room for their morning briefing. Now that they'd seen one citizen fall to whatever was wreaking havoc on the town, they were all on high alert, but they still lacked any sort of lead. They would have to split up again in an attempt to find the cause. With the quarantine in place, Alistair wondered why they didn't take more drastic measures. Surely their student covers weren't really helping them at this point, but Luca seemed insistent on keeping things as calm as possible. That meant not causing a panic.

Just as he'd promised, once he'd doled out surveillance targets to the others, he told Alistair that they would be going to the house Lakelyn and his mother had been staying in. They would use the excuse of keeping the children in town safe on the way to school as an excuse.

Alistair wasn't particularly unhappy with the assignment. He felt a draw to the young teen, maybe because of his resemblance to Alistair's first love, but also because he felt sorry for the kid. Just like him, Lakelyn was a boy whose choice was taken away from him, shipped away against his will. He wondered if there was a crush, or even a lover Lakelyn had left behind in Chicago.

He's way too young to have a lover.

Like a recurring infection, memories of Felix hit him as he entered the small yard partitioned off by the white fence—moments stolen at school in the boys' bathroom, in his bedroom while his mother self-medicated in the other room, moments of exploration that belonged to them only.

I guess that means I was too young too.

The house was a small, but well kept, cottage. The horizontal siding that wrapped the structure was painted a cheery yellow that matched the aesthetics of the white picket fence and potted plants that hung from the eaves of the porch. Most of them were wilted or dead, though. The lawn, too, seemed unkempt compared to the effort that had been put into the landscaping—flowerbeds, birdbaths, a small stone bench in the corner of the yard.

"So what sort of information will actually help?" They were climbing the stairs to the porch when Alistair finally thought to ask.

"Anything about the town," Luca said. His tone even now, and businesslike. "Things he's seen people doing that seem strange. A list of people who act the way his mother did. Also, if it's not too sore a subject, more information about his mom wouldn't hurt. How long she's been acting strange. What she was doing when he first noticed the change. That sort of thing." Luca rang the bell.

"Yeah, I'm sure that's exactly what he'll want to talk about."

"Just anything you can get." Luca's hand came to rest on the back of Alistair's neck for a second and it seemed like he was trying to encourage him. Or comfort him. Either way, it was a surprise.

Alistair recognized the man who opened the door. He'd not spoken with him, but he'd seen him at the barbecue, though there was nothing else that had stood out about him. He was in his late thirties and wore a yellow shirt buttoned all the way to his chin, looking comically country-proper.

"Well hey there." Despite their unannounced visit, the man beamed at them like there was no one he wanted to see more. "What brings you around this way?"

"Does Lakelyn live here?" This man was obviously not related to the younger boy, his hair and complexion much too dark. But Alistair remembered Lakelyn mentioning that other families shared the house with him, and now that he was looking at it, it seemed too small for more than three or four people.

"He sure does. He's getting ready for school, but you can come in and see him off if you'd like." The friendliness never wavered here, and it was starting to make Alistair uncomfortable.

Thanking the man, Alistair and Luca followed him inside, and immediately they could see there was something wrong. When Lakelyn had said that three other families shared the space, he thought maybe he'd meant a few other couples. But the house was teeming with people, adults, kids, crying babies. In just the living room, Alistair counted at least twelve people, and he could tell by the sound echoing through the home that there was more.

"We're real tight knit in these parts. You city folk probably couldn't understand even if you tried." He was laughing as he spoke and led them down the hall to a small room in the back. There, they found Lakelyn with four other kids younger than him. He was in the middle of tying up one little girl's hair into a ponytail, the other three chasing each other in varying states of undress.

"Kayla! Stop chasing your brother and put your pants on!" Lakelyn finished the ponytail and snatched one of the girls up by her arm. "What did I just say?" Reluctantly, the girl called Kayla shuffled over to a pile of clothes near the open closet and began digging for her pants. "What are you doing here?" He looked mortified when he saw Alistair and Luca in his doorway.

"Don't be like that, now, Lakelyn," the man in the yellow shirt said. "It's not every day we get visitors. Be sure to show them the kind of hospitality they deserve, you understand."

Lakelyn just made a face as the man turned and left, never pausing to help him with the kids.

"What do you want?" Lakelyn's voice was hard, but his face was red, and Alistair could tell he was hiding his embarrassment with the bite in his voice.

"Well, I was hoping--" Alistair had to step out of the way as two other kids ran into the room from the hallway, screeching and laughing as they jumped on top of Kayla in the pile of clothes. "--that we could talk some more. You know. Like yesterday."

"If you want to talk to me, you're gonna have to wait until I'm done getting these little shit heads to school." He pushed past both Alistair and Luca, stomping toward the living room. "Dylan! Shannon! You have five seconds to get in here and get dressed!"

Alistair looked wide-eyed at his teacher in the boy's wake, and immediately knew they had little choice. It took nearly an hour to get each of the children clothed, brushed, and organized. Alistair could only imagine what breakfast had been like for them. Lakelyn was a tiny hurricane that swept through the rooms, gathering the stragglers and wrestling them into their clothes if they wouldn't do it willingly. When they were finally ready and out the door, Alistair hung back with Lakelyn as Luca walked with the children several yards ahead of them, two of the older girls—maybe eleven each—holding onto his shirt tails and peppering him with questions. Even at a young age, women recognized Luca's appeal.

You're ten years too early, you little brats.

There were twelve of them. Twelve children, presumably all living in that tiny, three bedroom house. And as far as he could tell, Lakelyn had become their sole caretaker. He felt like he should be asking this boy questions, getting the information that Luca needed to help assess the situation, but it was hard to know which question to ask. So he walked with his hands in his pockets beside the younger boy until Lakelyn decided to break the silence first.

"Aren't you going to ask about the house?" He adjusted his backpack on his shoulders.

"Why? Is there something about the house you want to tell me?"

"It's not normal, though, right? I mean, I know there are places in inner cities where things like this happen. Kids end up raising themselves cause their parents are drug addicts or something." It was obvious that this had been building up inside the thirteen-year-old for a long time, so Alistair just let him vent. "But you saw them. Those adults were just fine. But they won't lift a god damn finger to take care of their own kids anymore! It's been like this for weeks."

"Why bother then, if you hate doing it so much? They're not your kids. You're not the one who should be responsible for them." Alistair couldn't tear his eyes away from the children clinging to Luca, waiting to decide if he should intervene.

"For someone as pretty as you, I thought you'd be a bit more compassionate." Lakelyn's cheeks betrayed him, turning pink as he looked at the gravel in front of him as they walked.

Alistair couldn't help but laugh. "Is that what you were thinking when I caught you staring at the barbecue? If I'd known privacy is a rare commodity for you I wouldn't have given you that half chub."

"Half chu—ugh!" The pink turned to red and seeped down into his neck. "What the hell is wrong with you?"

"Does your mom know?"

"Know what?" He'd put a little more distance between himself and Alistair.

"That you like boys." Alistair was still grinning about the boy's innocent reaction. He was obviously a virgin.

"I don't...particularly, I mean."

"It's fine if you like both. Have you got a crush back home?" These weren't really the questions he was supposed to be asking, but he was more comfortable talking about crushes than he was about this kid's mom who might be looking like their zombie friend from the compound as they spoke.

"N-not really. I mean, there are some people in my school who I think are cute, but I don't talk to them or anything."

"Well if you want a bit of advice, when you get home, talk to them. All of them if you want. Tell them you think they're cute. Kiss them. Experiment with them. Do all the things you fantasize about."

"That doesn't really sound like the sort of advice you're supposed to give to someone my age."

"Well, I mean, don't be an idiot. Use protection, stay away from people who are ten years older than you. All that normal stranger danger stuff. But you're a cute, normal kid. There's no reason for you to not enjoy yourself."

The boy was quiet for a second, and when Alistair looked at him he could see the "he said I was cute" all over his face. Lakelyn really was a cute kid. Even if he went home and fucked the kid from third period, the worst that could happen is their parents would find out and send them to camp or something. He would never have to worry about hurting his lover, though. Not the way Alistair did.

"If you ask really nicely, I could help you with your first kiss." Alistair kissed the air between them and laughed when Lakelyn pulled a face.

"Yeah, I'll wait, thanks." His face lit back up though, and Alistair couldn't stop himself from ruffling the kid's hair.

"You better make it count, then."

"Oh, I will." He swatted Alistair's hand away and straightened his back. "I've already got plans, you know. It's going to be the best first kiss ever."

"Just be prepared to knock your teeth together."

Alistair got no information about the town from Lakelyn. Instead, he listened to the boy tell him about the girl from his math class last year who sat in front of him. About how her hair used to pool on his desk and always smelled like flowers. And about the boy from gym who could do more push-ups than anyone else in class, whose arms were already "the size of my thigh." Alistair was skeptical since they were all thirteen or fourteen. But he remembered how some boys hit puberty faster than others, and the way they'd stood out.

After they'd dropped the kids under five off at the church where one of the pastors had set up a daycare, they took the others back to the community center—to the same room where Lakelyn's mother had turned the day before. Alistair felt bad leaving him there, but the boy smiled at him and mumbled a soft "Thanks for listening to me. Can we meet again to talk?"

For the first time in what felt like ages, Alistair felt a warmth inside himself as he smiled, and after ruffling the boy's blond hair, he promised he'd meet him after school.

"So what did you find out?" Luca asked when they were finally alone.

Somehow Alistair didn't feel bad about failing his reconnaissance task. Lakelyn had obviously needed a friend to talk to, not a secret intelligence agent lancing information out of him. So as Luca looked at him expectantly, Alistair smiled and said "I found out he's bisexual, a Taurus, and that he's got a promising love life ahead of him when he gets home."

"Oh, well in that case, I guess our job here is done." The way he put his hands in his trouser pockets made it seem like he really was satisfied with the job Alistair had done, though the small twitch of his eyebrow gave him away.

"Don't be so grouchy. It's obvious that all the adults in that house are infected. No one would move way out here and live in conditions like that unless they had some sort of illness or addiction. And, the best I can tell, the only thing these people are addicted to is small town charm." He turned to look up at the man beside him, enjoying the way his grey eyes cast down the bridge of his nose at him. "So what now? Do we arrest them for being sick?"

Luca's hand slipped from its pocket and moved to Alistair's face where one thumb brushed over his cheekbone. "Now we find out who's infecting them."

"That sounds awfully intentional for a parasitic infection."

"Parasites can be pretty crafty, kitten. Maybe I'll give you a lecture about them sometime." A quick wink later, Luca was walking back toward town.

"Sounds riveting..."

Alistair trudged after him, hanging back to enjoy the way the man's pants fit perfectly around his ass.

20: BASTIAN

The church looked a lot like a barn, white-washed with a steeple built at the front peak of its roof. Shipton had asked Cole and Bastian to look into the food delivery system used by the city—try to find some point of contamination that could have caused the initial infection. Instead of heading to the general store where most of the groceries were purchased in town, though, they went to the church to meet Sabin and Berlin, just as they'd agreed.

Bastian wondered what they might need from the church, but, after hearing Sabin's plan from the night before, he had a vague inkling. Unfortunately, he didn't really like the idea of it.

Around the church was a low fence, corralling the vegetable garden and small playground that made up the front lawn of the grounds. As they approached, they saw that Sabin and Berlin were already there, Berlin leaning against a carved horse which was attached to the ground by a spring. He was grinning at Sabin as they approached, bouncing lightly on the spring.

"Stop being an asshole, Berlin." Bastian didn't even bother asking him what he'd been saying to the other boy. He could tell by the look on his face that he was giving their other teammate a hard time.

"Why do you always assume that I'm the one doing something wrong?" The tattooed boy only seemed mildly offended.

"Because you usually *are* the one doing something wrong."

"I was just reminding him that getting whatever he needs from the church might be harder than he expects. It's a well-known fact that anything that's been touched by the devil can't pass the threshold of a church." He grinned at Sabin again. "And seeing as witchcraft is the devil's magic, I was trying to see if he'd place a bet with me to see if he'll make it inside."

"Isn't gambling a sin?" Sabin narrowed his eyes at his partner, and Bastian could see the effort it took for him to *not* hex the stupid smile off his face.

"He's right," Bastian agreed.

"I don't care. I'm already a sinner. I never said I wasn't. But being a sinner and being devil-kin is very different."

"Whatever, Berlin. I'm tired of all your stupid superstitions. Let's just get whatever it is we need and get on with our day before Shipton finds out we're not where we're supposed to be."

Bastian reached for Cole's hand. His quiet lover had seemed tired that morning, and while Bastian was sure it was because he would have to feed soon, he'd not pressed the subject, afraid of upsetting him.

"All I need to do is fill *this* up with holy water." Sabin waved a small glass bottle back and forth between his fingers.

"Hold on a hot second, here. You can't just use *holy water* in some shady witchcraft bullshit." Consciously or not, Berlin put himself between Sabin and the church doors, as though he were the protector of some hallowed grounds.

"Um, yes I can. And I hate to break it to you, but holy water's not that rare of an ingredient for a lot of spells."

"There's no way I'm letting you go in there and steal holy water for your devil work."

"Berlin..." Bastian pinched the bridge of his nose and wondered if Sabin could whip up some sort of Xanax spell. But before he could finish chastising his friend, Cole spoke up instead.

"He's doing this to help us. Would you give it a rest?" It wasn't unusual for his mood to harden a bit as he grew hungry— another sign that he was avoiding the subject of feeding.

Bastian readied himself as he saw a response formulating in Berlin's head, but before his friend could say anything they were interrupted.

"Can I help you folks?" A few yards away, one of the heavy wooden doors of the church had swung open, and a man who looked to be about Professor Shipton's age stood in the threshold. At first he seemed to be dressed like a normal citizen, but then Bastian's eyes fell on the collar of his shirt. He wore a denim-blue button up shirt, not unlike the sort they'd seen other men in the town wearing, but it had been fitted with the white notch of a clerical collar.

To Bastian's surprise, it was Sabin who approached the deacon first, his hand outstretched. "Yes, sir. My name's Sabin, and these are my friends. We're here with the class from The University of Nebraska."

"Oh, yes, I remember seeing you at the barbecue yesterday. I'm Emmett Hartford. I'm the youth pastor here." He shook Sabin's hand, though they could see his eyes counting the piercings in his ears. "Still can't believe this quarantine though. What bad luck for you."

"We were just in the wrong place at the wrong time. How are *you* holding up?"

Bastian wasn't sure why he was surprised to see Sabin holding such a normal conversation with a stranger. It wasn't that Sabin *couldn't* talk to the rest of them; he was actually quite sharp-tongued, but he rarely sought out contact.

"I've not slept a wink, to be honest." The bespectacled pastor gave a nervous laugh that hid an obvious panic he'd only just come to terms with. "But to be honest, I'm shocked by how well everyone else has taken it." He shook his head. "I guess I just expected more of a reaction from people. Then again, this town has been a strange place for a while now."

"Strange how?" Bastian moved forward, putting himself in the circle of their conversation.

"Well," the man scratched his fingers through his brown, short trimmed hair. "I guess it started when our head pastor built those tents. He said it was for a revival, and I guess he was right. People started flooding into town. A couple families every day. But things have just seemed... odd, I guess, since they got here." The man sighed, then shrugged, as though he'd done it a thousand times. "Who knows? Maybe I'm just upset because with the tents up fewer and fewer people have been coming to service inside the church any more. Almost nobody comes here these days."

"Well," Sabin said, his voice sympathetically positive. "I know it's not Sunday, but maybe *we* could come in for a quick service. If it's not too much trouble."

Pastor Hartford laughed good-naturedly. "Maybe if you were all about ten years younger you could enjoy the sorts of services I give."

"Then could we just trouble you for a quick blessing? I think it would be comforting considering what's happening right now."

Hartford seemed uncertain for a moment, maybe even suspicious. And who could blame him considering how they all must look—Sabin in particular. But then he smiled. "I think that's a great idea." Turning, the Pastor pulled the bolt from the floor that held the second half of the wide doors in place and pushed it open.

Through the arched entryway, they could see down the middle aisle of the church, the simple wood floor ending at a raised stage backed by simple but brightly colored stained glass. Pews disappeared from their line of sight on either side of the walkway, and the ceiling rose all the way to the top of the building, the rafters which supported the arched room bare inside.

"I'll wait out here." Berlin shoved his hands deep into his pockets and didn't budge.

"Seriously?" Sabin already had one foot inside the door, proving Berlin's superstition wrong, when he turned to look at his teammate. "You're the one always going on about this stuff." He waved vaguely inside the church.

"I said I'll wait out here." His voice was harder this time.

Bastian took Cole's hand again and sighed, leading his lover up the steps. "Don't worry about it, Sabin. I think it's a denominational thing." Bastian had known Berlin for years, and, despite all of his religious talk, had never once seen him step foot inside a church. He rarely talked about his reason, though Bastian had heard him say once that he wasn't holy enough to enter God's house. He'd never gotten his friend to explain what *that* meant, though.

"Whatever."

Sabin walked inside, and Bastian was only a few steps behind him. The air inside the open room was cool, though he didn't see any obvious signs of air-conditioning. It was peaceful feeling, and he wondered when *he'd* last been in a church. With a lurch, Cole's hand was jerked from his grip, and the peaceful feeling was broken. Turning, he saw his small-framed boyfriend standing just outside the threshold of the building, his hands wringing themselves and his face looking paler than normal.

"Cole?" He looked panicked for a second, and Bastian took a step toward him, his hands reaching out to provide whatever his lover might need. But the black-haired boy matched his step backwards.

"Sorry. I think I forgot something at the hotel." His voice was steady, but quivered in Bastian's ears as the lie reverberated off it. "You guys go ahead. We can catch up with each other in a bit."

And before Bastian could say anything else, the boy turned and jogged down the stairs and walked quickly for the gate, his eyes on the ground in front of him. Bastian watched him leave, then caught Berlin's eyes which seemed a bit wide.

"Bastian." Sabin's voice drew his attention back inside the church where he and Pastor Hartford waited. He didn't say anything else, but his expression reminded him that they had something important to do.

Cole would have to wait.

21: COLE

A dull ache hummed through Cole's body as he fled the church, doing everything he could to keep from breaking into a run. As he passed the gate, he refused to turn around, not wanting to know what sort of expression his lover might have. He also didn't want to know if Berlin had seen what happened.

What if he did see? What if he's already told Bastian?

His hands shook as he crossed the street, then a small grassy field that rested between two houses, trying to find someplace private to collect himself. He didn't care where he was going, he just wanted to be out of the sight-line of the church. It wasn't until he rounded the backside of a squat building that he found himself at the tents where they'd held the barbecue. Seeing nobody else around, he walked through the tall grass until he was in the shade of the canvas. The tables they'd eaten at were gone now, replaced by rows of white plastic chairs where the townspeople would congregate for church service. Sitting down in one toward the center of the tent, he felt a small reprieve, happy that someplace where church was held would allow him.

Berlin had been right. It was hard, even then, for Cole to understand what had really happened, but as Bastian had led him through the door, the building itself had stopped him from entering. It had felt like a thousand hands had shoved him away before he could pass one toe over the threshold. He pressed a hand against his chest, like he could still feel the remains of the ethereal force that had shoved him away.

Berlin had said that anyone touched by the devil wouldn't be allowed inside the church. He'd spent every day since Marla had found him trying to believe that no matter what he was, he wasn't evil. But now—

"I'm afraid service isn't until this evening."

Cole jumped in his seat, turning to see the man they'd met at the barbecue the day before—Pastor Blackholly, he remembered.

"Oh, no, I'm sorry, sir." Cole stood up, ready to move on to his next sanctuary. "I wasn't waiting for a service or anything."

"Just looking for a quiet place to think?" There was something soothing, and possibly knowing, about the man's voice, and Cole found his urge to flee ease.

"Yes, actually." Just like with the other people in the town, Cole felt close to this person, like he might go out of his way to comfort him. He didn't hate that idea.

"It's a shame you had to come here at the same time as this horrible quarantine. Everyone's so scared they might get sick like poor Margaret did." He shook his head solemnly as he took the seat in front of Cole, turning so he could look at him, his arm resting on the back of the chair. "Has the situation left you feeling uneasy?"

"Of course," Cole lied.

"I wish you could have come and enjoyed the town in better times, Colvam. Things would have been much easier that way."

"I'm sorry, what did you call me?"

"Your name *is* Cole, isn't it? Did I get it wrong?"

"Well, I thought—" He wasn't sure what he thought. It had sounded strange, but not wrong. "No, I'm sorry. I guess I'm just hearing things."

"I'm sure you have a lot of things on your mind. Maybe about where you belong or who you belong with?" Blackholly's voice soothed the tensions inside Cole, and he wondered how the Pastor seemed to know exactly what he was thinking.

"Yes. How do you know these sorts of things?"

The pastor laughed softly. "We've all dealt with these problems. But we realized that the people we should be with, are the ones like ourselves. No one will ever be able to understand you the way *your people* will understand you."

"I don't understand. What do you mean by 'my people?'"

Blackholly smiled, slowly this time, and simply said "Most of us can't enter that church anymore either."

Cole stood up, his chair teetering behind him, threatening to fall over. What did he mean by that? How did he even know about it? And if he was saying that he couldn't enter either, then wouldn't that mean—

"Cole!" Bastian's voice broke the panic that was sloshing around in Cole's head. Following the sound of his voice, Cole saw his lover jogging toward him through the grass. "What happened?"

Turning back, Cole found the chair in front of him empty. Pastor Blackholly was gone. What *had* just happened?

"Cole." As he approached, Bastian took his shoulders, turning him to look him in the face. "What is it? You look pale."

Cole swallowed, took a deep breath and smiled as apologetically as he could. "Sorry. I'm okay. I just needed a second to myself."

Bastian stared at him for a long moment, but seemed to understand that his boyfriend wanted a bit of privacy. "As long as you're okay. I can't force you, but you know I'll listen to whatever you have to say, right?"

"I know." Cole pressed himself into Bastian's chest, wondering how this *couldn't* be where he belonged. He hugged him tight around his rib cage. "I'm okay. I just spooked myself."

"At the church? How?" Bastian's arms closed around him.

"What Berlin said scared me."

Bastian huffed and kissed the top of Cole's head. "He needs to learn to keep his stupid mouth shut. One of these days I'm going to shut it for him."

"He's just worried about you." Cole could feel the invisible feathers brush his hands where they rested on Bastian's wide back. He wanted to rake his fingers through them, as though to show the church that he didn't need to be inside to have a little piece of heaven at his fingertips. But that was stupid. He was starting to sound like Berlin himself, thinking of Bastian in such angelic ways.

The sound of feet in grass drew their attention to where Sabin and Berlin had caught up to them.

"You guys done having your moment?" Sabin sounded inconvenienced, but not angry.

"Sorry. Did you get what you needed?" Cole loosened his grip on Bastian, though he still leaned against him as one arm draped over his shoulders protectively.

Sabin held up his now-full bottle and waved it triumphantly at him. "Now all we need are some hairs to test with. We should each try to collect a few hairs from as many people as we can today. We'll meet in our room tonight after lights out to test them. Alright?"

Behind the pierced boy, Cole saw Berlin watching him, his eyes harder than usual. He was quiet, which was startling somehow. As they agreed on their meeting time and parted ways, Cole wondered if Berlin had, in fact, seen what had happened at the door to the church.

22: ALISTAIR

"So we're just leaving those kids with teachers who might flip out on them the way Lakelyn's mom did yesterday?" Alistair had been surprised when, after dropping the children off at the community center, Luca had caught Alistair by his hand and lead him away. Not that he'd *wanted* to spend his day in a room full of shouting, sticky-handed children.

"I'm not too worried. The replacement teacher isn't as far gone as Margaret was." Luca was still holding onto Alistair's hand as he led him down the street.

It was stupid, but the familiarity with which Luca used the woman's name annoyed him. The *last* person he should be jealous of was the woman whose neck he'd broken, and the last person he should be jealous *over* was Luca Shipton. The man was narcissistic, arrogant, and Alistair hated how he talked like he was bound to fall for him. Alistair's affection and attention were to be coveted, not expected. Unfortunately for his pride, though, the draw he felt toward the man was becoming harder and harder to fight.

"How would you be able to tell that?" Alistair asked as he snatched his hand away from his teacher, narrowing his eyes when the man turned to smile at him.

"Call it intuition."

"Well then we'll blame your intuition when those kids get turned into zombie chow."

Luca only laughed. "Alright. If they're hurt I'll take full responsibility. How's that?"

Alistair only grunted. "If we're not staying there, then where *are* we going? I mean, this mission is actually going to start soon, right?"

"What are you talking about? This mission has been a great success so far."

"Oh yeah. Huge success."

Luca only put his hands in his pockets and led Alistair to a small room at the back of the general store. It looked like it might have been where the security cameras were held, but a system like that seemed unlikely for a Trumbull, so Alistair assumed a lot of the equipment had been brought in with them.

There was an old, boxy computer set up in the corner that probably belonged to the store-owner, but the two laptops and the wall of radio equipment were definitely out of place. Milo sat at one laptop, tapping away while Jett sat on a desk against the opposite wall, slouched so low he might as well lay down, his phone out and blasting laser noises from some game he was playing. Kiyiya was hunkered under the desk, his head resting on Milo's shoe.

"Oh, thank god you're here." Jett groaned as he sat up. "Please tell me you have something more interesting for us to do."

"Well, that's going to depend on what our new friend Milo has found."

Of course they would have Milo holed up in some makeshift intelligence station. He was alright with a gun, and was a great tactician, but he was at his best when he was behind a computer.

"Nothing too surprising yet." Milo handed a folder over to Luca, the thing held together with a rubber band to hold the all the pages in. "These are all the confirmed missing persons reports. Surety levels are at about 98.7% right now."

"Excellent." Luca flipped through the pages and, over his shoulder, Alistair looked at each of the pictures. He recognized a few of them, but there were so many.

"How do you know all these people are here?"

"I've been keeping an eye on things." Milo opened the spare laptop and Alistair saw a grid of video screens—street views, candid office shots, the auditorium with the children.

"What the hell? They had a camera system like this?"

"Nah. I planted all of these." Fishing in his pocket, he pulled out a bullet-shaped device with a lens on one end, the other end formed into a sharp point. "I have an air gun that plants them wherever I want and they send the signal back to me wirelessly."

"Well that's handy. And a bit creepy."

Milo set the bullet camera down on the desk. "Well it's better than having to do the footwork myself. I've verified most of these people visually, but there are a few who I found medical records for so we can make an accurate ID."

"It's alright. We don't need a positive ID for every single one of them. Given these numbers, we can probably assume that almost everyone is infected."

"I've also been reviewing call records for the weeks prior to the first reported case. There must be some reason that they're all congregating here."

"You're very thorough." Luca didn't seem to have much else to say. When he spoke up again he changed the subject completely. "Alistair, why don't you hang out here for a few minutes? Jett, I'd like you to come with me."

"I thought Marla didn't want me to leave your sight." It wasn't that Alistair *wanted* the teacher to stay glued to him, but he found himself wondering just how close Luca was with the other boy.

"Well, Marla doesn't need to know *everything*, right?" He winked at Alistair as Jett jumped down from his seat.

"Please, anything that'll get me out of this closet for a while."

"Excellent. Kiyiya, you stay here with them." At Luca's order, the dog whined and laid his head back down. Alistair had seen the animal perk up when Alistair asked Jett to leave with him.

"You know, I'm not your dog sitter," Milo said, giving Jett and Luca a tired look.

"Don't say that. He likes you and you'll hurt his feelings." Jett grinned at their teammate, not even bothering to pause as he followed Luca out of the tiny room. "Besides, he's *your* babysitter, not the other way around." With a waggle of his eyebrows, he closed the door with a definitive click.

Milo sighed, but only turned back toward his screen. And, despite his complaint, Alistair saw him slide his shoe off and begin rubbing the dog's side with his socked foot.

"So is this where you've been since we got there? I was just thinking that I'd not seen much of you the past few days." It was rare for Alistair to be alone with Milo.

"Yeah. These are the sorts of places I usually end up. Guess it comes with the territory."

Alistair nodded and looked around the room, leaning against one of the tables and wondering how to entertain himself in such a small room. The walls were lined with shelves that held tools, extra receipt paper, and files that looked like they were older than he was. Milo had built his little surveillance room over the top of the store's supplies.

"Do you think these people actually believe that we're a bunch of college students?"

"It's hard to say. I have no reason to think they don't yet. But until we know what their *plan* is, there's no way to be sure."

"Plan? I thought we were just here to take care of this outbreak stuff."

"Well, what else could we call it other than a plan? We have a few hundred people migrating here, possibly *after* becoming infected. Which would mean that they didn't *catch* this illness from someone *in this* town. Something's drawn them here. And if they're all being drawn into the same spot, then it must be for some reason. I doubt this illness or parasite just *likes small town charm.*"

Alistair hadn't even considered the possibility that they were congregating for a reason. "You think it's like a cult or something? They draw people in and then infect them?"

"There's no way to tell at this point. I'm hoping we'll find something in the phone records. Some way that they were contacted and brought here. This town has an almost non-existent internet footprint, so they must be getting information out to people somehow. It's just a matter of finding their tracks."

The creepy overcompensation he'd seen in the townspeople since they got there was suddenly much more alarming.

"I'm gonna go to the front of the store for a second and get a pop or something. Do you want anything?" Alistair needed some air. And needed to look in the eyes of one of the townspeople to see if he could tell what, exactly, they might be thinking.

"No. I've been living on junk food from this place. I think I'm over sodas for a while."

"What about you, dog? You want something?" Kiyiya looked up at him without raising his head. "Is that a 'no?'"

"Could you bring a bottle of water back for him? I think his bowl is empty."

"The way Luca and Jett talk to him I thought he'd answer for a second. I'll be back." Alistair closed the door behind him as he reentered the store. They were definitely a funny trio; Luca, Jett, and Kiyiya. As he browsed the shelves of groceries and candy, he wondered to himself how long they'd been together. They seemed close no matter how he looked at it, though. And the more time he spent with them, the less he worried that Luca may be involved with Jett the way he was with him. The idea of Luca harassing the blue-haired boy seemed more and more ridiculous. Still, his stomach churned when he saw them acting so friendly.

Eyeing the old shop owner where he was stocking canned soup down one of a dozen small aisles, Alistair browsed through the limited offerings. Haven provided each of them with a small allowance, probably to trick them into thinking things were better than they actually were. He was pulling a cold bottle of water out of the coolers against the back wall when he caught a hushed voice he recognized right away.

"So you just want to wait until they try to take him?" A thread of annoyance ran through Luca's words.

"Of course we'll not let them take him," Jett said, the usual cocky tone to his voice gone, replaced with a steady, sure quality. "But striking at the heads of a hydra will do nothing. We have to wait for our chance to strike the heart."

"And when will that be? When things have escalated more than they already have? You're starting to sound like Clairemonte."

"Please, we're in this for infinitely different reasons. Remember, I'm here to help. Just trust me on this."

"And if more of them start defecting?"

"Don't worry, I'll handle all of it once their leader shows himself."

"I just think it's getting too close for comfort."

"Things were too close to comfort from the beginning."

Alistair heard shoes scuff the linoleum floor, and he bolted for the back room again. He wasn't sure what he'd just heard, but it definitely wasn't good, and it definitely wasn't meant for him to hear. His face must have shown the shock that was still rolling in his gut because when Milo looked at him, his brows furrowed. Before he could ask anything, the door behind Alistair opened again.

"Hey, Legs." Jett popped his head through the door and smiled at Alistair. "Mind hanging out in here for a few hours so I can go stretch my legs? Luca said he'll be back for you before school's out so you can go meet your boyfriend."

Before Alistair could answer, the blue-haired boy, in a perfect imitation of their teacher, winked at him, thanked him, and disappeared. After the initial shock wore off, Alistair's face flashed hot with anger.

"It's pointless getting angry at him," Milo said from where he was still scrolling through lists of data on his computer. "Arguing with him is like shouting at a brick wall."

"You been doing a lot of shouting?"

"We've been stuck in this closet together for two days. Patience has run thin, yes."

"Great."

Alistair wasn't sure whether he should tell Milo what he'd heard. He spent most of his time with Jett these days, whether they were arguing or not. And what was worse, back home he spent most of his time in the labs with Marla and her science goons. He had no reason to particularly trust any of his new teammates, but out of the three of them, Milo definitely seemed like the most compromised. So he kept the conversation he'd heard to himself, figuring he would get the chance to tell Bastian and Berlin later. He would just have to decide how *he* felt about what he'd heard. Somehow, Luca being a villain was a pill that was becoming more and more painful to swallow.

For hours, Alistair tried to find ways to occupy himself. There was only so much he could do on his phone since the quarantine line Marla had set up around the town included a signal blocker of some kind. He didn't bother asking how Milo was able to get past it, figuring that Marla had either *let* him, or he was just smart enough to sidestep it. Kiya wasn't even any help. A few times, Alistair had tried rolling up paper and tossing it to one side of the room or the other, hoping he would maybe go after it. A few times the dog's tail thumped against the floor, but he never even lifted his head off Milo's shoe.

When the door opened again, Alistair was surprised by how happy he was to see Luca. He might be a conniving sexual predator, but at least he was the ticket out of that closet. He almost felt bad for leaving Milo there, but the other boy seemed used to the tiny, dark space.

School would be letting out in just a few minutes, and as they walked back toward the auditorium, Alistair thought the streets seemed unusually empty. The sky was blue and the sun was warm on his face as they walked; there were even sounds of birds chirping and stalks of corn rustling on the other side of some buildings. But it still felt eerie, somehow.

The man beside him was quiet, his face turned up a little, like he was soaking in the rays of the sun—something that seemed way too innocent for him now. Alistair wasn't particularly surprised to learn that he was sneaking around behind their backs—less surprised that Marla seemed to be involved in some manner—but it still felt wrong in his stomach. One thing was clear, though. Whatever they were dealing with in this town, it *wasn't* an illness.

"Don't tell me just a few hours in confinement broke you." Luca was grinning at him as they neared the auditorium.

"At least the company was better in there."

Luca laughed, which was both annoying and dreamy somehow. "You know, one of these days you're going to hurt my feelings for real."

"I look forward to it."

"If only you treated me as nicely as you treat that boy Lakelyn."

"You know, you and Jett both seem pretty interested in my relationship with him." As he said those words he remembered what he'd heard the two saying in the shop. They'd talked about waiting "until they try to take him." Was Lakelyn the "him" they'd been talking about? That might explain why Luca was going out of his way to facilitate Alistair spending so much time with him.

"I just like seeing this sweet side of you, that's all. It's good to know that underneath that prickly, gorgeous exterior of yours, you have a nice soft spot."

"I hardly think talking to some kid counts as a soft spot. He has good information. He just got attached to me because he's going through puberty and I make him feel funny in his pants."

"Who could blame him, though? You make me feel funny in my pants, too."

A small pulse of satisfaction threatened to blow the distrust Alistair had felt toward his teacher away. He *liked* the idea of having Luca to himself—having the other man desire him from his core. He wanted that sort of power over him, and he didn't want to share him with anyone else. The strength of that need scared him.

"You know, I'm getting pretty sick of your sexual harassment. If you want a student to molest, why don't you stick to Jett since you two are so close?"

"Alistair. Are you jealous?"

He didn't even have to look at him to know how he had the smug grin on his face that always turned Alistair's knees soft. "Of course you'd be arrogant enough to think that." The words were hardly out of his mouth when Luca's hand closed around one of the Alistair's thin wrists, stopping him instantly. When he turned, ready to snap at the other man, he saw a smile softening his face that was different than what he was used to. It was still cocky for sure—something that seemed woven into the fabric of who he was—but it seemed gentler than usual.

"I'd be pretty happy if you were jealous." His thumb brushed over the small knob of bone on Alistair's wrist, sending goosebumps up his arm. Alistair opened his mouth to argue, but Luca pulled him close, an arm wrapping around the small of his back and pressing the length of their bodies together. He was still trying to catch his breath when Luca's lips brushed over the curve of Alistair's ear. "One day soon you'll fall for me. Then you'll come begging for me to take you." Alistair started to push away, and for a second he thought he wasn't strong enough to free himself, but then he was sure he just didn't want to get away. "And when you do, you'll be mine forever. And you won't have to worry about someone like Jett taking me away."

As Alistair's mind reeled, trying to figure out what he should say—how he actually felt—Luca's free hand moved to cup his jaw and he pressed a slow kiss to the boy's cheek. Then he let him go, his fingers brushing his side as he slid away and began back down the street, heading toward the community center like nothing had happened.

After a second to steady his legs, Alistair followed, more confused now than ever.

When they arrived at the community center, Luca took his leave, though Alistair didn't believe for a second that they were really alone. The man was good at hiding though, and they both hoped Lakelyn would be more forthcoming if he thought he was alone with Alistair. The boy looked surprised when he saw him waiting, and smiled when Alistair offered to help him walk the younger kids to the church where the youth pastor held after-school daycare. The blond boy seemed visibly lighter once they had dropped them off, and Alistair thought he was much too young to look so exhausted.

"So, was there something you wanted to do?" Even though Alistair liked the kid, it was still hard for him to know how he should handle him.

"Not really." Lakelyn just seemed happy to be relatively alone, and Alistair could respect that, so instead of pressing for conversation, he walked him back to the general store where Milo was holed up and bought them some sodas, chips, and candy.

Since they had a haul to go through, they went back to their spot behind the silos to feast. Like the day before, the sky was clear and the wind rolled across the field of corn and right into their faces, bringing with it the smell of greenery and diesel— probably from the military trucks they could still see stationed on the horizon.

For a few minutes they sat quietly, snacking on KitKats and barbecue chips. Then Lakelyn flicked the lid of his Coke into the field.

"How hard do you think it would be to get past all of them?"

"Hard enough that trying would be a bad idea."

"What do you think they'd do to stop someone? Would they shoot them?"

Alistair thought for a second. He wasn't sure *what* he thought they would be capable of. With Marla at the helm, though he felt like he could escape with nothing much worse than a tranquilizer.

"Probably not. But you might spend a long time in federal prison, and you're too cute to go there."

Alistair tried not to laugh when he saw the boy beside him blush at the compliment.

"Well, I feel like I've been living in a prison for the past month anyway. Maybe it wouldn't be that bad."

"Don't even think about it, brat. I'm sure they'll get things taken care of soon, then the quarantine will be up and you'll get shipped out to whichever hospital your mom was sent to. All you'll have to worry about is chasing hot nurses and swiping Jell-O from the coma patients."

"I don't think they give lunches to coma patients." Lakelyn smiled despite himself.

"Alzheimer's patients then."

"That's pretty brutal."

"Look, kid, you've gotta learn to take life by the horns and all that cliché stuff. If you want something, take it. Don't let people stand between you and the thing that will make you happy."

Lakelyn laughed this time. "I think Hartford and Blackholly would be upset with the advice you're giving me."

"Let me guess. Preachers?"

"Hartford was the one who took the kids. He's more relaxed than Blackholly. That guy gives me the creeps."

"He's not like, you know..." Alistair made a lewd gesture with his free hand, worrying that the preacher had a nasty habit of touching kids.

"No! Oh God, no. He just—he's like my mom was. And the other adults. Really into the town and stuff. My mom always seemed worse when she came back from his sermons."

"Did you ever go to them?"

"No." Lakelyn polished off the bottle of Coke in his hand. "Only the adults go. They're always at night."

"Do you think this guy could have been the one who invited your mom out here?" Alistair knew his questions were getting a little too specific. He worried that if their conversation started sounding like an interrogation Lakelyn would close up on him.

"I doubt it. I mean, it may seem weird to have all these people coming out here, but it's not really *that* weird for my mom. She's been into some really culty stuff for as long as I can remember."

"Cults? Like Satan worshipers or something?"

"No way. She's at the opposite end. For years she's thought she was some sort of spiritual warrior out to save people from demons. She's tried doing exorcisms on me a *few* times."

"Seriously? What for?"

Lakelyn's face flushed red, and he refused to look up at Alistair. "For some stuff she found on my computer. Stuff with guys."

Alistair suddenly felt less guilty for hurting the lady. "That sucks." Alistair wasn't sure what else to say. He tried to remember what he had wanted to hear when he was thirteen. "She didn't, like, hurt you or anything, right?"

"Nah. Mostly it was a lot of praying and having her friends hold hands around me and flick water and oil on me. But what about you?" The boy looked at Alistair through his bangs. "I mean, are you..."

"What do *you* think, kid?" It was a struggle to not laugh as Lakelyn looked back at his feet when Alistair gave him a single, lovely brow-raise. "You can't let people make you feel guilty for it, though. Even if it's your mom."

"Was your mom okay with it? Was she mean about it like my mom?"

It was hard to say why Alistair was surprised by the question. It was the obvious progression of this conversation. But thinking about his mother wasn't something he liked to do much. It seemed wrong to brush this kid's questions off, though, so he sighed and leaned back in the grass, liking the way it pressed into his elbows.

"Yeah, she was kind of a cunt." Lakelyn choked on his candy beside him and Alistair managed a smile. "I don't see her anymore, though. So I don't let it get to me."

"Was it because you're gay?" The word "gay" stumbled on Lakelyn's lips in a way that made Alistair revel at his innocence.

"Probably didn't help." Alistair knew his mother had a lot of reasons to hate him. A single mom with a toddler who broke her fingers on a nearly monthly basis had all the reasons in the world to dislike her freak kid. He wondered if she'd ever taken him to the hospital to figure out what was wrong with him, or if she'd kept him a secret in true X-Men fashion. Either way, he wasn't about to drop her a line to find out. And when a kid that broke everything you ever gave them started breaking people, how many choices did you really have left? The obvious answer was to get rid of the problem. "You can't let shitty parents stop you from being who you are though. You know, all the trendy 'it gets better' bullshit.

Just do what you want. Eventually you'll move out and she won't be able to say anything about it."

Lakelyn nodded and was quiet for a long time, both of them taking a few minutes to sunbathe and forget about the weird shit spiraling through the small town.

"How old were you when you got a boyfriend?"

Alistair laughed, but didn't bother opening his eyes, the sun making it easier to forget that this was definitely *not* the sort of questioning that was supposed to happen. "I guess I was about your age."

"What was his name?"

"You know, you really are a nosy little brat." Alistair struggled to hide his smile, but when he cracked an eye and saw his new friend chewing his thumbnail nervously he let a short laugh out through his nose. "His name was Felix. He was cute. He looked a lot like you, actually." Lakelyn looked at him so fast Alistair thought he might get whiplash. "Don't get ahead of yourself. Felix was taller than you and much more strapping."

"Thanks." Lakelyn tore some grass out of the ground and tossed it at Alistair.

"He was good though. He used to hang out with me even after my mom pulled me from public school."

"Why'd she do that?"

"Don't get too nosy, now." He lightly shoved the smaller boy, grinning as he toppled over in the grass. "You've already used up all my good graces on the boyfriend story."

"Whatever." He pushed back, kicking Alistair's knee playfully. "So are you guys still together?"

An unexpected lurching in Alistair's stomach made smiling a little harder, but he managed to hold onto at least a shadow of the expression. "No. There was an accident and he was really hurt. I left town a little while after that."

"Was he okay? He didn't die, did he?"

"No. He survived. But he had lots of broken bones. I don't think he'll ever be at a hundred percent again."

"And you just left?" The indignation in his voice was a familiar sound.

"Well, I didn't have much of a choice. I was *sent* away." He took a breath and closed his eyes against the bright sun again, wanting the warmth to ease him. "Besides. I didn't really want to see him after that since it was my fault he got hurt."

Alistair hoped the air that hung between them would stay quiet, but inevitably, Lakelyn asked, "What happened?"

"So nosy!" Sitting up, Alistair gave him a small shove again, this time making the boy slide a few feet down the slope of the hill. "This isn't about me and my romantic history. This is supposed to be about you and this weird-ass town."

Lakelyn got up and tried brushing the grass stains out of his pants. "Well I don't know what else to tell you about this place, other than if someone offers you a glass of Kool-Aid, say no."

"Isn't that reference a little old for you? Shouldn't you be making jokes with emojis or something and not referencing mass suicides from the seventies?"

"This is exactly why I hate it here so much. It's not exactly the most modernized place in the world."

"Ah, a kid after my own heart."

"I have to get back to the church. Pastor Hartford can only keep the kids for a few hours."

Alistair stood, stretching a little to hide the sincerity of his words. "You're a good person for taking care of those kids, you know."

"Well if I don't then no one else will. Hartford comes by in the evenings sometimes to help out, but there are other houses like the one we're staying in, so he has a hard time dividing himself between all of us."

"He sounds like a good guy." Alistair wondered if it was possible for the town to have a sole survivor, so-to-speak, who's over the age of eighteen. He definitely sounded different from the others, but if he wasn't infected, then *why* wasn't he?

"Yeah. But it's still nicer to have someone closer to my own age to talk to about it. He's always giving me the supportive father treatment. It just ends up getting on my nerves most of the time."

"I can't blame you. Want me to help you walk the kids back to your place?"

"Nah. The older girls won't want you to leave if you come back with us."

"Jealous?" Alistair winked at him and then laughed when he gave him a scathing look in return.

"It would be cool if we could hang out again tomorrow though." Lakelyn was obviously trying to keep the indifferent tone to his voice, but Alistair saw the small bloom of pink on his cheeks and couldn't help but smile.

"Sure. I'll pick you up from school again. Get out of here. I'll clean up all the wrappers."

Lakelyn didn't argue, and with an awkward wave he left, disappearing around the fence and the silos. When he was gone, Alistair laid back in the grass again, closing his eyes against the afternoon sunlight. He felt bad for the kid, which was unlike him. Maybe it was because he reminded him of himself—too young to be saddled with such a large burden. Of course, every single member of Haven probably had some sort of sob story from their past. Haven wasn't exactly a resort. The people who went there were just like him—feared, unwanted, mistreated. He never saw a reason to bring up his past because everyone else was in an equally bad spot, and pity parties just weren't his thing.

"Be still, my heart." Luca's voice broke the peace Alistair had found and he cracked an eye to watch the man approach from the same direction Lakelyn had left in. "Sunbathing just like the sweet kitten you are."

Pulling one hand from where he'd been pillowing his head, he flashed Luca his middle finger.

"Now, now. You can't fool me anymore after that doting heart-to-heart you just had."

"So not only are you following me, but you're eavesdropping too? Have you looked up the definition of 'skeezy,'" lately?"

Luca laughed, and like the day before, sat down in the grass beside him. "Well, aside from awkwardly flirting with you. He *did* have some interesting things to say."

Alistair wondered if Luca was avoiding the subject of Felix out of kindness, or if he was just holding it like an ace in his sleeve for later.

"So we're going to look into Blackholly now?"

"I've had my eye on him from the start, but we'll definitely be trying to catch one of these midnight sermons he has.

Alistair felt an uneasiness weigh him down against the grass. Even with Luca sitting beside him, talking in a way that seemed open, he couldn't shake the conversation he'd overheard between his teacher and Jett. They knew *something* about the town, and it was clear they wanted to keep whatever it was to themselves.

"You know." Luca's voice had dropped in pitch, much as it had on the road before they'd picked up Lakelyn. The man leaned back, turning on his side to look down into Alistair's face, his broad frame propped up by one elbow like he weighed nothing at all. "I'd wanted to wait until I had things finalized." Calloused fingers pushed a small rope of hair out of Alistair's face. "But I'm negotiating with Marla right now to have the children in town evacuated. I feel like things may get dangerous soon. I thought you might be more comfortable knowing they were safe."

As far as Alistair could tell, he managed to keep his face lax, refusing to give away any emotion to the other man. But inside, his heart sputtered against his ribs. He was sure Luca was doing this to impress him, possibly as some part of his campaign to eventually trick him into bed, but despite that, it was impossible not to feel grateful. He imagined the face Lakelyn would make when he heard the news, his freckled cheeks plumping against his smile, his eyes turning into little crescents of joy. He wanted the chance to tell him that he could go. And despite any ulterior motives, looking up into Luca's steel-grey eyes, he wanted to trust that he was doing this because he was a good person.

"Luca?" His voice was soft, not a whisper, but a subdued, yearning call.

"Hm?" Fingers traced the frame of Alistair's face, from his hairline down to the soft corner of his jaw.

"Do you know what's happening here?" His tone was steady, but he plead with his eyes. *Please. Please tell me the truth so I can trust you.*

Perched above him, Luca was silent for a few long moments, looking back and forth between the pleading green orbs, then he bent forward, leaving a slow kiss to his forehead. "I don't, kitten."

Liar.

23: BASTIAN

It was nearly one in the morning, and though Bastian laid reclined in bed with Cole's check on his chest, they were both fully dressed. They hadn't spoken in at least an hour, but Bastian knew his lover was still awake—his thin fingers still fidgeting with the front of his shirt. He got the impression that Cole was nervous, but Bastian refused to acknowledge why. Berlin had filled the smaller boy's head with stupid lies and paranoia, and if he didn't stop, Bastian was going to have to stop him by force if need be.

Glancing at the clock, he saw that it was 12:58, and he brushed his hand through Cole's hair, pleased to be able to see his horns again since the glamour spell had worn off. It was novel to see him without them, but he preferred the boy the way he was meant to be.

"It's time. Do you have the samples we got?"

Cole sighed and sat up, stretching just enough to ease the tension Bastian had been feeling. "Yeah. They're on the desk."

Getting up, they collected the folded piece of paper they'd used to keep track of the dozen hairs they'd managed to pluck from different people in town. The open walkway outside their room was quiet, the parking lot eerie in its emptiness. When Berlin let them into the room beside theirs, they were surprised to see Milo present as well, sitting on the edge of one mattress, the giant black wolf-dog laying with his body curled behind him as though protecting him.

"Sabin let him know after we split up." Berlin gave a short, quiet explanation, all of them knowing that he and Cole still spent very little time in the same place at the same time.

Bastian looked at Cole, silently asking him if he was going to be okay with the set up, but he only shrugged, gave a reassuring smile and said, "It's fine."

It was easy to tell that he wasn't fine, though. He hadn't been fine for most of the day, and unlike last time, when he'd sat eagerly watching Sabin prepare his spell, this time he hung back, leaning against the dresser and watching a spot on the carpet. Then again, everyone seemed solemn in the room, even Sabin who sat on the floor, grinding something in his mortar and pestle, seven small stone bowls lined up in front of him. The pierced boy smiled at him when he approached, though he looked exhausted.

"You got some?" He set his mortar down to accept the folded piece of paper from Bastian, which he opened up to inspect.

"Yeah. About a dozen of them. You okay?"

He waved his hand at him. "Yeah, yeah. Magic is just time consuming and tiring. What about you?" He nodded toward Cole.

"I don't know. He's been freaked out since this morning at the church. No matter how many times I ask, though, he won't tell me what happened."

"Hm." Sabin looked at Cole again, his eyes resting on him for a long time before he looked back down at his work.

"Do you have any idea?" Bastian pressed.

"Maybe. But we'll talk later."

Bastian wanted to press him, but before he could say anything else, the door opened, a bang making everyone in the room jump as the knob hit the wall. Alistair looked spooked as he hurried inside.

"Luca's missing."

"Shouldn't you be happy about that?" Berlin quipped as he settled back down on the bed he was reclining on.

"Not when he might be out planning something shady!"

"He's with Jett." Milo didn't bother getting up, one hand stroking Kiyiya's head like it was already a habit.

"What do you mean 'he's with Jett?'"

"He said something about some midnight service the church does. They went to check it out."

"Scheiße. That son of a bitch..."

"That is a little weird, though." Bastian left Sabin where he was on the floor. "I mean, shouldn't we investigate as a group? And since when had we heard about a midnight service?"

"I found out about it today while I was doing some recon with one of the kids," Alistair said, his hands moving to his hips as he shook his head. "That asshole, swooping in without even saying anything to us. He's being secretive. Him *and* Jett. I don't trust them."

"I don't think any of us do, actually. Which is why Milo brought us some of Jett's hair. We're going to test them too."

Bastian wondered when everyone had become so suspicious of each other. Maybe he'd just not been as perceptive as he should have been. But if Sabin's spell worked, then they could at least get things out in the open.

"So this is supposed to work?" Alistair marched over to Sabin. "You can tell us who's evil and who's good?"

"More or less." He shrugged. I'm about done, though, so if you guys want to circle up we can get started."

A quiet gravity fell in the room as they all took a seat in a circle around the line of bowls. Bastian made sure to position himself between Cole and Milo, and wondered what was up with the dog when it followed Milo down to the floor and leaned against the boy's back, panting lightly in Bastian's ear.

"Do we have to hold hands and chant or something?" Berlin sat to Sabin's left despite his snide remark.

"I mean, if you guys want to hold hands, you can. But it won't make a difference." Sabin took a moment to snap a picture of his line up from a few different angles with his Polaroid. He didn't bother checking the shots, though, tossing them aside as soon as the popped out of the camera.

"Let's just get on with this. If Luca is out at some secret meeting, then I need to get back before he shows up." Alistair seemed more irritated by their teacher's secrecy than Bastian expected. It seemed personal with him, somehow.

"Alright." Sabin pointed at the cup on the far left, a milky-white liquid in the bottom. "This bowl covers our Nordic and European spirits. Ground horn from that white stag we relocated, mixed with distilled water." He moved down the line. "Water from the Ganges River, a holy place in Hindu culture. It covers our South Asian nasties. This one," he tipped the bowl forward so they could see a dark red paste. "This is the paste made of poisons. This is what that black widow was for." He looked at Bastian and Cole, as though to explain himself to them in particular. Producing a lighter and a white piece of paper, he turned the talisman toward the others. Across the front, in broad black strokes were several Chinese characters.

"I didn't know you could write in Chinese," Milo said, sounding impressed.

"Don't flatter me. I know exactly as much as I need to do a spell." Holding the talisman up, he lit the corner, watching it burn for a few seconds before dropping it into the bowl on top of the paste. They all watched it burn for a few moments, then Sabin took a small mortar to it and mixed the soot into the paste. "Taoist exorcism paste. If you eat it, it forces the evil spirits out. If it doesn't kill you, anyway."

"You're kidding." Berlin's face was stuck in a permanent grimace.

"You can test it if you don't believe me."

"I'll drown myself first, thanks."

"That's a shame. I've always wanted to see it in action." He lifted a small chip of something that looked like bone out of the next bowl. "This is from Western Africa. A lion's bone bound with cowrie shells." As he turned the chip over, they could all see the small domed shell attached to the side with twine. "The shell draws the spirit in, and the bone traps it."

The next bowl had a small bundle of herbs Bastian recognized from Native American culture. Since living in America, he'd seen it show up in movies and TV shows. Sabin lit it and let the smoke coil slowly into the air between them.

"And of course, here's our holy water." He tilted the bowl slightly, the clear liquid easing toward the lip of the vessel."

"What's the last bowl for?" Bastian asked.

"Well, that one is to cover *South* American spirits." Picking up the bowl, he handed it to Berlin, then positioned the other boy's hands so he was holding the bowl under Sabin's chin. "Hold it there for me, would you?"

"Please don't throw up in it." Berlin looked like he was struggling to keep his hands from shaking, but he held the bowl steady.

"I'm not gonna barf in it." As he spoke he produced a rag and a needle. Using the lighter, he rolled the needle over the flame. "Most South American gods expected blood sacrifices. So the concept is that blood offered freely has a great deal of power behind it to repel evil."

"Blood?" Bastian took Cole's hand without really thinking about it. "You're not going to hurt yourself are you?"

"No." He shrugged. "Well yes. But it'll be fine. Blood is usually offered from the cheek, tongue, or foreskin." A ripple of disgust passed over the room. "Luckily, I've been thinking about getting my tongue pierced for a while."

"Woah, woah, woah! Hold on a second!" Berlin started shouting as soon as Sabin leaned forward, but he couldn't manage much else before the other boy forced the sanitized needle through the center of his tongue. "Ooooohh! No!" Berlin's hands shook now, but he lifted the bowl higher as blood flowed from the puncture wound, staining Sabin's bottom lip and chin. "Du spinnst wohl!"

Cole's hand tightened around Bastian's, but nobody else said anything as Sabin let the blood drip into the bowl for a few moments before producing a small barbell and sliding it through the hole the hollow needle had made. His fingers were bloody when he was finally finished closing up the new piercing. As he wiped the blood from his chin and hands with the rag, Berlin stared at the bowl holding a half inch of blood like *he* might barf in it.

"Hand me that cup of ice, would you?"

Letting go of Cole's hand, Bastian did as he was asked, turning and collecting the cup from the corner of the desk. With one hand, Sabin took the bowl from Berlin, returning it to the lineup, and with the other he popped an ice cube into his mouth, crunching it up before speaking again.

"Metal." Alistair said it almost to himself, nodding in a show of his newfound respect.

"So yeah. That should cover that region. Which means," he paused to eat a few bits of ice in quick succession. "That we have the whole world covered here." He looked proud, even as Berlin's face tried to regain some color.

"I feel like I'm going to Hell just for being in the same room with this shit." The tattooed boy crossed himself again as he looked over the bowls.

Sabin ignored Berlin and carried on. "So, in concept, if any of these hairs came from people who are either not people, or possessed by some sort of evil spirit, this line up will tell us, *and* give us a good idea of what sort of baddie we're dealing with. And to be thorough—" with his still slightly stained fingers, Sabin plucked a few hairs from his head. "This will be our control."

"How do we know you're not doing some sort of spell to keep your hair from reacting?" They were all getting tired of Berlin slowing things down.

"Well do *you* want to provide the control then?"

"Are you kidding? This is exactly *why* I keep my head shaved. So weirdo Satan-worshipers like you can't steal it and use it in voodoo dolls or something."

Sabin only smiled at his roommate, and, unfortunately for the tattooed boy, he'd chosen to wear shorts to sleep in. In one swift motion, Sabin snatched some leg hair off the other boy's shin, making Berlin yelp and recoil.

"Heads up, leg hair works just as well."

Bastian had to rub his nose to hide his grin.

"Now, as I was saying." Moving from one end of the bowls to the other, Sabin dropped one of his own hairs and one of Berlin's leg hairs into each container.

Bastian found himself holding his breath, squeezing Cole's hand, waiting to see if anything happened. When a few seconds had passed after the hairs had fallen into the small bowl of blood, they all sighed in unison.

"There. Satisfied?"

Berlin only grumbled.

For a few moments, Sabin separated out the hair samples they had all collected, a few of them—like the mayor, the two pastors, and the woman who had attached Alistair—were set aside. Then there was the collection Cole and Bastian had brought, a mix of townspeople, only a few hairs from each person.

"Okay, let's start with our friend, the mayor. Milo managed to swipe this one." With tiny scissors, Sabin cut the hairs in half until he had enough for each bowl. "Here we go."

The room stilled again as every eye focused on the bowls in front of them. The hair floated in the river water, settled in the soot of the Chinese Talisman, and just bounced off the shard of lion bone. Cole's hand squeezed Bastian's hard as Sabin dropped one piece into the bowl of holy water and they all caught their breath in unison. As the hair touched the surface of the clear water, bubbles began rising from the bottom of the bowl, as though the whole vessel had begun to simmer. The hair twisted as foam formed around it, and then dissolved, leaving the one black hair Sabin had offered it, and the small curl of leg hair—undamaged.

Jaws dropped across the room, but Sabin and Cole both looked severe, their mouths pressed into thin lines and brows creased.

"This is what I expected."

"So what does this mean?" Alistair spoke up, his eyes wide with wonder.

"It means we're probably dealing with demons. Old-fashioned Biblical demons."

"What? But those are just myths." Even after seeing some of the crazy things Haven had exposed him to, Bastian still had a hard time accepting something as fanciful as demons, Hell, or Heaven.

"Says the guy with angel wings. I've been telling you this from the beginning, Bastian." Berlin was quick to defend his own beliefs, obviously bolstered now by the evidence.

"We don't know that."

"Could we just check the others please?" Cole raising his voice was rare, so even Berlin shut up as the smaller boy shouted over him.

"Do we really need to?" Alistair shrugged. "I mean, I can't imagine the evil spirits of the world are having some sort of reunion in the middle of Nebraska."

"Well I think we should still test them all!" Cole's hand was shaking where he held onto Bastian's, though his voice was steady.

"I agree." Another surprise. Of everyone in the room, it was Milo who took Cole's side. "From a scientific standpoint it's important to cover all our bases, and reaffirm as much as we can."

"Well, it can't hurt at this point." Sabin said. "We can skip the other bowls for now."

One after the other, Sabin dropped each hair individually into the small bowl of holy water, and one after the other, they each sizzled and disappeared. They were maybe ten hairs in when one of them broke the pattern and stayed floating atop the liquid, drifting over to where Sabin's hair still sat.

"Who is that?" Cole's voice shook now and he leaned forward to get a good look. "What color was it?"

"It was one of the samples I kept separated." Looking at the paper he'd taken it from, Sabin's eyebrows rose. "Looks like it's Hartford, the youth pastor. I guess it's good to know that a few people made it through all this unscathed."

Bastian recognized the paper he and Cole had brought their samples in, but instead of watching as Sabin began dropping them in one at a time, he looked at his lover. Cole was shaking harder by the minute, his face sallow and pale. He wanted to reach out and touch his cheek—lend him some of his own color, but Sabin finished their contribution before he could do anything, and when their teammate turned the folded paper out showing that it was empty, Cole pulled his hand away from Bastian and pressed his knuckles to his own lips, hiding what Bastian thought was the smallest quivering of his chin.

"That's it," Sabin said, popping another ice cube into his mouth and crunching it noisily. "Out of every sample we got, Hartford was the only one clear. That means probably ninety percent of this place is full of people possessed by demons. The mayor, the head pastor, the ladies running the temporary school. Every single one of them."

"Bathroom." Cole muttered a quick explanation, then got up and bee-lined for the small, closet-sized room that held the toilet.

24: COLE

The voices of his teammates became muffled as he closed himself in the small room. He knew that Bastian, at least, was probably suspicious of him, but he had to get out of there. Dropping the lid on the toilet he sat down, took a deep breath through his nose, then covered his mouth to muffle the sob that shook him.

He had mixed one of his own hairs into the samples they'd given Sabin.

There had been suspicions from the very beginning about what he was. Deep down he probably already *knew* what he was. But to see it proven right in front of him, to sit holding hands with someone so much kinder and stronger than he could ever be, was too much. Leaning forward into his own lap, he let the shaking roll over him, felt the hot tears roll down his nose before melting into the fabric of his pajama pants.

What would happen when the others found out? Bastian kept saying that he was a good person, no matter what he might be, but would he feel that way knowing—*really knowing*—that he was a demon? That he was literally a creature from Hell? He laughed a little into his lap, wiping his nose with his sleeve. He hardly even believed in such a place, but in his gut he knew it was true. He could feel that darkness inside him—the darkness which manifested as the hunger that followed him, that made him hurt people.

Taking a deep breath, Cole leaned back and looked at the ceiling, trying his best to scrub the tears from his face. If he went back out there with red, swollen eyes, Bastian would fuss over him, and he just wasn't ready to tell him. He wasn't ready to decide if Bastian really might be better off without him. The answer he refused to give actual form to sent another sob through him, and he covered his face again.

He had to stop.

Once he'd calmed the convulsive shaking in his ribs, he cleaned his face with some tissue and flushed the wad of paper. When he let himself back out into the room the others were talking about what needed to be done, but he could feel Bastian watching him as he washed his hands. As he took his spot beside his lover again he offered him a smile, but despite his best efforts, he could feel how tight it was.

"Are you okay?" Bastian was whispering as his hand brushed along the back of Cole's arm.

"I'm not feeling real well." Cole offered, knowing that might be vaguely true enough that Bastian wouldn't be able to detect his evasion.

It seemed to work, since Bastian rubbed his back and looked concerned but didn't say much else.

"So should we tell Shipton?" Berlin looked star-struck, his eyes wide with wonder even after the minutes that had passed since Sabin's spell. He was probably just pleased to have his paranoia validated.

"No." Alistair was the first to speak up. "I don't trust him. He's up to something. Him and Jett, both."

"I agree." Milo took the redhead's side. "I've thought for a while now that they had something more going on than what we've been told."

They all turned to Bastian, obviously wanting his truth barometer to tell them exactly where their new teammates stood. His wings shuttered a little—something Cole noticed they did when he was nervous—and he shrugged.

"I don't know," he said. "I've not really had a chance to talk to them."

"Well you should." Alistair seemed alight, motivated in a way Cole had never seen him before. "We can get Bastian to ask them some questions and then we'll know for sure if they're lying."

"Are you sure you're not just having a lover's spat with him or something?" Berlin—usually so eager to jump onto conspiracy band wagons—seemed to be the only skeptical one now.

"I don't know about this," Bastian said, his attention torn between the worry he was obviously feeling due to Cole's behavior and his friends' demands. "Even if we know they're lying, it won't explain what they're actually planning."

"We don't need to *know* what they have planned! We need to stop whatever they're doing!" Alistair's voice grew shrill, and he seemed to realize that he was overreacting, because he cleared his throat and pushed his hands through his hair to calm himself. "Look, I'm just saying that if they're up to something, they could be putting us in danger." He hesitated a second. "I overheard them talking today. I think whatever has this town under its control is targeting someone. I think it might be this kid I've been talking to. But it could be anyone. Maybe it's Hartford since he's not possessed. Maybe it's one of us. Like, this is important. We have to figure out what they're planning."

"It's unusual for you to care about stuff like this."

Cole didn't want to admit that he agreed with Berlin. Seeing his usually blasé teammate getting so fired up made his anxiety spike. If Luca and Jett *did* know that they were after someone, shouldn't they have warned everyone else?

"Just because I usually let other people fuck up their own shit doesn't mean I'm going to ignore it when they're fucking up *my* shit. Besides. I heard them mention Marla. I think she's in on whatever is going on."

"That's a lie." The words were out of Cole's mouth before he realized he was going to even say anything. The others quieted and looked at him, but he could tell by the way Alistair's mouth pinched, he was ready to argue. "I'm not saying that Marla doesn't keep secrets from us, but she wouldn't keep something from us that would get someone hurt. Especially one of us."

"Look." It was obvious that Alistair was trying to measure his words. "I know that you have some sort of mommy complex for Marla. She saved you, gave you a home, blah, blah, blah. But she is keeping us prisoner. And if you have any notion that Haven is anything more than a cushy prison, then you're delusional."

"Marla is a good person." Cole said it again, his heart aching at the idea of losing her as his safe place, because even if Bastian turned his back on him for being a monster, he knew that Marla never would.

"Marla had me shot with a tranquilizer when I told her I wanted to leave, Cole. She kept me prisoner in my own damn body. How is that good?"

"She did it for you! To protect you! You might not mean to, but if she let you go, you could hurt people. *I* could hurt people. We're all here because we're dangerous."

"Guys, I think we need to calm down." Bastian raised both hands between the two. "Losing our heads right now isn't going to help us."

"Oh don't give me that load of shit, Bastian. Du nimmst nur seine Seite, weil er dich ficken lassen kann."

"Sprechen Sie nicht so über ihn!"

Cole's heart hammered in his chest as the two started shouting at each other in German. He didn't regret defending Marla, but if Alistair got this angry at him for defending his mother, then how angry would he be to find out the truth about him? Berlin already hated him for what he was. If both of his teammates agreed, wouldn't Bastian be obligated to stand with them? He'd already estranged himself from Milo. And as he looked at Sabin he saw his teammate eating his ice and watching the others argue like it was some Pay-per-View prize fight.

When they finally died down, it was Milo who spoke up, his voice steady and mild the way Cole remembered it being before he'd begun his spiral. "I think whether Marla might be involved or not doesn't affect our situation right now. I also agree with Bastian. Knowing whether they're lying to us or not won't really be of much help to us now. It's obvious that they're doing things behind our back, so lying is sort of a given. For now, I think we need to figure out what exactly these people want. Whether we get that information from Shipton or from the people of the down directly doesn't matter. We can't do anything until we know what sort of leverage we might have. While the rest of you look into that, I'll work with Sabin to figure out how to reverse whatever is going on here."

"You mean how to perform exorcisms," Berlin said, almost sounding excited.

"In layman's terms, yes. We need to figure out if exorcising these things is even an option. With Reverend Blackholly holding secret sermons in the middle of the night, it's only logical that he's probably in a position of power, so let's focus our attention on him and the mayor for the time being. Alistair, you seem close with some of the kids, so see what else they know while we figure out a way to keep them safe in things come to a head."

Despite their misgivings, no one else seemed to have a better plan than the one proposed by Milo, so they all exchanged looks but agreed.

"Well, since we have a leader now, I guess I'll take off," Alistair said, hoisting himself up off the floor. "The last thing I need is for Luca to catch me out in the middle of the night."

A few muttered goodnights passed between them as the redhead left, and for a second, Cole wanted to run after him, either to continue defending Marla or to escape his lover—he wasn't sure which. Bastian's hand on his back felt suffocating, though.

"We should go too."

That was the last thing Cole wanted to hear from his winged lover. Going back to their room meant they would be alone. And that meant that Bastian would start asking questions. Still, he let the taller boy pull him to his feet.

"Actually!" Sabin scrambled to his feet before they made it to the door. "Bastian, I wanted to ask. Do you mind if I take a few of your feathers?"

"What?" They were at the door already as Bastian turned around.

"Well I was thinking they might have some sort of magical property." Sabin gave him the sweetest smile he could manage—a look that was slightly damaged by the dried blood at the corner of his mouth.

"Um. Well, sure, I guess." Bastian turned to look at Cole. "Give me just a second, then we'll go."

Cole knew what that meant. It meant "give me a second, then I'll be available for you to tell me everything that's bothering you." But Cole didn't want to tell him. He didn't even know how to begin. But he nodded and watched Bastian walk back to where Sabin was keeping all of his ingredients. Berlin followed immediately, complaining that Bastian shouldn't give up a part of his body to witchcraft.

"Cole."

It was impossible not to jump as Milo interrupted Cole's internal panicking. It had been weeks since they'd last talked in relative privacy.

"Hey," he said, not really sure what else he could offer.

They were both quiet for a few moments and Cole watched him rubbing mindlessly behind Kiyiya's ears as the dog kept to his side.

"Seems like he's taken a liking to you, huh?"

"Oh. Yeah." Milo smiled a little as he looked down at the black dog. "He sleeps on the foot of my bed at night. Jett says it's because I spoil him."

"I'm not surprised he likes you. You've always been really good at spoiling people."

A weight fell between them as the words left Cole's lips. Milo had been so gentle when Cole first met him, but he'd lost some of that. Cole had *taken* some of that from him. Guilt filled Cole's gut and his weakened tear ducts stung. He should apologize to him.

"I have something for you," Milo said before Cole could form his apology. "Here."

Holding his hand out, Milo deposited three small glass tubes of medicine into his palm. "I know you don't really need this anymore. But I've tweaked it a little. And it could help if there's an emergency of some kind."

It had been a long time since he'd taken any of Milo's medicine, but just that minute he could feel the hunger squirming inside him and he wasn't ready to sate it.

"Thank you." Cole tried to infuse as much gratitude as he could into those two words. As his fingers wrapped around the small bottles, though, his eyes moved to where Bastian and Sabin were talking. Everything hurt inside him—especially when he looked at Bastian.

"You know he would love you no matter what happened, right?"

Cole looked back at Milo, whose eyes looked sad even as he smiled at him. He swallowed, angry because he knew that Milo was probably right, and sad because that meant that *he* would have to be the one to decide what was best for him. And if that meant separating, then it would be up to Cole to do.

"Yeah, I know. Thank you, Milo. You really are a good person."

Milo smiled a little more convincingly and patted Kiyiya on his flank as the dog stood, prepared to leave. "Yeah, I'm getting there."

It was a gentle way of letting Cole know that the effects of the toxins were still dissipating, and that soon enough, he would be back to normal.

"Goodnight, Cole."

"Goodnight."

Cole's chest felt a little lighter as his friend left the motel room, and he pocketed the medicine before Bastian got back to him.

The room Cole and Bastian shared felt even tinier as the door closed behind them. Cole had never felt claustrophobic before, not even when they'd been trapped in the cave at Lechuguilla. He had to figure out what he would say.

"Cole." Bastian had that soft, understanding tone to his voice, and it made everything squirm. "Cole," he said again, his hands catching Cole's arms in wide but impossibly gentle hands. "Look at me."

He tried to not shake as he looked up at his lover.

"What's going on?" As if Cole's skin was connected directly to his heart, every place Bastian's fingers touched made the pounding lump of pain inside him quiver.

"Nothing," Cole said weakly, not even able to keep his eyes on his lover's. He wasn't ready. He wasn't ready to find out what would happen. He didn't even know what he *wanted* to happen yet.

"Liebe." His hands moved to Cole's cheeks, holding his gaze steady. "We both know that's not true."

It was too much. He wasn't going to be able to stay silent under that gaze, so instead, Cole dug his fingers into the fabric of Bastian's shirt and pulled him down toward him. It felt like ages had passed since they'd last kissed. Of all the things they did, kissing was one act Cole guarded most in his attempt to shield his lover from the poison inside his body. But if he kissed him, then Bastian wouldn't be able to ask him any more questions. For a second, the blond seemed to revel in the sensation he got so rarely, then he pulled back, murmuring Cole's name.

"Please Bastian. Just kiss me right now." He saw his lover waver a little, trying to decide what he should do. His distraction was obvious, though after a moment he wound his arms around Cole's waist, nearly lifting him off the floor as his mouth descended on his again.

Even as guilt twisted his stomach, Cole told himself that it was okay. He would surrender himself to his lover. He would let himself drown in Bastian's touch, and he would tell him afterwards.

And after all, he reminded himself, this might be his last chance to feel Bastian's hands on him.

So he wrapped his arms around the taller boy's neck, hooked his ankles behind his back as he was lifted off his feet. Bastian carried him to the bed, lowering him to the mattress before covering his body with the strong expanse of his own. Cole knew Bastian wanted this for a long time, and despite the warning bells ringing in his head, Cole had to admit he'd wanted it too. Bastian's mouth left his and traced a scorching path down the front of his throat, banishing for a few seconds the abhorrence he felt toward his own existence, and in thanks Cole raked his fingers through the blond's tangled curls.

"Bastian, I love you." He said it like an apology, murmuring over and over as Bastian's hand pushed his clothes away from his body like he was brushing away sand from some hidden treasure.

His shirt was pressed up under his chin, his pants were pushed down to his knees, and as one broad hand moved under the curve of Cole's lower back, hot lips traced the already swollen head of Cole's dick. A shiver ran down his legs, and his lover's hand guided the arching of his back. He told himself he was just letting Bastian do what he wanted—allowing him to sate any desire he might have—but Cole pressed into him, the very center of his soul struggling to get closer to the winged boy.

With one hand stationed at his hip and the other supporting Cole's helplessly undulating spine, Bastian held the smaller boy brutally still, his tongue tracing circles around the head of his cock, his lips wrapping him in soft heat, his teeth sending sparks through his body as they scraped the sensitive skin of his shaft. It took only minutes before Cole's legs jerked, thrashing in an attempt to find purchase on the sheets of the bed, needing to push himself further into the heat of his lover's mouth, needing just a little nudge to tip over into bliss.

"God--" his hands clenched fistfuls of his lover's hair, straining as he felt the pressure of his orgasm building, like the tide pulling out to sea before the wave hits. Then cool air replaced the mouth that had promised him release, and his whimper was cut off in his throat as fingers wrapped tight around the base of his cock. "Ow." He winced and squirmed, trying to come back from the brink he'd been pushed to. "Bastian, what are you doing?"

"You can't come until you tell me what's going on." There was a teasing quality to his expression and his voice, but Cole could tell that he was serious. His gut ached as he tried to wriggle out of his boyfriend's grip, his hands moving to pry the other boy's grip loose.

"Bastian, hold on. Wait a second." Panic infused his veins in a wash of ice water, but the more he struggled, the harder Bastian's grip became.

The blond didn't let go, instead pressing Cole's legs further apart as his mouth descended on the sensitive skin of his inner thigh. His tongue sent sparks of electricity through Cole's body, but when his lips latched onto the delicate skin and sucked an agonizing bruise into his flesh, Cole realized he wasn't shaking from pleasure any more.

When Bastian came up for air his voice was low and lacked the tenderness Cole was used to hearing in it. "Just tell me, and I'll make you come harder than you have in your whole life."

Despite the painful ache of Bastian's fingers squeezing his dick, Cole's head dropped back to the pillow when the other boy's lips sucked another dark bruise into his thigh.

"It hurts. Let go." When a small sob hiccupped out of Cole's throat, Bastian finally paused.

"Why are you like this?" Bastian's voice was so quiet that Cole almost didn't hear it over the sound of his own pounding heard.

When Cole was finally released he clamped his legs shut.

"I spend every second worrying about you," Bastian continued, propping himself up over his recovering lover. "All I think about is you and what I can do to help you." His face was grim and Cole could see tears forming in his eyes as his jaw set hard around his words. "I want to help, but you shut me out every time. You won't even let me feed you. We've done blood tests for Christ sake, and you still refuse. Why am I not good enough? Why were people in a fucking subway enough, but not me—" The words were barely out of his mouth when Cole struck him hard across his face.

The room was silent for a second, the echo of that one slap seeming to take ages to die away. Bastian knelt above him, pain much greater than an open-handed strike called for contorting his face. Cole had been reluctant to tell Bastian details about the time he'd spent before Marla had found him. Suddenly he regretted the few things he'd let slip.

"You sound like Milo." Cole's voice trembled as the words shook off his lips. "Are you listening to yourself?"

"Are *you* listening to *your*self?" Bastian pulled away, moving back to sit on the mattress. "Cole, do you trust me at all?"

Did he? How could he trust those feelings when he'd heard them from Milo while under the influence of his toxins? And even if the toxins had no effect on him, how could he be sure Bastian would *keep* loving him when they had to finally come to terms with what he is?

"It's complicated."

Bastian pressed his hands into his eye sockets. He'd always hated that answer.

"Dammit, Cole. That means the answer is 'no,'" Bastian swung his legs off the side of the bed and pushed his hands so hard through his hair he looked like he might pull it out. "I get that you're scared, but Jesus. I can only tell you that I love you so many times. What else can I do to make you believe me? To make you trust me? Du machst mich wahnsinnig."

The narrow bed felt vastly empty all of a sudden, and shame burned across him as Cole pulled his pants back up around his waist. He knew Bastian was angry—that he had every right to be—but anyone could say "I love you." Millions of people said it every day, and millions of people didn't mean it, even if they thought they did.

"I'm sorry, Bastian; it's just not that simple."

"It *is* that simple." He turned to look at him again, the pain on his face making Cole's stomach churn. "What else is there? Why do you believe every bad thing that someone else says, while the good things I say never reach you?"

"Because the bad things people say about me are true!" Cole felt his bones shaking inside his body. "You couldn't possibly understand, because you jumped off a cliff and got *those!*" He pointed at the wings folded against Bastian's back like they were the cause of every bad thing in his life. "Because you look sweet, and line up with what people expect from an *angel*. Even if you aren't, even if there isn't even such a thing, people treat you differently. You tell the truth and help people. I prey on people and get violent if I don't. I have horns and see in the dark. I'm made to be in the sorts of places where bad things happen." Cole didn't realize he'd started crying until he tasted the salt at the corners of his mouth. He wiped the tears from his face with one brush of his arm. "How can that not bother me? How can I keep myself from believing there's something bad inside me when I check every box? When I can actually feel it in there?"

He brought his trembling fingers to his face, pressing them hard against his brow to try and alleviate the misery that pounded in his head. Bastian was quiet for a moment, and when he spoke again he had the soft tone that Cole recognized. It always lulled him into an easy, comfortable state. If he let himself, he would nestle into the safe space Bastian created for him and he would put off the truth for another day. That's all this past month had been— procrastination. He'd told himself over and over that he would decide whether or nto he was right for Bastian, and every day he put it off for just a little longer.

Now, having seen part of his own body sizzle and vanish on the surface of something meant to be holy—meant to represent everything that was good in the world—he knew he couldn't put it off any more. When Bastian's fingers brushed over his shoulders, Cole slapped them away.

"Don't touch me." It was hard to see Bastian's expression through the tears in his eyes, but he figured that was for the best. Seeing the way he'd hurt the man who had shown him so much love would only dampen his resolve. As he got up, he twisted out of Bastian's reach again, the blond trying desperately to catch him.

"Cole. Where are you going?" Bastian was on his feet as soon as Cole was.

"Please, Bastian." He was backing toward the door. "Just for tonight, please just let me figure this out."

"Liebe, it's not safe out there. Stay here. If you need time, I'll go stay with Berlin and Sabin."

"I can't. Just, give me tonight. I promise, I'll have an answer. Just, please wait for me."

Bastian's arms hung at his sides like they were made of lead, his face pale and his mouth open in some unfinished plea.

Not wanting to give his heart the chance to waver, Cole opened the door to their room and let himself out into the night, trying to convince himself that when he came back, he would know what to do, and he would have the strength to do it.

25: ALISTAIR

The room was still empty when Alistair returned to his bed. That was good—at least it was supposed to be good. Stripping down to his short boxer briefs, Alistair reminded himself that Luca was part of the problem—someone to be suspicious of, not someone to worry about. But he didn't like the idea of Luca sneaking away in the cover of night. After all the anger he'd felt toward him, when had the man's presence become so comforting?

This was unlike him.

Alistair turned over in his bed, the scratchy blanket rubbing his bare legs. He wanted to be wrong about Luca. He wanted to forget the conversation he'd heard. He wanted to believe, instead, in the man who sat beside him and stoically comforted him.

He stilled as keys scraped into the door, the yellow light of the street lamp washing into the room for a few moments as Luca let himself in, his movements nearly silent. Alistair kept his eyes shut, not sure yet if he wanted to call the man out on his suspicious behavior. In the silent room he listened to the rustling of cloth, punctuated by the sound of a belt buckle, his breath freezing in his chest for a few moments as he sensed Luca still at his bedside. He was watching him sleep, and for a moment, Alistair hoped the man would slide into his bed, press the heat of his body against his back, give him some reason to think that he wasn't betraying them. Then Luca stepped away, the sound of his own blankets marking his retreat.

A humiliating surge of disappointment seemed to hit home the severity of Alistair's situation. He didn't just want Luca to touch him, he wanted Luca to care about him enough to tell him what he was doing. He wanted Luca to love him. Alistair was falling for him—hard. Too hard if he was going to be honest. It had to be the town, though. It had to be the way he'd been forced to talk about Felix. He was confused.

And before he fell any harder, he had to find a way to get out. Even if Marla kept him sedated in the back of one of their medical trucks until the mission was over, he felt like that was safer than letting himself slide any further down this rabbit hole.

26: COLE

The sun was just breaking the horizon, lighting the fields that stretched out beyond the revival tent a soft yellow. Cole had expected to find the people from town there when he'd made his way to the makeshift chapel during the night, but it had been empty. The whole town had been silent, so Cole had sat in one of the many rows and waited. It was hard to say what he was waiting for exactly, but when Blackholly's voice broke the silence the way it had the day before, Cole knew this was who he'd come to find.

"Welcome back, Cole." The man stood only two rows behind him, his hands in the pockets of his tan slacks, the sleeves of his white shirt rolled up to the elbows and his black tie loosened slightly, like he'd just come from working elsewhere.

"Hello, Reverend." It was hard to tell if he was happy to see him or not, his heart stumbling through an uneven rhythm.

"You look like you have some questions. I'm sorry I kept you waiting."

The mere fact that this man seemed unfazed by Cole's horns answered at least one of those questions. For the past two days, Bastian and Cole had gone to Sabin early in the morning for their glamour spell. It seemed like they hadn't been fooling people as well as they'd thought.

"You're not with your friends?" He asked the question like he knew the answer already. Blackholly strolled down the row of chairs to the main aisle so he could face Cole more directly. "Is it because they found out that you're like us?"

Cole's heart raced at the affirmation, but he had to know for sure. He had to hear it out loud. "And what are we? Exactly?"

The smile the reverend offered was soft, his eyes warm and kind, and as he took a seat beside Cole he brushed a fatherly hand through his hair. "We're kin. That's what we are."

"We're demons?" His voice cracked a little, though he didn't hate the feel of the hand resting against the back of his head now. "Like real life demons from Hell?"

"I can tell by the way you say that that you don't really know what it means." He moved his hand to Cole's shoulder, his elbow resting on the back of the chair. "Hell is not the sort of place you imagine it to be, and demons aren't the sorts of monsters you're thinking of either. We merely have a job to do, and we do it. And right now, our job is to help you."

"Me?"

"Of course. What did you think we were doing here?"

What *did* they think they were doing? All they'd determined was that these people were demons. They'd assumed from there that they were planning to hurt people.

"I don't know. I guess I thought it would be something bad?" He felt foolish saying it out loud.

Blackholly only smiled at him, the aged creases at the corners of his mouth comforting Cole somehow. "We're not here to hurt anybody, Cole. We've come here to find *you* and take you home with us."

"What?"

"You're not supposed to be here, Cole. I think you know that already. You were sent here by accident."

"'Sent?' By who? What for?"

"I'm afraid I don't know those answers. But back home there are people who do. If you come with us, everything will be answered."

"Go with you? Where?" He thought he might know the answer to that, but it seemed too extraordinary to be true.

"Back home."

"What, to *Hell?* Are you kidding?" He stood up, ready to leave, but the older man caught his wrist, his grip firm, but gentle.

"Cole, sit down. Let me finish explaining."

"What is there to explain? You say you're not up here to hurt anyone, but this isn't what you actually are, is it?" He gestured toward the middle aged man holding his wrist. "Reverend Blackholly is a real human, right? You're just using his body?"

"That is true, yes."

"And the ones who turn into monsters?"

"Please, Cole. I'm not trying to hide anything from you. Just sit down and I'll explain everything."

Reluctantly, Cole sat back down, folding his arms over his stomach against the cool morning air of fall. The demon occupying the reverend's body seemed relieved.

"It is true that we are borrowing these vessels. But we treat them well, and it's only temporary. My real name is Mammon."

Cole studied the man's face, as if he would be able to see the demon inside him if he looked hard enough.

"What about that lady from yesterday? And I saw another one of your vessels that had turned into a monster. You said you don't hurt them."

"It is never intentional. But, unfortunately, human bodies were not made to hold spirits as strong as ours. They deteriorate over time, and some are stronger than others. The weak ones corrupt first."

"That *is* hurting them, though! Why take vessels if you know they could become corrupt? Why not just come on your own?"

"Unfortunately, we are not permitted physically on this Earth. So we must take vessels to do our works."

Cole's hand moved to his own chest, where he felt his heart thumping under his sternum.

"Don't worry. That is not a vessel. Unlike us, you are here in the flesh."

"How, though?"

"I'm sorry, but only my lord could answer those questions for you. He will be waiting to tell you everything when we bring you home."

Cole's brain whirred in his head, trying to process everything Blackholly—no, Mammon—was telling him. Was he really considering leaving with these people? Was he *really* considering going to *Hell?* But wasn't that where he belonged?

"That blond boy." Mammon's voice broke Cole's train of thought. "He's your food source?"

Cole's face flashed hot, and before he could say anything to defend himself, the older man continued.

"It requires a great deal of power to keep your form here on Earth. But back home, you will be where you were meant. Your body will not need such crude sources of fuel."

"What do you mean?"

The reverend smiled at him. "When you return with us, you will no longer feel the hunger you battle with here."

Cole couldn't imagine living a life without the twisting appetite always ready to overtake him. The life this demon offered him could be his chance to get away from that, away from the pain he felt and the uncertainty. It would get him away from the future he saw where Bastian finally left him—finally saw him for the monster he really was. If he left right then, without going back to see his lover, then he could free them both. He could free Bastian and Milo. He could ensure they would both eventually find happiness.

"We are your family, Cole. The sooner you come with us, the sooner you'll be home where you belong. And the sooner we can release these humans' bodies back to them. Everyone will be happier. You just need to come with me."

Cole swallowed. He had to make his choice.

27: ALISTAIR

Despite the late hours Luca had kept the night before, Alistair heard the other man stir at 6am, just as he had every other morning. Alistair had barely slept himself, his head spinning too fast, trying to process all of the new information. He kept still as Luca quietly slid out of bed and shuffled toward the shower. The man seemed to have a pretty structured routine for the morning, and always made a shower top priority. It was kind of cute to imagine the usually put-together man groggy and delirious from sleep, though Alistair had yet to see it for himself.

A mild ache squeezed his gut. What was he doing, thinking about Luca's morning routine and how intimate it felt to know it when the man had just snuck away to a midnight demon meeting? He had to get out of that town, or he had to get Luca out of that town. Either way, he knew he couldn't stay with the man for another day. Despite his cocky attitude, the teacher had begun to worm his way into Alistair's heart, and he didn't like it.

Once he heard the shower running, Alistair threw the covers off himself. Across the room, partially hidden behind the fat television, he propped up his cell phone, the camera pointing at his teacher's bed. If Marla found out that they'd slept together, then she would definitely separate them. It was win-win. If she removed

Luca, then the traitor among them would be gone. And if she removed Alistair, then he wouldn't have to decide how he felt about the man and his betrayal at all.

"And if he gets hurt while I'm fucking him, that'll just be a perk," he mumbled to himself before starting the recording.

Alistair didn't bother changing clothes, figuring the low riding, short boxer briefs he wore were flattering enough. They made his legs look long and his hips look narrow, two things his partners always seemed to like. Though, admittedly, it was rare for him to have sex wearing so little. Most of his encounters were with clothes shoved aside in the corners of bars or clubs. In bathrooms and other places Alistair worked to forget. Doing it in a bed would be a nice parting gift, since—if Marla has her way—this may be the last time he has sex ever again.

He positioned himself at the corner of Luca's bed when he heard the shower turn off, his heart racing uncharacteristically. Luca paused when he reentered the room, one towel wrapped low on his waist, another draped over his wet hair. After an initial moment of surprise, he smiled and strolled over to stand in front of his student, his hands idly drying his hair.

"You're up early," he said, his voice low from disuse and his eyes scoring sharp lines down Alistair's exposed body.

"It gets lonely in here when I wake up and you're already out of bed." He knew Luca would probably see through his fib, but as he spoke be brushed one foot up the man's toned leg, tracing the swell of his calf, then rubbing his toes over his knee before pushing the ball of his foot up the front of his thigh, lifting the towel with it.

"You should be careful, kitten. Tempt me too much and you might regret it." Despite his words and his smile, Luca's chest rose as he took in a deep breath against the expert caress.

"Are you saying you *don't* want me to touch you?" Alistair's own heart skipped a beat as his toes passed over heated skin.

He gasped as Luca's hand caught his ankle, mere inches from his target. The teacher tutted him as he tossed his foot aside and stepped closer to the bed, looking down the straight line of his nose at the younger boy.

"You're playing a dangerous game, Alistair. We've been teasing each other until now, but push me too far and I really will take you."

Alistair knew that no one could ever truly *take* him the way he wanted. He was too strong, too dangerous. But the way Luca said it, his voice heavy with promise, sent a jolt straight to the core of his body, and he knew Luca could probably see the swell in his minuscule shorts. The man moved a knee onto the corner of the mattress, pressing between Alistair's legs until he pushed into the erection that jumped against the man's thigh.

"Hm. It looks like that might be exactly what you want."

It was hard not to squeeze the other man's leg to the point of bruising as Alistair's hands moved to Luca's muscled, bare thigh, his hip rolling forward into the pressure. He did want it. All of his plotting aside, getting removed from the mission was only a side benefit. At his core, Alistair had wanted this man to take him since he first saw him in the bar in New York.

One long-fingered hand caught Alistair's chin and turned his face up to look at him. He was smiling, the expression unlike the normal teasing grin he gave him. This look was deeper, sharper, and it drained the will power from Alistair's body. He couldn't even tease him anymore, he only bit his lip to keep himself from begging.

"I don't want any misunderstandings, Alistair." A thumb brushed over his bottom lip, easing the red line from the boy's teeth. "So why don't you prove it to me. Show me just how badly you want me."

As Alistair let Luca's thumb part his lips, his tongue lolled out, obediently passing over the calloused digit that thrust softly against it. Locking his eyes with Luca's, Alistair's hands moved to the towel at his waist, carefully undoing the simple fold that kept it up. He slid to the floor with the fabric, kneeling in the narrow space Luca created for him by stepping away from the bed. He felt like he was worshiping him, and for a second, he thought that was exactly what Luca deserved.

Then his eyes traced down the long lines of his torso. He'd only caught glimpses of his naked body before. Even as Luca had stoked him to completion back at Haven, or watched him fondle himself in the shower, he'd been dressed in his impeccable suits. He was so much more arresting now, standing bare and perfect in front of him.

Luca stood powerfully still as Alistair's hands pushed up his thighs before wrapping around the base of his already growing cock. He felt the muscles in the man's hips tense slightly, but there was no other reaction, save for the hot swelling against his palms as he pulled gently on him. When he saw the man's eyes shut for a second and heard the short, hushed grunt in the back of his throat he leaned forward, guiding the searing head of his dick to his parted lips.

Alistair had learned a few tricks over the years, but as he felt the other man's fingers thread through his hair, he found it hard to remember them. The fact that his hands had begun to shake didn't help, so he kept to what he knew best. Luca gathered Alistair's long hair in one hand, wrapping it around the width of his palm and squeezing just hard enough to be felt, though he did nothing to change Alistair's pace. Instead, he hummed as the younger boy rolled his tongue across the head of his prick, tracing the ridge before pushing forward and scraping his teeth along his shaft just hard enough to make him jump.

Despite knowing that he could tear himself away from Luca at any time, Alistair relaxed his neck, letting the hand in his hair guide him, pretending that he really was helpless. It was shameless of him, having such a fantasy, but his own body responded so perfectly to the release of control. He ached against the soft material of his shorts, and as Luca began a slow thrust into his mouth, he dropped both hands to his lap, kneading himself through the fabric, whining around Luca as the head of his dick brushed the back of his throat.

"So beautiful," Luca breathed above him, his hand tightening just a little in his hair before brushing a few fingers down his cheek as a reward for the whimper he got in return. "You feel so good, but you don't want it to end like this, do you?"

Alistair brought his eyes up to look at Luca, whimpering as he eased out of his mouth, strings of spit drawing lines between them.

"Why don't you go ahead and tell me what you want me to do?"

The shaking in Alistair's hands hand spread to his whole body, his fingers pressing into his shorts still, his dick jumping and weeping against the cotton. No one had ever turned him on like this, and at that moment he'd even forgotten the camera. He'd forgotten their mission, or his plan to escape. He'd forgotten that this was a set up. All he wanted at that moment was for Luca to keep going.

"I want you to fuck me, Luca."

The man grinned at him, even as his own arousal growled in his chest. "Good boy." His wide fingers cleaned some of the moisture from the corner of the boy's swollen lips. "Why don't you get on the bed now? Show me where you want me to fuck you."

He took a step back, and for a moment, Alistair thought his knees wouldn't hold him. They shook as he stood, and it was a relief as he crawled onto the bed. He bowed his back and pressed his chest into the mattress as his ass rose shamelessly into the air, his hands pushing the thin fabric of his underwear down over his hips. He felt the bed dip behind him and pressed his cheek into the mattress as he looked behind him. Luca kneeled there, hand fisted around the flesh that had been thrusting into his mouth only seconds earlier. The head of his dick shined dark and wet from his saliva, and Alistair tried to stifle a whimper at the thought of that thick spear pushing inside him.

Freed from his shorts, Alistair spread his legs, shamelessly reaching between them to outline exactly where he wanted Luca to touch him.

"So immodest." Luca's fingers traced fire down Alistair's back, coming to rest on the two dimples where the swell of his ass began, then Alistair jumped as he felt one slicked thumb press against his opening, beginning a firm, slow motion against it. He leaned over Alistair's narrow body, planted a kiss behind his ear. "Keep touching yourself, kitten. Do it until you're just about to come, then I'll give you everything you want."

Alistair didn't have to be persuaded. Pressing his face into the sheets, he wrapped both hands around his already quivering prick and rolled his hips back against the thumb that kept pressing against him, but refusing to penetrate him. As a pleading sound tumbled from his mouth, almost ready to flat-out beg for him to push *anything* inside him, Luca eased one long finger into his waiting passage. He'd been so ready for it that there was no discomfort, and he let out a long keening sound into the bed. How was a single finger making him this crazy?

Luca must have had lubricant hidden somewhere within arm's reach, because as Alistair pulled helplessly at his own dick, Luca had worked his opening until it was pliable and slick. And when the man leaned over him again and nipped at the curve of his ear, Alistair felt every muscle in his gut tense.

"Are you close, Alistair? Hm? I have three fingers inside you already. Are you going to be able to handle me when I fuck you for real?"

"Do it," Alistair heard himself plead before he'd thought of what to say. "Hurry, Luca. Please, please, I want it."

"Mmm. You *have* gotten nice and soft here. Do you think you can take it?"

"Yes! Please, hurry."

In response, Luca pushed his fingers hard inside him, chuckling in his ear when Alistair shrieked in delight. "How do you want me to do it?"

"Hard!" Alistair's hips wagged against those fingers. "Hard, and deep. Please!"

"Alright."

As Luca shifted behind him, Alistair released himself, moving his hands to fist the sheets instead. With one hand moving to the back of Alistair's neck to hold him still, Luca guided Alistair's hands back to his straining cock.

"Don't stop touching yourself."

Alistair feigned obedience, but he didn't stroke himself, instead just holding his throbbing member in his hands. If he wasn't careful he might fall over the edge as soon as Luca entered him. He had to calm himself down. He had to be in control so he didn't hurt him by accident—despite his big talk, he didn't want to hurt anyone. Then Luca's hand moved to squeeze around Alistair's fingers, moving them for him as he pushed into him in one long stroke. The movement was so sudden that Alistair's breath was pushed from him and sparks began skipping across his field of vision. Immediately, Luca was moving inside him, hard and deep just like he'd asked, his free hand working Alistair's around his suddenly over-sensitized prick.

"Luca! Oh god, stop!"

He was losing his control, he could feel his muscles clenching all over, his orgasm eminent. If Luca didn't stop, Alistair would end up breaking him.

"Please! Please, I'm coming, stop!"

Luca didn't stop, driving harder into him instead, and in a moment of panic, needing to still the swell of ecstasy, he yanked his hands away from Luca's grasp and jabbed his elbow back into the man's ribs, harder than he'd meant. Hard enough to break bone. His heart stopped a second, but Luca didn't. He pressed down against his back and in the split second before the blinding, fuzzy light of orgasm washed over him, Alistair realized that he really, truly couldn't move.

He heard himself scream, felt his toes curl and his feet thrash as they sought purchase on the sheets, but as his muscles tightened around Luca, there was no shriek of pain, no miserable sound of bursting blood vessels. Luca only hammered into him harder, riding him through his orgasm. Alistair shook so hard he thought he might fall apart, helpless, hot tears of euphoria streaking his face. As the shaking stopped, Luca's steady thrusting slowed and he gave Alistair a few moments to catch his breath, his body still spasming and squeezing around him where they remained connected.

Luca lay with nearly his full weight on Alistair's narrow body, panting softly in his ear, and when the boy pushed against the mattress to get up, he found himself trapped under the man's chest.

"W-what happened to me? What'd you do?" He must have been fed sedatives at some point. He shivered in the face of his helplessness, trying to steady his breath. But when Luca chuckled low in his ear he felt his body tense, squeezing around the shaft that kept him speared to the mattress.

"I gave you everything you wanted, kitten. You wanted to be helpless, didn't you? And so here you are, trapped, pinned down while I fuck you."

"Y-you drugged me?" He couldn't deny the shiver of arousal that shook his body at the thought of being *truly* helpless under this man.

"No, love. You seem to forget that I work for Haven. I've been with them since I was fifteen. Just like you and your friends, I have my own secrets."

Luca's arms snaked around Alistair's chest, one hand moving up to hold him at the front of his throat, not squeezing, just keeping him steady, like a promise that he could hurt him and that he wouldn't all at once. Alistair's voice cracked as Luca slid slowly out of him, pausing as the head of his dick stretched him wider before starting a slow, torturous push back inside. The pace was so measured that Alistair thought he may cry, his arms trapped folded against his chest, held in place with one of Luca's powerful arms.

"They called me the boy of stone when I was a child," Luca said, his voice rumbling against his neck. "I am the proverbial immovable object, Alistair. Your strength will not move me, it will not hurt me. So I'm going to make every one of your fantasies come true."

Holding him maddeningly still, Luca finally sped up his powerful thrusts, his mouth kissing and biting the curve of Alistair's shoulder, drawing bruises on his freckled skin, and Alistair only sobbed in helpless pleasure, weakly begging for more when he could find his voice. He had never been driven to a second orgasm before, and as his body shook with the promise of one, he pressed his head back against Luca's hard shoulder.

"Oh god, Luca! I can't, I can't. Too—it's too much." He was incoherent, his vision clouding and his ears ringing as his orgasm tightened every muscle in his back, forcing him to bow in Luca's unyielding arms.

He heard the man growling something into his ear, but everything was coming through cotton now, and when he felt Luca's grip tighten around him, threatening to squeeze the very air from his lungs, the coil snapped, and he convulsed as a few weak threads of cum drew lines across the mattress, his body having little left to give. A few hard thrusts later, Luca stilled inside him, his body pulsing, marking him in places no one else would see.

When Luca's grip around him loosened, Alistair found himself unable to support even his head, and he shivered against the soiled mattress as Luca combed the hair away from his face. He wanted to laugh, basking in the immense glow of bliss, but his ribcage also shook against the threat of tears, his entire body overcome.

"You're perfect," Luca murmured into Alistair's ear as he waited several long moments before pulling himself out.

For a second, Alistair wanted to stop him, wanted to stay connected for a few more seconds. He was hot and freezing and lay spent on his stomach as the man behind him kissed lines over his shoulder and back.

"Stay still. I'll get a towel."

The air around him seemed cold as Luca retreated from the bed. What had just happened? Alistair had never considered that Luca could be a member of Haven the way he and his friends were. He'd always assumed that anyone with powers would be kept as prisoners the way he was, but Luca seemed to have free reign. But more importantly, why hadn't he said something? All those times that he'd flirted with Alistair—the minutes he'd spent watching Alistair touch himself in the shower—he could have just taken what he wanted. There was a thrill of fear in Alistair's gut that he'd never felt before. There was actually someone who, without the help of sedatives, could overpower him, *hurt* him even. It was terrifying, and thrilling all at once. He closed his eyes, trying to quiet his mind, when he heard a distant shrieking.

Jumping where he lay, he pushed himself up to one elbow and saw Luca, a towel in one hand, Alistair's phone in the other, standing in all his naked glory, smiling as he watched the recording.

"Oh my. You're even sexier on camera."

Alistair lunged for the other man, shouting for him to give the phone back, but his legs still shook, and they gave out the moment Alistair's full weight landed on them. Luca caught him with one arm draped and laughed as he dragged him back to the bed.

"Give me my phone back," Alistair demanded as he was dumped unceremoniously onto the bed.

"And pass up such a great show? Let me guess. You thought you'd show this to Marla? And then what? Were you hoping to be taken out? Or were you wanting me to be removed?"

Alistair glared at the bed sheets. "Either would have been fine."

"I'm hurt, you know." His grin didn't give his words any weight.

Alistair thought he should have called the man out, told him he knew about his secret conversation with Jett, and the secret town meeting he went to. But his plan had backfired on him. With his brain still reveling in the afterglow, his body still burning where Luca had touched him, he was even less willing to believe that Luca could be a traitor than he was that morning. He didn't want him to be the enemy.

Setting the phone down out of Alistair's reach, Luca put a knee on the bed, lowering himself down over Alistair again so he was propped up on one arm over him.

"Do you really want me removed *now*, Alistair?" Using the towel, he wiped the mess from the boy's chest and stomach. "Now that you know what I can do for you?"

"Sex isn't everything." Alistair was a little surprised to hear himself say that, but he believed it in that moment. He didn't just want Luca to fuck him, no matter how good it had been. He wanted to be able to *trust* Luca. He wanted Luca to care about him enough to tell him the truth.

There was a long pause, then Luca smiled at him, the expression soft, like the one he'd seen on the road the day before. "I'm glad you feel that way."

He brought a hand to Alistair's chin and for a second man leaned down like he would kiss the redhead. Instead, despite the way Alistair's eyes lowered, fixed on his lips, Luca pressed them to the boy's forehead.

"Just trust me, kitten."

Alistair had never felt as unsure of his own feelings as he did right then, lying naked on his teacher's bed.

28: BASTIAN

It was well into the morning when Bastian finally decided to leave his room. He'd stayed as long as he could stand, wanting to be there when—*if,* he reminded himself—Cole came back. But it was nearly nine o'clock and he'd not heard anything from his lover. Bastian slipped out the door after peeking through the curtains to ensure the coast was clear. Sabin and Berlin were staying only one door down, but he didn't want to risk being seen with his wings in full view. Berlin opened the door quickly once he knocked.

"It's about time," Sabin said. He'd obviously been waiting to do the glamour spell for them. "Wait, where's Cole?"

"Du siehst nicht so gut aus," Berlin muttered as he closed the door behind him.

"He left last night."

"What do you mean 'he left'? We're practically walled in, where could he have gone?" Sabin waved him over anyway, preparing to do the glamour spell while they talked.

"I'm not sure. We argued last night and he left. He said he needed time to figure out what he was going to do. I think he might leave me."

Sabin groaned. "That stupid boy. What did you fight about?"

"I don't even really know!" Bastian pushed his hands through his hair. "He's always been uncertain about us because of the stupid toxin thing. But I feel like he's keeping something else from me. And he won't tell me what it is. He doesn't trust me at all. I don't know what to do." He realized too late that he sounded hysterical, though he managed to regain some composure when both of his teammates looked at him like he'd lost it.

"Well, listen. I'm pretty sure I know what's gotten him all messed up here, and had you paid proper attention to him last night you would've probably noticed too." Sabin flipped through some tokens in a small canister, pulling out a tiny bit of wood with some markings carved into it.

"Excuse me? I pay *very* close attention to him."

"Well not the right kind of attention, apparently." Laying the paper-thin sliver of wood on his newly pierced tongue, the token caught fire there in his mouth and he blew lavender smoke over Bastian's wings. "*Recensere.*" He used his hand to guide the smoke around his wings, and slowly they vanished, as if being lost in a fog. "When we were putting those hairs you guys brought into the holy water, he was white as a sheet. He looked like he wanted to throw up."

"So?" Berlin's initial response seemed to give Bastian pause. If Berlin thought it didn't matter, then it probably *did.*

"I think he snuck one of his own hairs into the sample you guys gave me."

All three of them were quiet for a few moments before the realization seemed to dawn on both Bastian and Berlin at once.

"I think he's upset," Sabin continued, "because he finally got definitive proof of what he is."

"No." Bastian swallowed hard. "Marla said he wasn't a demon."

"No, Marla said she didn't *believe* in demons, though I've always known she was wrong on *that*. And besides, didn't we prove last night that they're real?"

"I knew it." Berlin seemed inappropriately excited. "I *told* you! He's a demon, that means *you're* an angel. And I'll bet *anything* you were kicked out of heaven for boning hell spawn."

"Berlin, this isn't the time for your stupid stories!"

"God." It was hard to tell if Berlin was even listening as he spun out of control into his own little world. "That means that you've probably *really* truly been in heaven. Let me touch you again. It's like an indirect Heaven kiss."

Berlin grabbed for Bastian, but the blond shoved back against him him so hard that the tattooed boy stumbled and looked annoyed.

"This isn't funny, Berlin!"

"Listen, Bastian." Sabin's voice was low and steady. "I wanted to do that test last night because I already had the suspicion that we might be dealing with demons. I've sensed powerful magic coming off the people of this town since we got here. I had a feeling it was demon magic, but I wanted to be a hundred percent sure. And, it's the same sort of magic I've sensed from Cole since I met him."

Bastian sunk onto the nearest bed, needing to sit down. "He's been saying from the beginning that he feels something evil inside him. And even *I* felt it when I first met him. I just thought... You know, I just figured it was because of how he ate. I thought the evil was from the damage he's done to people in the past to sustain himself. I never thought he was *actually* evil."

Sabin closed the box he'd gotten his glamour token from with a snap loud enough to make Bastian jump. "Well if that's how you feel, then you probably shouldn't bother going to look for him."

"What?"

"He probably left because he was afraid of you finding all this out. He probably thought you would assume he was evil if you knew, and here you are proving him right. So I guess it was a good thing he left when he did."

"Hey! That's not what I'm saying!"

"Really? Sure as hell sounds that way."

Bastian stared at his teammate for a long time. Wasn't that what he was saying? If it wasn't, then what *was* he saying?

"Look. Cole's a demon." Sabin tucked his box away, storing it beside a hundred other little boxes that now piled so high on the counter outside the bathroom that the mirror was nearly blocked. "We know it now. But Cole was also a demon yesterday, *before* we knew. He was a demon last week, and a month ago. He was a demon when you told him you were in love with him."

Bastian felt his heart rate pick up, mimicking the flutter he felt when he was close to Cole.

"He's exactly the same person now that he always has been. I know that he was my friend then and he's my friend now. For me, being a demon has nothing to do with it. What about you?"

Sabin was right. It didn't matter if Cole was a demon, or an angel, or a human. Cole was the one person who made his body ache with adoration. He couldn't imagine a life past that day, or mission, without him. If he wanted Cole to trust him, then he needed to remain steady. He needed to love him unconditionally, no matter what he may be.

"Will you help me find him?"

Sabin smiled at Bastian's new resolve. "Yeah, come on."

"Who knew Sabin was such a good pep talker," Berlin grumbled as he replaced his tank top with a long sleeved shirt. "When does the abstinence only seminar start?"

Sabin only smiled at him as he tied his shoes. "Don't be upset because my public speaking skills are higher than a third grader's. We can't all be stuck playing in the sand box."

"Oh, big smart witch kid. Where's the anonymous questions box? I want to ask you why my shitty roommate is being such a prick."

"I'll look by myself if this is how you guys are going to be." Bastian left the room, but, unfortunately, they both followed him.

Hoping he could get lucky a second time, Bastian first went to the revival tent, expecting to find Cole there like he had the day before. The white fabric billowed slightly in the wind, creating a steady thumping sound as the heavy material jerked against the metal poles holding it up. The rows of chairs were empty.

At least Berlin and Sabin seemed to be capable of getting along in public, but the harder they looked through the town, the more Bastian realized there wasn't much of a public to get along in front of. For a town bursting at the seams with extra people, the streets were dead. They saw a few people inside stores, talking to the workers behind the counters, but nobody was on the roads. Despite his feelings toward Cole, knowing what these people were made the situation all the more unnerving.

As they made their way further toward the center of town, they passed the church where they'd collected the holy water the day before. Like the rest of the town, it was quiet, but sitting on the small porch at the top of the stairs was Cole, his horns standing out in stark contrast to the darkness of his hair.

Relief burst inside Bastian's body, rushing down to his fingers and toes as he hopped the gate leading to the churchyard, too impatient to bother with the latch. "Cole!"

The other boy turned to look at him over his shoulder, dark circles hanging under his eyes. For a second, Bastian wanted to snatch his lover into his arms, squeeze all of the uncertainty out of him, but he stopped himself at the base of the steps. They both stared at each other for a long time, then Cole glanced back through the open doors of the church.

"It's pretty in there."

Looking past the exhausted boy's figure where he sat with his legs crossed, Bastian peered into the shadow of the church. He'd been in there briefly the day before, but hadn't paid much attention. The walls, floor, and ceiling were simple, bare planks. The pew benches were unembellished, and the podium at the front had no decoration. The only point of color was a small circle of stained glass, installed on the far wall just below the sharp angle of the pitched roof. It was hard to make out the design, but it shone with deep reds and blues, rays of gold radiating out from the center.

"It is," Bastian said, fighting his urge to shake Cole—demand to know where he'd been all night. From the look on his lover's face, he figured the boy needed a little longer to figure it out himself. "Cole, your horns..."

"It doesn't matter." He kept still, watching the window at the far end of the church. "We know what they are now, and they know what I am. I won't surprise anyone."

"You'll surprise Hartford if he comes back here." Bastian climbed the handful of steps between them.

"Not anymore. I was told he was taken care of last night." Cole chuckled through his nose as he looked at Bastian again, obviously guessing that his words might have elicited a certain amount of shock. "I mean he's become a vessel. They haven't hurt him or anything."

It was obvious that Cole had been in touch with one of the town members during the night, but at the moment, Bastian was more frightened by the empty look in his lover's eyes. Where he usually saw pinpricks of light—tiny pools of the universe—he saw nothing. Cole's eyes were dull, and Bastian couldn't help but wonder if he'd already lost him to that town.

"Cole. You look tired. Why don't we go back to our room? You can rest a while."

The other boy watched him for a minute, his eyes passing over his shoulder to look toward the road where Berlin and Sabin waited. When he looked at him again, Bastian saw tears gathering on his lashes.

Bastian opened his mouth, ready to tell Cole whatever he needed to hear, when his pocket buzzed. Cole had left his phone in the room the night before, but when Bastian looked over his shoulder he saw Berlin and Sabin both fishing their phones out of their pockets as well. With connection to the outside shut down by the quarantine, he felt his stomach sink as he swiped his screen.

It was a message from Milo: Emergency. Meet at community center.

29: ALISTAIR

Luca had won the struggle over the phone, something Alistair would have to work very hard to get used to. He'd pushed, shoved, squeezed, and even tried hitting him in order to get the phone back before his teacher had managed to send the video to himself. But Luca had stood stone-still, not even swaying as Alistair had done his worst. He had been completely steadfast. Even in broad daylight, walking down the sidewalk that led them to the auditorium, Alistair felt a shiver of arousal run up his back. Luca really was unshakable, and he really had just held him down and fucked him senseless.

It was hard to wrap his brain around, especially since Alistair rarely—if ever—considered sleeping with the same person a second time. Now, he felt like he'd hardly even scratched the surface of his desire for Luca.

"Have you talked to Marla yet?" Alistair needed to interrupt his own train of thought.

"About?" Luca had been walking quietly beside him, his hands in his pockets and his posture just a little more slouched than normal.

"About having the children removed from the quarantine." He tried not to let the annoyance show in his voice. Had Luca just said that to impress him? His gut twisted, and for a second he wondered if he'd walked right into Luca's trap. It wouldn't be the first time a guy had suddenly become less appealing after getting what he wanted.

"Oh." He stood up a little straighter. "No, I haven't had the chance."

Alistair bit his tongue. He didn't know how to tell him to hurry the fuck up without giving away the information they had about the town. Somehow, after the morning they'd had, it felt harder to keep it a secret. His face flushed. If anything, he should just be annoyed that his plan to get rid of Luca had backfired. Instead, he felt foolish since he was actually glad he'd failed. When had he started enjoying the other man's company so much?

No.

He took a breath. He couldn't let a bit of earth-shattering sex distract him from what he needed to do, which included getting the hell out of there. His plan to get Luca removed had failed. That was fine. He would just have to refocus his efforts. If he couldn't get out early, then he would need to speed up the whole mission. The sooner they took care of the people in the town, the sooner they could all get out of there. Of course, speeding things along would be harder if he wasn't able share their intel with Luca.

He wanted to pull his own hair out.

Why was everyone making this so complicated?

"Make sure to talk to her about it soon. If things get dangerous around here, it would be best if they weren't around."

Luca hummed a half-hearted answer and said "Yeah, I guess that would be for the best."

His words felt cold, especially after the few glimpses he'd allowed Alistair to have of the softer side he seemed to hide with his coy attitude.

Sharp words were forming on Alistair's tongue when the community center came into view. He hadn't considered how quiet the streets had been on their walk until he caught sight of a man shuffling into the open doors of the low, wide building. There was something about the man's gait as he walked that sent pin pricks down Alistair's arms. His spine straightened, and he picked up his pace a little.

"Luca, did you see that guy?" He didn't wait for his teacher as he jogged across the street and up the walkway to the glass doors. Before he'd gotten to the entryway, he heard screams funneled down the bare hallways, bouncing off the linoleum floors and drop ceilings. Cursing under his breath, Alistair sprinted into the building, his sneakers squeaking and the heels of Luca's shoes sounding behind him.

Entering the auditorium—a room usually humming with the sounds of kids talking—he felt the blood drain from his face. Children cowered in corners and ran in a scattered panic as adults from the town pursued them, the fronts of their shirts and dresses stained with the black, tar-like vomit Alistair had become far too acquainted with. Luca nearly crashed into him as he came to a stop behind him.

There were at least five of them—men and women from town who had turned into the gurgling, putrid monsters Alistair was becoming far too familiar with—each snatching at children who scurried out of their reach. In the back corner, Alistair saw a man he recognized immediately as the Mayor, his black-stained hands wrapped around Lakelyn's throat. The boy's body lay over the top of Shannon—one of the kids Alistair met when he'd visited Lakelyn's home. The girl was screaming, pinned under the weight of both Lakelyn and the Mayor.

Alistair blindly reached behind him just long enough to slap Luca's chest. "Call for help!" Then he took off across the auditorium. His hands crushed the bones in the mayor's arm as he wrenched it off the boy's neck. The man howled as he recoiled, one arm dangling crookedly as he turned his attention toward Alistair.

"Don't kill anyone!"

He heard Luca's words and glanced in his direction just in time to see him catch one of the possessed women by her throat as she rushed toward him. Alistair could tell, even from the distance, that he was not squeezing hard enough to hurt, but no matter how violently the woman fought, no matter how viciously she clawed at his arm which held her at length, Luca didn't budge, his skin didn't break—he didn't even flinch. He saw his teacher pull out his cell phone for help just before the mayor—his jaw crooked and gaping—lunged for him again.

Lakelyn lay on his side now, coughing and catching his breath as Shannon sobbed in his ear, shaking him to get up. She could have only been six, at most, and Alistair wondered—for the fraction of a moment before the mayor's good hand caught his shirt—what this might do to her in the future. Then his attention was pulled inexorably back to the black, gurgling cavity that had once been a human mouth.

Pain didn't seem to slow these demons down, and the mayor's broken arm dangled unused and forgotten at his side, even as he lurched and snapped his teeth at any exposed flesh he could reach. This was the greatest struggle Alistair ever faced in a fight. This was why he preferred fighting monsters instead of men. How could he fight this *human being* without destroying him?

For the time being, he would just have to keep him busy. Dodging the man's one good hand as it clawed for him, Alistair led him away from Lakelyn and Shannon. He had had to keep him occupied. He had to keep all of them occupied. Grabbing a pack of crayons he found on the floor, Alistair threw it toward one of the other adults. It was a much older lady, one he recognized from the parking lot dinner they'd been fed their first evening there. The crayons caught her in the side of the head, the corner drawing blood from her deteriorated skin, and then her black eyes turned to him.

Good. If I get them all chasing me, then Luca can get the kids out.

His teacher still had one of the vessels in his grip, which meant he only had two more. Ducking and dodging to keep himself just out of reach, Alistair led his two new friends through the auditorium, toward the men in pursuit of the older children. One of the vessels he tripped—which thoroughly captured his attention— and the other he clothes-lined. They would all be bruised pretty badly, but no one would be dead, and that was the best he could hope for.

As he led his small, unhappy parade of zombies toward the doors of the auditorium, he looked back toward Luca, who was no longer on his phone. He had the woman who had attacked him trapped now, wrapped in arms that wouldn't budge. He had the situation completely under control.

But he wasn't moving a muscle to do any more.

Alistair wanted to shout at him to get his ass in gear, to do *anything*, but when Luca looked at him, there was something cold in his stare. Alistair faltered for just a second under that gaze, and that's when the mayor caught a fistful of his hair and dragged him to the ground.

He'd never been particularly interested to know what it felt like to be inside a horror movie, but he was sure at that moment, that he knew. His eyes opened around the pounding light knocked loose when his head crashed into the floor—gurgling, screeching human shells descending on him, reaching and clawing for him.

"Luca!" He felt fingers break under his palms as he fended off their grasping hands. Every bone he felt snap struck him in his gut like an arrow of guilt. "Please! Do something!"

He managed to shield his face, but broken, grinding fingers continued to claw at him, and hot lines of pain rose up on his skin. If he fought back, he'd hurt them; if he did nothing, he wouldn't be making it out of the auditorium alive. It was hard to tell what the right choice was. It was hard to know whose life was worth more.

Just as he began to think that it was his responsibility to lie still and die obediently, noise erupted from the doors of the auditorium. It was hard to tell what was happening as the woman—whose hand was crumpled yet still somehow grasping at him with raw, exposed bone—was yanked away from him by some unseen hand. Another vessel toppled away from him, rolling a few feet away and not moving to get back up.

As the halo of grasping hands broke around Alistair, he was able to see his teammates swarming into the room, black lines drawing themselves in arcs through the auditorium, binding the townspeople and forcing them to the ground. Cole and Bastian appeared at Alistair's side, and Milo covered them, a sleek black pistol in hand. It was obvious by the low "thp" sound coming from the gun that it was shooting darts and not bullets. Whatever was in those bullets had enough punch to knock one of the retreating men off his feet. By the time Alistair was sitting upright, he saw the final, putrid citizen dropping to the ground, turned to a limp sack of meat within the binding of Berlin's slithering tattoos.

Even after so many years, he still loved watching those black lines as they retreated, snaking their way across the boy's dark skin, finding the scarred lines of his body where they would settle and remain until called for again. When they were back in place, Berlin helped Milo check on the unconscious townspeople. Cole was asking if he was okay, his voice worried as Bastian pressed some sort of fabric to his bleeding arms. But he didn't even feel the pain, every thread of his senses reaching across the auditorium, past Sabin—who was dragging a limp woman toward their teammates—to Luca. The man's eyes watched Sabin for a moment before falling on Alistair, and just like before, something was closed off about them. Alistair felt stupid, suddenly, for letting himself feel different now that he'd felt Luca's body on him—now that he'd felt Luca inside him.

Why didn't you help me?

He was foolish for even thinking the question. He couldn't even tell yet if Luca was on their side at all, why would he expect the man to put himself in danger to help him? Because he'd been flirtatious? Because he'd been kind?

Because he'd made love to him?

"Come on, Alistair." Cole's hands were surprisingly persistent as he pulled the taller boy to his feet. "Milo and the others have this under control. We need to get you cleaned up."

"Wait." Alistair finally felt his head begin to settle. "I have to check on Lakelyn." His eyes scanned the room, and he found Sabin sitting with some of the kids, one of the smaller boys in his arms, sobbing into his shoulder. They all huddled together, most of them crying or scurrying away when Berlin passed them. Unsurprising considering his powers were the flashiest. In the crowd, he saw Lakelyn, his arms wrapped around Shannon, rubbing her back consolingly.

"They're shaken up right now," Bastian said, blocking his way, even though he knew Alistair could move him if he wanted. "Let's go find the doctor so he can have a look at all of them."

It was obvious that he wanted the doctor to look at Alistair first, and he would have argued if the heat of pain hadn't started radiating up his arms again.

30: ALISTAIR

The small supply closet had seemed cramped when Alistair had been inside it with three other people, but now, with the whole team packed inside, it was downright claustrophobic. Berlin sat on a shelf at the back, Sabin sat cross-legged on the small writing desk that hadn't been consumed by Milo's computer setup, and the rest of them stood shoulder-to-shoulder behind Milo and his computer screen. Jett was missing, though Luca said he was taking care of something for him. Alistair had thought to press his teacher for more information about their missing teammate, but was too distracted to think on it. It seemed to be the same for the others.

Both Marla and Venja filled the screen, wearing black uniforms that looked similar to those worn by Haven guards. While their faces were drawn and serious, Marla's lacked the sort of worry Alistair could see from his own house mother.

In the hotel room the night before, they had all talked about keeping their findings a secret until they knew where the loyalty of their new teammates might lie, but after the attack on the children, they'd agreed through stolen whispers that they should let Marla know. If she knew what they were up against, then maybe she would be able to give them some way to handle the situation that didn't involve calling in the Vatican.

"Well if they all chose this place to congregate then they must have a leader," Marla said. "And if they have a leader, then they probably have a goal."

Alistair could hear Berlin grumbling behind him. "Besides starting the apocalypse?"

"More than that," Milo seemed comfortable knocking ideas back and forth with Marla, so the others let him do his thing. "We need to find a way to reverse the infestation. Keeping them sedated will work in a pinch, but we need a way to get whatever's inside them out without harming the person."

Alistair knew Milo was speaking in general terms, but he still felt a sting in his gut. Of course they needed a way to fight them without hurting anyone, but he knew that any one of his teammates could have done more to help those people than he had. He thought about the horrendously broken bones he'd watched the doctor fuss over, and the look of fear on the man's face as he'd sent them out to the quarantine line to receive better treatment. Alistair wondered if their cover was completely blown at this point. Then again, with the number of turned citizens, it was hard to tell if they were fooling anyone anymore.

"I think you've all done a fine job of keeping those people safe." Venja's voice eased something in Alistair, something she'd always had the power to do. He knew that, while she was addressing the group as a whole, those words were meant for him.

Everyone, on both sides of the camera, was quiet for a few moments. If they couldn't find a way to de-possess these people, then nothing would truly be resolved. For what felt like the hundredth time since their fight in the auditorium, Alistair's eyes found their way to Luca's profile. He was solemn, his eyes slightly downcast. He had called for backup. What else could Alistair expect from him? Still, he felt like there should have been more.

"It might be prudent for us to see what these things want." Marla's tone was grim, but resolute, and Berlin immediately blew up in response.

"You mean we're negotiating with demons now?" The tattooed boy's disgust mirrored what Alistair was feeling, and he was glad *someone* was willing to speak up. "What we need to do is get some priests in here that are trained for this sort of thing. We're a monster cleanup crew. We're not qualified for this shit."

"We know this is a bit outside the norm for you guys." Venja was playing Good Cop, like she always did. "But until we can get someone else inside, we need to have a plan."

"If we're worried about the safety of these people, then we need to have the kids removed." Alistair didn't raise his voice, but the others grew quiet while they waited for their teachers' responses.

"I'm afraid the risk of removing anyone who isn't seriously injured is too dangerous."

"Are you shitting me?" Alistair pushed his way to the front of the group, so he was leaning over Milo's shoulder. "You just said we need to keep these people safe. None of the kids are possessed and they're in very *obvious* danger here."

"We can't know that for sure." Marla had the soft finality to her voice that he heard sometimes when being scolded.

"So taking the obviously possessed ones is fine because they have a broken arm, but these innocent kids aren't allowed out? For Christ sake, they're *living* with some of those monsters."

"I'm sorry, Alistair. But if you're that worried, then funnel that passion into the mission. We need to figure out what they want *now,* so we can get this mess cleared up." Beside her, Venja looked uncertain. If anyone would want to keep children safe, it was Venja, but somehow she seemed willing to bend to whatever Marla wanted.

"This is ridiculous."

"That's enough, Alistair. You guys have my orders: find out what they want. If we can give it to them, then we might be able to clear this up without anyone else getting hurt."

Alistair clenched his teeth. How did she always manage to say things that felt like barbs aimed right at him?

"Luca." She seemed unconcerned by any offense the redhead might be feeling. "You have your orders. Locate their leader. Find out what they want and negotiate the best deal possible."

"Right."

"The others don't seem aggressive, so continue as you have been. They likely know that you aren't college students, but if they're willing to stave off violence, then we'll meet them on that."

Some murmuring passed through their cramped group, but no one else spoke up for real.

"Milo, contact me directly if there are any changes."

"Yes, ma'am."

"Be safe." Venja's words felt like a desperate line she was throwing out to them before the connection was lost.

The room was quiet for a long time, though Alistair couldn't tell if the others were thinking the same thing. How could she think it was okay to leave kids like Lakelyn and Shannon trapped in here with these monsters? Twice, already, these possessed *things* had targeted the community center. It was starting to feel like it was all on purpose.

If he couldn't get the kids out, he would at least remove them from the awful, cramped house they were living in. Shoving his way through his teammates, Alistair left the small room, ignoring the calls for him to wait.

He'd just made it to the street outside the shop when Luca caught him by the arm, narrowly avoiding the bandages wrapped around the wounds he'd gotten.

"Let go of me."

"Where are you going?"

"To help the kids, since no one else seems interested in taking care of them." He tried to wrench his arm out of the man's grip, his guts running cold as he realized he couldn't.

222

"You know that's not true, Alistair."

"Yeah? Then what was going on back in the auditorium? Huh? You sure did a whole lot of standing around for someone interested in protecting *anyone*." He'd not meant to bring that up. That wasn't even the real problem. He should have focused more on the big picture, but instead, his feelings were prickling and raw over the way Luca had just stood back and watched him be dragged to the floor by monsters.

Luca looked taken aback for a second, but frowned. "You're right. I should have done more." He finally released the younger boy, who stumbled without the resistance anymore. "The kids will be fine, though. Once we give their leader what he wants, everything will be fine."

A vague sense of disgust passed over Alistair, and for a second he thought that this wasn't the man he'd met, or even the man he'd slept with, any more. He'd imagined Luca being much more righteous than this, much more willing to fight the system. But there he was, bowing down to Marla the way everyone else did.

"Whatever. You guys can go kiss their asses all you want. If Marla won't let the kids leave, then I'm taking them back to the motel with me. I refuse to let them stay in a house with any more of those monsters."

Luca didn't chase after him this time. It disappointed him a little, but didn't matter. It was stupid for him to let the closeness he'd shared with Luca color his expectations. It hadn't meant anything. They hadn't even kissed. He would do what he thought was right, and after everything was over, Luca would leave again, and Alistair would forget about him, just like he'd forgotten about the other trysts he'd had in the past.

31: BASTIAN

Walking back to the motel seemed strange after the conversation they'd had with Marla. If it hadn't been clear before, it was now—whatever was possessing the people of this town knew they were on their scent. Considering they were dealing with demons and monsters, he thought there would be more of a climax at this point. If the other members of the town were possessed, and had just seen a few of their own turn into those...*creatures,* wouldn't they want to do something to cover their tracks? What were they waiting for?

"Feels weird," Berlin said, mimicking Bastian's thoughts. "Shouldn't we be going after the leader or something? I don't like heading back to that stupid motel for the night. This shouldn't be the time for sleeping."

The clean up after the attack on the community center had taken nearly the whole day, and now the sun was low in the sky.

"Well, if Marla wants us to negotiate, then we're sort of at a standstill until we can figure out what they want." Milo sounded matter-of-fact, but there was something in his tone that suggested even he didn't agree with their absent leader.

As had become habit, Bastian glanced at his lover, always seeking to gauge his comfort level whenever Milo was nearby. But as he looked at his black-haired boyfriend, he saw something far more despondent in his posture. The boy jumped a little as Bastian slid his fingers around Cole's chilled hand. As if he were reliving the argument they'd had in the motel room the night before, Bastian thought his boyfriend's eyes looked flat, somehow—those little pinpricks of light he always saw there gone, burnt out.

Their comrades were still discussing their leader's choice, but in that moment, it didn't seem to matter very much.

"Guys, we'll catch up with you in a bit." Bastian didn't wait for his friends to question his choice before turning off the shoddily paved road that would take them back to their quarters. From behind him he heard Luca shout for them to be careful, probably just to fulfill his responsibilities as their caretaker on this mission.

Cole questioned him weakly, but didn't resist as Bastian led the other boy through town, trying to find someplace quiet where they could talk. Even as the sun was setting, casting a yellow light down empty streets that should be teeming with the people who Bastian knew were bustling inside the quiet buildings, it was impossible to feel alone. As the days had gone on, he had seen fewer and fewer people in town, making him think that things would be coming to a head soon, whether they were ready for it or not.

"Bastian, where are we going?"

"I just want to talk in private for a bit." He wasn't sure where he was going either, but when he saw the white fluttering of the revival tent through the buildings, he figured it was as good a place as any. Before they finished crossing the grass to the shade of the pavilion, Cole stopped, digging his heels into the sod.

"I don't want to go in there."

Bastian looked at the rows of chairs and then back at his lover, the boy's dark brows knit softly on his forehead. "Alright." He held Cole's free hand with his so they stood face to face. He watched the other boy for a few seconds until Cole's eyes wavered and fell to the hem of his shirt. His body ached seeing his lover look so uncertain in front of him. He had to help him, and at that moment, supporting him was all he could do.

"Cole, I want to apologize again. What I said last night was wrong. Thinking I have the right to force you to tell me anything is *wrong*. If you need time, or space, or anything else, I'll give it to you." He could hear his own voice strain under his effort to hold himself to that standard. "But I love you, Cole. I know there's something happening, something to do with this town that's changed things. Please, will you let me help?"

Bastian's heart hammered harder than it had when they'd been fighting those creatures in the auditorium. His hands shook where he held onto Cole's, but he didn't pull away.

"Please, Cole."

He knew that if he let Cole continue spiraling down whatever path he'd set himself on, the boy would eventually slip out of reach. He squeezed his hands, urging him to feel the panic brewing inside him. Urging him to feel how desperately he needed to hold onto him. Finally, Bastian saw Cole's jaw tighten just a little, followed by the telltale pools growing in his eyes.

"Please." Bastian's voice was so quiet he wondered if Cole heard him that time, but the boy leaned forward, pressing his forehead against Bastian's chest, hiding the small sniffle he heard.

"I talked to one of them last night." Cole's voice was weak where he spoke against the Bastian's shirt.

"One of them? You mean one of the townspeople?"

"No. I mean, yes. But I wasn't talking to the person. I was talking to the demon who was inside him. They really are possessed, and they're possessed by people like me."

Bastian moved his hands to his lover's shoulders, rubbing his arms in an attempt to sooth him. "No matter what, you aren't the same, Cole. We both know you wouldn't hurt people the way they are."

"But I *am* the same. I am, Bastian. I put my hair in with the others. It reacted just the same way. I'm a demon. I'm evil, I can't stay here with you guys. I don't want to hurt you, I just—"

"Cole, stop it!" Holding him tight by his shoulders, Bastian gave him one small shake, startling him at least enough to stop the hysteria that was winding up inside him. The boy blinked tears from his eyes and Bastian lowered his voice as he continued. "Listen to me. Sabin knew you did that. But he'd suspected from the moment he met you that you might be a demon. We all have, haven't we? Whether Marla wanted to say it out loud or not, we all knew to some degree." He watched as Cole's face began to crumple under his building despair, but Bastian smoothed his hands over both of the boy's cheeks, threading his fingers into the hair between his ear and the base of his horn. "We knew, Cole, but we're all still here, aren't we?"

It felt a little cheap to recycle the words Sabin had given him that morning, but he needed Cole to understand. He needed those words to give Cole the same confidence they'd given him. Cole was silent for a while, his hands coming up to hold onto the sides of Bastian's shirt as his eyes dropped again."

"There's more, though." His words were soft, his voice flat as the hopelessness seemed to continue consuming him. "All of these people who have been possessed or hurt, it's all because of me. It's my fault."

Bastian's head fell back, despite his best efforts to stay supportive. He wasn't sure what else he could say to break Cole out of his looping cycle of self-hatred. "Cole, Liebe. You can't keep blaming yourself for everything. Not everything is your fault."

"You don't understand, Bastian." When Cole looked at him again, his tears were gone, replaced by a heavy-lidded expression of exhaustion. "They're here to get me. Marla wanted to know why they were here, and what we could give them to make them go away. It's me. They're here to bring me home."

In any other circumstance. Bastian may have thought Cole was just panicking again—letting his paranoia get the better of him—but the ice that dumped into his gut told him that wasn't the case anymore.

"Who told you that?"

"Blackholly." Cole shook his head. "No. The demon *using* Blackholly. He's called Mammon. He told me everything. He told me that they were sent here to bring me home because I'm their family." Tears gathered in the boy's eyes again. "He told me if I went home that I wouldn't have to feed on anyone anymore."

"Cole—"

"He said the sooner I go, the sooner these people would be released. If I had just gone with him this morning, then those people in the auditorium would have been fine. No one would have gotten hurt. If I had just gone with him—" The tears that overtook the barrier of his lashes traveled familiar trails down his reddened cheeks, and Bastian struggled to find his voice for a second.

The whole world seemed to be slowing down for a few seconds, like it was losing its spin, leaving a lurching feeling in his stomach.

"You aren't *going* to go with him. Right Cole?" It felt like everything really had stopped as he waited for his lover's answer. He wasn't even sure if his heart was beating any more when the boy pressed his forehead into his chest again.

"No, I'm not."

Bastian felt faint as the lie reverberated inside his head.

The last rays of light from the setting sun disappeared under the horizon, and for a second, Bastian felt like it had taken his heart with it.

32: ALISTAIR

It was dark by the time Alistair reached the small, fenced house. He took the steps of the porch in two long strides, and with one shove, the door swung open despite the lock Alistair heard splinter the wood of the frame. Inside, cattycornered from the entrance in the unlit living room, stood the parents. Shoulder-to-shoulder, forming a tight circle in the middle of the room, the adults watched each other, not sparing even a second to glance in Alistair's direction, even after his noisy intrusion.

A shiver ran up Alistair's spine—a feeling that might keep him from enjoying horror movies any more. He waited for several long seconds in the doorway, waiting for them to react, waiting for them to even notice him, but their eyes only passed between one another. No one moved.

Taking the chance, he began edging past them, watching their faces as he crept toward the hallway. Their jaws were loose, almost to the point of hanging open, but their eyes were alert, intense. A queasy feeling rocked his insides when he realized that this is what the townspeople must be doing now that they'd retreated from the streets. They *knew* that Alistair and the others knew what they were, and they clearly saw no reason to hide it anymore.

Trying to shake off the feeling of spiders running over his skin, Alistair strode past them, his feet loud on the hollow floor of the raised house, the whole structure vibrating under the pounding of his feet.

"Lakelyn!" The back of the house was quiet—quieter than it should ever be with 12 kids.

When he pushed open another locked door in the back, a wave of shrieks erupted from the four children left in the small bedroom. Lakelyn was heaving one of the smaller kids out the open window. They all froze, Shannon's eyes peeking in over the window sill.

"What are you doing?"

Whether Lakelyn liked Alistair any more or not, he didn't seem to see him as a threat, because the boy just huffed, then finished pushing the four-year-old out the window, Shannon waiting to help him down to the ground. He was waving one of the other kids over when Alistair reached for him.

"Lakelyn! Tell me what's going on?"

The boy slapped Alistair's hand away from him before he could make contact, taking a definitive step away from him.

"Don't touch me!" They were both quiet a second, his words striking something inside Alistair that made him feel ill. "And shouldn't I be the one asking that question? About this whole damn town? About *you* and your *classmates?*"

Alistair wasn't surprised that their cover was blown after the fight they'd had in the auditorium.

"Are you like them?" The boy's voice was quieter now, a tiny tremor making it sting all the more.

"Of course we're not, Lakelyn. We're here to keep you safe. We came here because we knew something was going on. We've only wanted to help you."

"What are you? What are *they?*"

"I guess... we're sort of like superheroes. But the grownups in this town are something much worse." He didn't want to scare him more than he already was. "But we can reverse it. And your mom and all the other parents are going to come back and be good as new." He wasn't sure if he was lying or not, but he knew he was expressing his own true intentions. It seemed to satisfy the children a little, because the tension in Lakelyn's shoulders seemed to relax. "Now, please, tell me where you're going."

Lakelyn watched him for a few more seconds, as though he were trying to decide if he believed in superheroes, but after the things he'd seen that day, his skepticism must have been weakened. "We're leaving," was all Lakelyn said as he picked another child up, lifting her high enough that she could swing her legs over the ledge.

"There's a quarantine, Lakelyn. They won't let you leave. Come with me instead. You can come back to my room with me. I'll keep you guys safe."

"No offense, but I saw you break the mayor's arm like it was made of toothpicks." He was pushing the last child out the window. "I don't want anything to do with whatever bullshit is going on between you and the grownups." With the last child lowered down to the ground, Lakelyn jumped up onto the windowsill himself, prepared to jump out into the night. Alistair reached for him again in a moment of panic, not wanting to let him slip away, but the boy yelped and fumbled his way out the window before he could lay a single finger on him.

Is he really that scared of me now?

It wasn't surprising, but as he leaned out the window, it hurt seeing the untrusting eyes the children turned up to him, huddled together in the grass, looking smaller in the dark of a new night than they had a moment ago.

"See ya." Lakelyn had a hint of disappointment in his voice as he took one kid's hand and led him away from the house.

This wasn't anything new—seeing those he cared about, those who used to find a safe place with him, turn their back. It was a pain he shared with all the boys who lived in Haven—

rejection, fear, suspicion. But whether or not Lakelyn would ever look at him again the way he had behind those silos, Alistair had to stop him. Crawling through the window, he jumped down to the grass and hurried after the small pack of quiet children. They walked quickly, huddled together in a lump of tiny, shaking bodies, following a road that would lead them out of town. And there wasn't much town for them to get through.

"Lakelyn!" Alistair jogged up to where the oldest boy was leading the pack. "Look, I know you're scared. But trust me, staying with us is your safest option. Please, just come back with me. We won't let any of these—"

"No! I'm tired of just sitting back and letting everyone else make choices for me. I let my mom drag me here. I let the adults force me to take care of everyone. I let you trick me into thinking you were like me..." His voice trailed off a little, the light from the rising moon illuminating the slight blush on his cheeks. "I got into this mess because I didn't stand up for myself. Well that's what I'm doing now. They took my mom out on this road. I'm going to go out the same way she did."

"She went out on a *stretcher,* Lakelyn. I'm serious. What you're doing is dangerous."

"What are they going to do? Shoot us? We're kids. If they let anyone out it's gonna be us, and then you guys can be free to do whatever superhero bullshit you want. But we're done."

In all likelihood, the boy was probably right, but for some reason, Alistair couldn't let go of this kid. He could let him out of his side. He would be the one to save him, and he would prove that he could do something without destroying what mattered most. "I'm not *joking!* You need to *stop!*" In a moment of desperation, Alistair snatched the boy's wrist up in his hand, forcefully separating him from the other children.

Lakelyn stumbled as Alistair dragged him away from the others, a cry rising from his throat. When Alistair released him, the blond pulled his quickly bruising wrist to his chest and staggered away, his eyes huge.

Alistair let go of him like the boy's tiny wrist had scalded him, his hands shaking.

"Just stop!" The cool light reflected in the tears that formed in the boy's eyes. "Stop trying to help me!" They looked at each other for a long time. "This is what happened to Felix, isn't it? You hurt him?" His voice was quiet, and he didn't sound like he was waiting for an answer.

"Lakelyn, please; I just want to keep you safe."

"We'd be safer away from you and your friends, I think."

Lakelyn was just a kid, just some horny thirteen-year-old boy he'd met a few days ago, but somehow, in that moment, the rejection struck something deep inside Alistair. His soul hurt under this little boy's distrustful gaze.

Waving for the other kids, Lakelyn began leading them away again, the road continuing past the last houses into the field of corn. Swallowing the lump that felt like broken glass, Alistair followed them, determined to do what was right, even if his chances of redemption were gone.

"Stop following us!" Before Alistair could catch up, the children broke into a run, the youngest stumbling to keep up.

Then a spotlight landed on them, and the blond began waving his arms over his head. "Here! We're here, help us!"

"Lakelyn, stop!" Alistair pushed himself into a sprint.

"Please, you need to let us out! We're not sick!"

Knowing that it would be harder to catch Lakelyn than the others, Alistair forced himself between the younger children and their leader. He spread his arms out in front of them, blocking their path, and watched them stumble to a halt, clutching at each other and drawing in a few of the littlest ones as they caught up. He didn't care if they were scared of him anymore. He would be their worst nightmare if it meant they stayed safe.

"Move and I'll break your little necks, you got it?"

They froze under his gaze, some of them on the brink of tears when the crack of a rifle shattered their sniffling and the rustling of corn. Screams erupted from the children as Alistair whipped around in time to see Lakelyn topple to the ground, his legs tangled under his body and a fine red mist dissipating in the moonlight.

Moments passed, the sound of the hysterical kids seeming to drift away, muffling out as though Alistair were sinking into the ocean, cold pressing in around him. It wasn't until the spotlight which had stayed trained on Lakelyn's body moved to Alistair that he realized he'd been walking toward the boy.

Lakelyn lay on his stomach, his arms splayed out to either side, his legs in crooked lines and his cheek pressed into the road. A single red bullet hole marked the smooth skin over the boy's left eyebrow, his blue eyes open and staring unseeing at the asphalt. The pale, blond hair that haloed his head seemed to glow under the guards' light as blood pooled around the gaping exit wound at the back of his head.

Alistair had seen dead bodies before, but this one was not processing in his brain. He was still staring at Lakelyn's face, trying to accept that the boy he'd met and talked with—the boy who had asked his advice and who had kept children he'd not known before moving to Trumbull safe—was dead.

"You have ten seconds to move away from the quarantine line. Failure to cooperate will be met with lethal force if necessary." The tinny sound of the speaker shook the silence of that tiny road, and Alistair's ears rang with the violent fury that was condensing inside him.

Raising a hand to shield his eyes from the spotlight, Alistair stepped over the boy's splayed legs. "Did you give *him* that warning?" His throat stung with the pitch of his voice. "Huh? Did you tell him you were going to fucking murder him?" The ground beneath him began passing faster, his feet moving from a walk to a jog, then to a run as his eyes locked onto the base of one of the towers. It was made of metal poles, like a repositionable hunting station. Massive black trucks blocked the road, and Alistair saw the scurrying of lights as he ran toward the base of the turret. He could demolish it all.

There were no more warnings.

Before Alistair could reach his target, he heard a sound much softer than the horrible discharge that had taken Lakelyn's life, but the pain that erupted from his shoulder knocked his feet out from under him. He was aware of his head smacking the gritty, cracked road for only a few seconds before things went black.

33: BASTIAN

Cole's lie could have meant any number of things. Knowing something is a lie never got him closer to knowing what the truth was. It could have simply been the boy's uncertainty that tinted his words, or it could be that Cole planned to leave him. Bastian didn't have the courage to ask. Instead, they walked silently back to their room, and as they crossed the threshold, Bastian wondered if it was the last time they would share a space like this.

When he refused to let go of Cole, his lover turned to look at him again. One small, cold hand moved to Bastian's cheek.

"I love you, Cole." He wasn't sure what else he could say to him to make him stay, but the anguish that rolled inside his body must have shown on his face.

"I know," was all Cole said as his fingers hooked behind the blond's neck, pulling him down into a quiet, sad kiss.

The soft press of his lips hurt, and in an attempt to force the boy to stay with him, Bastian's arms wound around his narrow body. Unlike the night before—when Cole had seemed scared and unsure—Bastian sensed a matching desperation in his lover now. Thin arms wound around his neck and his mouth opening to meet

Bastian's tongue. For a moment, Bastian thought the soft sounds the boy made as he tried to catch his breath were sobs.

The bed bowed beneath their weight as Bastian lowered Cole onto the scratchy comforter. If this was going to be their last time, he wished he could have at least given him someplace more comfortable—someplace that could accurately represent what he truly thought Cole deserved. He knew—in those quiet moments marked only by their shared breath—that Cole may never believe he deserves anything more than that drab, rundown motel room.

Desperate hands pulled at the hem of Bastian's shirt, and the blond rose up on his knees long enough to yank it off. His heart hammered as he watched Cole squirm out of his own clothes with matching fervor. When Bastian lowered himself against his lover again, he was drawn in by hands that seemed starving.

"Cole, wait." His chest ached as soft lips kissed across the corner of his mouth and down over his chin. "It's been a while since you've fed. Slow down a little." The boy was too frantic, and Bastian knew the last time he'd fed his lover properly was before their departure for Trumbull. Bastian would give him anything he needed, but he didn't want to confuse his lover's frantic hunger for something connected to the heart. He had to know that his words and his actions were being felt properly.

Cole's hands moved to either side of Bastian's face, drawing his eyes down to lock with his.

"Milo gave me medicine," Cole said, his voice soft and quivering. "I took some last night. I don't want you to feed me, Bastian. I want you to make love to me. Make me feel it."

Bastian's chest twisted under the sorrow—barely concealed by arousal—in Cole's voice. They had nearly died together; they'd felt the bond of another life together; they'd embraced dozens of times, and yet Cole hadn't *truly* felt the love Bastian had for him. He pressed his forehead against Cole's, tears stinging his own eyes. What could he possibly do to make him feel what he'd been trying to give him all along?

Not sure what else he could possibly say, Bastian cradled the boy's head and kissed him. They both seemed to take a moment to savor the feel of the other—the shape and pliancy of yielding mouths, the heat as tongues touched then twined together. As they each drew the other closer, Bastian tried to transmit the adoration, the tenderness, the *yearning* he felt for his wavering lover.

There was no teasing this time—no suggestive words used to make Cole blush. There were only gripping hands which drew the other closer. As pale legs spread for him, Bastian found the boy's opening soft to the touch already. He'd learned early on that their bodies were not made the same way. This is how Cole fed, so of course his body would open up—would heat up and relax in self-preparation. This is what Cole was made to do. As Bastian slid one finger into him, watching the boy's head fall back in satisfaction, he hurt—because this is what Cole hated most about himself.

Working a second finger into the mewling boy, then a third, Bastian held himself up on one elbow, kissing his lover's face and his open, gasping lips. He murmured his love over and over like a prayer, hoping that if he said it enough then maybe Cole could one day love himself even half as much as Bastian did.

When Bastian's name slipped from Cole's lips in a soft, whispered plea, the blond obeyed, moving over the boy's splayed body which wound around him in acceptance. Bastian's wings folded over them, creating a sanctuary of feathers, shrinking their world down to where their bodies were meeting. Cole arched against him as Bastian felt the softened ring of muscle open up for him. He groaned low in his throat as his lover's heat enveloped him, tremors passing over the pale skin he explored with his fingertips.

Buried to the hilt inside the horned boy, Bastian traced his fingers up the curve of his waist, his thumbs brushing peaked nipples as his fingers thrummed over his ribs. He watched Cole's eyes flutter as his reddened lips parted in an attempt to catch his breath. His hands paused at his chest for only a moment before continuing their journey up under the boy's arms, guiding the supple limbs up over his head. Soft skin, thin wrists, cool and trembling fingers—Bastian laced their hands together and pressed them into the mattress, leaning down until their chests touched and their lips passed over each other. Their shared kiss was slow as they savored the feel of their bodies being connected.

"I'd be with you forever if you'd let me." Bastian's whisper reverberated in the shell of his wings.

"I know, Bastian." His voice was weak, cracking slightly as his body clenched and shivered. "I want that too—"

Bastian closed the distance between them, stealing the other boy's breath before he could continue—before he could give him any reason to leave. He wouldn't let him say it out loud. Instead, Bastian swallowed the other boy's cries as he slid almost completely out of him before pushing back in with one strong roll of his hips.

Cole moaned and squirmed where he was pinned beneath the larger boy, his legs wrapping around his waist, his hands squeezing his lover's where they were held above his head. Bastian set a maddeningly slow pace, refusing to let either of them stray too close to their climax. Minutes passed, fading in and out of flurries of movement punctuated with rests where Bastian let his desperate lover come down off his high. As long as this didn't end, they wouldn't have to make a decision.

Bastian's restraint was growing weak, though. As he left a trail of purple kiss marks across his lover's neck, he felt his end come onto him suddenly. Releasing Cole's hands, he wound his arms around the boy's ribcage, squeezing him tight enough that he may break. When Cole's nails bit the back of his neck where he had gripped him, he knew the other boy was doomed as well.

He breathed in the scent of Cole's skin and sweat, moaning deep against the crook of his neck as he buried himself as far as he could manage inside him. The sweet sound of Cole's cry and the helpless shuddering of his body underneath him made Bastian's heart ache. As stars burst behind his own eyes, he felt Cole shoot wet ribbons of cum between them. Before he'd even caught his breath, Bastian moved one hand to touch the slick traces of their lovemaking. He needed to feel the evidence of Cole's ecstasy— needed to know that he was the one who gave him this feeling.

Neither of them tried to separate, but after several long minutes, Cole's hands came to Bastian's cheeks, guiding his face up to look him in the eyes. Then he kissed him, long and slow and chaste. Bastian tried not to guess whether the sweet kiss meant "goodbye."

34: ALISTAIR

The window in the motel was still dark when the pain in Alistair's shoulder brought him around. For a second he thought he was bleeding out on the rented bed, but when he found his limbs numb and weighted, he realized what had happened. He'd not been shot at all. The soldiers had used a bullet on the innocent boy trying to get help, but had switched to tranquilizers for him.

A different, deeper sort of pain twisted Alistair's guts as the image of Lakelyn's body came tumbling back into his mind, the rifle blast echoing in his ears. A low, keening sound like something from a dying animal filled the room, and a moment later Alistair realized that sound was coming from him. Why hadn't he done something sooner? Why hadn't Marla evacuated them when she had the chance?

Tears dampened the hair at Alistair's temples as he lay helpless again, waiting for the strength in his limbs to return. He might as well stay that way, he thought, staring at the ceiling. He did about as much good either way. He could feel the weight of his misery pressing him into the bed, but when the door opened, letting in a grey light of morning—when Alistair saw Luca's broad figure approach him—he finally crumpled under that weight.

"Luca." The warbling, pathetic sob that escaped him as he said his teacher's name would have mortified him if not for the pain he felt. "Luca." He tied to raise his arms, wanting the larger man to collect him, to hold him close and drive out the misery he felt.

"Shh." The brunette sat on the edge of Alistair's mattress, one hand moving to brush the hair back from his forehead. "Just rest a bit longer."

"They shot him." Somehow, Luca's presence shattered whatever composure had been left, and now Alistair's ribs ached and shook around his sobbing. He wanted to wind himself around Luca, to let the man protect him from the pain that was threatening to tear his brain apart. Heat radiated from his shoulder, but in that moment he would have taken any physical pain over the ache in his heart. "Luca, help me."

"I know, Alistair. But sometimes casualties are part of the mission." There was something distant about the way Luca watched him. Alistair hoped it was his own form of mourning that dulled the gleam he normally saw in his eyes, but somehow the man leaning over him seemed too cold, too distant. Even the way he dressed seemed wrong. Instead of a button up shirt, he wore a fitted black t-shirt, black pants, and a gun holster around his shoulders. Despite the clothes that said he was preparing for something, despite the cold stare, Alistair needed him.

Alistair needed the Luca who would take control, who would know exactly what he needed whether Alistair was aware of it or not. He needed the Luca who would trap him inside his arms and force him to submit to the calmness he needed.

"Please, Luca, I can't do this. It hurts. It hurts too much. I need you." Somewhere inside him he felt the ghost of shame, but his soul was crumbling under the weight of Lakelyn's death, Felix's injuries, and the loneliness he'd felt since he was old enough to know people were afraid of his touch. He needed to forget those things, even if it was only for a few moments. "Please, hold me. Touch me, fuck me if you want, just *please* make this stop."

When the man clucked his tongue at him, Alistair thought ice water had been poured over his body.

"So pathetic. One little country bumpkin dies and you're ready to fuck your way into oblivion. "

"What?" Alistair's voice squeaked out of him as he blinked the tears from his eyes and finally saw the way Luca's stare was narrowed at him.

"Oh, please, Alistair. You think I can't tell that you've seduced more men than you can probably remember? Letting them fuck you in back rooms and filthy toilet stalls just so someone can erase your memories for a few sweaty minutes." He stared quietly at him a moment, as though reading his face like a book, then he grinned. "And the rougher, the better, right?" He ran one finger down the center of Alistair's chest, raising goosebumps on his skin. "Because way down, deep in here, you want someone to punish you for what you are."

"Stop it!" Alistair struggled to swat his hand away, his body refusing to follow even the simplest direction. This wasn't something Luca could have read in his dossier.

Luca shook his head slowly, his hand moving over the boy's hip. "People like you are so infuriating. All this power, and you're wasting your tears for that useless boy."

"Don't you dare say another word about him!"

"I think it's time for you to accept what you are, Alistair. You were spared because you have purpose, just like I do. And if you want, you can help me fulfill that purpose."

"Fuck you and your purpose!"

Luca actually laughed, then his hand caught Alistair by the chin, his grip unyielding as the boy did everything he could to will his body out of the grips of both his teacher and the sedatives. As Luca leaned over him, Alistair felt bugs crawling across his skin, and as his hot tongue passed over his lips, he tried catching him between his teeth.

"So much potential," Luca said as he sat back up, looking pleased with the redhead's attempt at defiance. "Too bad you'll go to waste." Then he stood up and turned for the door.

"Get back here," Alistair spit. "I'm not finished with you!"

"Adorable. Really, pet. But I have something very important to collect now. I'm afraid all my time to play is gone. You stay there and rest, though. Maybe when this whole mess is sorted out you'll change your mind. I could take you away from Haven, just like you've always wanted. Think about it."

The door shut as Luca disappeared onto the streets of the small town. Everything inside Alistair shook, but his sorrow was replaced with rage now, and luckily, he knew how to handle that a little better.

35: COLE

Bastian had torn himself away for a few moments to get a wet rag from the bathroom to clean them both, but had returned to Cole's side immediately after. For the rest of the night they stayed like that, the two of them simply lying, limbs twined together, holding onto each other. They should have been sleeping. It seemed like the calm that had taken over the town would be gone soon, and rest was always vital to a mission, but neither of them seemed capable of sleep at that point.

The heat that Bastian had poured into their love-making still radiated in Cole's chest, but the flame seemed fringed in ice. He wanted to stay with Bastian. In fact, the thought of leaving him sent a surge of nausea coursing through his system. However, the idea of being welcomed by people like him—of not having to fight the hunger that occupied so much of his life—was so seductive. And without him there, Bastian may be heartbroken, but for how long? Surely he would recover, and after time he would find someone more suited to him—someone who hadn't been spawned in the actual, literal, *biblical* Hell.

Then Bastian's arms tightened around him, as though he could sense the self-loathing radiating off of him. Lips brushed his forehead as Cole's cheek rested on his lover's wide chest. How could Bastian calm these horrible waves crashing inside him with such a simple gesture? How was Cole supposed to leave that behind when all he wanted was to dive even further into it?

In the wake of that touch, his mind cleared for a few blissful seconds, then Bastian's chest rumbled under his cheek as he spoke softly into Cole's hair.

"I want you to stay, Cole." His breath was warm against his scalp, but before the horned boy could answer, Bastian continued. "But all I can do is love you. I can't make you love yourself. So—" His voice cracked a little and he had to pause. "So you need to do whatever is going to make you happiest with yourself. You understand?"

The heartbreak was obvious in Bastian's voice, though he'd done a valiant job of hiding it. As he opened his mouth to answer, Cole still wasn't completely sure what he was going to say, but before anything could slip out a burst of static from the bedside table made them both jump. Their radios sounded off in echoed unison.

"We have a situation." Shipton's voice was edged with alarm. "Suit up and meet me in front of the motel office. Two minutes."

If he was ready for them to drop the student act, then something had definitely gone very wrong. Thoughts of love and goodbyes evaporated as both boys leapt out of bed, going for their mission packs with a practiced efficiency. With their black jumpsuits pulled on and zipped up the front, Bastian pulled special cords that closed off the slits built into his to facilitate his wings. The neck snaps were closed, the resistant material protecting all their vital spots. For the next thirty seconds, the clacking and cocking of guns sounded in the small room, neither of them speaking as they strapped their pistols to their hips and under their arms.

Before leaving they checked the others jumpsuit and holster straps, but as they finished patting each other down they paused,

Bastian's hands on Cole's cheeks. He looked like he wanted to say something, but then pressed his lips into a thin line, leaned his forehead against Cole's and kissed him. It was quick, lingering for only a few seconds, but Cole could feel the blond's ardent plea.

"Let's go," he said, before releasing Cole and heading for the door.

The parking lot of the motel was dark, save for a handful of still-working street lamps—tiny specks in a sea of broken bulbs. The others had already assembled, but Jett was still missing, and now Alistair was gone as well. Shipton stood directly under the lamplight, no matching jumpsuit, though he'd shed his suit, wearing now a simple black t-shirt and black pants tucked into his boots. He reminded Cole of the soldiers who stood guard back at Haven and he wondered if the man had a history in the military. It would make sense, being affiliated with Haven. A grey shoulder holster held two pistols tucked tight against his ribcage, the rig not unlike their own.

"Where are the others?" Bastian asked before Cole had the chance.

"Jett is performing a special task for the mission, but Alistair was wounded. He's going to be fine," Luca continued as the others came in more tightly around him, obviously shocked. "After our meeting with Marla he went for the kids, but just ended up provoking the vessels that were staying with them. He was knocked unconscious, but I arrived in time to get him out okay." He paused, his brows knitting in concern. "But there was a casualty. That boy, Lakelyn."

Cole's hands moved to cover his own mouth, muffling the gasp of horror that escaped him. He'd not grown close to any of the children the way Alistair had, but the thought of any child hurting—let alone being killed—twisted his insides. He looked at Bastian, wondering if he was thinking the same thing. This was exactly what Alistair had been afraid of. This is why their teammate had asked Marla to evacuate the children, but she'd refused.

She'd refused, and now one of them was dead.

"The other kids ran." Shipton shook his head, a hand moving to his brow, seeming angry with himself. "They scattered while I was tending to Alistair."

"We should contact Marla," Milo said. Kiyiya was at his side, just as he had been every time Cole had seen him since they'd gotten to Trumbull, but now the dog sat behind him, leaning against his calves, his head hung low, his eyes trained on their teacher.

"No." Shipton's voice wasn't loud, but it was final. "If we tell her then the soldiers will find out. There could be a panic and they could dissolve the quarantine line. If they rush the town then more people will die. Before we do anything else, we need to find the children. We'll split up, comb the town, and bring any kids we find back here. Berlin, you stay behind." Before the dark-skinned boy—his uniform sleeveless to give room for his tattoos to propel themselves from his exposed skin—could protest, their leader continued. "You stand the chance of providing the strongest defense if anyone comes for the children once we deposit them here. The rest of us will split up."

Bastian gathered Cole's hand into his. "Cole and I will check the churchyard first. The youth pastor said they kept some of the youngest ones there sometimes. The kids will probably go to places they're familiar with."

"No. No partners. We don't have time. The town isn't big, but there's still a lot of ground to cover."

Cole felt uneasy about going on his own, and judging by the soft squeeze Bastian gave his hand, he probably felt the same. But Shipton was right. They needed to find the children as soon as possible, and that meant covering as much ground as they could. Still, Bastian continued to squeeze his hand until Cole gave him a nod. He felt bad that his lover was so scared to be separated from him now. He probably thought that Cole would slip away into the night—run away and never been seen again. Cole was still not completely sure what he was going to do, but this had nothing to do with that choice. He would help find the children first, and worry about his and Bastian's fate once he knew they were safe.

He offered a soft smile to the winged boy, hoping to reassure him. He was reluctant, but eventually Bastian released his hand.

"We'll all meet back here in one hour, whether we've found the kids or not." At Shipton's order they all synced their watches, then turned away from each other and left.

36: BASTIAN

Bastian, like the others, had spent enough time in the town that it had begun to feel normal. However, as he walked alone through the still night, the place seemed more alien, and far more dangerous. The air was cool and still save for the occasional breeze that sent a quiver through the stalks of corn. The streets were still empty, though from windows he could see light and figures watching him. He shuddered under their vigilant stare, and wondered what it would take to tip them over the edge. What were they waiting for? And how long would they wait?

Cole had gone toward downtown, while Bastian had made straight for the church, still convinced that the children would go there. When he got to the small playground, he saw no signs of them, though. When he checked, the arched doors were unlocked, so he pushed them open and let himself in. Pulling the small flashlight from his chest pocket, Bastian flashed it around the room, checking between the pews where a child might crouch to hide. No one was there, and when he checked behind the building, all he found was shaggy overgrown grass.

He moved down the street, heading for the water tower that stood like an inverted teardrop in the night, watching over the post office situated near its base. He ducked his head inside a mechanic's garage on the way, the brick walls crawling with vines. There were dozens of nooks and hollows for tiny bodies to shelter themselves, but again, he found nothing.

He went on like that, carefully checking each building and swatch of grass between them, eventually coming to the post office, whose doors were locked. Cattycornered across the street was another warehouse, the whole structure made of silver sheet metal. He crossed the intersection, his feet crunching tiny rocks that had come loose from the aged road.

He'd kept quiet during his search, not calling for the children, worried he might provoke the quiet vessels filling the residential homes into action. So when the metal door screeched as Bastian forced it along its rusted track, he flinched, checking over his shoulder but seeing only silent yards, and beyond those, the expanse of corn and the dots of the quarantine towers. The building had looked like an oversized shed from the outside, so Bastian figured it should be full of junk, or grain or any number of useless things. Instead, he found an open space with chairs set in in rows facing the far end of the rectangular building. There were dim lights at the far end—lanterns that lit up the space like some sort of makeshift church. In the circle of their light he saw several rows of chairs toppled onto their sides, three bodies lying in the chaos, either unconscious or dead.

"Took you long enough." A familiar voice sounded from the shadowed corner at the far end of the building, and when Bastian moved further into the room, he saw Jett leaning against the metal wall, looking worse for wear.

Bastian hurried to his new teammate's side, whether he fully trusted him or not. His clothes were disheveled and stained with an uncomfortable amount of blood, some of it brown and crusty on his nose and lip.

"Hold still." Kneeling beside the blue-haired boy, Bastian eased the now-stiff fabric of his shirt up to assess the severity of his injuries. What he found, instead of the open wound the surplus of blood suggested, was a fresh purple scar that ran from his bellybutton to his sternum.

Jett laughed, though the sound was a bit tired, and Bastian could only guess what sort of face he'd made. "Sorry, Braveheart. Looks like I ran to my own rescue. Didn't mean to steal your thunder."

"You can heal yourself?" He made another quick once-over of his teammate's body, looking for any other injuries that could have soaked his clothes in blood.

"Pretty cool party trick, huh? If you're good, maybe I'll teach you how to do it someday. Help me up."

"And here I just thought you liked catching things on fire." He helped the other boy to his feet even as he said, "You should rest a bit longer."

"We don't have time for that. Luca's probably going after your beau as we speak." He stood on his own feet, refusing Bastian's offered shoulder. "Let me guess, he had you all split up?"

"What are you talking about? He said you were busy with a separate part of the mission. We have to let him know what happened."

"He lied to you, man. I've been stuck here since last night, and whatever goose chase he has you on now is just a distraction."

"What are you talking about?"

"He's one of them now."

"No, that's not possible. I would have known if he was lying."

"Look, that lie detector you got in your noggin," he pressed a finger into Bastian's forehead for emphasis. "It's not fool-proof, alright? The demon that snagged Luca's body is a powerful one. They have ways around those things."

"I didn't know you were an expert," he said, swatting the other boy's hand away from his face. "If my lie detector doesn't work, then why should I believe *you*? I'll have you know that we have some reasons to suspect you as well."

Jett laughed, a hand moving to his gut like the action pained his recently healed injury. "Look, we can sit here all day and argue about which side I'm on. But I'll bet you money that at this very moment, that asshole in Luca's body is leading your boyfriend straight to Hell."

Bastian paused. He still wasn't sure if he should believe this boy or not, but he did know that the other demons in that town had been trying to talk Cole into leaving with them. Was it a coincidence that Jett knew that?

"Bastian!" A clatter sounded at the entrance to the warehouse, and both boys jumped as Sabin ran into the room, nearly falling over the back row of chairs. "This is a trap! Luca's possessed!"

The three of them were quiet for a few seconds as Sabin took in the bodies on the ground and the bloody state of their teammate.

"Looks like you're a bit late to the party, Blue Eyes, but you can help me." Jett leaned himself against the wall again, still seeming to be regaining his strength. "Our friend here didn't' believe me when I told him Luca was a walking talking man-suit now."

"B-blue eyes?" For the first time ever, Bastian saw color splash across Sabin's face. "Fuck off, okay? How do we know you're not one of them too?"

Jett tilted his head, his eyebrows moving up his forehead in a tired expression. "Do I *feel* like one of them?"

Sabin scowled, but didn't reply until Bastian demanded to get some straight answers.

"You remember how I told you I could sense the demon energy here? That I wanted to do that experiment just to be sure it wasn't my imagination? Well, when Shipton showed up tonight, he reeked of the same shit. But it's fresh. I haven't sensed this on him at all until tonight."

"That's because he wasn't possessed until last night," Jett said. "We came *here* because this is where Blackholly was holding his midnight sermons. They caught us spying though, and overpowered us. I was kept hostage. He was pumped full of demon juice and sent on his way. Sent to get *your* boyfriend. So we need to stop yakking and go do something, or your sweetiepie's getting a one way ticket to Pitchfork City, okay?"

Bastian wasn't sure if he could trust Jett, but he did trust Sabin, and if Sabin said that Luca was compromised, then he believed him.

"Alright." Bastian brought one hand up to the tiny radio in his ear.

"Surprise," Sabin waved his hands in mock excitement. "He deactivated our radios. Milo's on it already, though. He should have them back up by the time we rendezvous with him."

"Tick tock, tick tock. Your cutie-pie is waiting for you." Jett seemed impatient, but insistent on waiting for Bastian to make a choice.

"Alright. Forget the rendezvous. When he gets it back up he'll radio us. We go straight to find Cole and Shipton."

"A heroic choice."

"Can you walk?" Bastian didn't want to say out loud that he would leave him behind if he couldn't.

"On your order, Braveheart."

"So what, are nicknames your 'thing?'" Sabin didn't wait for the injured boy as he turned and led the way out of the warehouse.

"Careful. Feisty turns me on." Pushing himself off the wall, Jett followed.

"This really isn't the time, you two. Flirt after Cole is safe."

Once they were outside, Bastian broke into a run, not caring if the others would be able to keep up. When they split up,

Cole had been heading toward Main Street. That's where Bastian would start.

37: COLE

In the first few months of his time at Haven, Milo had shown Cole as many things as he could. He'd tried to get him as acclimated to life above ground as was possible spending most of their time in the main facility. But when they'd arrived in Trumbull, Cole had distinctly remembered photos Milo had shown him of tiny downtown areas just like the one at the heart of this small community. He remembered seeing postcards and calendars with pictures of quaint streets lined by colorful shops.

Unfortunately, it was dark now, and he was alone, and there were hundreds of possessed people hiding *somewhere* in the town. Somehow, the place seemed a bit creepier considering the situation. Now, under the sparse light of half working streetlamps, Cole felt more like he was in one of the games he and Bastian played than a postcard. Not quite as scary as Silent Hill, but when the wind blew, making the American flags hanging outside the store window snap and wave, he felt a chill crawl under his skin. He couldn't imagine a child running around on their own on such an eerie night.

They must be much more frightened than I am.

The entrance to the general store where Milo had set up shop in was open when Cole gave the handle a tug, so he let himself in. There were a few lights on at the back, but it was obvious at the store was closed.

"Hello?" Cole tried to keep his voice soft, not wanting to seem intimidating in case some of the kids *had* come to hide there. "It's okay if you're scared. I'm not here to hurt anyone." Cole checked each aisle, hoping to find a few of them chomping down on some candy. He wasn't so lucky.

At the back of the store, he found the door to the storage room sitting ajar. Inside, all of the computers were shut down and most of Milo's papers were gone, but there were still a lot of nooks and crannies that would be perfect for housing tiny, frightened children. So Cole checked under each of the desks, moving boxes to see into every corner.

"Please don't be scared," he tried again.

"I'm afraid I've already checked here."

Cole knocked his head on the underside of the desk as Shipton's voice startled him out of his crawl space. "Jesus, you scared me."

"I'm sorry, but I need you to come with me." Taking Cole's arm, the teacher pulled him through the store and back onto the street. "I've found something concerning at the community center."

"Why didn't you radio us?" Cole had a queasy feeling in his gut. There was something about the feel of the man's hand on his wrist that Cole didn't like.

"Have you not checked your radio? They're malfunctioning."

As he followed their teacher, Cole reached up to touch his radio and found that he'd been right. No connection was made with any of his teammates. How had it defected in such a short period of time? As they neared the auditorium, Cole found the same quiet atmosphere hanging over the town, the crunching of their boots deafening in the midst of such full silence. The hallway just inside the auditorium was dark, and the sound of the door latching behind them echoed off the linoleum floor. To their right, a set of double doors would lead them into the main room where the children had been assembling for classes, but Luca passed those doors. He led Cole further into the building, to a place where Cole realized he'd not been before.

As the sickening smell of Sulphur hit his nose, Cole wondered how they'd missed searching this area.

"Shouldn't we wait for the others?"

"There's no time."

Before Shipton had finished pushing the final set of doors open, Cole knew he'd been duped. The room, like the rest of the building, was lit only by sparse fluorescents, the majority of the power still off for the night. The room was empty, scrapes gouged in the floor suggesting some sort of heavy furniture, possibly metal shelving, had been dragged out. In the center of the room was a wide hole, maybe six yards across, jagged but round, like a giant die had punched an eyelet into the ground. Only a foot inside the opening was a black, rolling mass that could have been smoke, were it not rippling and ebbing like water. The churning inside the void seemed to reflect itself inside Cole. Just like that black mass, he could feel something coiling inside him, and the closer he got to the dark pool of smoke, the more it stirred.

"This is it, Cole."

When Cole turned again, finally ripping his eyes away from the vein that seemed to drive its way straight to the heart of the earth, he saw Blackholly standing beside his teacher. Then his eyes turned to Shipton, and he felt his shoulders sag with realization. He didn't bother asking for an affirmation from the man that used to be his teacher.

"You said you'd give me time to decide." He looked back at Mammon instead.

"I did. Unfortunately, our time here is running out." He walked to where Cole stood, bringing both hands to the boy's shoulders. "It's time to make your choice."

The pit at Cole's back felt uncomfortably close, the lump he'd grown familiar with growing in his throat again. How was he supposed to leave Bastian behind? More townspeople filed quietly into the room behind Shipton, and he wondered if he would get the chance to say "no" at all.

"Listen to me." Mammon drew Cole's attention back to him. "I knew you before you were sent here. Before you were cast out, you were Colvam. You held a position in our ruling class; you were greatly loved by our people."

"Ruling class?" Cole tried to rake his brain for memories, but like last time, something stirred in him at the sound of "Colvam." Had that really been his name?

"We mourned your loss. Our Lord *still* mourns for you. Please, come home. The life you left behind was so much better than this wretched over world."

"Why did I leave?" The question hadn't really occurred to Cole until that moment, and he saw an uncertainty pass over Blackholly's face as Mammon formulated his answer.

"You were led astray. Deceived into giving up the future you were set to inherit."

"By who?" Cole's heart was racing now, a sort of distant déjà vu rolling over his body.

Shipton stepped forward now, his voice rising in the room that was now full of at least a dozen other vessels. "We don't have time for this! Just shove him in and get on with it!"

"That's enough, Harborym." Mammon gave him a long sideways stare, and the other man stilled but remained unhappy. Blackholly's face softened as he looked back at Cole. "You were drawn away from us by a devotee to the Tyrant Lord."

Cole could feel the confusion on his own face. Harborym, the impatient demon residing in Shipton's body, cut in.

"A groveler. An ass-kisser who gave up their free will because they were too frightened to stand up for themselves."

"Are—are you talking about angels? Are you telling me an angel talked me into leaving?"

Harborym reflexively spit on the ground between them at the mere sound of the word.

"'Angel' is a human word, Colvam. But so is 'demon.' In reality there is little that sets us apart from one another, save for our alliances."

Cole felt a smile creep on his face.

"This is hardly the time for amusement." Harborym seemed to have little in the way of patience.

"So Berlin was right."

Blackholly's head tilted just a little, and Mammon said, "Pardon?"

Cole just shook his head, though. "Nothing. I've made my decision."

It was strange to associate *Berlin* of all people with the warm sensation that spread through Cole's chest, but if what he said was true, then that meant the dreams he'd had about Bastian were also true. That meant the love he had for Bastian was true. It was real. If he had left everything behind to be with Bastian, then that was where he belonged.

"I'm going to stay." He could feel the tension in the room growing, but he refused to back down, instead raising his chin just slightly. "I'm sorry. I know you've done a lot to bring me home, but this is where I'm meant to be."

Silence.

The whole room stood still, and for several long moments, Cole willed them to keep their word. Then Harborym stepped in, using Shipton's hand to snatch Cole up by his arm.

"I've had enough of this. Lord Ashmodai made a mistake when he chose you." Yanking Cole toward the opening in the floor, Shipton's grip was unbreakable, even as Cole shouted and dug his heels into the ground.

"You said I could decide!"

"Shut up! I've known you were trouble from the beginning. I told my cousin to choose someone else, but he had to have *you.*"

"Harborym, calm down," Mammon said, hurrying after him, their followers edging forward but holding for a direct command. "You know Lord Ashmodai won't tolerate Colvam's rough treatment."

"Then he should have come himself! Do you think I *like* wearing this meat suit?"

As the words left Shipton's mouth, a flurry of motion poured into the room—a blur of black Mylar and red hair—and Shipton's body lurched and tumbled away from Cole as Alistair struck the man full-force in the side of the face. The man-turned-demon groaned as he pushed himself off the floor.

"So you're not so indestructible when you're caught off guard, huh?" Alistair shook his obviously sore hand out, a grin on his face as he positioned himself between Cole and their teacher.

"Cole, run!" Milo had appeared in the doorway now, Kiyiya at his side and his pistol raised as a shower of tranquilizer darts began dropping the vessels encircling the room. The men and women scrambled over each other, trying to reach the brunette before he could mow them down, but Milo's aim was too good, and his trigger too fast. They fell atop one another as Mammon caught Cole by the wrist.

"Harborym, handle the strong one."

"Oh, is that your name, you piece of shit?" Alistair jeered as he eased back toward the door. It was obvious the demons inside Blackholly and Shipton were the leaders. They were the strongest. Which meant separating them would give everyone else a leg up. "Why don't you come take care of me like your daddy said?"

Shipton's eyes were hard as he wiped the blood from his lip, and the demon inside him was hot-headed enough to fall for Alistair's bait. He followed when the other boy turned and sprinted from the room.

Then the space was quiet. In the few seconds that passed, Milo had successfully darted the remaining vessels, leaving them in piles around the perimeter of the room. Now it was just Cole, Mammon, and Milo who had the demon leader in his sites.

"Let him go."

"Your violence surprises me," Mammon said, even as he pulled Cole's body between himself and the scope of Milo's gun. "We've not hurt anyone."

"I don't care. If you think you can take him against his will, then I'll be as violent as need be."

"You're playing a dangerous game, child. I can crush you without even touching you. You and your friends are alive right now because of my good will. Lower your weapon."

"No! I'll shoot you first. Maybe I'll even use a real bullet this time."

"Milo, stop! Please, both of you." Cole turned as best he could with the demon's hand gripping his arm, but he lowered his voice. "Mammon, you told me that demons weren't bad people. I believe you. I believe that we're *both* good people. So, please. Just let me stay here. Show them the kindness you've shown me. Just let me go."

The demon seemed to consider his proposition, the bruising fingers around his arm softening. Then the loud echo of the main doors slamming open reverberated into the room, baleful after its trip down the long corridor. Bastian's voice hit Cole's ears before the sound had died away.

"Cole? Are you in here?"

Just hearing his voice sent waves crashing through Cole's body. He'd made the right choice. He knew he had. He belonged wherever Bastian was, and when Cole felt the demon's grip on him tighten again, he shoved Mammon away, shouting for his lover. Mammon stumbled, and Milo took his opportunity. A low "THIP" sounded from his gun, but Mammon's hand rose as if by reflex, and the air between his outstretched arm and Milo seemed to bend, distorting the room around them. Cole found himself thrown to the ground by the force behind him, sliding several feet on his stomach before regaining himself. But that blast had not been aimed at Cole. It had been aimed at Milo, and the room shook with the force of the boy's body hitting the wall, the steel beams behind the crumbling drywall bending under him, a dull cracking sound filling Cole's ears as he watched his friend's body fall limp to the ground.

In the quiet that followed, footsteps filled the space, and when Bastian and Jett came around the corner, Cole could hardly see them. Bastian's voice came as if from underwater, every one of his senses waiting for Milo to give some sign that he was okay. Cole pushed to his feet, stumbling toward his friend.

"Colvam, listen to me."

As he sank to the ground beside Milo's deathly still body, Mammon eased toward him again, arms reaching for him. His friend didn't move. His friend who had given everything to him in an attempt to help him—in an attempt to set him free—lay still and absent. Cole had done nothing but take from the boy whose face grew paler by the second. He'd poisoned him and broken his heart, but still Milo had been ready to give up his life for him. Shaking fingers touched the other boy's crooked glasses. Then a crown of blood radiated from his chestnut hair, the deep red staining something inside Cole.

"Milo." His throat felt like sandpaper as the name tore out of his body, so quiet he could hardly hear himself. Something hot surged in him and his eyes moved to Mammon, some sort of recognition showing in the demon's eyes. "You killed him."

Cole stood, the very air around him shaking as waves of red-hot ire crashed out of his body—from his gut out through his fingers and eyes and mouth. Moving toward the demon, everything else inside him drained out, leaving only the fire, and from the corridor, just at the edge of his periphery, he saw Bastian coming toward him. Before he could reach him, another wave of anger swelled from Cole's body, and the blond stumbled, fell and was shoved back into the corner where Milo's body lay.

"Peace, cousin!" Mammon had raised his hand toward Cole again, a softer version of the force he'd used on Milo neutralizing him. "It's been too long for you! You're no longer disciplined enough for this!"

Cole didn't need discipline. He could feel the raw, hostile power infusing his body, making every thread of his being thrum with potential—with the potential to decimate another person.

Words formed in Cole's mind, but never made their way to his lips. Instead a low rumbling growl shook the room, and everything went red. Mimicking the other demon's gestures, Cole raised both hands toward Mammon, urging the hatred he felt out through pathways coursing down his arms. The room shook and bent, and then there was a deluge of rubble as the ceiling collapsed. Pale dust flooded the room as chunks of concrete flew from the gaping hole made in the side of the building, but as things settled, Cole saw Mammon leap through the laceration, Blackholly's body gliding through the air as if carried by an invisible hand.

Through the madness mutilating what was left of the soft feelings Cole could hardly recall, he thought of Bastian hovering over him, white regal wings spread out to save his life. Now, as Cole willed his body to follow the man he would see crushed into small pulpy hunks of flesh, his back split open, dark, oily replicas of his lover's wings unfurling and pushing him into the night.

38: ALISTAIR

It was hard to hide the shaking in his legs as Alistair ran from the auditorium. After Luca had left him lying in the motel room, he'd forced himself out of bed and into his jumpsuit. The drugs had lost a lot of their strength, but he could still feel the weight of the sedatives in his limbs. As he'd stumbled out of his room, he'd found Berlin waiting outside looking antsy and pissed. Then, when Sabin and Milo had doubled back to them with news of the busted radios and Luca's possession, everything had begun to make sense—his talk about a purpose, his harsh words, and the sudden change in his attitude.

"Why are you running, kitten?" Luca sounded amused, like the pursuit was a game to him—a game he seemed confident he'd win.

Before they'd split up, Milo had come up with a plan. Alistair wasn't sure how the pieces would come together, but he knew his role, and he had a personal score to settle. He was to occupy Luca and eventually lead him to the church. He wanted to do a lot more than distract the demon who had hijacked his teacher's body, and as soon as the weak wobbly feeling in his legs died down, he would find a way to satisfy those desires. Until then, he would have to evade him.

When Alistair ducked between two houses, Luca slowed to a walk. "Don't be upset, sweetheart."

Alistair could hear the man's boots rustling through the grass as he rounded one of the buildings. He needed a few seconds to rest. The yard at the back of the small building was overgrown and had lopsided hedges along the siding, tall enough that they blocked Alistair completely when he slipped between them and the flaking paint of the house. He'd inched his way nearly halfway to the other end of the building when the back door flew open, blocking his route. He froze, holding his breath as men and women filed silently out of the house. They seemed entranced, walking through the doorway, then running across yards toward the center of town. He had counted ten of them when the stream finally stopped, but he didn't dare move until he was sure they were gone.

"You know," Luca's voice called from nearby, though the foliage made it impossible for Alistair to pinpoint him. "I always hated coming up here, but you really made it all worthwhile." Bushes rustled nearby where Luca checked inside them. "My offer still stands, you know. I'd be happy to take you home with me. What do you think?"

While Luca distracted himself with his banter, Alistair shimmied past the back door and continued behind the hedge until he escaped to the far side of the house. Pressing himself to the wall, he called back to the man following him. "So you really are just a parasite, huh? No wonder I noticed a sudden decline in quality."

Alistair jumped the low fence separating the yard he was in from the next, then ducked behind a shed when he was on the other side. A few moments passed, then he heard the distinct sound of Luca jumping the fence. He was like a bloodhound, his pace slow as he walked the perimeter of the yard.

"Oh come now. I didn't hear you complaining when we were fucking you senseless."

Alistair's face went hot. Every word the man had spoken in their encounter, every brush of his hand, every thrust of his body flashed through Alistair's mind. Was it the demon who had done that to him? Had this demon been the one to wring such devastating pleasure from him? Then he remembered the soft look he saw in Luca's eyes that morning. It had only been for a few moments, but he'd seen it. It was a look that he was sure this demon couldn't counterfeit. And he had just said "we." Surely, there had been at least some of Luca present that morning. The question was whether there was anything left of him now.

"What's wrong, Alistair? Does it upset you to think that you fucked me too? You should really be thanking me, though. Without me, Luca probably wouldn't have touched you at all. Being inside his head gives access to all sorts of goodies. If only you knew how much he hates laying his hands on sloppy, used goods."

Another wave of embarrassment hit Alistair. "Fuck off!"

He'd played right into the demon's trap, and before the words had even fully left his mouth, the shed against Alistair's back splintered. The concussive force of the blast sent him belly first into the grass. Turning over once the debris had settled, he watched as Luca stalk over the remnants of wood. Before Alistair could do anything else, ghostly cords seized his body. As if moved by dozens of unseen hands, Alistair was picked up and flung several yards before tumbling back to the ground, landing on his back, rendered immobile.

"So easy." Luca clicked his tongue at him as he strode up to his side, one hand outstretched toward Alistair, controlling the invisible binds which kept him pinned to the ground. "All that strength trapped in such a weak little body. Maybe I should stop playing around and just squeeze you until you burst."

The demon's fingers bent, forming a slow fist, and the cords around Alistair's body tightened, pressing the air from his lungs like a closing vice. The constriction was slow, obviously intended as entertainment for the demon. Then Harborym chuckled and tapped one finger to his brow.

"I can still hear him in here you know. Poor Luca. He's telling me not to hurt you. How sweet. Maybe if I kill you it'll break what's left of him and I can keep his body for good. It's such a nice fit after all."

Alistair locked eyes with him, and for just a second he thought he saw a flicker in the grey pools that was not Harborym, but a hint of the emotion he'd seen flash in his eyes before: the tenderness Luca let slip sometimes.

"Like hell you can keep him." Alistair's voice was hoarse, fighting for air, but he would not let this demon walk away with the man he just realized he didn't want to give up.

Somewhere inside of Alistair was a mental lock, a levee put in place by his fear and his guilt that kept his strength from ever reaching its full potential. He didn't need it any more. Luca would not be hurt by him and would not let him hurt anyone else. Like he was breaking out of twine wrapped tight around his body, Alistair flung his arms outwards, causing Harborym to stumble as the invisible cords binding him shattered. Feeling power radiating through his muscles, Alistair stood sneering at the demon, "That body you're borrowing might be indestructible, but it looks like your baby-dick ghost powers aren't."

Harborym was shocked for a second, then he smiled. "Guess I'll have to take care of this the old fashioned way, then."

39: BASTIAN

Chunks of concrete and metal shavings from the blasted trusses of the roof were still falling when Bastian got back to his feet. He ran to the opening, shielding his eyes from the dust in an attempt to see Cole. He'd flown. Not only had he grown wings like his, but he'd been able to use them. Even after practice, Bastian hadn't been able to get more than a few feet off the ground. The sky above them was empty, though he heard something that might have been Cole shouting in the distance, but it sounded more animal than human.

"Bastian!" Jett's voice interrupted his vigil, and when he whipped around to look at his new teammate, he found him crouched beside Milo.

Bastian hurried to the unconscious boy's side, his fingers going immediately to the soft spot under the curve of his jaw. There was a very faint pulse, despite the wide pool of blood that had formed around his head.

"We have to get him to Marla." He shifted, looking over the boy's body to decide the best way to carry him. Chances were good that he had broken bones, so moving him would be dangerous.

"There's no time," Jett said, his hand stilling Bastian's movement. "You'll have to do it."

"Do it? Do what?" He could hear the panic rising in his voice. "I can't treat him, Jett. I'm not a doctor!"

"Listen to me." Jett's hand caught him by the bend of one wing, a squeeze forcing him to meet his stare. There was something powerful in his gaze, and when he spoke again, his voice was low and calm. "He won't make it all the way to the quarantine line. His injuries are too severe. If you move him now he *will* die."

Bastian's hands shook as he tried to measure his breathing, and Jett's hand moved to the back of his neck in a show of reassurance.

"He's not going to die, understand? You're going to heal him. Just like magic, okay?"

"What are you talking about? I can't do anything like that."

"You didn't think you could fly either, did you? Until these stupid things showed up, right? There's all kinds of stuff in here that you haven't found yet." He jabbed his finger into his head again.

His words steadied something in Bastian. Jett was right. Bastian didn't know what he was capable of. Not really. He didn't know how Jett could have any better of an idea than he did, but if they didn't do something soon, Milo would die. If moving him wasn't an option, Bastian was willing to try anything.

"What do I do?" Despite his resolve, his voice still shook.

"Attaboy." Jett smiled and shifted so he was shoulder to shoulder with Bastian, then he guided his still trembling hands to their teammate's barely moving chest. "Now, have you ever made people do things? Like willed them to follow your orders, even though they had no reason to?"

Bastian jerked his head to stare at the boy next to him as the night in the club came rushing back to him. All those weeks ago, when he'd gone to collect Cole from the nightclub—the same night they'd confessed to each other—he'd told the man who was forcing himself on Cole to leave. No he remembered the glazed look that had passed over his face—the way everyone else on the upper floor had seemed affected too. They'd all gotten up and filed back down to the dance floor; but how could Jett have guessed something like that?

"I'll take that deer-in-the-headlights look as a 'yes.'" He smiled a little and looked back down at Milo, guiding Bastian to do the same. "This is just like that time. You need to will this body to do what you say. Demand that it goes back to how it was before the injury. Tell it that you are the master of everything on this Earth and that it must obey."

What is he talking about? This is crazy.

How was he supposed to will anything to change? Scaring some people into doing what you want is one thing, but how could he make bones heal just by ordering them around? He tried to focus. He pictured the shattered bones in his back, and the open wound in his skull. In his head he imagined them shifting and stitching themselves back together. He imagined Milo sitting up and being fine.

But nothing happened.

Every second that passed was a second wasted, and Bastian could feel the movement of the other boy's chest grow weaker and weaker. Finally, he looked back to Jett.

"This isn't right. We *have* to get him to Marla."

Now, when Jett's hand latched on to the back of his neck his grip was hard, painful even, and his voice came out low through his teeth. "Listen to me, Bastian. Did you see what happened to Cole? Let me tell you a secret. If this boy dies, you will never get your cute little black lamb back. If Milo dies, Cole is going to the dark side for good. You got me? So you better fix this kid or kiss your sweetheart goodbye."

The look of fear he'd seen on Cole's face over the past day fell juxtaposed to the creature he'd watched fly away a moment ago. Cole had been afraid that being a demon meant being evil, but Bastian knew that wasn't true. Yet as they knelt in the ruined auditorium he was sure that Cole was trying very hard to *kill* the demon he was chasing. That meant killing the vessel along with him. Bastian didn't want that, not for Cole. Not for the sweet boy who murmured so helplessly in his ear when they made love, who wanted to badly to be good that he would let himself suffer for it.

He wouldn't allow that.

He would not let Cole fall, and he would not let Milo's death be the anchor that dragged him to Hell. This time he didn't imagine the other boy's bones healing—he got angry, igniting the familiar burn of righteousness in his chest. Just as he had in the nightclub, the ember of that feeling vibrated out of him, his mouth hot with what he thought must be magic.

"Get up!"

Maybe he was imagining it, but the air around them seemed to shudder, a wave moving with the vibration of his voice, but as it died away there was only silence.

For several long moments nothing changed, then under Bastian's fingers he felt a heavy thump, followed by a steady heartbeat that had been almost gone a moment ago. Bastian held his breath as Milo's ribcage heaved, still-pale lips parting to draw in air. Bastian only had a few seconds for the wonder to set in before a loud keening sounded from the dog on Milo's other side. Kiya jumped up, leaping over Milo's body and onto Bastian's lap, crying as he licked his face over and over. Jett clapped Bastian's shoulder and laughed in his ear.

It wasn't until Kiyiya stepped on Milo's stomach causing the boy jerked and groaned that Bastian realized the extent of what he'd done.

"What the hell, you stupid dog?" Milo's voice was hoarse and his movements were stiff, but he moved, his hands reaching up to shove the massive dog off of him. The shove only made Kiyiya transfer his frantic licking from Bastian's face to Milo's, the high whining still matching his wagging tail.

"How'd I do that?" Bastian had been asking himself more than anyone else, but Jett squeezed his shoulder again.

"Guess there's more to the angel package than just some pretty wings, huh?" The blue-haired boy winked at him, but before Bastian could ask him how he could possibly know any more than he did, Milo's voice rose in a panic.

"Where's Cole?"

"Hold it right there, Sleeping Beauty." Jett pushed Milo back down before the boy could try sitting up. "You're not going anywhere. Kiya, give me a hand." Without missing a beat, the huge black dog sat down on Milo's chest, making the boy groan under his weight. Then Jett turned to Bastian. "You need to go get your boyfriend and give him a love Xanax now. I'll get this one up and walking. Seeing him on his feet should help."

"How, though? I mean, if every person in this town is possessed, it's only going to get harder from here. How do we fight that many?"

Jett rolled his eyes and slapped the dog on the side of his ribcage. "You just brought a boy back from the brink of death and you're wondering what you could possibly do?" He shook his head. "Ever watch The Exorcist?"

His smile crinkled the corners of his eyes, and Bastian couldn't help but smile back. He was right. The memory of the power he'd felt tingled inside him and poured into his growing confidence. If he really was an angel, then who better to fight demons than him? In a burst of certainty, Bastian stood and bolted through the opening Cole had made in the wall, jumping the debris in a handful of strides.

40: COLE

Cole's body hummed with a sort of violence he'd never felt before. His back burned where the wings had sprung from his flesh, but the sensation was dull and only fed into the simple goal he had set before himself. He would kill Mammon. He would take revenge for what the demon had done to Milo, and he would not let anyone stand in his way. He had spent too long being helpless and ashamed of what he was. What he was gave him power—it gave him a way to make the world bend to his will for once in his life.

The night sky was scattered with stars as they both rose into the air, and he could see the halo of military vehicles and turret lights that ringed the town. He wondered for a moment if they were watching them, training their guns on them as they spiraled higher and higher.

"Colvam!" Mammon slowed, but did not stop as he turned to watch his pursuer. "Please calm yourself! I don't want to fight with you!"

You should have thought of that before hurting my friend.

That thought never made it to Cole's lips, his body seeming incapable of forming words anymore. Instead, his hands pulled both pistols from his hips, and he fired. In a spark of light, each bullet seemed to ricochet off an unseen barrier as Mammon rose a hand between them.

"You're embarrassing yourself!" Mammon's temper seemed to flare now, his diplomacy gone. "It's one thing to have you betray us with one of those mindless devotees. Now you're getting this attached to *humans?* You're tarnishing your name, *and* Lord Ashmodai's name!"

Somewhere in the back of his mind, Cole recognized that name, but the nagging memory was brushed aside with another barrage of bullets. Mammon shot toward the ground again to avoid the volley, Blackholly's body moving more nimbly than would be expected from a man his age. Cole followed, diving after him and trying to keep him in his sights as he went.

Bullets poured from Cole's guns, and when they clicked uselessly he dropped them and pulled the spare set from under his arms. The holster was loose and flapping in the wind after his wings snapped one of the straps. Mammon swooped and spun, more experienced in flight than Cole was. His body seemed to know how to propel him and take simple directional commands, but he felt clunky and awkward in the sky. By the time they reached the ground, he'd nearly emptied his second set of guns. The rage that had blinded him seemed to be ebbing, and he was able to guess he had maybe three rounds left in each gun. That was better than nothing, but their value was diminished by the demon's ability to block bullets like they were pebbles.

Cole's wings trailed behind him once both men landed in the field beside the revival tents. They were heavy, and the way they dragged through the grass sent shivers up Cole's spine. As he tread his way toward Mammon, the demon matched his steps, looking furious even as he retreated.

"You can only run for so long, Mammon." Cole's voice felt like ice on his lips. "I might not remember a whole lot, but I'm pretty sure I'm stronger than that human body you're stealing."

"Perhaps, but are you stronger than three hundred human bodies, Colvam?" He snapped his fingers, and for a few seconds the wind simply blew between them.

Was that it?

He knew better than to turn his back on the demon ahead of him, but any derisive amusement he'd felt died in his throat as a sound rose from the buildings behind him. A white noise of movement grew—doors and windows and books—then there was the rustling of grass. Catching his breath, Cole watched as dozens of townspeople—vessels carrying lesser demons inside them—swarmed the field. They didn't attack, but formed an ever-thickening ring around him and their leader.

"Didn't your boss tell you not to hurt me?" Cole tried to sound tough, but the fire he'd felt was going out. Fighting a few hundred demon-possessed people would be hard enough, but doing it without hurting the innocent humans who had been hijacked would be impossible. With the flames doused, he also remembered that even Mammon was in one of those people.

"Unfortunately, he did, but accidents do happen."

"What happened to all that 'bring you home,' brotherly love talk? Huh?" As he bought himself time, Cole wondered if the lower demons could fly the way Mammon had. With his wings that were feeling weaker as his adrenaline fell, escape was possible but growing more unlikely by the second.

"You *were* my brother, Colvam. But that was when I still thought you had been *taken*." He seemed to need a moment to steady his voice. "But seeing you here, it's obvious that you were not taken hostage. You are a deserter. If I thought for one second that you felt remorse for what you did, for your betrayal to our lord, then maybe I would care a little more about Ashmodai's orders to keep you safe." Mammon seemed full of bluster now that his backup had arrived. "For your crime of choosing some loyalist guard from the enemy territory over your own people, you will either face death here or incarceration back home. I'll let you decide which you prefer."

The grass shuttered against Cole's legs as a cool wind blew between him and the other demon. Somehow, six bullets and a weak pair of wings was going to have to sort this out for him.

41: ALISTAIR

Knowing that Harborym was unable to use his creepy poltergeist powers on him gave Alistair a leg up as he sprinted toward the church again. He'd effectively killed time and while his extremities still tingled they didn't feel as weak. Hopefully the detour had also given Berlin the time he needed to get into position. Of course, whether their plan worked or not would depend almost solely on catching the demon off guard. Alistair had proven it was possible, but he wasn't ready to bet everything on it happening again.

At the very least he seemed to have the demon's attention, though he was starting to think that Harborym had seen Star Wars too many times. As they ran, the demon used the Sith Lord force-throw like it was going out of style. Potted plants, rocks, mailboxes, garbage bins—he sent a constant barrage of debris in Alistair's direction. As he turned onto the home stretch, a groaning of metal interrupted his sprint, and Alistair planted his feet just in time to catch the two-door pickup truck Harborym had fired at him. His fingers latched into the twisted metal of the hood and his feet dug potholes into the road as he caught the vehicle. In the next heartbeat he swung the thing and hurled it in Luca's direction like a hammer thrower. His aim was perfect.

When Harborym raised Luca's arm to defend himself, the truck slammed into him, crumpled, and fell dead to the ground in front of him. Harborym seemed surprised, yet pleased. When he sauntered out from behind the vehicle he was beaming.

"Yes. I could definitely get used to this body."

"Well don't get too cozy. I don't plan on letting you keep it, you fucking tape worm."

Then the chase was on again.

When Alistair jumped the small picket fence surrounding the church, he didn't see Berlin, which could mean that things were going exactly as planned, or that he'd flaked out and wasn't there at all.

"What's this, kitten? You're seeking sanctuary? I didn't take you as the religious type." Luca followed right behind him.

"Yeah, that's real funny coming from *actual* Hell-spawn!" He bee-lined for the open doors of the church, jumped the stairs at the front porch and slid feet first into the cool darkness of the building.

Just like Berlin had said, the demon stopped before entering. Alistair had been skeptical at first, thinking his usually paranoid teammate was just drawing from superstition again, but the way Luca's lip curled as he paused just over the threshold made it all seem more plausible.

"What's wrong? Afraid a bit of holy spirit will rub off on you?" Alistair took the moment to catch his breath.

"Oh please, I can tell you don't believe in any of that bullshit. I smell way too much sin for you to be a good little Christian boy."

"Well good thing I don't need to be, huh? Since you're stuck out there and I'm safe and sound in here."

Harborym grew still, then moved his hands to rest on the top beam of the doorframe. He leaned his weight into the frame and narrowed his eyes at Alistair, the grey orbs passing over his face like he was reading a book. Then a slow smile played on his lips.

"You know, Alistair," the demon began, his tone softening to something that might be mimicking sincerity. "I'll say it one last time. My offer still stands. We don't have to fight like this. You could just come back with me."

"With *you?* Yeah right." Alistair wondered what Berlin was waiting for. The townspeople who had run out of the house he'd ducked behind hadn't been the only movement they'd seen in town. Men and women had spilled from the buildings like angry wasps from a rustled nest. They'd seemed uninterested in him and Luca, but maybe Berlin hadn't been as lucky.

"And what's wrong with me? What have I done to you?" He gave Alistair a smile that sent chills down his spine. The worst part was, they weren't bad chills. This demon was *inside* Luca's body, which meant he had every ounce of charisma the man possessed at his disposal, and he definitely knew how to use it. "Are you upset that we're here to take your friend back with us? Or are you upset because I snatched your boyfriend's body?"

The heat that flashed across Alistair's face surprised him. He'd had sex with Luca already—hell, he'd fingered himself in front of him—but there was still something distressing about a committed word like "boyfriend."

"Ah, I see." Harborym leaned his forehead onto Luca's arm where he held the door frame. "You're upset that I was hanging around when he fucked you. Have I ruined something important to you? Did you think it was some sort of sacred act between the two of you?" He paused to take in Alistair's reaction, but save for the tightening of his fists and the reddening of his cheeks, Harborym got nothing. "Of course, you've never even considered that you could have a *real* lover, have you? After Felix? After you broke his ribs, and his shoulder? After you tore all the blood vessels in his poor little dick." He stuck out his bottom lip. "Sad, sad Alistair. Your mommy put so much cough syrup and Valium in you that you almost died. All doped up when the other people in town came to your house for some good old-fashioned mob justice."

"Shut up!" Alistair hadn't realized how badly he was shaking until Harborym smiled at him.

"You can't hide things from me, Alistair. I can see every one of your secrets. I can also see how bad you want out. How bad you want to get away from Marla. What you did to Felix doesn't mean anything. Come with me and you will be someplace free of judgement. You'll have the power to do anything you want."

Somewhere, in the darkest corner of Alistair's mind, the offer was tempting. He *didn't* want to stay with Marla. He *did* want to have the freedom to do what he wanted without some nosy parental figure breathing down his neck. Despite that, he also knew there was something about Luca—there was some sort of possibility with him. Not as a guardian, or as someone who would pity him. Luca was someone who could challenge him. He could push him to be better, and he could do it without patronizing him. Luca could be a partner—he could be what a lover was supposed to be—an equal and a guide at the same time. Alistair wouldn't go anywhere with this demon. He wouldn't let him take Luca either.

"Get fucked."

Before the demon could answer, inky black strands, which were wound into a thick log-sized cord, slammed into his back. The cord burst like waves crashing on a rock, newly released tendrils moving to the frame of the door. The wood of the frame creaked as they dug in, using the doorway as leverage as they pressed against Harborym's back, trying to shove the demon inside the church.

Just as they'd planned, the demon inside Luca's body had been caught off guard. The man stumbled, lurching forward before he could harden his body. His hand seized the door frame, but by the time he caught himself he'd already stepped one foot inside the church. Steam rose from his skin—every part of his body inside the sanctuary quivering. The demon howled and pushed against the net of tattoos at his back. Berlin *had* been hiding somewhere on the grounds outside.

Harborym was too fast, though, and now stood rock-still. Alistair grabbed the man by his arm and pulled, digging his heels into the soft wood of the floor until it began to break apart.

"Let go of him!" Alistair shouted as he yanked and twisted at the unmoving arm.

Harborym laughed, though his teeth were pressed so hard together that he sounded pained. "You think you can move this body that easily? You have no idea what I'm capable of inside this man."

"Yeah, well you don't know what I'm capable of either!" Alistair began to sweat under his efforts. He'd never struggled like this before, but he pushed himself. He opened up every safety valve he'd ever set for himself and with a jerk Luca's arm straightened and the man faltered, having to take another step forward to catch himself.

A growl rose in the demon's throat as more of his body was forced inside the church, steam billowing from part of his neck as he craned his head away to protect his face.

"You're not taking him away from me!" Alistair wrenched his arm, wood buckling and pushing toward the doorway. The building creaked and groaned under the three forces battling at its doorstep. "Luca, please, don't let him do this to you! I need you!"

The demon jerked and all at once, his resistance was gone. Alistair tumbled back into the church, dragging his teacher's body with him. Luca landed hard on top of Alistair's slight body and then shook, convulsing for a few seconds as steam gushed from him the way it had from the hairs dropped in the holy water. As Alistair pushed the man over, moving to his knees to look down at him, he saw a black smoke trickle from Luca's clenched teeth, then his mouth snapped open and a mire of charcoal-colored sludge poured out of him. It looked thick like liquid, but moved like a dense smoggy vapor. It rolled off him and onto the ground, then like a massive ghostly slug, darted across the fractured wooden floor and out of the church.

Alistair watched it until it was gone, then Berlin appeared in the doorway, his tattoos still slithering back into place and his breath short. "Did you see that? Was that the demon? Did it work?"

Alistair looked down at the man lying unconscious on the church floor, and pressed his hands against his broad chest. Beneath the ribs, Alistair felt Luca's heart pounding and heard his breath wheezed through his throat.

"Luca?" He ran his hands up the sides of the man's neck, holding the curve of his jaw as he turned his face toward him for a better look. "Luca!" He shook him a little, then small mercurial pools peeked through his eyelashes and a second later they curved into tiny crescents as he smiled up at him.

"Hey, kitten." He sighed, as though even talking was hard work. "You're stronger than you look."

Alistair's breath rushed from his body in relief and for a second he dropped his forehead to his teacher's chest. It was hard to put into words, but there was something about the dopey grin the man had given him that assured him Harborym was gone.

"Aw, babe. Don't cry. I'll be fine."

Taking in deep breath through his nose, Alistair took a moment to appreciate the man's smell—sweat and hints of cologne—then he sat back up and smacked his cheek just hard enough that it might sting. "Stay here." Alistair stood and turned to Berlin, who was watching on from the doorway. "Come on," he said, striding past him. "We need to help the others."

Berlin glanced back at their teacher's prone body, obviously surprised, but he didn't argue. From behind him, Alistair heard Luca call for him, telling him he was heartless for leaving him without a kiss. He just smiled. Luca deserved at least this much punishment for getting himself possessed in the first place.

42: BASTIAN

The sky was empty as he scanned the expanse for any sign of his newly-winged lover. He'd noticed the first night they'd arrived in Trumbull—when he and Berlin had followed Sabin to the post office—that it was darker here than in the city. Now the moon hung low on the horizon and was only a sliver of light, doing nothing to help illuminate the town, or the aerial battlefield over his head. It wasn't until gunfire broke the silence of the night that he was able to spot them—two small figures wheeling in the sky, wide dark wings blocking out the stars as Cole pursued the other demon.

Reminding himself to stay confident, Bastian spread his own wings wide, and with one strong push down, he lifted himself off the ground. His back protested from the effort, and after only a few long strokes the ache proved too much, and he spiraled the several yards back down to the earth.

Why is this so hard for me? How could Cole do it right away?

He was just about to try again when another round of bullets drew his attention back to his lover. They were descending, shooting toward the ground like the shadow of a comet, both forms disappearing beyond the buildings surrounding the auditorium rubble. Bastian would have to catch up with them on foot.

Tucking his useless wings back against his body, Bastian ran. He passed the mayor's office and the general store, but the moment he turned onto a residential street, the doors to the houses around him burst open, lines of people spilling out into the night. Bastian stilled, the road ahead of him teeming now with scores of possessed men and women. He waited, but they seemed uninterested in him, all of them tromping over yards in a direct line toward whatever destination they had. It was when he realized they were traveling in the same direction he'd seen Cole and Blackholly going that his feet started working again.

The vessels were single-minded in their objective, but when a few of them caught sight of Bastian as the blond caught up to them, a small group halted then turned to block his path.

This was it. Bastian squared himself and finally accepted what he was. He was an angel, they were demons, and angels always triumphed over demons. He would cast them out and save the lives of the humans who had been taken as vessels.

If only he could figure out how that worked.

The demons didn't seem interested in giving him time to figure it out, and they lunged for him in unison. Bastian leapt back, one pump of his wings giving him the thrust he needed to put space between them. As they pursued him, he cycled through every horror movie he'd ever seen, and suddenly found himself wishing he'd paid more attention when Berlin had woken him up at night afraid that Alistair or one of the new guards was actually a demon trying to get at him through his dreams. He vaguely remembered him talking about ways to exorcise whatever evil force he thought was controlling them at the time, but now the details were fuzzy.

Bastian caught one of the vessels by the forehead as the thirty-something-year-old man rushed him. "Be gone, demon!" He tried to mimic the serious and theatrical way he'd heard priests say those words in movies and YouTube videos. The demon just growled and snapped his teeth at his wrist. He glided backwards again, trying to avoid actually engaging with the vessels who bayed and snarled as their hands grabbed for him.

He hoped there wasn't some important incantation he was supposed to know.

In a weak attempt to mimic Berlin, Bastian brought two fingers up in front of himself and drew a cross, adding a "the power of Christ compels you," for good measure.

Still nothing.

Like a pack of hunting wolves, the five vessels spread out, a few of them running to Bastian's side. When he turned to block their advance, their cohorts hooked their fingers into his wings. Pain rippled through the limbs to his back as fistfuls of feathers were ripped out of him. He didn't even try to stop the shout that tore from his throat, and when he turned, extending a hand in an attempt to grab them, he felt the uncanny heat inside his mouth again.

"Let go!"

Two of the demons closest to his outstretched arm went rigid. Their heads lolled back and their eyes rolled toward the sky, as the air rattled out of their lungs. From their open mouths, a thick black mass of smoke drained out of them, both men collapsing into their own footprint. Once it had coagulated into a single mass of liquid vapor, the expelled demon slithered back toward the Community Center.

The other vessels took pause, and for the first time that night they seemed to come out of their hive-mind trance. Tapping into the sensation he'd just felt, Bastian turned back to the two demons who had acted as decoys and aimed his outstretched fingers toward them. He didn't speak this time, but inside himself he demanded they release the bodies they'd attached themselves to. He ordered them to let go of their prisoners. Just like the first two, they crumpled, black seeping from them before the disembodied spirit retreated back to the hole in the floor of the auditorium.

The last demon froze when he turned his eyes on it, the woman's arms dropping to her sides. She stared at Bastian for a long time, then her head tipped back and she collapsed. The demon had exorcised itself—it seemed strangely pleased to be gliding its way back home as the black mist coasted along the asphalt.

I guess some of them still have some sense.

The other vessels had long since left Bastian behind, but he still knew the general direction he'd seen Cole and Blackholly fall, and he was sure he would find the others there with them.

Bastian cut across yards following the trodden grass left by hundreds of feet. He knew where he was heading—the place where Blackholly liked to congregate his followers, where he often found Cole drawn to—the revival tents. There was something profane about a demon posing as a revival pastor; turning what many humans saw as a place of peace and worship into an assembly of demons. Then again, since when had he cared about things like that? As he hopped fences, he wondered if his new-found identity had anything to do with these strange feelings of righteousness.

As he jumped the last fence that stood between himself and the expanse of grass that butted against the cornfield, a rumbling of noise began—snarling, shouting, the clamor of bodies, and then gunshots. Bastian sprinted the last hundred yards, his heart in his throat. A gunshot meant one of two things. Either Cole's guns had been taken and used against him, or he'd shot an innocent person in an attempt to get at the demon inside. Both of those options horrified him.

The field opened up in front of him as he took the final corner around a low-lying warehouse, the commotion dauntingly loud now. A breeze hit Bastian's face, wind-blown by the heaving of Cole's wings. His horned lover was airborne, his black wings beating furiously against the pull of hands that latched around his leg. He kicked the grasping mob that crawled over each other in an attempt to get to him, pointing his pistols at men and women who clawed at his clothes. He never fired, and Bastian was sure then that the shots he'd heard earlier had been warning shots—bullets fired into the air or the dirt in an attempt to scare the demons away.

I haven't lost him yet...

Clenching his fists, Bastian sprinted for the mass of undulating bodies. He jumped, pushed down hard with his half useless wings. The force sent him over their heads before landing feet-first on top of a half dozen of them. They tumbled to the ground, toppling the men and women around them like writhing dominos. When Bastian felt his feet hit the ground he threw his hands out and with one word tearing through the heat inside his mouth, banished them.

His throat burned hot as fire, and his voice seemed to echo even in the open space. Bodies dropped around him, like grass blasted flat with Bastian at the epicenter. Cole tumbled in the air before crash-landing a few yards away. They both held still, catching their breaths and watching each other with a matching wonder in their eyes. Bastian could tell just by looking at him that his momentary violent madness had dissipated. Cole's eyes were dark, but alight as he looked over the scores of unconscious bodies at his lover who stood powerful and triumphant above them.

Without a word, Bastian closed the distance between them in two strides and another beat of his wings. As if floating, he descended on his lover where he lay in a swath of black feathers. Cole didn't resist as Bastian hoisted him to his feet, and before the demon could say a word, Bastian clasped his lover's shoulders. He wondered for a moment if he would get the soft unsure Cole from the past few days, or the rage-drunk Cole he saw blast the wall of the auditorium to bits. Whichever one it was, he wouldn't let him throw away the best parts of himself for the sake of some demon lord.

"It's over, Cole. It's done; I've sent them all back. Milo's alive, and he's in the auditorium waiting for you." He took a breath, still a little scared to continue—worried that exposing his true desires would frighten Cole. "And I know I told you I would let you decide if you should stay or go, but I lied." His hands moved to Cole's face, cupping his cheeks as he lowered his forehead to the shorter boy's "Don't go. Demon or not, *good* or not. I don't care which one you are. Just stay. I can't let you leave."

He held his breath, terrified that the possessive hunger he felt for the other boy would scare him—would remind him of Milo's obsessive deterioration. Instead of shrinking away, Cole's hands moved to rest on his lover's wrists, his fingers shaking softly.

"Milo's okay?" Tears filled Cole's eyes, but never fell.

"He's okay." His words puffed out of his chest on a breathless laugh as he pulled Cole into his chest, his arms wrapping around the smaller boy's neck. He brushed his lips across the black hair at his chin. "He's going to be just fine. He's already talking."

Cole's hands fisted the fabric at the back of Bastian's suit, and he could feel a slight tremor in the smaller boy, the dark feathers of his wings quaking where they lay limp off his back like a cape of glossy plumage.

"Thank God." His voice murmured against Bastian's chest.

As the words left his mouth, the bodies at the edge of the field shifted. On reflex, Bastian thrust himself between the movement and his lover, his wing spreading wide to shield Cole from whatever was coming. On the far side of the field, Blackholly pushed his way out from under several of his fallen comrades. Bastian waited, wondering if the man had just recovered quickly or—

"Really, a demon thanking *God*. You truly have become pathetic, haven't you?" Mammon still held full control over the pastor, and as he shook the grass out of his clothes he stepped over the unconscious figures around him. "Did you actually think your little exorcism would work on someone of *my* standing?"

289

"We've sent all of your demons back where they belong," Bastian said, trying to sound more authoritative than he felt. "You should go, too."

"Don't make me laugh. A servile little *foot soldier* like you shouldn't even be allowed to speak in our presence."

Bastian dare not soften his stance as he felt Cole's hands holding his jumpsuit. But what could he say? In the silence of his floundering, the demon continued, pacing a steady path toward them.

"You came to our lands as a guard, little more than a *servant*, to your lord's envoy. You came to bring us gifts and instead you stole from us."

An eerie sense of déjà vu fluttered in the back of Bastian's mind, but any memory he had of his past life was still too distant from him.

"Whatever happened back then doesn't matter anymore." Despite having a human body, Mammon was still intimidating. The way he spoke, the way he held himself—chin raised, eyes and shoulders hard—made Bastian's stomach churn. "I won't let you take him back. He's mine now!"

Mammon snorted. "I don't think you understand the gravity of what you've done, boy. You have stolen from us, and from Lord Ashmodai. Believe me, our Lord will not rest until—"

Brushing past Bastian's protective wing Cole surged forward before the other demon could finish his threat, his hands reached toward Mammon, seizing him and lifting him into the air with invisible cords. Bastian didn't move, scared for a moment that Cole really might kill this man. Instead Mammon just hung there, grunting as though someone were choking him about the neck.

"Listen to me." Cole's voice was low, but Bastian could hear a slight quiver in it that proved he was not really one of them. It wasn't a quiver of fear, but one of acknowledgment. He understood the power he was holding that second. He knew how easy it would be to abuse, and how much he didn't want to do it. "I don't care what you or your Lord wants. As long as Bastian wants me here, this is where I'm staying."

Another strained moment passed, then Cole's arms dropped to his sides, and the pastor's body fell with a muffled thump. Sputtering, the demon struggled to untangle himself from the heap of bodies.

"Harborym and I will *not* allow you to disrespect our lord! We will not return without his prize!" The demon's composure seemed gone, thrashing now as he struggled back to his feet.

"Sorry for the bad news." Before the demon could say anything else, Alistair and Berlin entered the field from the shadows between two of the adjacent houses. "But your body-snatching friend is already on his way home."

The demon took pause now, his expression grim as he took stock of the two and their claim.

"Go home, Mammon." Cole's voice was softer now, but his back was straight as he stood between Bastian and the other demon. "Tell your lord that you did everything you could, but that I will not be returning."

The demon hesitated, his eyes darting between the four boys who now surrounded him, weighing his options. When he spoke, his voice had lost some of its strength.

"You have no idea what your refusal will cause. Lord Ashmodai will not allow this sort of petulance. Just know that whatever happens next is *your* fault." With that, a tremor passed through the man's body, his head craning back as the black spirit ejected from his mouth.

Blackholly crumpled as the spirit raced back toward the auditorium.

"We need to find a way to close the portal," Cole said, following the demon at a run.

Bastian and the others followed close behind, and even after Cole lost sight of the dark cloud that used to live inside the pastor's body, he didn't slow down. It wasn't until he pumped his wings, propelling himself through the hole in the side of the building that he paused. His feet landed hard on a debris-strewn floor. Where the portal used to be, there was now just a hole in the foundation with churned up dirt marking the bottom.

"It closed up on its own." Milo's voice was weak, but when Cole snapped his head around to look at him, the brunette smiled at him. Blood still stained the boy's clothes and matted his hair, but he was sitting up, one arm draped over Kiya to help support him. Jett and Sabin sat cross-legged on his other side. "Hey," was all he said in response to the look of pure relief Cole could feel on his own face.

It was hard to not throw himself at his friend, but Cole refrained, not wanting to hurt him. Instead, when he ran to the other boy's side, he dropped to his knees in front of him, small hands cupping the boy's face. His cheeks were warm, and the laugh that bubbled from him brought tears to Cole's eyes. Not only was he alive, but he was Milo again. The darkness Cole had planted inside him no longer clouded the honey color of his eyes— his smile was loving. Overcome, he collapsed into his friend's shoulder and cried. As Milo's hand soothed his back he heard his teammates catch up to him.

"This one sure does cry a lot," he heard Jett say.

The brunette's frame jostled just a little with laughter. "It's okay." Milo said, his voice tired but light. "It's one of his better qualities."

They would have to find a way to let Marla know the demons were taken care of, and they would have to make sure the residents of the town were alright once they came-to. But for now, Cole just hung onto the first friend he'd ever made. For the time being, he was content with just that.

43: COLE

The plane ride back to New York was painfully quiet, everyone trying in their own way to process what had just happened. It hadn't taken long for the soldiers at the quarantine line to come in—followed by swarms of medical officers with stretchers—and secure the unconscious bodies that lay strewn about the town. Marla had insisted that Milo and Professor Shipton ride back with a medical team, but had let Cole on the plane with the others. Apparently, once one teenager sprouts wings, it's less worrisome when another one does it. They were certainly inconvenient though, and Cole had to leave one of them hung over the armrest, letting it spill into the center aisle. The other lay along the backs of the seats beside him, draped lightly over Bastian's body where the boy leaned into him, his head on Cole's shoulder, dead asleep.

"I guess all of that exorcism stuff takes it out of you." Sabin turned in his seat, finally giving up the stack of photos he'd taken of the damage done to the community center. He'd even gotten some shots of the swarms of medical staff carting people out of town on stretchers. Now, he shook his head as he looked their teammate over. "What am I supposed to do with him stealing my gig?" He smiled when he said it, but Cole could see a hint of envy in his friend's blue eyes.

Cole laughed. "Well, he may think he's hot stuff now, but Bastian wouldn't have pierced his tongue for the sake of a mission."

Sabin waved his hand, dismissing him. "I wanted to get it done anyway. Besides, in the end I didn't prove anything we didn't already know."

Sabin wasn't one to get sentimental, but Cole was sure that hidden in that phrase, was all the reassurance he needed. The witch was too sharp to have missed the turmoil Cole had been in, but by dismissing it he had made it clear that what Cole was didn't actually matter.

"I guess you're right," Cole said, resting his cheek on top of Bastian's head, the gesture drawing a look of disgust from the witch. Cole only laughed as Sabin recoiled from their PDA, the sense of relief still clouding his mind in a rosy glow.

"Well, just make sure you guys keep your molting in check. I don't want to find your fluff in my drinks and body creases." He sat down with a definitive motion, only to turn around again a second later. "But you *will* give me some of your feathers, right?"

"Sure."

Cole sighed once he was alone with Bastian again, turning his nose and mouth into the blond waves that tickled his face. Rationally, he thought their situation should feel stranger than it did. Having definitive proof that he was a demon had shaken him, yet knowing that Bastian truly was an angel hadn't made him bat an eye. Maybe it was because Bastian already felt so angelic. He was kind and righteous; he was gentle. Cole had seen him crack, though. The night they'd fought he'd seen a side of Bastian he'd never expected—impatient, pushy, angry. A few weeks ago, Cole wouldn't have expected to find those traits in his boyfriend.

They weren't bad traits though.

They were human traits. Just as Cole could be good even while being a demon, Bastian could be imperfect and still be an angel. Neither of them were a perfect representation of what they were supposed to be, and maybe that was what had drawn them together in the first place. They were both flawed. Somehow, that made it easier for Cole to allow himself the happiness he'd run away for in the first place.

He relaxed and tried to let his newfound identity settle over him. Sliding a fingertip along the shaft of one long, black feather where it draped around Bastian's shoulder, Cole felt a shiver run up his own spine. Mammon's words played in his head. He'd told them that whatever happens next would be *his* fault. It was impossible to know what else they might be planning, or whether this Lord Ashmodai person would even care enough to chase after him. Surely, if Cole had been some sort of underling to this lord the way Mammon and Harborym were, then he wasn't worth the effort.

He would just have to wait, and hope to be forgotten—hope that no one else would get hurt.

Beside him, Bastian shifted, nestling his cheek further into his boyfriend's shoulder, then he grew still again. Cole took a breath and rested his head back against the chair, letting the exhaustion weight his eyelids. They would all just have to wait and hope for time to heal things.

44: ALISTAIR

Alistair would never admit to what he was doing. He was absolutely *not* waiting around the dining room for Luca to be released from his debriefing. They would all have their turn, but Marla seemed set on talking to their new teacher first. It made sense, but Alistair was definitely *not* desperate to hear whether the man told her what had happened between them.

Berlin seemed less worried about their upcoming meeting with Marla. He sat at the table, shoveling cereal into his mouth with one hand and scrolling through his phone with the other. He had little to worry about. As for Alistair, he wondered if Marla would bring up his tryst with Luca or what he should say to her about Lakelyn. He'd tried to keep his mind from lingering on the boy or the sight of his lifeless body on the moonlit road. A jolt of pain clenched the muscles of his stomach even now as he steered his thoughts away from it.

He worried that Marla would have some sort of punishment in store for him after rushing the quarantine line like he had. It made him scared to bring it up. But at the same time, Lakelyn deserved more than someone tucking their tail. He deserved justice—whatever that might look like.

"Berlin!"

Alistair heard his friend's spoon drop hard into his bowl as Sabin rushed into the room, looking excited and holding a small, carved box in his arms.

"What?" The tattooed boy leaned back in his chair as though to put distance between himself and the witch, suspicion edging his voice.

"Look," Sabin began, taking the seat across from Berlin. He placed the box between them "I know I was kind of mean to you while we were staying in Trumbull, and I just want to apologize." His hands sat atop the box where two lying dogs were embossed in silver.

Alistair thought the carvings that wound along the sides of the cube looked Celtic.

"Okay." Berlin still watched him suspiciously.

"You know, there's a lot more to magic than piercing tongues and bugs and stuff. So I want to show you something you might like."

Finally, Berlin leaned back toward the table, his expression changing to something a bit more curious. "Like what?"

Even Alistair was interested now. Tossing his phone to the couch, he got up and moved to stand by Berlin, looking over his shoulder as Sabin slid the box toward him.

"Look, nothing in the box." Sabin opened the ornately carved chest, which was only about a foot across, and swept a hand over the velvet-lined interior. Then, he produced a small gold crucifix and placed it inside.

"What are you doing with that?" Berlin was uneasy again, but leaned closer when he closed it.

"It's *magic*, Berlin. You can't rush it. Now, concentrate." He didn't say what they should concentrate on, but he waved his hands over the box like a fortune teller at a fair.

Despite the witch's exaggerated showmanship, even Alistair leaned in close, watching the box. Moments passed, then a snap sounded from inside the container, and the thin silver plating that formed the dogs shifted, the sound of wood scraping metal silencing even their breath. The dogs stretched, sat up, and then reared back on their hind legs. Another beat of silence passed even after they'd stopped moving, and Alistair realized his mouth was hanging open.

"What just happened?" Berlin's eyes were huge, his own mouth slack.

"Open it," Sabin urged, smiling as he slid the box toward their teammate again.

Berlin looked uncertain but fascinated as his fingers brushed over the lines of silver that had seemed alive moments ago. They all leaned in close as broad fingers unlatched the box, the hinges creaking a little as he cracked it open.

"Oh just open it already!" Reaching across the table, Sabin yanked the lid open, and a swarm of scuttling legs erupting from inside the box.

Spiders scattered on the table and a shriek stung Alistair's ears as Berlin toppled backwards, his chair tipping with him as he scurried away from the box. A light flashed, and then Sabin's laughter filled the room as Berlin tucked tail and sprinted away as soon as his feet were under him. When Alistair looked back at the witch, he was gently shaking a Polaroid, his camera sitting on the table.

"How'd you do that?" Alistair didn't particularly like spiders, and stepped back as the little black bodies began spreading. Seeing Berlin scurry away had definitely been worth it, though.

"I told you," Sabin said around a smile as he admired his new picture. "It's magic."

Alistair just shook his head, still unable to keep the smile from his face. When he was done admiring the photo, Sabin scribbled something on it with a marker he pulled from his pocket, then slid it into the box and closed it. The dogs on the lid laid back down as the witch produced a jar and began gingerly catching his spiders again.

When Alistair raised a credulous brow at him he looked slightly offended. "I don't want them to get hurt," he explained. "I have to put them back in their terrariums." He picked each one up carefully with his fingers, or offered his palm for them to climb onto, always careful not to squash any of them.

"No wonder Berlin thinks you're so weird."

"I'm doing him a favor. Compared to me, everything else will seem manageable."

Before Alistair could say anything else, the intercom dinged and Marla's voice came on over the speakers.

"Sabin, report for debriefing."

Alistair's stomach clinched, but if Sabin was worried his face didn't give it away. The pierced boy just looked up, like he could see the voice around them and then smiled a little at Alistair.

"I guess that means she's done with Shipton," he said, looking knowing. "Guess I'll go drop my spiders off." He held his magic box in one arm, the jar of spiders balanced precariously on top. "I think we're all on the same page, Alistair." He turned at the door to look at him, his hand at his side waving almost imperceptibly. Alistair felt the pressure in the room change, his ears popped, and when Sabin spoke again his voice was lower and distorted. He sounded muffled, like Alistair's ears were full of cotton. "We all have things we don't want her to find out about. We'll keep your secrets for you if you keep ours, yeah?"

"Of course," was all he could manage to say.

Sabin smiled and the heavy blanket of air lifted. "Cool trick, right?"

Alistair wondered if Sabin had just cast some sort of silencing spell around them, but in the face of his own ignorance all he could do was nod and wish his friend good luck.

Waving a hand toward him like he didn't need luck, Sabin left the room.

45: COLE

"Ow! Bastian, that's my wing." They both huffed and paused where they were shifting on Bastian's bed.

After the plane had landed, they'd both been sent down to the labs along with Luca and Milo. Milo was checked over by the doctors and deemed to be perfectly healthy, if not bruised and exhausted. Luca had been sent for a CAT scan. As for Bastian and Cole, their wings were measured and compared to one another. Blood work was taken for the hundredth time, and then Cole was hit with a barrage of questions—the same questions Bastian had been asked after their time in Lechuguilla. Obviously, they were trying to not only figure out what they were, but whether they were the same thing.

Cole remembered what Mammon had told him—that "demon" and "angel" were both words used by humans, that they were more or less the same save for their alliances. He wondered if the tests they did in those labs would ever be able to prove something like that.

When they had finally been released back onto the dorm level, Bastian ate ravenously, his new found powers having depleted any reserves he might have had. Then it was Cole's turn to eat. He wasn't starving yet, but he told himself that he wouldn't let himself get that bad any more. When he was hungry he ran the risk of hurting people, and if Bastian was willing to always keep him fed, then he would just have to accept his lover's gift to him without feeling guilty. He would have to accept that Bastian gave because he loved him.

Feeding was a little more complicated with yet another set of wings clogging up their space. The bed was crowded, even while Cole tried to keep his tucked close to his body where he lay. Bastian's hands and knees still caught them between his weight and the mattress on occasion, and every time it happened a sensation like getting hit in the funny bone would radiate down his spine.

"Sorry, sorry." Bastian was panting where he knelt over Cole.

Neither of them had been shy about ditching their clothes once they'd shut the door behind them, and now Cole felt his heart race as he was left with an unhindered view of his lover perched over him, arms and chest taut from the effort of holding his weight off of him. Trailing down the lines of his body, he saw how much effort he was putting into taking things slow, even as his cock strained and pulsed slightly against his stomach when he caught Cole's black eyes looking at him.

Despite his obvious desire, Bastian's brows were knit into soft lines of concern. Without meaning to, Cole had trained his boyfriend to worry all the time—to question his every move and to wait and see if Cole would fall apart. That wasn't what he wanted for them.

In a moment of confidence, Cole pushed against the blond's shoulder, pivoting him and laughing as they shifted, wings tangling, until they had swapped places.

"Lay your wings out like this." Cole pushed the white plumage out to either side of Bastian's tanned body, his own thighs spread across his hips, bracing himself on the bed out of reach of the delicate feathers. "There, see? They're both out of the way now." He tucked his own wings tight against his back as he pressed down with his hips, catching his breath as his own body pulsed in time with Bastian's.

"You're so beautiful like this." The angel's voice was labored as hands moved up Cole's thighs to grip his narrow hips, guiding his undulating motion.

The reverence Cole heard in the other boy's voice made something shake inside him and he felt the telltale pinpricks of fear—fear that Bastian was under some negative influence, or that being a demon meant he wasn't good enough for such a sweet feeling. Instead of giving it any room to germinate, he smiled at his lover and simply said, "Thank you."

Bastian seemed to understand the meaning of the smaller boy's gentle acceptance, and the smile he gave him was so radiant that Cole thought he should look away.

"I love you," Bastian said, his voice soft now, his thumbs rubbing circles on Cole's inner thighs.

Bringing one hand down to touch Bastian's cheek, Cole opened his mouth to return the words, wanting them to convey the true depth of the feelings he had. Before he could say anything, a mood-shattering banging came from the door. They both jumped and paused, looking at the door and trying to remember if they'd locked it. After a few seconds of quiet, they smiled at each other like two kids skipping school. Cole leaned down, his hands spreading over his boyfriend's chest, but before his lips could meet Bastian's, Berlin shouted through the door, banging louder this time.

"Bastian! I need you!"

"You have got to be kidding me." Bastian dropped his head back against the pillow as Cole slid off him, pulling the blankets up around his naked body.

"Go talk to him," he said, smiling at the annoyed slouch in his lover's shoulders as Bastian sat up and found his pants.

When he opened the door, Berlin pushed his way in, his eyes huge and a thin sheen of sweat on his forehead.

"Sabin turned a crucifix into a swarm of spiders!"

"Are you kidding me?" Bastian looked like he wanted to shake his teammate until he had brain damage.

"It's serious this time, Bastian! He did it right in front of my eyes, like magic!"

"Of course it was like magic, Berlin, he's a *witch!*"

Their English deteriorated until they were shouting at each other in German, their arms waving and faces going red. Cole just smiled and pressed his cheek into the pillow that still smelled like Bastian as he watched his boyfriend and his best friend fight in a way that made them seem like brothers. He'd made the right choice to stay, and when the endearment of their raised voices made Cole laugh to himself, they both finally quieted and looked at him like he might be making fun of them.

He wasn't sure how to tell them that their stupid fighting made their hidden dorm feel like a real home with a real family inside it.

He would just keep smiling until he figured it out.

46: ALISTAIR

Alistair didn't see Luca before he was called in for his own debriefing. When it was finally his turn, Marla sent a guard to collect him, as though she really worried he wouldn't go. The thought had crossed his mind, but something inside him needed to hear what she would say to make the death of an innocent child acceptable. He'd not talked to any of the others about Lakelyn's death, not ready to deal with their sorry looks or consoling words, but he needed to know where she stood.

When he was finally sitting across the desk from her—listening to her lament the dangers inherent in all missions, demoting Lakelyn's murder to an unfortunate accident—his feelings iced over. Even when she said the man responsible for the boy's death would face conviction, none of it seemed to matter. Nothing he did or said would change the situation. Whether that man went to jail or not—whether he'd actually been ordered to shoot the boy or not—wouldn't bring Lakelyn back.

If he tried to fight Marla, he would just end up comatose in bed again, so instead of arguing, he simply stared at her, watching as she tried to smooth over what she'd done. They would all go on with their lives, doing their parts to keep each other's secrets from her, but in the end they were just prisoners in a posh dungeon. Just like the man who had shot a little boy because he thought it was his duty, they would all keep marching in line, doing as they were told. As long as they played Marla's game they would be treated well, but the moment they stepped out of line—Alistair already knew what that meant.

At the end of the debriefing—after Alistair had walked her through the days they'd spent in Trumbull—Marla told him they would try to plan more chaperoned outings for him and his teammates, but that he was still forbidden to go out on his own. She was probably offering him that olive branch because he'd left out the parts of their mission that included fucking his *current* chaperon. It had been a gamble since he wasn't sure what Luca had told her, but judging by her reaction, he thought his teacher might have had enough sense to keep it private as well.

Venja caught him in the hallway after the debriefing and tried to comfort him, but even her words failed to reach the parts of him that were still hurting. He let her hug him, and he promised he would go to her if he needed someone to talk to, even as he knew he never would. He told her whatever he needed to just so she would let him go. All he wanted at that moment was to get back to his room where he could sit alone.

Things seemed promising as he stalked back to his room—the hallways were empty, his other teammates occupied—but the solitude he was hoping for shattered once he got to his bedroom. Sitting on the edge of his bed, Luca smiled at him when he came in, the usual teasing edge to his grin softened just a little.

Alistair paused as the door clicked shut behind him. "What are you doing here?"

"Just wanted to see you." Luca's voice was low, and Alistair could hear the underlying meaning. He had the same tone Venja had out in the hallway.

"It's awfully brave of you, sneaking into a student's room with all the cameras watching."

The sly quality of his grin returned and Luca shrugged. "I have my ways around that."

"I guess you would, given your position." Alistair didn't approach him, his emotions muddled now that Luca was back in a setting where he rubbed elbows with Marla. With everything churning inside him, it was hard to tell what he'd felt while in Trumbull.

"I think you already know that I haven't told Marla anything." His tone dropped again, like he wanted to make sure Alistair heard his sincerity.

Alistair *had* heard it, and it made his stomach flip. "Have you seen a doctor?"

"Yes. I was poked and prodded as soon as the plane landed. Scanned and cleared and released into the wild." He chuckled and Alistair wondered if the relief he felt had shown on his face. "Alistair."

The redhead had only just realized he'd been looking anywhere but at his teacher when the command he heard in his name drew his eyes back to Luca. His teacher patted his knee like he was calling a pet.

"Come here."

Alistair didn't argue. He walked to the man as though he had no choice in the matter. Bracing one hand on Luca's shoulder, he slid onto his lap, one knee on either side of him. Face to face, Alistair looked evenly into his eyes, waiting to see if they would give him the answers he wanted. Luca's hands gripped him at the bow in his lower back, his fingers locking with each other and forming a support to hold him in place.

"I'm sorry about what happened to Lakelyn. If I had made the children more of a priority, then it would never have happened. As the leader of the mission, I should have been more careful."

Alistair had thought those words wouldn't be important, but hearing them from Luca made the pain soften, even if it was only the tiniest bit.

"Were you in there still? Did you know what was happening?"

"On and off," the man admitted, not mincing his words. "I remember you asking about the kids, but things had gotten very foggy by then."

"And before that?" Alistair felt small in Luca's lap, his voice quiet as he laced his fingers together, needing to hold onto them to keep from shaking.

"If you're asking whether or not I was the one to make love to you, then yes. That was me."

Alistair's face went hot as Luca used the words that he'd scolded himself for thinking so many times since then. Had they made love? Alistair had been trying to tell himself that wasn't the case.

Luca continued. "I'm just sorry that he was there with us. I knew what had been done to me. I knew that Jett had been kept hostage. It just didn't seem to matter at the time. I can only guess it was because that demon was messing with my head already, but I was the one who touched you. I want you to know that."

"It doesn't really matter," Alistair dismissed.

Luca's hand moved to his chin, gripping his cheeks with his fingers and thumb and turning the boy's face to look at him. "It does matter, Alistair." Luca chuckled. "We both knew we were made for each other the moment we met in that bar, don't you think?"

"You had a shitty way of showing it if that's how you felt."

"I admit, I played a dirty game with you. But it was at least a little fun, don't you think?"

"You mean *except the* part where you were possessed by a demon and I was forced into an unexpected threesome?"

"Yes, except that."

Alistair took Luca by the wrist, pulling his hand down away from where he was still holding his face.

"What now? Since the mission is over, will you go back to California?"

"It sounds like whatever is going on between your friend Cole and those demons isn't done yet. We'll be staying at least as long as it takes to sort that out."

It was hard not to smile as Alistair nodded.

The grin Luca flashed him sent a tingling through his stomach and down to his thighs. "So, now that your little heart has been saved from breaking, you're going to let me fuck you again, right?"

"You arrogant prick. Here I am actually spending my energy being worried about you and you just—" Before Alistair could finish his complaint Luca's fingers hooked behind his neck and pulled him down into a kiss far softer than his teasing would have suggested.

As Luca pulled away slowly he let his lips linger against Alistair's, murmuring so low the vibration tickled the overly sensitized skin. "No complaining. Be a good boy and let me love you."

Alistair nodded as he found his voice. "Slow this time," he said, shocked by the immediate spike in his desire.

"Whatever you want, kitten."

The fingers at the back of his neck spread, gripping the soft curve and guiding him back down into a longer kiss. Alistair hummed like a purring cat as he pressed his body into Luca's, spreading his legs and rolling his hips down against him. He opened his mouth in a soft gasp when he felt the man harden between them, and Luca took advantage of the opening. Alistair thought he would melt there on top of him as his tongue traced the soft lining inside his lips.

The man tasted like honey and spice, and as Luca's arms moved to grip the narrow lines of his back Alistair's whole body began to heat up. It wasn't unusual for Alistair to make out with men he met in clubs and at bars, but he'd never felt like he was being consumed before. Every place Luca touched felt weak in comparison to the sure grip he felt from the man's lightly calloused hands.

Alistair raked his fingers through Luca's loosely styled hair, then pulled it just hard enough to make the man gasp. Luca looked surprised as his head tipped back, but after a moment of shock he grinned, seeming to like the rough play.

"Be gentle with me, kitten," he teased.

Part of Alistair wanted to do exactly the opposite. He'd never been presented with the opportunity to let loose on someone, and for a second he thought that might be fun. It wasn't what he wanted or needed though—not just then. He wanted to forget the power he had to hurt other people. If he were helpless, then he would have none of the dark corners that lurked in his mind. He brought his lips down to hover just over Luca's where the man's neck craned back against the pull in his hair.

"Make me." He purred the words across his teacher's lips.

With a low rumble in Luca's chest, the man hooked his hands under Alistair's arms. Standing, he lifted him up like a child, then tossed him unceremoniously onto the mattress. He'd provoked him on purpose, but Alistair still gasped in surprise as he was handled so fiercely. Luca was prowling toward him on the mattress when he opened his eyes, and Alistair felt himself still under the man's gaze. Hooking two fingers under the silk of his neck-tie, Luca pulled it loose.

"Too bad I can't tie you up with this," he said as he slipped the dark blue tie from the collar of his shirt. "I guess I'll have to hold you down the old-fashioned way. Lift your hips."

On command, Alistair planted his feet on the mattress and lifted his body, giving Luca the chance to pull the thin house pants from his narrow hips. Alistair rarely bothered wearing underwear under them, and was already growing hard beneath the man's sharp grey eyes. The teasing look Luca gave him when he found the boy sans his underwear sent goosebumps across Alistair's skin. Continuing the show, he pulled his shirt off over his head, making sure to arch his body in a way he knew was flattering.

When the man had propped himself up over Alistair's body, the redhead pushed his hands along his flexed forearms, tracing the muscles there before sliding fingertips under the rolled sleeves of his button-up shirt.

"Take this off before you teach me a lesson," Alistair said, his voice sultry as he gave Luca his best doe eyes.

He wasn't sure what their relationship was yet; he had no idea what to expect in the future. For now, he trusted that his teacher was on his side at least enough to keep their trysts a secret, and as Luca exposed the pale skin of his chest one button at a time, Alistair was happy with just that.

When Alistair's hands moved to the buckle at Luca's trousers, the man caught him by the wrists and tutted him softly.

"Patience, now."

Crawling over him, Luca positioned himself so he sat across Alistair's thighs, one hand pushing the boy's wrists into the mattress above his head. Heat spread through Alistair's body, even as the cool air made his nipples peak where he was left fully exposed beneath his teacher. For a few long moments Luca just admired him, his eyes licking over his body in a way that seemed palpable. Alistair tried to keep his breathing steady, but he was already panting softly even though he'd not been touched at all.

One finger came to the redhead's lips, and he swiped his tongue over the calloused pad before it trailed over his chin, down the center of his chest, and finally to his belly button. Taking his time, Luca spent long moments drawing constellations between the freckles that stippled his chest, always making sure to avoid touching him where he really wanted. Alistair's limbs had begun to tremble, and he was sure Luca could feel it where he sat pinning his legs down. He was so hard he ached, his dick jumping and weeping every time Luca's fingers inched toward the swollen head where it lay against his stomach.

"So pretty," Luca cooed. His finger moved back to the boy's chin, tilting his head up as he leaned forward, rewarding his student's patience with a soft, long kiss. "Now why don't you squirm for me a little, hm?"

Alistair's head fell back against the bed, exposing his throat to the man whose lips were kissing a hot trail over his pulse point. When teeth pressed into the soft curve of his shoulder he jumped, his arms straining where the man held his narrow wrists in one hand. His heart thumped low in his groin as he found himself trapped.

"Fuck, Luca." He wasn't sure what he was asking for, but his body writhed under its newly-found constraints. He couldn't come like this—he'd be mortified. Luca hadn't even touched him properly, yet his prick strained and seeped, leaving a smear of precum on the smooth skin of his stomach.

The man chuckled against his shoulder where he was sucking on the light bruise he'd left with his teeth. "Patience," he reminded him.

Luckily, Luca's wandering mouth and fingertips pulled away, giving Alistair the few moment's he needed to calm himself. Keeping the boy's wrists pinned to the bed, Luca moved from where he'd been sitting across his legs. He knelt beside him as he slid one hand from the boy's knee to his hip.

"Now, spread your legs nice and wide for me, Alistair."

Alistair wasn't shy. Planting one foot on the comforter, he spread his knees apart, his hips tilting toward the man who knelt beside him in a silent plea to be touched. A broad hand brushed the inside of his thigh, moving down into the heat where his legs met. Luca's steel eyes watched him intently, reading every jolt and shudder that passed through his body, and when Alistair's lashes weren't fluttering, he matched the man's stare. When fingers pressed against Alistair's opening, the boy moaned and pressed his hips toward the promise of something more than Luca's teasing.

His skin felt cold when Luca pulled his hand away long enough to reach into his back pocket. Never pulling his eyes away from Alistair's face, he produced a small packet that he tore open with his teeth. With practiced eased, Luca squeezed the clear contents of the packet onto his fingers. Alistair actually laughed where he was restrained against the mattress.

"Were you carrying lube around in your pocket?"

Luca didn't seem insulted by the humor in the boy's voice. He smiled proudly down at him, instead. "Call me an optimist."

"Pervert," he teased, smiling as he pressed one hot cheek into the cool skin of his own arm.

"Look who's talking." Luca drew his knuckles up the inside of Alistair's thigh, only turning his now slickened fingers toward the boy's skin when he could touch him directly. He chuckled when Alistair's hips jerked then pressed into his fingers. "All wound up and I haven't even gotten started yet."

"Then maybe you should stop teasing me and get started already." Alistair's voice shook a little as he chastised the older man, and he was rewarded with a deep slow chuckle and the persistent push of one finger inside him. "Fuck." His head dropped back to the bed and he hummed in satisfaction as his hips swiveled to match the slow thrusting the man had begun inside him.

What he'd thought was relief quickly turned into torture. Luca worked so slowly that Alistair wanted to scream at him. Ages past before he worked a second finger into him, then minutes more before he finally crooked his fingers to stroke the bud of nerves inside him. Alistair's hips jerked and thrust toward those fingers, but the more he squirmed, the slower Luca went.

By the time Luca had worked his body open—three fingers twisting and thrusting inside him—Alistair thought he was going to lose his mind. He was sweating and panting, his legs unable to hold his weight anymore.

"Enough!" He'd meant to sound annoyed with the man's teasingly languid pace, but the word had torn from his mouth, sounding more like a sob than a command.

Alistair was relieved that the man above him seemed to be satisfied with his show of desperation. Slowly, he slid his fingers out of him only to circle them around the softened ring of muscle.

"Do you remember what I felt like in here?"

His teasing struck a sensitive chord in Alistair, and his chest ached a little. He must have glared at the man, because Luca chuckled apologetically and released his wrists, his hand sliding down the length of his arms until he was cupping the redhead's cheek. When he continued, his voice was low, his lips brushing softly over Alistair's.

"Don't forget that it was still me who held you. You felt so amazing, I could never have let anyone else have you for real."

Luca kissed him again, long and slow. His tongue filled the boy's mouth, laving stripes of heat along the roof of his mouth and flat of his tongue. The kiss seemed to blanket him in a swath of fire and goose bumps. He'd barely noticed his teacher undoing his trousers until the man had settled himself between his thighs. Alistair turned his head, trying to catch his breath as he felt the dull heat of Luca's dick pressing into him, but his teacher caught him by the chin. Forcing his face back toward his, Luca devoured him, swallowing the pitiful moans he wrung out of the slender boy beneath him.

Alistair trembled, his over-sensitized passage squeezing around the man who filled him until even his breath had nowhere to go. When Luca's hips met the splay of Alistair's legs—unable to go any further—he finally released the redhead's lips. He stayed like that for a few moments, letting the boy adjust, though his eyes never left his face.

"You're the worst," Alistair said when he finally gathered enough breath to speak.

Luca only chuckled at him, then watched with satisfaction as he rocked his hips. Alistair's hands fisted the blanket beneath him, a tearing sound punctuating the motion as his head dropped back.

"Hold onto me."

Alistair's head was a mire of pleasure and fog, the command lost before it had been processed. When Luca pried his hands away from the comforter and hooked them around his shoulders he managed to come back to himself a little. Luca's movements were slow but powerful, knocking soft cries from his throat as he set his pace. Alistair could feel the muscles in the man's shoulders flex where his arms draped around him, but the redhead kept his hands balled up tight. It was instinct to keep from grabbing people, and his body refused to let his crushing grip latch onto anything.

"Alistair, hold onto me." His voice was stronger this time—more commanding—though his student only managed to shake his head drunkenly.

With a grunt of frustration, Luca's arms hooked under the bend of Alistair's knees. Bracing his hands on the boy's slender back, he hoisted him off the bed. Alistair shrieked in surprise as he was lifted from the mattress, his hands latching instinctively onto the man's back to keep from falling. Luca held him up for a second, a smug grin curving the perfect line of his mouth, then he used the boy's own bodyweight to drive him down hard where he was still buried inside him.

Alistair's back bowed on its own, and he clawed at his teacher's shoulders as he drove into him without mercy. As deliberate and teasing as he'd been moments ago, Luca now matched that with power and appetite. He drove into Alistair's quickly unwinding body with a vigor that borderlined violent, wringing sounds from Alistair that even *he* had never heard. Unable to do anything more than hang on for his life, Alistair panted and cried against Luca's cheek, begging him to give him respite and give him more all at once.

With his hands acting as Alistair's only support, Luca was left to bite and suck at the pale, freckled neck exposed to him. He breathed hard in the boy's ear, now, growling low in his throat as he slammed into his shaking body.

"You're mine now." The words seemed to come through clenched teeth, and Alistair could only nod feebly.

When one arm released Alistair's leg and moved to hook around the boy's back—his hand gripping hard at the back of his neck—the redhead felt his whole body tense. Fingers clawed at his teacher's shoulders and the man supported him as his back formed a trembling arc in his arms. The cry that erupted from him with his orgasm was met with a low groan as heat surged from Luca's body, filling Alistair's and leaving a mark in him he hoped wouldn't be erased.

As the pulsing of his own orgasm eased, cool air moving between them to touch the lines of rapture he'd painted across their chests, Alistair's whole body lost strength. He was nearly limp as Luca's arms deposited him back onto the mattress, his deep panting breath releasing a soft laugh as he pulled the boy's tangled hair out from under his shoulders. Propping himself up on one elbow, Luca stretched out at Alistair's side to catch his own breath.

When Alistair managed to see straight again, he found Luca watching him, and for a second he wasn't sure if he wanted to kiss him or hit him. Instead, he scoffed a little and said, "Was that all you had?"

"Are you *asking* for me to spank you?" Luca's hand came up to squeeze the boy's cheeks again.

"Don't threaten me unless it's a promise." Alistair smiled when Luca leaned down to kiss him.

Alistair's extremities tingled for a long time as he came down off the high Luca had driven him to, neither of them seeming interested in getting up or getting dressed. Luca's fingers traced lines over his student's body and Alistair wondered if "boyfriend" was the right word now. He'd certainly made it seem like he didn't want Alistair having flings with anyone else, but perhaps it was too soon for any sort of label.

"What did Marla say to you about Lakelyn?" Alistair asked, the barriers in his mind weak in his teacher's presence now.

"We spoke very little about him," Luca admitted.

"I'm not surprised. What about his mother?"

There was a pause in both the man's words and his wandering fingers. "The people who were taken out of the town are still being kept for research purposes."

"Is that legal?"

"Who knows."

"Luca?" Finally, Alistair turned to look his new lover in the face. "Did you know what was happening in that town before we got there?"

The steady gaze he got back from his teacher was a complicated mix of emotions. He could almost *see* him weighing his desire with his responsibility. When he responded, his voice was soft.

"We had our suspicions."

"Did Marla?"

"I think she knew more than any of us did."

"Do you trust her?"

Luca sighed and rolled onto his back, looking at the ceiling now. "I think Marla has an endgame that none of us can be sure of. Whether that makes her untrustworthy or not is hard to say."

Alistair turned over, settling himself in the crook of the man's arm who accepted his weight without hesitation.

"Are you staying to help her?"

"I think she's keeping me here for that reason, but I'm not staying to help her." He looked down the line of his nose where Alistair's face lay close to his. "I'm staying to make sure that you and your friends aren't put in jeopardy while she tries to accomplish whatever it is she has planned."

Alistair's cheeks flushed, and he snorted to hide the warm embarrassment he felt kindling inside him. "How chivalrous."

Luca met his teasing with a soft chortle. "Trust me, kitten. Marla's not the type to make small plans. When she dreams, she dreams big. We're just going to have to wait and see what it is she wants to do."

For a few moments, Alistair considered asking Luca if they could just leave together. Surely, someone of Luca's standing could sneak him out, and together they would be an unbeatable team. He could see in the distant look the man had, however, that Luca wanted to stay. There was some facet of Marla's scheme that he was invested in, though it was impossible to tell whether he was invested in helping or hindering her.

ABOUT THE AUTHOR

While Michelle Kay's social circle in high school was full of artists, Michelle realized early on that she had no passion for drawing. In exchange for free pictures, she began writing fanfiction about her friends and favorite characters, giving them away as gifts, jokes, and bribes. Eventually, her interest in Boys Love lead her to pursue original stories about men kissing, falling in love, and doing some of that other stuff...

Working as a librarian, Michelle gets to spend most of her day surrounded by her favorite things—books! When not at work, she uses her free time to play video games, read, and unsuccessfully tame her wicked cat, Lucius. (Yes, named after a certain Malfoy.)

You can find more about Michelle at her website:
HisPrincelyDelicates.com

ABOUT THE COVER ART

Cover art done by Ero-Pinku

http://www.ero-pinku.com

Made in the USA
Charleston, SC
02 February 2017